# Praise for the novels of Maisey Yates

"Yates brings her signature heat and vivid western details to another appealing story in the excellent Gold Valley series.... Fans of Kate Pearce should enjoy this."
—*Booklist* on *Rodeo Christmas at Evergreen Ranch*

"Yates's outstanding eighth Gold Valley contemporary... will delight newcomers and fans alike.... This charming and very sensual contemporary is a must for fans of passion."
—*Publishers Weekly* on *Cowboy Christmas Redemption* (starred review)

"Fast-paced and intensely emotional.... This is one of the most heartfelt installments in this series, and Yates's fans will love it."
—*Publishers Weekly* on *Cowboy to the Core* (starred review)

"Multidimensional and genuine characters are the highlight of this alluring novel, and sensual love scenes complete it. Yates's fans...will savor this delectable story."
—*Publishers Weekly* on *Unbroken Cowboy* (starred review)

"Yates' new Gold Valley series begins with a sassy, romantic and sexy story about two characters whose chemistry is off the charts."
—*RT Book Reviews* on *Smooth-Talking Cowboy* (Top Pick)

# MAISEY YATES

# The Troublemaker

CANARY STREET PRESS

CANARY
STREET
PRESS™

Recycling programs
for this product may
not exist in your area.

ISBN-13: 978-1-335-60080-6

The Troublemaker
Copyright © 2023 by Maisey Yates

Second Chance Cowboy
Copyright © 2023 by Maisey Yates

This is a work of fiction. Names, characters, places and incidents
are either the product of the author's imagination or are used fictitiously.
Any resemblance to actual persons, living or dead, businesses,
companies, events or locales is entirely coincidental.

For questions and comments about the quality of this book,
please contact us at CustomerService@Harlequin.com.

Canary Street Press
22 Adelaide St. West, 41st Floor
Toronto, Ontario M5H 4E3, Canada
CanaryStPress.com

**Printed in U.S.A.**

# CONTENTS

To Oregon, the only place I've ever lived.
The place I love best. I will never tire of describing
the mountains, the lakes, the sunsets.
Just like I'll never tire of seeing them.

# THE TROUBLEMAKER

# CHAPTER ONE

HE WAS THE very image of the Wild West, backlit by the setting sun, walking across the field that led directly to her house. He was wearing a black cowboy hat and a T-shirt that emphasized his broad shoulders; waist narrow and hips lean. His jaw square, his nose straight like a blade and his mouth set in a firm, uncompromising manner.

Lachlan-McCloud was the epitome of a cowboy. She was proud to call him her best friend. He was loyal; he was—in spite of questionable behavior at times—an extremely good man, even if sometimes you had to look down deep to see it.

He was...

He was bleeding.

Charity sighed.

She had lost track of the amount of times that she had stitched Lachlan McCloud back together.

"I'll just get my kit, then," she muttered, digging around for it.

Not that there was any other reason Lachlan would be coming by unannounced. Usually now she went to his house for cards or for dinner; he didn't come here. Not since her dad had died.

She found her medical bag and opened up the front

door, propping her hip against the door frame, holding the bag aloft.

He stopped. "How did you know?"

"I recognize your *I cut myself open and need to be sewn back together* walk."

"I have a…*need to be sewn back together* walk?"

"You do," she said, nodding.

"Thank you kindly."

She lived just on the other side of the property line from McCloud's Landing. One of the ranches that made up the vast spread that was Four Corners Ranch.

Thirty thousand acres, divided by four, amongst the original founding families.

Her father had been the large-animal vet in town and for the surrounding areas for years. With a mobile unit and all the supplies—granted, they were antiquated.

Charity had taken over a couple of years ago.

Her dad had always understood animals better than he did people. He'd told her people simply didn't speak his language, or he didn't speak theirs, but it didn't really matter which.

Charity had known how to speak her dad's language. He liked chamomile tea and *All Creatures Great and Small. Masterpiece Theatre* and movies made in the 1950s. Argyle socks—which she also loved—and cardigans. Again, something she loved, too.

He'd smoked a pipe and read from the paper every morning. He liked to do the crossword.

And just last month, he'd died. Without him the house seemed colder, emptier and just a whole lot less.

It was another reason she was thankful for Lachlan.

But then they'd both had a lot of changes recently. It wasn't just her. It wasn't just the loss of her father.

Lachlan was the last McCloud standing.

His brothers, resolute bachelors all—at least at one time—were now settled and having children. His brother Brody was an instant father, since he had just married Elizabeth, a single mother who had come to work at the equestrian center on McCloud's Landing a couple of months back.

But Lachlan was Lachlan. And if the changes had thrown him off, he certainly didn't show it.

He was still his hard-drinking, risk-taking, womanizing self.

But he'd always been that way. It was one reason she'd been so immediately drawn to him when they'd first met. He was nothing like her.

He was something so separate from her, something so different than she could ever be, that sometimes being friends with him was like being friends with someone from a totally different culture.

Sometimes she went with him and observed his native customs. She'd gone to Smokey's Tavern with the group of McClouds quite a few times, but she'd always found it noisy and the booze smelled bad. It gave her a headache.

And she didn't dance.

Lachlan had women fighting to dance with him, and she thought it was such a funny thing. Watching those women compete for his attention, for just a few moments of his time. They would probably never see him again.

She would see him again the next day and the day after that, and the day after that.

"What did you do?" she asked, looking at the nasty gash.

"I had a little run-in with some barbed wire."

He was at the door now, filling up the space. He did that. He wasn't the kind of person you could ignore. And given that she was the kind of person *all too* easy to ignore, she admired that about him.

"We've gotta stop meeting like this," he said, grinning.

She'd seen him turn that grin on women in the bar and they fell apart. She'd always been proud of herself for not behaving that way.

"I wish we could, Lachlan. But you insist on choosing violence."

"Every day."

"You could stop being in a fight with the world," she pointed out.

"I could. But you know the thing about that is it sounds boring."

"Well… A bored Lachlan McCloud is not anything I want to see." She jerked her head back toward the living room. "Come on in."

He did, and the air seemed to rush right out of her lungs as he entered the small, homey sitting room in her little house.

She still had everything of her father's sitting out, like he might come back any day.

His science-fiction novels and his medical journals. His field guides to different animals and the crocheted afghan that he had sat with, draped over his lap, in his burnt orange recliner, when at the end of his days he hadn't been able to do much.

She had been a very late-in-life surprise for her father.

She'd been born when he was in his fifties. And he had raised her alone, because that had been the agreement, so the story went. Amicable and easy. Which made sense. Because her father had been like that. Steady and calm. A nice man. Old-fashioned. But then… He had been in his eighties when he'd passed. He wasn't really old-fashioned so much as of his time.

He'd homeschooled her, brought her on all his veterinary calls. Her life had been simple. And it had been good.

She'd had her dad. And then… She'd had Lachlan.

And there was no reason at all that suddenly this room should feel tiny with Lachlan standing in it. Because he had been in here any number of times.

Especially in the end, visiting her dad and talking to him about baseball.

She sometimes thought her dad was the closest thing that Lachlan had to a father figure. His own dad had been a monster.

Of course, the unfairness of that was that Lachlan's dad was still alive out there somewhere. While her sweet dad was gone.

"It's quiet in here," Lachlan said, picking up on her train of thought.

"It would've been quiet in here if Dad was alive. Until you two started shouting about sports." She grinned just thinking about it. "You do know how to get him riled up." Then her smile fell slightly. "*Did.* You did know."

"I could still rile him up, I bet. But I don't know that we want séance levels of trouble."

She laughed, because she knew the joke came from a place of affection, and that was something she prized about her relationship with Lachlan. They just *knew* each other.

She hadn't really known anyone but adults before she'd met Lachlan. She'd known the people they'd done veterinary work for; she'd known the old men her dad had sat outside and smoked pipes with on summer evenings.

Lachlan had been her first friend.

He was her only friend. Still.

He'd taught her sarcasm. He'd introduced her to pop culture.

He'd once given her a sip of beer when she'd been eighteen.

He'd laughed at the face she'd made.

"I do not want that level of trouble. I also don't want *your* level of trouble," she said. "But here you are. Sit down and bite on something."

"I don't need to bite on anything to get a few stitches, Charity. Settle down. I know what I'm about."

"You can't flinch, Lachlan, and sometimes you're a bad patient. So brace yourself."

"You could numb me."

"I could," she said. "But I'm not just letting you use all my supplies. I'm stitching you for no cost."

"Considering you normally stitch up horses, you should pay me to let you do this."

"Please. Working on animals is more complicated than working on people. People all have the same set of organs right in the same places. Animals... It's all arranged differently. I have to know way more to take care of animals."

"Yes. I've heard the lecture before."

"But you've never taken it on board."

"All right," he said, resting his hand on the coffee

table in front of her and revealing the big gash in his forearm.

She winced.

"Hardass doctor, wincing at this old thing," he said.

"It's different when it's on a person," she said.

Except it really was different when it was on him. Because he was hers.

He was special.

Seeing him injured in any capacity made her heart feel raw, even if she'd seen it a hundred times.

"All right, Doc."

"Okay," she said.

She took her curved needle out of her kit, along with the thread, and she poked it right through his skin.

He growled.

"I told you," she said.

She thought back to how they'd met. He'd been bruised and battered, and in bad need of medical attention.

His had been the first set of stitches she'd ever given.

She swallowed hard.

He winced and shifted when she pushed her needle through his skin again.

"I can't guarantee you that you're not going to have a scar," she said, her tone filled with warning.

"Just one to add to my collection of many."

"Yes. You're very tough."

"Oh, hell, sweetheart, I know that."

"Don't *sweetheart* me." He called every woman sweetheart. And she didn't like being lumped together with all that. She liked *their* things. Baseball and jokes about séances and *Doc*. "How is everything going at the facility?"

She had a hands-on role in the veterinary care of the animals at the new therapy center on McCloud's Landing. But everything had taken a backseat when her dad had declined, then passed. She was working her way back up to it all, but it was slow.

"It's going well. Of course, I am tripping over all the happy couples. Tag and Nelly, Alaina and Gus, Hunter and Elsie, Brody and Elizabeth. It's ridiculous. It's like a Disney cartoon where it's spring and all the animals are hooking up and having babies."

"The domesticity must appall you," she said. But she wasn't even really joking.

She continued to work slowly on the stitches, taking her time and trying to get them small and straight to leave the least amount of damage, because whatever he said about scars, she was determined to stitch her friend back together as neatly as possible.

"I'm glad they're happy," she said.

"Yeah. Me, too. It's a good thing. It's a damn good thing."

But he sounded a bit gruff and a bit not like himself. She had to wonder if all the changes were getting to him. It was tough to tell with Lachlan, because his whole thing was to put on a brave face and pretend that things were all right.

He'd tried that when they'd first met.

She had been playing in the woods. By herself. She was always by herself. Even though she'd been fifteen, she'd been a young fifteen. She'd never really gotten to be around other children. So she was both vastly older and vastly younger in many different ways. She liked to wander the woods and imagine herself in a fairy tale. That she might encounter Prince Charming out there.

Then one day she'd been walking down a path, and there he'd been. Tall and rangy—even at sixteen—with messy brown hair and bright blue eyes.

But he'd been hurt.

Suddenly, he'd put his hand on his ribs and gone down onto his knees.

She could still remember the way she'd run over to him.

"Are you all right?"

"Fine," he said, looking up at her, his lip split, a cut over his eye bleeding profusely.

"That's a lie," she said.

"Yeah." He wheezed out a cough. "No shit."

She'd never heard anyone say that word in real life before. Just overheard in movies and read in books.

Her father was against swearing. He thought that it was vulgar and common. He said that people ought to have more imagination than that.

"That is shocking language," she said.

"Shocking language… Okay. Look, you can just… Head on out. Don't worry about me. This is hardly the first time I've had my ribs broken."

He winced again.

"You need stitches," she said, looking at his forehead.

"I'm not going to be able to get them."

"Why not?"

"No insurance. Anyway, my dad's not gonna pay for me to go to the doctor."

"I… I can help," she said.

She could only hope that her dad was still at home.

He had a call to go out on later, but there was a chance he hadn't left yet.

"Can you stand up?"

"I can try."

She found herself taking hold of his hand, which was big and rough and masculine in comparison to hers.

Like he was a different thing altogether.

She'd seen the boys on the ranch from a distance before, but she'd never met one of them.

He might even be a *man*, he was so tall already.

He made her feel very small. Suddenly, her heart gave a great jump, like she'd been frightened. He made her feel like a rabbit, standing in front of a fox, and she couldn't say why.

But he wasn't a fox. And she wasn't a rabbit.

He was just a boy who needed help.

"Lean on me," she said.

He looked down at her. "I don't want to hurt you. You're a tiny little thing."

"I'm sturdy," she said. "Come on."

"All right."

He put his arm around her, and the two of them walked back to the house. Her father was gone. But his bag was still there.

"I've watched my dad do this a lot of times. I think I can do it."

"Your dad's a doctor?"

The best thing would be to lie. It was to make him feel better, not for nefarious reasons. It wasn't *really* a lie. But of course what this boy meant was a doctor for humans…and she was going to let him believe it.

"Yes. I've been on lots of calls with him. I can do this."

"Good."

She found a topical numbing cream in the bag and gingerly applied it around the wound on his forehead.

His breath hissed through his teeth.

She waited a few minutes before taking out a needle and thread. Beads of sweat formed on his forehead, his teeth gritted.

But when she finished, he looked up at her and smiled. "Thanks, Doc."

SHE LOOKED DOWN at the stitches she was giving now.

"That ought to do it," she said.

"Thanks. Hey, Doc," he said and he lifted his head up so that they were practically sharing the same air.

His face was so close to hers; close enough she could see the bristles of his stubble, the blue of his eyes, that they were a darker ring of blue around the outside, and lighter toward the center.

*What is happening?*

Her throat felt scratchy, and her heart felt…sore.

"Yes?" It came out a near whisper.

"I need a favor."

"What?"

"I need you to reform me."

## CHAPTER TWO

IF YOU NEEDED your car fixed, you went to a mechanic. If you needed surgery, you went to a doctor. If you needed to figure out how to be a better man, correct your crooked ways and otherwise redeem your mortal soul, you went to the Pope.

Or Charity Wyatt.

It made all the logical sense in the world as far as he was concerned.

Charity had been his bright and shining light for as long as he could remember. Well… Ever since that day he had come upon her in the woods, when he'd been broken and bleeding from his father's latest beating. That was how it had been, always, until Gus had run their old man off for good.

Gus, his oldest brother, who had nearly died trying to save Lachlan, who their father had been most certainly about to kill, and he wasn't being hyperbolic.

The McCloud family was a mess, and they always had been.

That was the thing. His brothers had always been messes. They hadn't had a chance when it came right down to it. How could they? They had never seen a functional relationship a day in their lives. Their father had been abusive, their mother had run away to escape it and hadn't been able, or willing—didn't really matter which—to take her children with her.

That had left them in the house of horrors, at risk and with no way out.

So yeah. They were messes. At least, they had been. And then… Something insane had happened. His brother Tag had found Nelly. Then Hunter had fallen for Elsie Garrett, literally the girl next door. After that, Angus McCloud, the meanest and most messed up of them all, had gone and married Alaina Sullivan, yet another girl next door. She had been pregnant, basically making Gus an instant father. Then after that, Brody had taken up with a single mother, which made him an instant father, and suddenly everyone was happy, and the furthest thing from traumatized.

Marriage.

It hadn't helped their father one bit, not with the possessive, toxic feelings in his parents' marriage.

It was different for his brothers. It had *healed* his brothers. They'd found women who'd…soothed them somehow. He would never have believed it if he hadn't seen it with his own eyes.

Marriage had done what years of distance, hard work and drinking hadn't managed to do.

It made them happy.

There was, he'd decided, *love*. Which was the toxic, awful thing he'd never wanted.

Then there was *love* as his brothers had found it. Something that seemed a lot like a partnership to him. Something that didn't hook into your demons and pull the worst out of you, but smoothed it over and made you better.

He had decided that was the only way forward for him. But one thing he did know—he needed to change.

He was haunted. By his past. By his fear that someday the monster that lived in his father would awaken in him, too.

He knew his brothers figured their dad hated them. Hated their mom.

The problem was Lachlan knew different.

The scary thing wasn't their dad hating them. It was that…it had been love, as far as he'd been able to show it. Possessive, controlling. Harmful.

The scary thing was…he'd seen his father show remorse. And do it all over again. So what Lachlan knew was he had to be vigilant. To never let anything awaken that inside him.

And he knew he had the capacity for it. He did.

He knew one truly good person in this whole world. Truly good, truly pure, truly lovely, and that was Charity Wyatt.

It was why he was proud of her being the thing he'd tested himself against back when he was sixteen. Because he'd wanted her then. He could remember the moment he'd felt like…he'd wanted to keep her. All for himself. A wild, fiery sort of feeling that had made him think of his older brother, locked in that shed, and his dad looking on with cold, dead eyes.

So he'd become her protector. Her friend. He'd taken his sick, toxic desires and he'd made them into something new. He'd put walls up where they needed to go and he'd won.

She had shown him, all the way back then, that he could be like his dad.

She'd been his cure, too.

If anyone would know how to…change him, it would be her.

Granted, she had been his best friend for a number of years and had never even suggested that he change.

Their friendship didn't make any sense, not on paper.

She was *sweet*. She didn't have any artifice or cynicism about her. She was funny, but artless. He liked that about her.

She wore long dresses with tennis shoes and ankle socks, and he was only human, so particularly when he had first met her, he had wondered what it would be like to get past that innocent exterior. To be the one who taught her how to be bad…

But she was just too good. And there were so many bad and broken things in the world. So many dirty and degraded things. He among them. So he had promised himself—when he'd been seventeen years old—that he would protect her at all costs. Even from himself.

He'd made spare few vows in his life.

The first was to never subject a woman to the kind of obsessive bullshit his father had tortured his mother with.

The second was to never let his own damage harm Charity in any way.

Which was how, even with fifteen years of friendship with him, she remained as lovely and pure as she'd ever been.

Which was why he needed her help.

"Reform you?" She tilted her head and looked at him, blinking, her pale lashes, tipped with gold, fluttering as she did.

"Yes. I've been thinking about it. I'm going to start looking for a wife."

She tilted her head again. She was beginning to look like a particularly confused sparrow. "A wife?"

"Yes. A wife."

He stood up and looked around the place. He would be lying if he said the death of her father didn't have anything to do with this. Doctor Albert Wyatt had been a good man. One of the best ones that Lachlan had ever known. There was something about losing him, something about that particularly poignant passage of time, that had... It had done something to his heart.

There weren't very many people in the world he cared about other than his brothers.

He would die for Charity.

He'd been fond of her old man, too.

It was a weird thing, grief. He wasn't all that familiar with it. He had lived his life to a steady drumbeat of loss and change and fear.

Watching a good man die was a totally different thing.

"Why do you have to reform to get a wife? Shouldn't you marry somebody that likes you the way that you are?"

"Oh, like your fiancé?"

Her cheeks went a delicate shade of pink.

"Yes. Byron loves me for exactly how I am."

Byron. Stupid name. Stupid guy, as far as he was concerned. They'd met when Charity had gone away to school, which was the only time the two of them had ever been away from each other. Byron was taking over for his own father's veterinary clinic in Virginia, and he and Charity had had a long-distance relationship ever since.

He'd come to visit twice. Lachlan had taken against

him. No grown man who wasn't in a BBC production should wear that much tweed. He was somehow thirty and sixty-five all at the same time. While he could understand how that appealed to Charity's aesthetic, it didn't mean that he approved of it *for* her.

But then he wasn't sure he would approve of any man in her life.

Which was selfish, and a little bit ridiculous. Especially given his current mission.

"We should all be so lucky," Lachlan said. "Except the problem at the moment is I'm not husband material. I need to be made into husband material."

His brothers had met their wives before they'd had any kind of reformation. But wouldn't it be easier if he changed first? He wanted that settled thing. That easy thing. If he came to the table with a little more polish, that would be easier to find, surely.

He was determined to go about this in a somewhat scientific manner. He was going to fix himself, and start the process of searching the area to find a wife. A series of dates; that ought to do it. He'd never tried dating before. Hookups, sure. But dating, no. It had never interested him. It had never been his thing.

He was a goal-oriented kind of guy. And sex had been his goal, not relationships. But that was changing now.

"Well, *well*." She looked…bewildered.

"I don't like that look on your face. That look that suggests it will in fact be impossible to turn me into the kind of man that a woman could marry."

"Don't be too hard on yourself," she said. "You've never tried to be that kind of man before, so it stands to reason that you would be very bad at it initially."

"That's mean, Charity."

She shook her head. "Impossible. I'm never mean."

"That isn't true. I am singularly acquainted with your meanness. In fact, I think I'm the only person on earth that rates it. Ever. I like to think that makes me special. But this was particularly wounding, and I feel the need to call you out on it."

"Maybe it isn't your arm that needed numbing."

He laughed. "Oh, Charity, that's what alcohol is for. In fact, it's what I've been attempting to do for the last sixteen years."

"You can start with alcohol," she said.

He frowned. "I can what?"

"For the reformation," she said, suddenly looking at him very seriously. "You should stop drinking."

"Stop drinking?"

"Yes. At least to excess. It would probably be good for you to stop altogether at first. Do you really want to meet a wife with beer goggles on? It's one thing to drink when you…do the things that you do. To select a woman while…inebriated is certainly a choice that you can make when you're just spending the evening with her. But for your entire life?"

"Fair."

She took a step away from him and began to pace the length of the cozy little room.

The house was in order, as always. Her father's bug collection still hung on the wall, beetles and butterflies held in place with mean-looking straight pins. His knickknacks were everywhere, and she hadn't moved even a single one.

"What exactly are you looking for in a…wife?" she asked, her tone hesitant.

He couldn't really put it into words. All he had was the flash of a feeling. Something that swept over him, unfamiliar and nearly painful in nature. "Something normal."

A little line creased the space between her pale eyebrows. "*Normal*. I've never really given a lot of thought to normal. I don't think my dad was normal. I don't think the life I've had here has been normal. But it's been very happy."

"I think that's the difference between you and me. My life wasn't normal, and it wasn't happy."

She winced. "I know. I'm sorry."

"All right. So what else, Doc? I need you to fix me."

He had forgotten about the pain in his arm. She always did a good job stitching him up. She always did a good job repairing him.

He needed to get a step better than repaired now, though. He needed to change.

"No drinking," she restated.

"Fine," he said, because she really wasn't wrong. It was best if he went into this with eyes wide open and without any kind of negative effects on his mental faculties.

"You're probably going to have to…clean up your place a little bit."

"What's wrong with my place?"

"Nothing really. It's just a little bit sparse. I don't know that many women are going to look around and see much other than a project."

"What if she already has a place?"

"That isn't the point."

"What is the point?"

"You need to look like you're together. No woman wants to marry a man just to become his mother."

"You've put a lot of thought into this?"

"Of course. I'm planning on getting married. One of the things that I like about Byron is that he's extremely well organized."

"I didn't realize that you'd been to his place."

"I've seen it over video chat."

"Oh. Over video chat. Racy."

She frowned. "I don't know what that's supposed to mean."

"Of course not."

She was charmingly innocent. That was the thing. She'd been engaged to the same man for quite some time, and even if it was long-distance…he was sure that she wasn't quite as innocent as she seemed to be. But it was almost like double entendre and sexual tension never occurred to her.

It was part of her charm.

"I have *seen* his place," she said. "It's in perfect order. Like the rest of him. In order. And I *like* that about him. He has a plan, he has a place, he doesn't seem like he *needs* a woman, really, and there is something nice about that."

"Really? There's something nice about not being needed?"

"I don't know. Maybe it's because…" She looked a little bit embarrassed.

"What?"

"Because my dad needed me for everything. I helped with his business, I was homeschooled. I was very, very needed and there was something nice about that.

But there's pressure with that, too. I like the idea of not being needed quite so much."

"Okay. So I need to clean my place up."

"Make it cuter," she said.

"Too far, Charity. Too far."

She looked at him, her blue eyes extremely sincere. "You also need to stop…" She hesitated for a moment, which was very unlike her. "You need to stop engaging in casual intercourse."

"I'm sorry," he said, staring her down. "I what?"

"You heard me," she said, and if it had been anyone else, he might've thought that she was embarrassed. Charity was, down to her toes, practical. A veterinarian. He had never heard her be florid or fantastical about much of anything. She tended to be matter-of-fact. Especially about things like the facts of life. Hell, she assisted with countless animal births and lots of other nitty-gritty things.

Of course, it was different between people. Except he had a feeling that she would look at him with very wide, serious eyes and tell him it really wasn't that different at all.

"I'm just trying to be sure that I'm clear," he said.

"You're talking about finding a wife. And the way that you behave…"

"Do you judge my behavior?"

She shook her head. "I can't say that I understand it, but I've never judged it."

"I don't believe you. I think you judge me."

"No. I don't. But you asked me to reform you, and I think that it would benefit you to change your behavior completely. Maybe even put it off, for six months or so. So you can…court the lady in question. It will help keep your mind clear while you're looking for the one."

"I'm not looking for *the one*, Charity. I'm looking for a wife."

"Maybe that's part of where you need to start. I ask again, what are you looking for in a wife?"

It was a good question. One that he hadn't given all that much thought to. But he thought of the women his brothers had married. They were all… They were all pretty different. Nelly had a sweetness to her, while Elsie was tough, a farm girl down to her bones. Elizabeth was sophisticated, and Alaina would cut you as soon as look at you. They were all engaged with ranch life. All invested in Four Corners Ranch, and specifically with McCloud's Landing.

So that seemed like a pretty good place to start.

"I need a ranching woman. No nonsense. Perfectly fine if she comes with kids, maybe even preferable." He was thirty-one, after all. He was definitely old enough to have kids of his own. A ready-made family wasn't a bad idea, and it had worked out well for Brody, who seemed well suited to being a stepfather.

He'd never thought about being a dad. In fact, in the past he'd had a strong aversion to the word. To the *concept*.

But…his brother seemed happy with it. Settled. Seemed like it was the greatest thing that had ever happened to him.

"All right. Well, I guarantee you that a practical ranching woman, maybe with children, is going to need some evidence that you have…changed your ways. I think you need to stay away from Smokey's Tavern for at least six months."

That was stupid. Charity might know a few things about being good, but she didn't know how to meet potential partners. She'd been lucky stumbling over a guy in college. But he wasn't in college. "How the hell am I going to meet a woman if I can't go to the tavern?"

"Well, if you want a woman who's marriage material, I think you should avoid it."

"I *did* ask you to reform me."

"You did. Then you scoffed at every piece of advice I've given you."

"So basically, you want me to do the kinds of things that you do."

"Yes," she said. "It might actually benefit you to learn cross-stitch."

*"Cross-stitch?"*

"It's soothing."

"I don't want to be soothed."

"I think that you do," she said, her tone maddeningly sage. "Otherwise, you wouldn't be looking for a domestic life, and you certainly wouldn't be looking for a wife."

The truth was he was more soothed by being here than much of anything else he could imagine. It had always been that way.

"How are your stitches?"

He looked down at his arm. "Stitched."

She sighed. "I think you might be entirely held together by thread that I've put into your body."

That might be true. Hell, that truth might go deeper than she even imagined.

"Yeah. I can't dispute that. I have to get back. We have new guests coming up to the ranch."

About six months ago they had gotten an equine therapy center up and running on McCloud's Landing.

It wasn't really his thing. But he supported it. Again, if Gus wanted to do it, Lachlan was all about it.

"Okay. I'll be by later to do the inoculations on the new horses."

"Yeah. Okay. I'll see you then."

"Yeah. I'll see you then."

He nodded once and stood up, then put his hat on and walked out of the house. It was a pretty quick walk from Charity's place to the ranch, and he had decided to walk instead of drive on purpose. His head was full. Which was not a totally typical situation for him. No. He had spent his entire life doing his level best not to fill his head up with thoughts. Because they didn't serve him. Because they didn't do anything. Because they didn't matter.

Because there had been nothing in the world that he could do when he was a child to fix the situation that he was in. He'd just had to endure it. That was when he'd found out that there were a whole lot of things in the world that felt really damned good, and they didn't require a lot of thought. Things that did something to help blot out the pain that he experienced.

But he wanted more now. Maybe it was that he was getting older. For sure it was seeing the changes in his brothers around him.

Maybe it was just being so damned tired of waiting to see if the monster would ever wake up inside him; if he would ever transform into Seamus McCloud.

Yeah. It had been a long haul, waiting for that one.

It was one reason he wanted to approach the whole marriage thing like this. For his dad, love and marriage had been a ticking time bomb. The jealousy, the toxic nature of his parents' relationship, had him on a short fuse.

Love, that was the problem. That all-consuming love. Lachlan didn't want that.

He was pretty sure he'd figured out how to make it work for him.

Plan for a calm life, the kind of life that would never, ever let that monster out.

There was something about the way his brothers had turned out that gave him some hope.

Something had to.

# CHAPTER THREE

SHE HAD A stop to make before she could head over to McCloud's Landing. It wasn't one she was looking forward to. Even though it was just for a vitamin delivery, she had a feeling it was going to be annoying. For the most part, everybody in Pyrite Falls accepted her as a replacement veterinarian for her father. But there were those… There were those who just saw her as a child, and there was very little she could do about it. This particular rancher was one of them.

He didn't like to listen to her, and he didn't like to take her advice.

This was where she absolutely and wholly agreed with her father. Animals were simply better than people. Animals didn't care how old she was; they could tell that she was trying to help them.

She wondered… She really did wonder sometimes if there was any future here in Pyrite Falls. Not because she didn't love it—she did. It was her home, and it always had been. But that was the issue.

People had known her since she was a child, and often they treated her like a child. No matter what.

It was almost as if there was no way around it.

They looked at her, and they saw the little girl with pigtails who had tagged along with her dad on every call, and somehow never saw the grown woman who had been doing this work in her own right for years. It'd only escalated since her father died. When he'd been alive, they'd seen her as an envoy of his work—even though he wasn't the one doing the work—to a point. But now that he was gone they saw her as groundless. Rootless. As someone they couldn't necessarily trust.

Which would have been fine if she hadn't looked at the stable and seen one of the horses restlessly biting at his flanks in the stall. At least Ed agreed to let her have a look, but that was where any cordiality ended.

"He's got colic," she said, keeping her voice as firm as possible. "I need to do a rectal exam—"

The man's red face got even redder. "I think I'd know if the horse had colic."

"He's visibly struggling. This looks like an issue to me. I really think he should have a rectal exam so I can see if he's got an impacted or twisted bowel."

"Missy, I take good care of my animals and I haven't let him into the grain or anything."

"I believe you but…"

"I'll keep an eye on him, don't you worry."

"But I will worry," she said. "Because I think—"

"I don't need you to think on my animals. I didn't ask you to."

She kept thinking about what Byron had said the last time they'd talked.

It made her feel…uncomfortable. She didn't want to dwell on it. They had made plans for him to move here. That had been the idea. All these years. But most recently he'd asked her if she was open to moving.

What if she went to Virginia?

Her dad had been the biggest reason to stay.

Now that he was gone, she wondered…

Immediately, she thought of Lachlan, and her heart rebelled.

Lachlan was the single most important human being in her life.

*Is that right?*

Well… Byron wasn't part of her day-to-day life. It was an *important* relationship, but it didn't define her in quite the same way.

She had great affection for Byron. But she was well aware that there was an element of convenience to their connection. She didn't want to be alone.

Her father had been so very lonely.

She didn't want that.

She hoped to have children, and medically, she was coming to a place where that had to happen, or it wasn't going to happen. At least, not easily.

She and her dad had a lovely, quiet life here, but there had been a sadness to her father. He had given her stern warnings about relationships early on. Warnings that she had listened to. It was one reason that when she'd met Byron she had pursued a friendship with him. It wasn't until after graduation that she had suggested perhaps they consider whether or not it might be something more.

*Romantic* seemed a strong word.

She had a lot in common with him. Her dad had told her that was important.

She didn't know very much about her mother, except that she had been younger than her father. Wild. They had been different from each other, and they had wanted different things.

It had been a painful experience for her dad, she knew that, too.

She had vowed that she would always keep her head when it came to physical attraction. Not that she'd ever had any issues with it.

Byron was the only person she'd ever met that she could see herself settling down with.

Her dad had told her that the most dangerous thing was getting caught up in the passion of it all.

She didn't know what that meant.

He claimed that he had lost his head for a time, that in the end, it had caused him quite a lot of pain.

Charity couldn't imagine ever losing her head over a romance. What she had was better.

What would it be like to move away? To start a whole new life?

"Well, I don't like it," Ed said, snapping her back to the moment. "I'm going to see how he goes overnight and…"

"I advise against that," she said, but the words got stuck in her throat and sounded strangled.

"Young lady, I'm going to do what seems right to me. You forget I've got age and experience. Wisdom."

*You forget that I have a degree in veterinary medicine.* But she didn't say that last part out loud. As much as she wanted to.

"I have to make sure you know, Ed," she said, "that this is not a wise decision. It's going to put the animal in danger and I—"

"You just want to make more money. Line your pockets."

"If I wanted to line my pockets I'd do something other than be a veterinarian in a town that's so small I can count the local families on two hands."

"You think you're smarter than me because you went to school, but experience—"

"No, that isn't it, but I *do* know..."

"I have fifty years' experience ranching. You're making a mountain out of a molehill and involving yourself where I didn't ask you to. Now, thanks for the vitamins, but it's time for you to head out."

She felt helpless. Angry. What could she do if someone like him didn't listen? She was afraid the animal was in the early stages of colic, but he wasn't her animal.

But this *was* her...job. She knew what she was doing. And this man wouldn't listen.

She wasn't going to convince him to, either.

She ground her teeth together, trying to hold back the growl of anger building inside her. "Please call me if his condition doesn't improve."

She got back in the big mobile veterinary vehicle and wrapped both hands around the steering wheel, sighing loudly. Then she hit the steering wheel for good measure, the palm of her hand stinging.

Sometimes she wondered if she should start wearing suits. If maybe her dresses undermined her.

But it shouldn't. It didn't matter if she dressed feminine or not. She was qualified to do her job. She needed... Maybe that was what she needed.

She had been thinking about Lachlan's desire to be reformed. Maybe *she* needed to be reformed. Oh, not in the same way that he did. Not in the sense that she was heathenous or problematic in some way.

But she was maybe a bit too soft. Lacking in confidence. And if there was one thing that Lachlan Mc-Cloud had, it was a surplus of confidence.

Neither of them had ever sought to change the other.

He seemed to like her just as she was, in the way that she enjoyed how they were different. They amused each other; they filled something in each other's lives they didn't get anywhere else.

But he was asking her to help him change. Maybe she needed something similar. Maybe what she needed was a dose of his particular brand of swagger.

She tapped her finger on the steering wheel and considered that as she drove the short distance over to McCloud's Landing.

There he was, out working a horse, holding the lead rope in one hand, and his other—the one with the giant gash—was held down at his side. His muscles flexed with the movement. The sun was low in the sky now, flooding the arena with golden light, catching the brim of his cowboy hat, illuminating the mane and tail of the animal as she ran circles around him.

The idea of leaving here made her feel physically ill. Her stomach lurched at the thought, rebelled. All of her did.

She got out of the truck and scrambled over to him. "I'm ready for inoculations," she said.

She had her kit slung over her shoulder, held firmly down at her side.

"That's such an alarming sentence," he said.

"You know what I mean."

He grinned. She frowned.

"Do you have another bruise on your face?"

"I don't think so," he said, reaching up and touching his forehead, right on the bruise.

"You *do*," she said.

"No big deal," he said. "I bashed my head getting something out of the tack room."

"Maybe you should add being a little bit more careful with your person to your reformation list. If you're going to get married, I imagine that your wife would like to minimize the sickness part and maximize the health."

"You think so, Doc?" His lopsided grin made it impossible to be mad at him.

"Yes, I do," she said.

"Well, I will endeavor to be more careful. I was thinking about what you said about Smokey's, though. I think I have to go to Smokey's. Because I need to figure out which eligible women might make good wife material. The odds are there are some good ones at Smokey's. They aren't all buckle bunnies. Also, you know, being a buckle bunny doesn't preclude a woman from being a good wife."

She let his words wash over her, let them remain shallow and meaningless. That was what she did when he talked about his hookups.

It was this whole mystery to her, and she was okay with that.

She knew the mechanics of sexual intercourse. Obviously. She was in medicine. She saw it, simply, as a biological function. Though there were men like Lachlan who seemed to take that as a challenge. To treat it like a *daily* biological function, rather than one reserved for procreation.

She saw it as a *distraction*.

Something that he did rather than spend evenings at home in the quiet.

She often thought that the quiet might do him some good.

She didn't want to be lonely, but she also knew that it was important to know how to be alone. She sometimes wondered if Lachlan didn't know how to do that. If that was his problem. Well, she imagined he had more than one problem.

Which she didn't mean in a mean way. Who didn't have their share of problems? She was lucky, because her dad had done such a good job of protecting her from the difficulties of life. He'd experienced a lot of pain and heartbreak in his own, with friends and peers and partners. He had done everything he could to insulate her against that. She had been very fortunate to have a father who loved her so much. Lachlan hadn't had that.

"Go on," he said. "We'll go do the vaccines."

"What about this beauty?" she asked, gesturing toward the glossy bay.

"According to the guy we got him from, he's good to go. I'll make sure to get you his medical information."

She nodded. "Thank you."

She still kept a paper file system, the way her father had always done. She was a bit of a Luddite, and she didn't see the point in changing. She used technology when it suited her.

She loved streaming devices that gave her endless options for British television shows. She was also pretty fond of smartphones, so that she could use video calling with Byron. But otherwise…she didn't see the point to all that rigmarole. She would rather just go through a physical filing system, which allowed her to really commit things to memory.

It felt more tactile and made her feel like she was more engaged with the patient. She didn't want to be scrolling through her phone looking at things while she was supposed to be speaking to people.

Some of that was just knowing the people around town. They wouldn't like it, either.

"I was thinking," she said while they walked to the stables.

"Yes?"

"I might need your help, too."

"Is that so?"

"I need more confidence."

"You need more confidence?" He looked at her like she was crazy. She actually understood that. He knew her, so he understood that she had absolute confidence in herself and her capabilities as a vet.

"Let me rephrase. I need to project more confidence."

"Why is that?"

"Because people here still treat me like I'm a child. I just went to Ed Forsyth's place to deliver vitamins, and he has an ailing horse. He won't listen to me. The animal is going to get worse, and when that kind of stuff happens I just get tongue-tied. And when I get all tongue-tied I can't…"

"It is very hard for me to imagine you being tongue-tied, Charity."

"Well, I'm not. With *you*. Don't you remember when we first met?"

"Yes. I don't really remember you being tongue-tied then, either. In fact, you dragged me back to your father's house, lying to me about the nature of his job…"

"I didn't really. You asked if he was a doctor. He was."

"You know that I meant a human doctor."

"Well… Yes. But I wanted to help you, and I didn't see another way to do that."

"You are perfectly willing to engage in any kind of workaround available to you to get what you want. You are stubborn, and you are very confident."

"But it doesn't come across," she said. "People don't... They don't see me the way that I *feel*. I think it's partly because of the way that I dress. Or the way that my dad taught me to dress? That sounds weird."

He looked at her. "I guess you just never really thought about it."

"That's it," she said, feeling illuminated. "I don't think about it. My dad always put me in dresses, so I wear dresses. Unless it's absolutely impractical to do so, of course. But I think it makes me look younger, which I think is impacting my ability to do my job."

"Alternatively, I could just go punch Ed Forsyth in the face."

"No. I don't need you to do that. *I* need the willingness-to-go-punch-someone-in-the-face energy that you have. I can't have you fighting all my battles for me."

Especially if she didn't stay. But she didn't say that last part. She wasn't ready to have that conversation with him.

But then... With him getting married...or at least planning to, he probably wouldn't care. It made her feel sad to think about it, though. She supposed that was what friends did. They grew up and grew apart. But she and Lachlan had had a lot of being grown up without having that happen. They were in their thirties. Their lives had been the same in many ways since they'd met. Until her dad had died. That had shifted *her* entire foundation.

She wondered if it had shifted his.

The biggest thing for him was probably his brothers getting married. It was completely understandable that it would make him take stock of his life and want to do things differently.

"Yeah. I'll help you. Though honestly, any woman willing to take a needle that size and jam it into a horse's ass has all the confidence she needs."

She held the needle up. "Okay. I need transferable ass-injection confidence."

Her cheeks immediately colored, because she did not say words like that as a habit.

Lachlan had introduced profanity into her life, but she had never truly adopted it. She had just collected his colorful sentences like guilty trinkets in the back of her mind. She had been fascinated by that part of him. By the way he was... Somewhat feral.

"Charity Wyatt," he scolded. "Such language."

A grin spread over his face and she wrinkled her nose, which was her knee-jerk reaction to these kinds of moments with him. It did something to jar the tension that always started to mount in her chest. It wasn't a feeling that she liked. And it was something that only seemed to be caused by Lachlan.

She was very good at pushing it aside. Ignoring it.

She administered the first vaccine, and Lachlan took the horse back to its stall. Then he got out patient number two.

"So what do you think are the core tenets of confidence?"

"Not giving a fuck what anyone else thinks."

She blinked. "I don't... I don't really care what anyone else thinks, though. I mean, I care to the extent that I need to be able to treat their animals, so I can't just disregard what they say or think, and I can't be rude. But it isn't out of…"

"You care what someone thinks about you. It's why you guard your language and dress the way that you do and… It's sweet, Charity. I think you care very much what your dad thought was good and bad and right and wrong. There's nothing wrong with that."

"That's very reductive," she said, frowning deeply at him.

"Don't go using those college words at me, missy. You know I don't have that fancy education you do."

"And we both know that you're not stupid."

"Do we, though?" He grinned.

"All right," she said, doing the next injection. "Bring me the next one."

They worked together to do all the rest of the vaccinations, and then she looked at him. "Now what?"

"I think we need to go to Smokey's. Where you need to oversee my reformation, and I can oversee your confidence."

"Again, why the tavern?"

"I need to make a potential list of candidates."

"Don't you have one already?"

He had the decency to look a little bit shamefaced. "I'm not good with names."

"Wow." She sighed. "Okay. Tonight we'll go to Smokey's. But then, I think we should go out to an actual dinner, and you can practice civilized conversation, while I practice my confidence."

"Okay. I'll put you down for civilized dinner later in the week."

"Perfect."

"Are you going to go change?"

She looked down. "No."

"Okay. Well, I am. So let's go to my house, and you can wait for me."

She got into his truck, and they drove across the property, pulling up to the little cabin that he called his home.

It was cute and cozy, but it was definitely a bachelor pad. When they had poker games there, she often baked in his kitchen, and had bemoaned his lack of utensils, and eventually, many of hers had ended up migrating to his place. To the point where half of his kitchen was filled with her things.

But it was about the most civilized thing going. They walked through the front door, and Lachlan grabbed the hem of his T-shirt and began to strip it off.

She redirected sharply and went into the kitchen, carefully studying the utensils that she had installed there as she listened to his footsteps disappear into the bedroom.

She turned to look at where he'd been standing and noted that he had thrown his T-shirt onto the floor.

She picked it up and found it to be slightly damp with his sweat. Which didn't disgust her really, but there was something about it that felt maybe not quite... It made her stomach feel a bit unsettled.

"Things like this," she shouted down the hall. "Things like this are what you mustn't do."

"I *mustn't*?"

"You left your T-shirt in the middle of the floor. That's what I meant by forcing a woman to be your mother."

"Wouldn't know," he shouted back. "Didn't really have one."

"Neither did I, Lachlan, so your motherless child sob story has limited effect."

She heard his crack of laughter through the closed door, and it made her smile.

He had taught her that. That sort of grim gallows humor. Taking things that hurt and turning them into a joke. She remembered when she had first noticed him doing that. They had been spending time together in the woods, while he hid from another of his father's rages.

*He can't take a joke. But I can take a punch, and a joke. Both those things will probably serve me well in life.*

She had just looked at him in horror.

*You can laugh.*

*I can?*

*Some things are so terrible, all you can do is laugh. Right?*

*I hadn't thought of it like that.*

*You learn. You learn to take joy where you can. Because God knows no one is going to give it to you. You gotta steal it.*

They had stolen a lot of joy together, in her estimation.

They had taken those sharp and awful things they'd both had to deal with in their lives and turned them into laughter. He had made a great case for why that could be a good thing.

She sat down on the edge of his couch, her hands in her lap. For the first time she really thought about him asking if she wanted to change her clothes. Did that mean she *should* have changed her clothes? Was there something wrong with them? He was supposed to be helping her be more confident. But suddenly, she felt less confident.

He appeared a moment later, wearing a dark button-up shirt that he had tucked into his jeans, and a different hat than he'd had on before.

"Was there something wrong with my clothes?"

He looked her over. "No."

"Then why did you ask if I wanted to change?"

"I assumed you might not want to go out in the clothes that you wore to work."

"I wasn't doing sweaty work."

"Yeah. You're right."

"What am I missing?"

He made a short, hesitant noise in the back of his throat. "Think about the kinds of clothes you normally see women out in. At Smokey's. It's not like you don't go out with me."

"I just don't usually notice things like that. It doesn't really matter to me. My dad essentially had the same wardrobe from 1970 onward."

"I think you're probably right. I'm not one to make a big deal out of clothes. But... when I go out, if I'm trying to project a certain thing, then I dress accordingly."

"What thing are you ever trying to project?"

"That I'm available."

She frowned. "Right."

"You look good. There's nothing wrong with what you're wearing."

"But there's also nothing right about what I'm wearing?"

"Since when do you care?"

She didn't know why. She hadn't really ever cared

before. But there was something about the way this had all… She just didn't like it.

"Doc, if you want to go home and change, I'll go with you."

"I don't," she said, furious now. Furious that he had made her feel anything about this at all. Furious that he had made her feel like she should care. She was just furious.

"All right, then, let's go. I need to get you a hamburger or something, because you're being a little bit feral."

"I am not."

"Okay. I'm sorry. We'll just go get a hamburger."

They got into the truck, and she noticed that he smelled different than he had when they had driven over. Like he put on cologne or something.

She sniffed a couple of times.

"Are you smelling me?"

Fire bloomed in her cheeks. *"No."*

Smokey's wasn't all that crowded yet, and when they went in, there were plenty of available tables. "Shall I go order for us?"

"I can order."

He went away to the bar. Sheena was making drinks tonight. She'd just started bartending at Smokey's a few months back, and she was undeniably hot. Somewhere around his age, with dark hair, a smoking figure and a full sleeve of tattoos on her left arm. He'd heard she didn't like locals, and she didn't really scream marriage material but while she got his order together he couldn't help but try to picture it.

"Hey!" She shouted across the bar at a couple of guys who looked like they were starting to tussle. They didn't respond, and she picked up an empty beer bottle and hurled it unerringly between the men. It hit the wall between them and shattered. Everyone stopped and looked at her. "Behave," she said, before turning to Lachlan. "What'll you have, McCloud?"

Well, she'd be interesting anyway. But he wasn't sure he was in the market for interesting. He was looking for a stabilizing influence and he had a feeling... she was not.

He went back to Charity with a beer for himself, and a Coke for her.

She leaned in and took a sip from the straw. And started to canvass the room. There were a lot of women here already.

"Any of them?" she asked.

"Maybe."

His eyes locked on the waitress. Dulce was her name. For some reason she felt an instinctive and intense dislike for that. And for her.

"No," she said.

"No what?"

"I don't think she's right."

"Do you know her?"

"No. But I just... She has a career. Don't you kind of want somebody who could dedicate themselves to your comfort?" He hadn't said that, but Lachlan was a rancher, and the way he talked about finding a wife— like it was a position that needed filling as a job—it made her wonder if he wanted something his ancestors would have chosen. He worked the land; she worked the house. That kind of thing.

But he frowned.

"I don't want a housekeeper. I want a wife."

That didn't make sense to her. What did he need a wife for if not completing the things he didn't want to do? She wanted to get married to Byron for companionship. But she knew him. He was a good friend. She knew he'd be…good at companionship.

Lachlan just wanted a wife. Any wife.

"What exactly do you want a wife for?"

"The change it's had on my brothers… It's completely unlike anything I could've guessed. I would've told you that they would be terrible husbands. But they're not. They've gone from being some of the most unpleasant assholes I've ever known to being…blissfully happy. I'm not an idiot. If I think that could be out there for me…"

"Are you unhappy?"

He looked at her for a long moment. "I'm a mess."

She looked down at her hands. "I've never thought that you were a mess."

"I think that's a lie. But it's a sweet one."

"Just one beer," she said, watching him lift the bottle to his lips.

"Damn. I forgot."

"I think one beer is probably fine."

"You don't think Dulce is fine?" he asked, and she had a feeling he knew full well he was needling her.

"I'm not trying to gatekeep your choices. I just…"

That was when Dulce appeared with two burger baskets filled to the brim with onion rings.

"Maybe I should consider Fia Sullivan," he said, as the bar continued to fill up and he looked around.

"Fia?"

"Yeah. My brother's married to her sister. The Sullivan girls are nice. Really, any of them…"

"Isn't she sort of in love with…"

"She *hates* him. If you ask her."

"Well… I'm not really up on all the gossip of Four Corners, but even I know that she's preoccupied with him."

"One thing I don't want is to be treading on Landry King's territory. Because he's an unpleasant son of a bitch."

He finished his beer and looked around.

"Coke," she said. "Order a Coke."

"You're a little taskmaster, do you know that?"

She spread her hands. "I'm just doing what you asked me."

"Your problem isn't confidence, Charity. Your problem is learning that you can take the confidence you already have and use it anywhere you like."

## CHAPTER FOUR

HE'D HAD A pretty good idea of who at Smokey's he would be considering before they'd gone out tonight. Dulce was in the running, even though Charity had expressed skepticism. He had always thought she was pretty. But had never really wanted to make drinking at the bar awkward by hooking up with the woman who served the drinks.

One point in her favor was that she wouldn't be bothered by his drinking, since she had already seen him do it lots of times.

She'd also witnessed every hookup he'd engaged in for the past few years, so he could see where she might not think he was the greatest bet. So there was that.

There were also a couple of girls who frequented the bar, but not often enough that they would be overly familiar with him, and he wasn't all that familiar with them. Lucy Carmichael and Lydia Holliday were pretty enough.

Charity was writing names on a napkin, which he felt like was maybe overkill. But he had asked her to overkill this endeavor. So he couldn't be disdainful of her now that she was. He also couldn't argue with her about the alcohol. He asked for her help. So he had to take it.

He supposed that could be true when it came to her

opinions on the waitress. But the thing was he hadn't asked her to choose him a wife. He had asked her to make him husband material.

Because she was all things bright and good and lovely, and he just...wasn't.

Suddenly, her phone lit up from where it was sitting on the table.

"It's Ed," she said.

She picked the phone up. "Hello? Okay. Okay. I'm on my way."

Then to Lachlan, "The horse is down. I have to help him get him up."

He started to stand, grabbing his coat off the back of the chair. "I'm going with you."

"You don't need to do that."

"I do. Anyway, I drove you."

"I need to stop and get the vet mobile."

"I'll take you right to it."

They helped each other. That was what they did.

They drove quickly back to the ranch, and he got into the mobile veterinary unit with her, and let her drive to Ed Forsyth's farm.

"I *told him*," she said furiously. "I told him."

"And this is why you need to get your confidence up," he said.

"That's what I said," she snapped. *"Dammit."* She put her hand over her mouth. "Sorry."

"Shocking. Twice in one day."

"You're a bad influence."

"I'm trying to be a *good* influence. Swearing notwithstanding."

They got out of the car, and she beat the path to the barn. When they were inside, she went straight to the horse's stall, where Ed was, standing over the horse. "I can't get him up myself."

"Luckily, she brought some muscle," Lachlan said.

The man looked up. "Hey there, McCloud. Appreciate you coming by to help."

He bristled on Charity's behalf. He'd called Charity out, after sending her away, and he wasn't even thanking her for rushing back. He was thanking Lachlan. Which made him feel that the biggest issue here wasn't her age, but her gender. That pissed Lachlan off.

"I'm just here to assist. Whatever Charity says goes."

"We need to get him on his feet. I'm going to take the lead rope in the front, if you can get the back end, Lachlan..."

"No problem."

Running an equestrian facility, he'd had plenty of experience with horses that had foundered because of colic.

"Okay," she said. "I'm gonna pull."

The horse was wild-eyed and struggling, and Lachlan worked in time with Charity, gently getting the horse back to his feet.

He went back down again, and they raised him back up.

"There we go," she said, once he found his feet. "There we go. Okay. Now I need to do an X-ray and I need to see if this is going to require surgery."

She set to work, giving orders and working with efficiency. She was amazing. Absolutely incredible at what she did. Seeing Ed humbled by her efficiency and brilliance was deeply satisfying.

She determined the horse didn't need surgery, just

medication, and they were able to get him settled, comfortable and stable.

Lachlan had always admired Charity. Hell, he let the girl stitch him up, and he trusted her before he trusted any doctor, but really seeing her in action like this... It was amazing.

Charity went back to the truck to log everything into her system, and then Lachlan turned to Ed.

"I would suggest that next time you listen to the lady," Lachlan said, looking at the older man with nothing but scorn in his eyes. He didn't care if the guy saw it. He *deserved* to see it. He deserved to feel ashamed of what he'd done. Of the way that he'd treated her, and put his animal at risk because he hadn't listened to her.

"It's just... It's not the way that I'm used to doing things," he said.

"Listening to the experts? She's the expert. That should be pretty clear."

It made him angry that it probably took a lecture from Lachlan to even get Ed to fully understand what had just happened.

She was good at her job, and the fact that this man would refuse to see it, even now that she had saved his horse's life, no thanks to his stubborn idiocy, made Lachlan want to tear the whole world down.

It was maddening that Charity needed to find the confidence to deal with people like this. Because it was maddening she had to deal with them at all.

He was snarling by the time they got back into the mobile vet unit. But Charity just laid her head back against the seat, looking exhausted.

"You okay?"

"I'm okay," she said. "Let's go back to your place. I'll drop you off."

Except… That wasn't what he wanted. He wanted to do something for her. Wanted to take care of her. She didn't have anyone left in her life to do that for her.

"I'll tell you what. Let's go back to your place. I'll either walk home later or I can sleep on the couch."

"Why?"

"Your dinner got interrupted at the bar, and you're probably still hungry."

"I don't know if I'm still hungry," she said. "You can't go making declarations like that."

"Well, if you are, I can get you something to eat."

"Okay," she said.

She didn't put up a fight at all.

He smiled to himself.

They drove back to her place. They had forgotten to leave the porch light on. Her dad would have done that for her. Left that light on. Lachlan looked at her and wondered if she was feeling as cognizant of the loss right then as he was.

"Thank you," she said, her voice scratchy.

"I'm sorry. It hasn't been very long since he died. I know it's hard."

"I appreciate you doing this. Because you know… *He* would have. He would have made me tea and asked to tell him about what had happened. He would have…"

"He would've left the porch light on for you."

"Yes. Exactly. I was thinking that when we pulled up."

"Somehow, I thought you might be."

"It's just a very sad thing when you realize that no

one's ever going to take care of you like that again. Because only my dad ever..."

She stopped talking, her words getting choked. He couldn't relate because he didn't know what it was like to be able to count on someone to take care of him at all.

But right then he felt her loss. He knew it must be devastating. How could it not be? To have had something like that and to lose it... It made his chest feel all torn up and bloody just thinking about it. Poor Charity. It made him want to wrap her in something soft. Give her whatever she needed. But definitely a cup of tea. No one had ever really taken care of him, but he could say that he hadn't taken care of anyone else, either.

His brothers had protected him. Especially Gus. But there was a hard edge to that reality. To the way that they had been with one another, always.

It wasn't the same as care in the way that she was talking about.

Gus had wanted to make him tough. It had been a matter of survival. Especially for Lachlan.

So he had taken his brother up on that. It was what they'd all had to do to survive living in the McCloud house.

Why have so many kids? Why have so many kids if you hated them so much?

Maybe their dad hadn't hated them, either. Maybe it was an extension of that same manic love he felt for their mother. Maybe all his feelings were just...

Poison.

The thought made Lachlan wince.

Maybe that was part of why marriage had been so

healing to his siblings. Maybe it was part of why having children fixed something inside them.

Because they were proving they could do it. Right and healthy and…not all that their lives had been.

Maybe proving it would fix this feeling.

It made sense.

It made a perfect kind of sense.

They got out of the large truck and started to walk toward the house, and Charity faltered, stumbling. He reached out quickly and grabbed hold of her arm, holding her so that she was upright and steady. She was so slender and small, his hand wrapped all the way around her forearm, his fingers overlapping. Her skin was soft. *She* was soft. He eyes glittered as she looked up at him in the darkness.

"That's why we need to leave the porch light on," she said. "I slipped on a rock."

"Be careful, Doc," he said, releasing her slowly. "I don't know how to stitch you up."

She laughed, a breathy sort of sound. "I'm definitely not letting you come at me with a needle and thread."

"As well you shouldn't. I am definitely not to be trusted."

She went ahead of him toward the house and he smiled, into the darkness, simply because it did something to ease the tension in his gut.

He could use that.

He was riled up from what had happened at Ed's place. He knew that he didn't see behavior like that because he was a man. He'd grown up around here, too. He'd been just a kid to all these older people. Not only that; they might have reason to distrust him because he was his father's son. Hell, he almost couldn't blame them if they did.

But he *didn't* get treated like that. Ed had even been happy to see him. Lachlan was able to be a man in his own right, sure and confident in his opinions because he had shown up and was a man. Which wasn't fair because she deserved respect.

That was what had him all tense. Having to look that bullshit straight in the face. He didn't like it one bit. He didn't like it at all.

Charity pushed the door open to the house after unlocking it and flipped open the light. It bathed the whole living room in a warm glow, and that empty chair in the corner felt like a slap to him, so he could only imagine how it felt to her. Poor thing.

"Have a seat," he said.

"You're not so bad," she said. "I guess this is why I keep you around and give you free medical care."

"Not to put too fine a point on it, but I am basically your lab rat."

He took the flower teapot off the stove and filled it up with water, sticking it on the back burner and turning it on high. "You can tell all of your clients that you've trained on an actual human. And before you tell me that animals are harder because different anatomy and *whatever*, you know that people will think that's impressive."

"Ed certainly doesn't think it's impressive. He doesn't think anything about me is impressive."

"He's sexist, Charity. There's not a hell of a lot you can do about that. If he refuses to listen to you, then he can pay the money to haul his horses over to a vet a couple hours away. Or he can pay the money to have somebody drive out to him."

"If I wasn't here there wouldn't be a vet," she said, her voice going flat and strange.

"No," he said, not quite able to read the tone in her words. "There wouldn't be. He's being an ass, and he's not appreciating what he has."

"If he does accept me, I suppose that the bottom line is he's doing it only because of his own comfort and convenience. That's kind of bracing."

"I don't know about that. But I don't really know that it matters. He should accept you because you're good at your job. He should accept you because I really do believe that if a man showed up and said he was a vet, he would. Not knowing him, not knowing that he trained under one of the best in the business."

"My dad *was* one of the best in the business," she said, standing and walking over to her father's chair. She touched the back of it, a sad smile touching her face. "You know, he was very lonely sometimes. I think you helped a lot. He had me, and he did appreciate it. But… He didn't have a whole lot of friends. And the ones he did have liked to argue with him. About all of his very firm and strident opinions. Which he liked. Because he liked nothing more than voicing his opinions whenever he got the chance."

"I know that about him."

"He liked you because you didn't get offended. He could talk to you about anything and you'd challenge him, but you didn't get angry. You just got more talkative."

"I didn't have a good father. You know that. Your dad was the closest thing I had."

"I think you were pretty close to a son to him."

The teakettle whistled.

He reached up into the cupboard and pulled out a mustard-yellow mug with little half-circle impressions all along the rim. It was one that reminded him of Albert.

He poured a measure of hot water into the mug and put a teabag into it before handing it to Charity.

"That isn't the right way to make tea," she said.

"Sorry. I don't know a different way."

"I appreciate it all the same. I really do."

"I might not be reformed yet, but I try my best for you."

She smiled. "I know."

He knew what he wanted the next step to be in his plan. "Tomorrow let's go on a date."

"What?"

"You mentioned that. Going out to dinner. I think you should go to dinner with me and evaluate my performance."

"Okay," she said slowly.

"I think I might ask Fia out."

"Oh."

"Yeah. I think she'd be a great wife. I want somebody that's interested in the ranch. Somebody that's invested in it. She really is. She's got her own responsibilities..."

"She's invested in getting the farm store up and running," Charity pointed out. "I don't know that you're ever going to get her to do work over here."

"It doesn't need to be over here. We have enough people. It's just...understanding. Understanding that this is important. That it's always going to be a high priority in my life."

"Right." She sounded skeptical, but she covered it with a slow sip of tea.

"Anyway. We can go to dinner in Mapleton. I'll make us a reservation."

"That's…fancy." She wrinkled her nose as if fancy was something foreign and concerning. He liked it. "Very fancy."

"Well, why not? It sounds fun. Fancy. You deserve it. Especially after the day you've had."

"That's sweet." She somehow made *sweet* sound suspicious.

"Do you have any…?"

"I have cookie dough in the fridge," she said.

He grinned and went to grab a cookie sheet, putting the oven on the appropriate temperature, which he knew, because Charity often brought cookie dough to him, much to his delight.

He put spoonfuls of dough onto the sheet, and as soon as the oven was preheated he put it in there and set the timer.

"I might have Byron out to visit soon," she said.

"You might?"

They kept their Bryon talk minimal and he preferred it that way. He had shared Charity with her father ever since he'd known her—that was fair enough.

When she'd gotten involved with Byron he hadn't liked it. He didn't like the idea that she had someone in her life who was that important to her, and he knew that wasn't especially fair but it was the truth.

"I am," she clarified. "I'm just waiting for him to give me exact dates."

"Oh. Well. Sounds good."

"It should be."

"Are you looking forward to it?" He didn't harass her about Byron, because he figured his issues with the guy were his issues. But for some reason, with him looking for a wife, and Byron coming to visit, maybe her marrying this guy seemed a lot more *real*.

It didn't sit right with him.

He told himself then and there it was because she didn't seem excited. He wasn't a huge fan of all-consuming love—thought it was dangerous, in fact. But it seemed like you ought to want to be with the man you were planning on getting hitched to.

"Yes," she said. "Why wouldn't I be?"

"I just can never tell when it comes to him. If you're all that excited."

"It isn't that kind of relationship. I really like him. I can talk to him the way that I did my dad. About all kinds of things. He's so interested in science and… He's very interesting. I enjoy talking to him."

He didn't say anything about passion, because he wasn't going to go bring that up. There were certain things they deliberately didn't talk about. Hell, for all he knew, she got super freaky with Doctor Tweed whenever they saw each other, or whenever they talked over video call.

The idea made him frown. Deeply.

He did not care for that. Not in the least. He would thank himself to never go pondering that again. He could see why it made sense for Charity to be with a guy like that. In a lot of ways, he could see that people might look at them and think they were alike. That they were the same. Because there was something sort of quiet and measured about him. Maybe a little bit old-fashioned, like Charity herself often seemed. But Charity had spark. Spirit. She was funny.

She wasn't really *old-fashioned*; she was just every inch *herself*.

Sure, he might give her a little bit of a hard time about her language, and sure, some of that was because she wanted to please her dad, who had *definitely* been old-fashioned.

But she was her; down to her bones, she defied description. She was his. That was all.

He didn't know what you called that. Beyond certainty.

Family, he supposed, in the way that other people saw it. He had often thought that. That he and Charity were like family. They had met that day, and they had been inseparable ever since. He had taken care of her; she had taken care of him.

But it was even more powerful because they had chosen it. He hadn't chosen to be born to a psychotic bastard who used his own wife and children as a punching bag. He hadn't chosen any of that. But he had chosen her.

That was just the way it was.

The cookies came out warm, and he let them cool for a moment before putting them on a plate and moving into the living room. Charity had gone and changed into some sweats, and was now sitting on the couch cross-legged, her blond hair loose and fanned around her shoulders, the old, tasseled lampshade casting funny shadows of warm light over her cheeks.

She was clutching the mug with both hands, but let one hand free to grab a cookie.

"That really is excellent," she said, taking a bite.

"Well, you made it. I didn't."

"Oh, I know that," she said. "I'm complimenting myself, but thanking you. It was… What a strange day."

"Yeah."

If he got married, he would lose these quiet evenings. This time with Charity. Because it wasn't like he could leave his wife at home and come here. He might think of Charity like family. But he knew that he would have a harder time convincing a wife of that. Not Fia Sullivan, though. Fia knew him. She knew Charity. Maybe it would be… Maybe it would be normal to her. Reasonable.

But by then, Charity would probably be married to Byron, and he would be bringing her cookies and tea, and maybe sitting in that armchair with an afghan over his lap in exactly the same way that Albert Wyatt had done. They would play board games, probably. Or maybe just talk about the weather.

Things were going to change. There was no getting around that. So he better make sure that he had something to fill his life when she was…

Hell.

The guy was coming to visit, too, which probably meant that they would actually take some steps toward getting married. He had always been a bit surprised that she hadn't hurried up and done it while her father was still alive. But it didn't really seem like her dad seeing her get married was her priority. It was more living out all of that sweet, quiet life she'd had with him, until she couldn't have it anymore, was the priority.

She hadn't wanted to change anything before then.

Now she needed something else.

*Great. Sit there and psychoanalyze her so you don't have to think about your own self.*

Whatever.

"I don't know that I like the beetles," she said.

"That's kind of random. But not even 'Hey Jude?'"

"Not the band. The beetles on the wall."

"Oh." He looked over his shoulder. At the bug collection hanging there. "You don't have to keep them."

"I guess not. But he loved them. They were his. I think he thought pretty highly of them."

"Yeah. But it doesn't matter. He isn't here to look at them."

Charity suddenly looked impossibly small and sad.

"I know that what you're saying is true. But... I kind of like the idea that he still can."

"I didn't say he couldn't," Lachlan said, suddenly feeling like his hands were too big and his tongue was clumsy. Because God knew he didn't have any experience dealing with people's fragile emotions.

He'd been there for Charity in the wake of her father's death, but she'd been oddly stoic during that time. Maybe because she had known it was coming. Maybe because so much of the mourning had been done in bits and pieces in the time leading up to his death.

It had never seemed to hit with a cymbal crash. Her father had slipped away, but the grief had continued on. A reverberating echo that sometimes grew and sometimes seemed to ebb.

Right now he could see that it was a swell, about to break over her.

"You could put them in a different room. That way,

if he wants to check in, he could check in on them specifically. You can put them in his bedroom."

"Yeah. That's a good idea," she said, smiling. "I'm sorry. I know it's silly. Given that I work adjacent to science, I guess I should have a more scientific mind about it all. But I can just still feel him."

Lachlan didn't care much about science one way or the other. It wasn't something he spent a lot of time pondering. But he knew what he felt. He knew that he felt a divine presence when he was out riding in the mountains, one that he'd often been angry at, because what the hell, man? If there was a big divine presence out there, why hadn't it intervened in his life?

It still comforted him. Even if he was sometimes mad at it. He'd rather have someone to be mad at than believe in nothing, frankly. So the idea that her dad was still around, that she could feel him… It didn't seem strange to him in the least. It seemed right. Reasonable.

Albert wouldn't like it. It would've been something they debated. It superseded logic, and Albert wasn't a fan of that. Lachlan was, if only because he had watched men do impossible mental dances to explain the terrible things they did. To justify them. He wasn't fond of men's logic. So he liked to believe that there were things out there that were beyond it. That were beyond their control and their understanding.

"Do *you* want them?" she asked.

"Do I want…what?"

"The bug collections. You can have them."

"Aren't I supposed to be finding a woman and convincing her to come and live with me? Because I feel like that might make it an uphill battle."

"Well… I know that. I'm sorry. It's just…"

"You know," he said, his voice suddenly feeling too harsh for the space. For the topic. "Yeah. I might like them. That way, your dad might have a reason to come and check in with me."

"He already does," she said, so confident in that.

"Well, I like it. So yeah. I'll take them, and I'll put them up somewhere. Any woman that wants to be my wife is going to have to deal with it, because they were a gift. From somebody really special."

Charity smiled, and right then he didn't know if he meant her, or Albert.

"Are you going to sleep here tonight?"

Silence blanketed them, and there was nothing but the sound of the house settling around them.

"You know, I think I'm gonna go ahead and walk home." He just figured he should. It seemed like the better part of valor at that moment, and he didn't even quite know why. "But I'll see you for dinner. Tomorrow night. I'll pick you up."

Because it was a date, after all.

"Okay," she said. She yawned and pitched her head back, then forward again, a lock of blond hair falling into her face. "I'm sleepy," she said.

"Yeah. I figured as much. Get some rest. See you tomorrow."

"See you tomorrow."

He reached out and snagged a couple of cookies off the plate and headed toward the door.

"Lachlan?"

He stopped and turned. There was something about the way the light shone on her just then, that made her look unfamiliar. She looked young, but not like she'd been when she was a teenager or anything, just…serene maybe. Like there was a halo around her.

"What?"

"Thank you. For taking care of me. It's just… It means a lot. I don't know if you really know that."

"You're welcome."

He opened the door, and a blast of chilly air hit him in the face.

He welcomed it.

He shoved the cookies into his mouth, then pushed both hands into his pockets and walked on with his head down, enjoying the press of the darkness around him.

There was light. There would be light. There always was.

And he was working on making some light of his own and he supposed that was a pretty good start.

# CHAPTER FIVE

CHARITY HAD ASSISTED with a difficult birth for a pig today, and had been rewarded by the intense adorableness that was a litter of piglets.

She loved piglets.

She loved animals. That was the thing. All of them, all kinds. The only reason she didn't have any of her own was that every animal in the vicinity was hers.

But sometimes she wished that she did have a puppy or a ferret. Or fox kits, even though she was morally opposed to the idea of taking a wild animal and domesticating it… But there were circumstances surely…

Her phone rang, and she startled. It was Byron. They had an appointment to talk; of course they did. It was weird that she had forgotten. That she had been thinking about animals instead of him. Or maybe not. It was pretty much the way her brain worked. She didn't think about him all that much when they didn't talk. She figured that was healthy.

Boundaries and all that.

She answered, holding the phone arm's length away from her face. "Hi," she said.

The vision of his pleasant face did soothe her. Made her feel calm and happy. He did that. He was like that afghan in her living room.

Comforting. Homespun. She didn't know how a

person could be homespun, but he sort of seemed like he was.

"I thought that I would call you and discuss the exact dates for my arrival."

"Oh yes," she said. "You know, I have a spare bedroom, so you don't need to worry about booking the room above Smokey's if you don't want to…"

"I appreciate that," he said. "But particularly with your father gone, I worry about appearances."

"Oh."

"I don't mean what people would think, it's just… It isn't that I don't trust you or myself. But staying away from the appearance of evil is important."

Byron was quite devout. She found it to be a charming part of his personality. His beliefs were very sincerely held, and while he mostly treated it as a personal part of his life, there were certain things that he was adamant about. He did not drink at all. And when it came to physical intimacy, he believed firmly that it must be between a husband and wife only. She didn't mind that. In fact, she found it to be sweet.

"Well, whatever suits you. I don't want you to be uncomfortable."

She wondered what he would think about Lachlan being at her house late at night.

The thought made goose bumps break out on her arms. It wasn't the same. He was Lachlan.

He wasn't her boyfriend.

He was her friend.

He had made her tea and cookies and…

She redirected her thoughts. To the conversation at hand. As was reasonable.

"Well, what is looking possible in terms of availability?"

"I'm thinking next week," he said. "It will also be a good flight time for me."

"Okay. That works well for me. I will still have work…"

"Of course. I'm happy to help you with anything you might need assistance with."

"Thank you," she said. "That's very kind."

He was very kind. Endlessly. She liked that about him. He was very… Well… He was a wonderful man. There was absolutely nothing about him that wasn't.

"I'm very much looking forward to it. Once I'm there we can discuss you moving here."

"I really did think that you wanted to move here," she said.

"I know we discussed that, and I am still open to it. I think this week will be a good chance for us to get our bearings. Maybe you can come to Virginia and visit me."

"I just have a harder time covering things than you, because I don't have any other person working my practice. Which is another thing. There isn't another veterinarian here." She thought about what Lachlan had said to her. About the way that it made her feel. She was the only one. If she left… If she left then somebody else would have to come and take her place, and it was difficult to get people to agree to come live in a place that was this small, this remote.

"I suppose it would be good to have two," he said.

It would be. There was plenty of work here. But then…there was also the chance to start over. With something totally new and different.

She was just so deeply unsure of what she wanted. If she wanted to change; if she wanted things to stay the same…

It was a change to think about marrying him. To think about having a husband, and eventually having children. Yes. It would be a change.

And there wasn't anything wrong with that. In fact, it was what she wanted. She just wasn't sure if she wanted a complete change—a move across the country—or if she just wanted to take it one step at a time.

It was so very hard to say.

But they would have the week. A week of him visiting for them to get a better idea of what they both wanted.

He was incredibly reasonable. That was one of the things she liked the most about him. Rational. He didn't lead with his feelings.

Whatever decisions they made, they would be so grounded in what was best. What they both cared about.

"All right. Send me your flight itinerary when you have it, and I will arrange to pick you up from the airport."

"Oh, no need. I'll get a rental car. Though I appreciate it. But that way I'll be able to get myself around."

"That's thoughtful of you." He was always thoughtful. "So we'll meet at my house?"

"Yes. I'll keep you posted."

"Thank you."

"I got a new German board game I think you'll like."

In college they'd spent a lot of time in the board game store just off campus, finding obscure strategy games to play in their group of friends, and it was something they both still enjoyed.

Lachlan found the games dull and incomprehensible. His words. But he'd only said it after she'd cornered the market on sheep. So she was pretty sure it had been sour grapes.

"That sounds great!" she said, suddenly more able to picture her time with Byron. It had been a while since she'd seen him and she was feeling nervous, which wasn't normal for them. But they were actually taking the next steps now, not just pushing the wedding off and off. Things felt more real. It was natural she felt a little nervous. "I'll see you soon."

She got off the phone with him and walked into her house. She was having dinner with Lachlan tonight.

That was suddenly the much larger thought on her mind. She had dinner with Lachlan all the time. But it was just funny because he had called this a date. It was a date, though, for her to evaluate his reformation.

His personal transformation into husband material, from whatever he was now.

It would be weird to think of him that way.

She knew what *she* wanted in a husband. Everything that Byron exemplified.

It would be weird to look at Lachlan and try to apply those same sorts of metrics to him.

And what was she going to wear?

The sweatshirt and skirt that she had on now wasn't going to work.

*Are you going to change?*

That stuck in her head. The thing that he had said to her yesterday when she had been wearing her long floral dress. As if there was something wrong with it.

He had said that he didn't mean that, but she couldn't get it out of her head now. Which was silly. And more than a little bit illogical.

She went into the bathroom and started the shower, looking at herself in the mirror while the water warmed up.

She didn't think about her looks all that often.

Her eyes were large, her nose small. Everything worked just fine. She wrinkled her nose, as if to prove to herself that it was fully functional.

She had always liked the color of her hair. It was golden, and she knew that a lot of people had to go to a stylist to get that color. While hers was simply there.

She wasn't overly proud about it per se, but if pressed, she would say that it was maybe her favorite feature. She had a very small amount of makeup to her name, just enough to sufficiently make herself feel formal at a wedding. A bit of pink gloss, some gold eyeshadow and mascara.

She decided to go ahead and get it out, because after her shower she would actually put some on.

She stripped her clothes off and hopped beneath the hot spray. For some reason she remembered yesterday when Lachlan had stripped his shirt off while walking through the house.

She hadn't looked at him.

On purpose.

She blinked.

She hadn't looked at him on purpose. That was an odd thought she wasn't entirely sure was true. She had just been interested in counting the different utensils in the kitchen.

It was just kind of a normal thing. He didn't really

possess any modesty to speak of, and it didn't signify to her one way or the other.

At all. It was just immaterial.

The water suddenly felt a little bit too intense, the pressure too high as the droplets slid over her skin.

She shampooed her hair and soaped up her body as quickly as possible and cut the shower short.

Then she went into her bedroom, swathed in a towel, and started to look around in her closet.

She mostly had long floral dresses, a denim skirt, a couple of pairs of jeans...

She saw a black dress in the corner and paused. She had bought it for something. She could scarcely remember what, and she hadn't worn it for years. It was midcalf, and a stretchy T-shirt material that was a bit more clingy than she usually went with.

She decided to go ahead with that, since it looked a little bit fancy. She put it on and grabbed her tennis shoes and socks and thought... They wouldn't work.

She had a pair of black simple ballet flats, and she put those on instead. She stood in front of the mirror and blew her hair dry, enjoying the way that it shimmered and fell with just a little more volume. She didn't usually bother with that. If her hair was wet, she usually just put it up in a ponytail and let it dry out of her way.

She put her bare minimum makeup on, and felt reasonably satisfied that she looked like someone who at least wouldn't be completely out of place sitting across the table from Lachlan.

Since when did she care about things like that?

She didn't. It was just a passing thought. People had passing thoughts all the time.

Her father was fond of telling her that when she had been very emotional or upset when she was an adolescent girl.

*These are just feelings. And feelings don't require that you do anything but feel them. It'll pass.*

Yes. Feelings were not an action item. She didn't have to do anything in response to them. And it was the same with thoughts like that. They were only thoughts.

It didn't matter what she looked like; that wasn't the point of anything. The point was to help him. And actually, she felt slightly more confident looking at herself right now. So maybe it was just a side effect of being able to help him.

Her phone buzzed where it was sitting on the bathroom counter. I'll be there in five minutes.

Ready.

And she stood and waited at the living room window. Waited to see his truck coming up the driveway. She was excited to go to Mapleton; she hadn't been in a long time, and they had great restaurants. She wondered what he had picked.

They almost only ever went to Becky's or Smokey's. The café or the tavern. And both essentially had the same kind of food; it was just that one had more alcohol, and since that didn't matter to Charity, which restaurant didn't really matter, either.

But this would be different. Totally different…and she was very much looking forward to it.

Then she saw it. The front of his big, black truck, coming up the drive, and a little flutter of excitement ignited in her stomach.

She found herself standing there, just smiling. She looked over at the chair where her father should've been. "I'll make sure to order the flourless chocolate torte. It has to happen, because it's a nice restaurant. And that's what you said. If it was a good restaurant, it would have a flourless chocolate torte."

Her eyes felt an immense amount of pressure behind them. Then she turned back, where Lachlan had parked and gotten out of the truck.

She watched as he walked toward the front door. He was wearing black jeans, a black button-up shirt and a black cowboy hat. And for just one moment she felt disoriented. Out of place in her reality.

It was like she was watching a movie, watching an outlaw walk with the horizon against his back. And it suddenly felt silly that she had thought she wouldn't look half so out of her league sitting across the table from him because he was…

He was him. Uniquely and utterly him, and she had never seen the light of him. Even having known him all her life, she felt right now like she had never seen anything like him. There was a well of insecurity that had bubbled up in her chest, and she didn't quite know what to do about it, because it was completely foreign to her. She didn't have insecurity about her looks, because her default was just not thinking about them at all. Except she had just spent a considerable amount of time thinking about them and now…

He was at her front door.

He knocked.

She scrambled over to it and pulled it open.

His eyes were startlingly blue, particularly with all the black.

His jaw was clean-shaven, and she couldn't remember the last time that had been true.

She wasn't sure she liked it. Except she did. Except she missed the way he usually looked. Except he looked special.

Special to go out with *her*.

"Hi," she said.

He didn't seem like he was having similarly frantic thoughts playing around in his head. Instead, he looked her over. Very slowly.

"You look nice," he said.

"Thank you," she said. And for some reason the words felt deflating. Almost disappointing. She had no reason to feel that way. As if she was expecting… What? Some kind of intense declaration? She didn't even want that. A declaration of what anyway? Something more than *nice*? That was ridiculous. She didn't need anything more than that. Anyway… What would that even be?

"Do you need a coat?"

"I don't think so," she said.

"Suit yourself."

They went to his truck, and he opened the door for her. "Chivalry? Good?"

"Yes," she said after pausing to think for a minute. "I think that's very good."

"Good. I'm glad to hear that I pass muster."

She climbed into the truck, and he closed the door firmly behind her. He got in while she was buckling, and she noticed that he smelled spicy again. That cologne.

She wrinkled her nose.

"I made a reservation for us at a place called Amuse.

Sounds ridiculously impressed with itself, but I figured that's what you want. Nobody wants to go to a restaurant with low self-esteem."

"I guess not," she said. "If it doesn't believe in its food, why should I?"

"Exactly. I don't want steak with imposter syndrome."

"Is there flourless chocolate torte on the menu?"

"Of course there is. I checked."

She felt a little bit warm, because that must mean that he remembered. That it was significant.

"I wanted to get one in honor of Dad," she said.

"Your dad really loved chocolate."

"Yes. He was a strange man. I know that. But I loved him all the same. I couldn't have loved him any more."

"If he was strange, then more people should be strange like him, Charity. Bottom line. He was a good man. He loved you more than anything."

She knew that; that was the really brilliant thing. She knew that her dad loved her so very much, and she also knew that a whole lot of people didn't have that level of assurance from their parents, or their parents really didn't love them enough at all. Like Lachlan's.

"I am going to get wine tonight. That's acceptable, right?" he asked.

"Yes," she said. "I would think that if you took a woman out to a nice restaurant that she would want a glass of wine."

"Not you, though?"

"I just never developed a taste for it."

"Fair."

"Anyway, Byron doesn't approve of alcohol."

"He doesn't approve of it?" She could hear the frown in his voice.

"No. He's coming next week. I thought that you might want to know that."

"Right. He… Bunking with you?"

"Oh no," she said.

"No?"

"No. He doesn't think it's appropriate."

"He doesn't… I… I don't really know what to say to that, Charity. For the life of me I can't figure out why it would be inappropriate for a man to stay with the woman that he's engaged to."

"Oh, he doesn't believe in that. That kind of thing. No cohabitation or anything before you're married."

"Or *anything*?"

Suddenly, she felt heat creep into the edges of her cheeks, a wholly unexpected and unfamiliar experience.

He made her realize it might seem strange to most people. But she'd known Byron for so long, and understood his background and convictions. She respected them. It didn't seem weird because she knew him, and now Lachlan was gawking at her like she'd told him the sky was green and the ground was made of taffy.

She didn't want to talk about this with him. She didn't want him to know. Suddenly, she felt small and embarrassed. Like there was a canyon between them filled with knowledge that she simply didn't possess.

It had never bothered her. Not before. But right now it made her feel silly. Lachlan was an expert in hedonism. Charity was anything but. It was just simply something they didn't discuss. It worked for them. But she had never… She had never talked to him about what she had or hadn't done with another person. It was too private. Too intimate, she assumed. And the minute that she was married, and she actually had done something, she'd likely feel the same way.

She knew the mechanics of it all. She knew there was nothing to be embarrassed about; it was just the… The personalization of it. The applying it to her. The getting close to thinking of it at all while sitting in a truck with Lachlan McCloud. It just didn't work for her.

"I don't really know what to say to that," he said.

"Don't say anything about it. It's not your relationship, and it's not your business."

"If you expect for me to adopt that level of… If you expect that that's what being reformed looks like, you are out of luck."

"I did tell you. I thought that you should likely abstain from physical…"

"I didn't think you meant once I found the person."

"Why not? Would it not be informative? If you had to actually get to know somebody rather than clouding your judgment with…"

"Clouding my judgment. How the hell do you know that would cloud my judgment? I'm not some green virgin, Charity. It's not like sex makes it impossible for me to think."

Her ears felt like they'd been scalded.

*Virgin.*

*Sex.*

She never really gave a thought to labels like that. They didn't matter to her. She didn't feel like she was a virgin. It was a strange, societal construct that didn't matter to her.

She had never been tempted to have sex.

It seemed…like a whole lot of unnecessary drama in her estimation. She knew that it had caused unnecessary drama in her father's life. She didn't like thinking about the fact that she was the product of a physical affair, but she knew that she was. Her father hadn't been married; he hadn't been in a committed relationship. It was difficult to reconcile that with the man she'd known.

The end result had been that he had ended up lonely, and she had ended up motherless. She'd never wanted that for herself. It had all seemed like a lot of trauma for what she just wasn't interested in. People did it because they had nothing else to do, she assumed.

It was just something that didn't factor into her life.

That was fine. She wasn't married. She wasn't in a relationship of that nature, and she hadn't wanted to have children yet. So…

But for some reason hearing him say that word made her unbearably conscious of the fact that—societal construct though it was—she was a virgin.

"You asked me to help you. Arguing with me isn't going to make it better," she snapped.

"Well, now that I know certain things about your relationship, I question whether or not you have a basis of knowledge from which you should be speaking."

"Which one of us is engaged? Which one of us managed already to find the person that they want to spend their life with? I did. You actually have no basis to be questioning me and what I think. Because clearly, what I think matters."

"Fine. I'll be pure and chaste just like Byron."

Those words rattled around inside her, and she found she didn't like them very much, particularly not when laden with the judgment that he had managed to slather on them.

"You are an intensely problematic human being," she said.

"Me?"

"Yes. It is a very good thing that you asked me to help you out, because I just don't think any woman would ever want to marry you. You're... You're such a..."

"Oh no. Are you about to say something scathing? You can't even get out *scathing*, it would end up sweet."

She would show him. She would.

"The fact of the matter is you use alcohol and... And sex so that you don't have to feel things. If you want to get married, don't you think that you should feel things?"

"That isn't even what I'm looking for," he said, skimming past the insults entirely. Maybe he knew that was what he used alcohol and sex for. Maybe that was why it didn't bother him to hear it.

"Then what is the idea?"

"It's going to... It's going to help me with that."

"Magically? Without you having to actually change yourself?"

He snarled, literally snarled like a feral animal and turned his focus back to the road.

"You're ridiculous," she said.

"Am I?"

"Yes. You're the one that asked for this, and now you're behaving like I'm punishing you."

"Well..." He suddenly relaxed his hold on the steering wheel. "It's fine. You're right. It's a crutch. All that stuff. I don't like the idea of trying to walk without it. But I'll live."

"Fair enough. I guess if you start dating Fia Sullivan then you just…"

She didn't even know what she'd been about to say really. That if he was so mad with passion for her that he couldn't hold himself back, they could proceed with their desires? Like she knew anything about that. She wasn't even sure she believed that was real.

She thought maybe people just wanted to satisfy their appetites and pretend that they couldn't resist a person because it sounded more romantic than the alternative.

Which was that they were like animals, completely driven by biological urges that they didn't have any control over. People just liked to make them seem more significant.

They were silent for most of the drive after that.

It was weird to be out of words between them. Usually, they could chat about anything, but for some reason the introduction of intercourse to the conversation had been like a bomb dropped in the middle of everything.

She felt itchy.

Finally, they arrived in Mapleton, and she was able to find words again because she could talk about some of the new businesses that had popped up; new restaurants she hadn't seen before. And then they were at Amuse, a tiny little restaurant housed in a cottage at the end of the main street.

There were cute little twinkle lights strung across the walkway in the front, and it was lit up like a fairyland.

She wasn't usually given to flights of fancy, but it was the kind of place that lent itself to that.

"I love it," she whispered.

"I hoped that you would."

Why? Why had he hoped that she would love it? This was just an experiment. They were on an official fake date, and she was supposed to be evaluating him through the lens of another woman. It wasn't supposed to be about her, or what she liked or wanted or anything like that.

"How come you hoped I would like it?" She couldn't stop herself from asking.

"Well, I didn't want to take you out to a place you didn't like."

"Yes, but none of this is for me."

"Charity, why can't it be for you? Yeah, I'm trying to figure some stuff out in my life, but you're not a prop. You're a person. You have to eat the dinner. You're spending the evening with me. You're not insignificant."

It was such a strange declaration, and it sat weird in the pit of her stomach.

"Well… Okay. Thank you."

They walked up the front steps and inside.

"Reservation for two, under McCloud," he said to the girl behind the podium.

"Of course. We put you over in the garden room."

They walked down the long hall and to a room at the back of the cottage. It had floral wallpaper and just one table in it, set up by the window. She hadn't known it would be…private like this. It was not quite like anything she'd ever seen before.

"The server will be with you shortly," the woman said.

She settled into the seat and smoothed her dress

down, looking around. "This is much…more than I expected."

"And if you were a woman I was on a date with?"

"I would be extremely impressed with your taste. I *am* extremely impressed with your taste. I didn't know that you… I didn't even know you knew about places like this. I've never seen you anywhere fancier than Smokey's Tavern."

"I have hidden depths, Charity. I'm sad that you didn't know that."

She had no reason to know it. Not one.

But she did now. Because they were on a date.

A date that was for another woman. A date that was like a dress rehearsal, but still.

She wondered then what Byron would think about this. If she had told him that she was going out to dinner with Lachlan, would he be…jealous?

The concept of jealousy was entirely foreign to her. She had certainly never thought of it in context with herself. She'd definitely never thought that Byron might be jealous. He was far too measured.

Lachlan was her friend, and he knew that. Lachlan was just her friend.

She grimaced internally. She didn't like that. *Just friends*. Like he was less important somehow than Byron. Which was absolutely not true. Of course it wasn't. No one was more important than Lachlan.

As of now, he was the person who had been in her life longest. He was her foundation. Her bedrock. Especially with the loss of her father, that connection to him was more important than anything else ever had been. He was one of the relationships that had made her. In fact, without him she didn't even know who she would be. There wasn't another person alive she could say that about. Not a single one. There was no *just a friend*.

Not with him. There never could be.

The server appeared then and brought them a very brief one-page menu. She perused it for a moment and decided on the house-made pasta with spring peas and butter sauce, which made her stomach growl just thinking about it. They were immediately brought a warm basket of bread, and Lachlan ordered the glass of wine he had mentioned earlier.

She got a sparkling water.

The bread practically melted in her mouth and she found herself making an extremely undignified noise as she chewed. "It's just so good," she said.

"So again, I get points?"

"Yes."

"Good. Tell me about yourself."

"What?" she asked.

"I am having dating conversation," he explained, very slowly.

"Tell me about yourself. That is an extremely open-ended question."

"Yeah. So that you can talk about yourself, but in whatever manner you want."

"That wouldn't work for me. It's just way too broad. You have to be like—tell me about your childhood. Or maybe even more specifically your fifth birthday."

"Do I want to know about your fifth birthday?" he asked.

"I don't know. Ask the question you want the answer to, Lachlan. That seems like it would be the better part of valor here."

"Okay," he said. "Tell me about your fifth birthday."

"Well…" She frowned. Because she actually had to think. "We set up a picnic table out back, and my father made me a cake. He used raspberries from the garden to color the frosting, and it was the most glorious shade of pink, tart and very pretty. He got me a stethoscope. Not a toy. A real one. I loved it. I used to put it on him, on myself and on all my stuffed animals."

"No friends?"

She shook her head. "No. You were the first friend I ever had, Lachlan."

He was her only friend. His brothers were friends, too, in fairness. She cared about them a great deal, and sometimes she felt like she might be part of their whole family. Which was a very good feeling indeed.

But no one else was Lachlan.

"Oh."

"What about you? Tell me about your fifth birthday."

He chuckled. "I don't remember it. Honestly. We didn't get birthday parties. So I can't say I really remember turning five, because we didn't mark it with anything. I think I maybe knew it was my birthday, and I imagine some kids wished me a happy one at school."

They knew each other. They had for a long time. So they didn't have "getting to know you" conversations, and just then she realized that meant there were certain things they hadn't talked about. Ever.

"I wished that I could go to school," she said. "I knew about the schoolhouse, and it made me feel so sad that I couldn't go." She looked down at her bread. "I mean, I loved spending the days with my dad, and I value the education that he gave me, which was so hands-on and rooted in nature. We would take hikes and he would show me which herbs were edible, and which plants could be used for medicine. We would sit out by the lake and work together. We read books and we talked about history and scientific discovery." She frowned. "I'm glad that we had that time."

"But you were lonely."

"Yes. He would hate to know that, because I know *he* was lonely. But I think because of that he never wanted me gone."

"He didn't really know your mother."

"No. He didn't. He knew… He knew who she was. But…" Her throat got tight, and she suddenly wished that she had been braver when he'd been alive. That she would've asked him more. Because now she was hungry to know the answers. Answers she could never have now.

"I don't know how they met. I don't know how my father, my sensible, socially awkward father, got himself into that kind of relationship. I don't know if he thought he was in love. I wish I did. I wish I had the whole story. Because I didn't ask for it, now I'll never know."

"I'm sorry," he said. "If it makes you feel better, most of the truths about my family are a mystery. Did my mother ever love my father? And if so, why? Did he ever think he loved anybody, and if not, why the hell did he get married? Why did he have so many kids? Did he like hurting people, or no? Did he wish that he could be better? Or did he hate us? I don't know the answer to that. I'm not sure that I want to. But I do know what it's like to have mysteries hanging over you that you won't get the answers to."

"I'm sorry," she said. "Those are very heavy questions."

"Well, it doesn't have to be like that. You just move on with your life, right? That's what I'm doing."

"If you can't tell me about your fifth birthday, then tell me about a good memory from when you were a child. You must have at least one."

He smiled, and there was something about that smile; something that took her insides and tilted them just slightly. It was a real smile. Genuine. Lachlan smiled all the time, but the thing was… It didn't reach deep. Lachlan smiled because he wanted to pretend he was happy. All the time. But she knew that his actual happiness was a whole lot more sparse.

But just now it was real. The happiness was real.

"Gus used to put me on his shoulders and run me around. I'm only four years younger, but you know he… He really took being our older brother serious. He looked out for us. Gus is my happiest memory."

"I'm glad that you had him."

"When I imagine him, it's from before the fire. Before he got burned." His smile slipped then. "He was trying to protect me. That day. My dad would've killed me… He…"

Her chest seized up.

"I know that your childhood was really tough. I know that nothing makes up for that. But isn't it wonderful that you have a brother that loves you enough to… He would have died for you, and he would've done it without being sorry."

He nodded slowly. "It's why I try not to run around being sorry for myself. Gus doesn't deserve that. He doesn't deserve me moping around about what I don't deserve. He went through all that for me. I can't dishonor him. It's a shitty tribute."

Their salads came, and they distracted themselves with that, followed shortly by the main course. Lachlan had gotten the steak, and she dug into her pasta happily. It gave them a slight break from the unexpected intensity of small talk.

She'd thought small talk was supposed to be easy.

"Are you thinking you might have dessert this evening?" the server asked.

"Two flourless chocolate tortes," Lachlan said.

When they were put in front of them, she smiled, her fork poised above the dark confection. "To Dad," she said, taking a big piece off the side.

"To your dad," he agreed, taking his own big bite.

She held her fork up, and he held up his and tapped it to hers, as if they were doing cheers with cake.

She laughed, then took a bite.

"Wonderful," she said.

"So how was that?" he asked.

She blinked. How was that? Oh. Of course. Because they were doing this thing to evaluate his spousal readiness, they weren't just having a meal. That conversation had been a rehearsal for him, not a real conversation. And of course, she knew that he really did mean the tribute to her dad; it was just… It was still part of this. And for a second she had forgotten.

"Very successful," she said. "I think that you've been very successful."

"Great. Glad that by your estimation I did a pretty good job, Doc."

"I guess when you get married your life will be like

this. An evening in instead of one at the bar, and restaurants instead of the tavern."

"I could marry Fia Sullivan, then it probably would be the tavern."

"Well, I'm sure that's fine. If that's what you want."

It felt weird, thinking about Lachlan going and doing this very thing with somebody else. Trying to insert another person into this position.

And she should be happy to think of it. Happy for him. But it just felt like this person—this exceptionally important person—was slipping further and further away from her.

He paid the bill—even though she protested—and they stepped outside.

She shivered. "It's freezing," she said.

He grinned, lopsided beneath the string lights above. Then he took his jacket that he had draped over his arm and wrapped it around her shoulders. "Should've brought your coat."

It was more of the chivalry. More of the chivalry that he was going to extend to whatever woman he ended up dating.

But his coat smelled like him, and it was very warm. And she found herself gripping the edges of it and wrapping it even more tightly around herself.

"Thanks."

They walked down the sidewalk together, the only sound their shoes on the cement.

The sky was clear and cold, the stars above twinkling, diamond white tonight instead of yellow.

His jacket was warm. So was his presence beside her.

He rounded to the passenger side of the truck and

started to open the door for her. And just then, a shooting star went across her vision. "Oh," she said.

"What?" He looked up, his gaze following hers.

"Shooting star. It's already gone."

They both looked down at the same time, at each other. The only light was a streetlight down the sidewalk a ways, and it was impossible to see his face in any great detail.

"Did you make a wish?" he asked.

Right then everything seemed to get slow. And there was something about the light that made her look at the features of his face a little bit differently. The way that it emphasized the sharp cut of his nose, the groove at the center of his top lip, the strength of his jawline. She hadn't made a wish. Because she had no idea what she would even wish for. It had never even occurred to her to wish for anything. Not once in her life.

"I don't wish," she said.

"You don't wish?"

"No. I had everything that I ever wanted. So there was never really much to wish for. I had my dad and I had you."

"You just said that you wish you knew more about your mother."

"Oh." Sadness welled in her chest. "I guess that's the beginning of wishing. When you're missing something that you can't get back. Because I didn't wish it before my dad was gone."

"I guess that's why I've always done a lot of wishing. Wishing my dad would drop dead. Wishing... Because you know my mom loved us. At least the best she could. And once that was gone, and I couldn't get it back... Yeah, I started wishing a whole lot."

"What do you wish for now?"

"Cold beer. A body that's sore and tired from work. Happier days, basically."

"Oh." She wondered if they were standing too close to each other, and she didn't even know what had made that occur to her. Except that her face felt warm, and her lips tingled slightly.

"If you had to make a wish right now, what would it be for?"

She didn't even think about it. It just came out. "More days like this."

Then her face really did feel hot, in earnest.

He nodded slowly. "That's a good wish."

She got into the truck quickly and he closed the door behind her.

She took his coat off her shoulders, and her stomach swooped.

He got in and started the engine.

"You're doing great," she said. "I think… I think you're going to do just great. You can definitely start dating."

"Thanks, Doc."

It had been a wonderful dinner. A great night. She had no idea why she felt sad.

# CHAPTER SIX

"I'M GOING TO invite you to tea."

"I'm sorry, what?"

Charity looked over at Lachlan, determined now in her mission. First of all, to find some equal footing after dinner two nights ago, but second of all, to actually do what she'd promised.

"I'm going to have you over to high tea. Because it makes sense. It's part of the reformation. My father believed in scrupulous table manners, and he put me through the rigors of etiquette."

"Etti-what?"

She laughed. "Come on. You aren't that ridiculous."

"You don't know that. Maybe I'm every inch this ridiculous."

"We will sit down and have a very civilized meal. At my house. We'll go over all the particulars of which fork to use and that kind of thing."

"I'm not sure if I'm insulted by this or not," he said.

"There's no need to be insulted. I'm being helpful."

"Yes. Very helpful. No alcohol…"

"Tea," she said, smiling broadly.

He looked at her like she had grown another head.

"Well?" she said.

"Fine. I guess we'll convene sometime after work?"

"Yes," she said. "I'll see you then."

She went about her daily appointments, and mentally planned the various things that she would prepare for her high tea with Lachlan. In fact, she thought about it all day. But that wasn't unusual. She often thought about Lachlan all day. He was like an extension of her in many ways. She couldn't explain that exactly; it simply was.

She didn't have a full day of appointments, so when she got home she decided to quickly put together a batch of scones and some lemon curd. But she forgot what a pain in the rear lemon curd was, and by the time she had finished whisking it, her arm felt like a limp spaghetti noodle. But everything looked lovely. However, she did wonder if Lachlan would really appreciate any of it. They were going to have a spread that had multiple pieces of silverware—because you didn't really get that at tea. But he could pull her chair out for her and put his napkin in his lap. That wouldn't kill him.

She would be picking Byron up at the airport in two days, and after that, their time together would be severely limited. So they might as well enjoy this now.

Why did she think about Byron like somebody coming to end something? It was a very strange thought. He wasn't that. Not at all.

But she didn't have time to ponder that anymore, because then Lachlan showed up.

"So my deep question to you," Lachlan said, "is if I should be offended that you clearly found my manners on our date to be wanting."

"It isn't bad. It wasn't lacking in the extreme. It's just that… You know, you could probably benefit from even more instruction."

"Was I not a gentleman?"

"You were," she said. "You gave me your jacket. You opened the car door for me. You could have scooted my chair back for me, however."

"Oh," he said. "My apologies, my lady."

"I'm not trying to be like that. I'm trying to do exactly what you asked me to do."

She looked at his face, and she could see that he kind of enjoyed this. Teasing her. Flustering her.

She knew this about him. She did. So she shouldn't actually be surprised at the way he was behaving. But she was a little bit.

She was selflessly helping him. Of course, the side effect of such selflessness was that she got to eat a scone and some lemon curd. But still. She had provided it all. He could settle down.

"All right. So what kinds of things do I talk about in such a civilized setting?"

"First of all," she said, moving over to the table, "you pull my chair out."

He did so, grinning down at her. "My lady."

"You said that already." She sat in the chair, and he pushed her up to the table. It was a bit abrupt, but funny, so she couldn't help but laugh, even though she knew he was being purposefully recalcitrant.

That was the problem with Lachlan. He was charming even when he shouldn't be. He had always been like that.

There was something that felt reduced inside her ever since that date. Some wall that had begun to crumble, that she didn't really want to examine.

She felt so...raw after that experience. Part of her wondered if she had simply suggested today because it was an etiquette lesson, rather than a replacement for something he would be doing with another woman, which had made her feel sort of hollowed out inside. And she didn't particularly like the sensation of being a Charity husk.

She skirted the edges of that enough, in the depths of her grief over her father. She didn't need to add to it. She just felt so raw. And this was the problem. Almost everything was beginning to feel like a loss. Like a new layer of grief. Even Byron's coming to visit, which should feel joyful, felt like a loss of time with Lachlan. A loss of her normal routine, and it jarred her.

She was extremely fragile in some ways and places. She didn't quite know what to do about it. Didn't quite know when it would resolve. If it would resolve.

"Now what?" he asked.

"Elbows off the table," she said.

He had his chin rested on his knuckles, his elbows firmly planted there.

He slid them off, giving her a sideways look. "I don't do that at restaurants."

"I know you don't," she said. "But it is still relevant."

"Fine. And?"

"Napkin in your lap. I did notice that you missed that one at the restaurant."

"I kept it on hand. I'm not gonna drop stuff in my lap like a five-year-old."

"It goes in your lap."

"Of all the dumb-ass things. Shouldn't your napkin go where you need it? I like mine right on the table. That way I can wipe my mouth with it, or my hands."

"Lachlan, I don't make the rules. I'm simply enforcing them."

"Of all the dumb-ass shit."

"Don't swear in the presence of a lady."

"Oh. I'm sorry. That's right. Except, you are ignoring the fact that you are one of the very few ladies in Pyrite Falls."

"Yet you swear in front of me all the time."

"You're made of hardy stuff," he said, reaching out to pat her arm. The lingering sensation the touch left behind made her feel uncomfortable.

She wrinkled her nose. "I am not *hardy*. I'm a lady."

"Okay. For the purposes of this moment, I will treat you as such. Do I get some tea?"

"Of course."

She poured him some from the pot.

"Oh. You put the teabag in there?"

"You do indeed, Lachlan," she said.

"Good to know."

"Another piece of etiquette."

"Lucky me."

"So then we talk about the weather. We never talk about religion or politics."

He snorted. "I wouldn't do that anyway."

"That is true. I've never known you to talk about either. You do talk about the weather a lot."

"In fairness, that is sort of religion and politics for a rancher. What the earth around you is doing." He chuckled. "And you can't do much about it. So again, commonalities."

"Dangerously close to a controversial statement."

"I take it I'm not supposed to be controversial?"

"Not right at first," she said. "Obviously, eventually you have to be somewhat controversial, because otherwise how will you ever get to know the person well enough to marry them?"

"Well, see, this is where none of this makes sense. I do a lot of… You know, I don't really know the women that I… You get the idea. But if I'm going to get to know one, why not open with the most controversial thing you think? See if they still stick around?"

"I don't know. Because you start with small talk."

"Did you and Byron start with small talk?"

"We had the common bond of being in veterinary school. When you have something big in common it's easy to talk to each other."

"All right. I can see that. So I find myself a woman who likes ranching—like Fia Sullivan—and we'll be able to talk about ranching."

"Well," she said. "Yes. I guess that stands to reason."

"Perfect. I just need to find somebody that I have some easy things in common with, and the small talk will be simple. And, you can assume that your controversial opinions might somewhat line up."

"Why is that?" she asked.

"If your life contains a lot of the same practicalities, you're probably more inclined to agree about other things, too."

"Probably a safe enough bet."

He stared at her. "We're pretty different, though. But you're a veterinarian. And I'm a rancher."

"That's true," she said. "But we're friends. It's different."

He put his elbows back on the table and rested his chin on his knuckles. "Why is that?"

"I don't know. That's just how it seems to work to me. We met, I stitched you up and we became friends.

Byron and I met, we started talking about stitching things up and we decided to date."

Except it was difficult for her to define the feelings at the moment, and that kind of struck her as odd. You would think that she would have something stronger in the way of feelings. You really would. Except it felt vague right now, and her memory of Lachlan was visceral. Even though it had happened much longer ago. But it had been emotional. Intense.

He'd been bleeding and bruised, and everything in her had broken.

*Because it's like an animal. When you see a wounded animal, it affects you. Deeply.*

Was Lachlan like a wounded animal to her? That seemed… That didn't seem right. He was more than that.

Of course, in her life, there was very little that was more than that.

"You're full of wisdom. Tell me about the forks," he said.

"You start on the outside and work your way in."

"And that required a meeting? I feel like that could've been a short text message."

"But at this meeting you got scones."

"True." A grin split his face, and his blue eyes lit up. Suddenly her heart felt like it dropped a foot inside her.

And it was like an alarm bell rang inside her head.

Lachlan was handsome.

Not that she hadn't noticed that before. He was objectively a good-looking man. Nobody who saw him would argue that point. Classically masculine, tall, broad-shouldered and square-jawed. Those were things that people generally agreed contributed to handsomeness. On top of that, he had extremely symmetrical features, which was scientifically proven to be more attractive than asymmetrical features. So just in a completely objective way, she knew that.

But this was different. This rearranged something inside her and couldn't be dispelled by the wrinkling of her nose.

He was handsome. And it made her cheeks feel like they were numb; made her lips feel like they were buzzing.

For a second she felt dizzy.

"What?" His smile faded slightly as he looked at her. And she wished that he wouldn't. She wished he would look away.

"Nothing."

"You look like you're staring at a whole ghost."

No ghosts. A ghost would be entirely less disconcerting than this strange moment she couldn't seem to dig herself out of.

This took some of her feelings from the date and put a name to them. And she didn't like it. She wanted to shrug it off like a coat that was too heavy, but she couldn't do it. She didn't know how.

She cleared her throat and grabbed a scone, taking a bite, and regretting that she hadn't paused to put curd on it or something, because it was just dry and felt like it got caught in her throat.

Acts of desperation were rarely smooth, and this was no exception. She coughed, and to her horror, Lachlan reached around the table and patted her back, then rubbed the center of her shoulder blades.

She froze.

His touch was warm and comforting, but there was more to it. She began to feel a strange tightening sensation in her breasts as they started feeling heavier. And as the feeling migrated from her stomach down lower, she jerked away from him and stood up. "I'm going to get some more tea."

"Okay," he said.

"Boil more water. I mean. For more tea."

"Cool."

"I'll… Yeah. Okay. You're doing great," she said, trying to smile.

"Thanks," he said.

"No problem."

"Glad to know I pass muster."

"You do. You definitely do." Except she didn't know why this had happened to her. This moment. Or why she couldn't shake it off. She was a professional at being around Lachlan without being affected. Except now…

Now she was far too aware, and she couldn't seem to get a handle on herself.

She went to the kitchen and turned on the water. She was tempted to run her hands beneath the cool stream to try and settle down some of what was happening inside her. It didn't matter that he was handsome. Nothing had changed. This was a truth that had always been so when it came to Lachlan, and she had coexisted just fine with him without fixating on it for a very long time, and there was no reason she couldn't continue to do that. And so she would.

She filled up the teapot and set it on the back burner. It felt symbolic. There were just some things you needed to put on the back burner. She was very accomplished at that. And she would keep doing it as long as she needed to.

She was being twitchy. Which was funny. Charity wasn't often twitchy. Today she was wearing another of her comically sweet outfits. A floral dress and white socks, with stockings underneath. Her blond hair was loose. He wondered if she ever went and got it cut at a salon or anything like that. That was a funny thing he didn't really know. It was just long, and he wouldn't be all that surprised to find out she trimmed it herself. Not because it looked bad. It didn't. It was just part of her shiny, wholesome-girl thing that she had going on.

For a moment he couldn't stop staring. When he had taken her on the date, it had felt…nice. They went out to dinner frequently enough, but typically at the tavern, or at the café. And somehow it felt different, making all that effort to drive her out there. She had put makeup on, her dress a clingier material than usual, showing off her slight curves.

Her breasts might be small, but they looked firm.

He gritted his back teeth together. He should not be thinking about her breasts. He had, in fact, made a study of not noticing her breasts for a great many years. Ever since he had gotten old enough to channel his testosterone in the directions he wanted to, and not in whatever direction it wanted to go. He was only human. As a teenage boy especially, he'd been fixated on her and had wanted to see her naked. But then, he could remember clearly wanting to see Fia Sullivan naked, too. And Arizona King, God help him. Because the King brothers would have cheerfully dismembered him, and he did not wish to have his limbs strewn as far as the east was from the west.

So yeah. There had been a time when he'd been your basic horny asshole, and he hadn't much been able to distinguish her from the other women in his life. But over the years, he had built a sacred wall around her. Put her up in a pristine tower where most especially his dirty thoughts could not reach her.

So why he was thinking about her breasts right now... The thing was there was a man coming here who would be thinking about her breasts quite a lot. And he was going to marry her. And, he'd probably already slept with her. Honestly. They'd been together for years...

That irked him. And it wasn't fair. She didn't belong to him.

That was the thing, he realized, as he tried to sort through his conflicting thoughts. The issue was that sometimes he felt like she did.

He was uncomfortable with the idea of things changing.

He wanted her to stay in the ivory tower. Where he and no one else could touch her.

So there.

And the firmness of her breasts didn't matter as long as she was up in a tower where he couldn't reach her. So he needed to quit thinking about the firmness of her breasts.

He was going to find a wife. One that he chose. He wasn't going to do this whole crazy in *love* thing his brothers had done.

And there were very good reasons for that. Reasons he was clear on.

But the problem was he kind of wanted to have his cake and eat it, too. He wanted a wife, and he wanted Charity. Right in the place she had always been. And that wasn't going to happen. Because Byron.

Honestly. *What a stupid name.*

"What is the deal with Byron's parents anyway? Who names their kid that? Were they insufferably into poetry?"

"I think so," she said.

"Oh."

For some reason, he hated that there was an explanation for the name. It just made him mad.

"They homeschooled all of their kids."

He frowned. "How many kids?"

"Nine. They're a very interesting family. Remember when I went to visit a couple of years ago? I met them then. His sisters are great, and his brothers are all very nice, just like he is. Everyone loves board games. At one point his mother and I were wearing matching dresses. Not on purpose. It was a little weird, though."

Given how much Byron reminded him of Charity's father, the whole thing felt a little bit strange. And he had to wonder how much of this was just her reaching for familiarity. She came back to the table and poured herself more tea, of which there was plenty in the pot. She hadn't needed to go fill up that stovetop kettle, and he wasn't exactly sure what had prompted her to do so.

Sunlight streamed in from the kitchen window and made her hair look like there was a halo around it. Sainted Charity. She was that to him.

*Sacred.*

The thought made him feel uncomfortable.

"So when does Byron get in?"

"In the evening."

"Great. Well. I look forward to seeing him."

He didn't. Not at all.

"Okay. Well. I'm sure you'll get to see him."

"Good times."

He couldn't quite sort through what was happening inside him, but he knew he needed to go ahead and get himself that date as quickly as possible.

## CHAPTER SEVEN

IT WAS A town hall day, which meant it was time to knock off work and head over to the Sullivans' for the big family meeting that they had monthly at Four Corners Ranch.

It was always a good time. Even if there was a big fight.

Hell, it was a good time almost especially if there was a big fight. If Fia Sullivan and Landry King were in the same place for a long enough amount of time, there would be a fight. He knew that there was history between them. Really bad blood. But when it came to considering dating her, he didn't mind that.

Sure, the Kings were insular, and it was entirely likely that if Landry got a burr in his saddle about it he might attempt to make Lachlan's life miserable. Along with the rest of his brothers, one of whom was an actual cop, which could bite Lachlan in the ass.

But the joke would always be on Landry, because Lachlan was so conditioned to life being miserable, that it wouldn't really signify.

They had a big tent set out over the lawn today because it was drizzling; tables were shoved underneath with excellent barbecue, pasta salads, potato salads, pies and other baked goods. Everybody turned out their best for the town hall meetings, and it was always a great time with better food.

There was a big old bonfire that was strong enough to reach back up and punch the rain in the face, but first, they would have to get down to the business of the meeting.

There had been quite a few instances of them all locking horns lately, what with the Sullivans pushing to complete a new building and open it as a store, and the necessity of permits and easements and newly excavated roads that would need to be paid for out of the community pot.

They all helped each other, and the way that they managed their cash flow among all the different branches got everybody through the lean times, kept it all running like a well-oiled machine, but that didn't mean there weren't occasional disputes.

It was just the way things were, especially when you had so many people working in one place. With very big personalities and very strong opinions.

They had taken a pretty decent infusion of cash at McCloud's Landing when they had started the equine therapy. But now the meetings were kind of a spectator sport, since they were done with their big change. It suited Lachlan just fine.

The meeting that took place in the big old barn next to the Sullivans' white farmhouse went off with only minor explosives. There was one near fight between Fia and Landry that was headed off by Fia's younger sister, Quinn, who laid out her plans, which would involve drawing a little less cash out of the pot. Provided she could pull it off.

"Timing," Quinn said, tapping her binder. "I'm just trying to nail down the timing."

Afterward, they all went outside to the big bonfire, and he wished that he would've invited Charity. She came sometimes, just to spend the evening and enjoy the food, but she wasn't really part of Four Corners, so it wasn't like it was mandatory. He just enjoyed her company.

She could've stood by to give him pointers on his behavior. His posture probably wasn't good enough to be approaching a woman that he was considering asking to be his wife.

That made him laugh.

Fia was standing over by the table filled with pie, her red hair captured high up in a ponytail, her green eyes still sparking with fury.

He had seen a similar look on his sister-in-law's face when Gus was irritating her.

Marrying a Sullivan didn't guarantee a peaceful existence, that was for damn sure. But there was something about the particular spark Alaina possessed that seemed to bring Gus to life. So maybe it would be the same for him.

"Howdy," he said.

Fia looked at him like he had grown another head. He supposed they didn't talk to each other all that often. But they had grown up together. They lived on adjacent properties. It wasn't like they were strangers.

"Hi," she said.

"Sounds like you guys are making pretty fair progress."

"Pretty fair. Slower than I would like. But the hideous weather kind of slowed down construction efforts, and then there's the whole issue of Levi Granger. And trying to get in to talk to him about an easement with his road. But Quinn claims she's going to handle that."

"Yeah. Granger is kind of an unfriendly bastard."

The man who owned the neighboring ranch was not big on cross communication. For him, ranching was not a group sport.

"How's everything going with…your thing?" she asked.

"Pretty good. I assume Alaina has filled you in a little bit."

"Yeah. A little bit. My sister seems pretty happy over there at McCloud's Landing."

"A miracle if ever there was one," he said. "Since nobody used to be all that happy over there at McCloud's."

"True. It's good. It's good to see Gus that happy."

"Yeah. Definitely. So. We're having a poker game over at my place tomorrow night. I was wondering if you wanted to come."

He had not in fact planned a poker game at his place for tomorrow night, but he *would*. Very quickly, as soon as he left here. Charity, Brody and Elizabeth, Tag and Nelly… Yeah. He'd fill up the chairs.

"Oh," she said. "I…haven't played a lot of poker."

"It's fun. And I'd love to have you."

She frowned. "Are you… Are you hitting on me, Lachlan?"

"If you have to ask, I'm not doing a very good job."

"Huh. Well… Interesting." She didn't sound thrilled,

but she didn't seem put off either. "I would love to come to the poker game. That sounds like a decent plan."

Maybe she was sick of pining after Landry, assuming that's what their deal was.

Sick enough that she was willing to take him up on this, even though she clearly thought it was weird. She was a pretty woman. A delicate build, but pretty generously endowed, freckles across her nose, wide green eyes. Yeah. He liked the look of her. It was more academic than it was visceral, but he supposed that was probably the best way to approach these sorts of things.

He didn't want or need to get carried away by anything, that was what he and Charity had discussed, and on that score, he did think she was right. He also was supposed to stay away from the alcohol tonight.

Difficult to do since that meant heading over to the kids' table and grabbing sodas out of the cooler.

"Okay," she said. "I guess I'll see you tomorrow."

"Yeah. Six o'clock. We'll have pizza."

"Great."

They stood there for a second, and okay, they weren't going to have an instant rapport. But hell, if she wanted to go on a date with him, she must be interested enough. So he'd take that.

After town hall ended, they convened at McCloud's Landing. "Poker at my place tomorrow," he said, grabbing a beer and sitting down at the table with his brothers. That was a fair moment to have a beer. It had to be.

"Okay," Gus said. "But we might skip. Cameron hasn't been sleeping, and Alaina is pretty tired."

Their baby was only a couple weeks old. Being an

uncle was a damned joy as far as Lachlan was concerned. All the cuteness without any of the sleeplessness.

"Well, her sister will be there, so maybe she'll decide to come anyway."

"Why will her sister be there? And which one?" Gus asked.

He looked deeply suspicious. And probably rightly so.

"Because I asked her to be. I asked her out."

"Son of a bitch," Brody said. "You can't go sleeping with Gus's sister-in-law. That's a mess waiting to happen."

"Who said anything about sleeping with her? I asked her out."

"We all know what that means to you," Tag said.

*"Deeply,"* Hunter added.

"Look, you all have gotten married. Settled down. Why can't I make a move toward settling down? Maybe my idea of what dating is has changed."

"Maybe," Hunter said. "But I kind of doubt it."

That just did it. It made him agree to Charity's celibacy demand. Then and there in his own heart because his brothers were assholes who didn't think he could, and damn them, he would.

"Look at Brody," Lachlan said. "He's a dad. If Brody can settle down and literally be raising a kid, why can't I start dating a little bit more seriously? In fact, I'm not having sex. Six months. No sex. Unless I get married first."

"What?" Brody just about fell out of his chair. "You. No sex. Six months."

"I asked Charity to reform me, and that was what she said I ought to do."

"Charity cockblocked you for six months?" Tag asked. "Well. That's a riot."

"It's not a *riot*, Tag. It is my attempt at getting some of the happiness that you all have."

Brody suddenly looked serious, which Lachlan didn't like at all. "None of us set out to get married. We fell in love."

"I mean, maybe you're all in love now, but you can't tell me that was how it started. Angus." He turned his focus to his oldest brother.

He had asked Alaina to marry him after she had found out that she was pregnant by a man who had abandoned her. Lachlan admired his older brother's protectiveness. But that was where it had come from. Alaina was the youngest of the Sullivan sisters, while Gus was the oldest of the McClouds. They cared for each other a great deal now; that much was obvious. But as far as love went…

"Nope," Gus said. "I've been in love with her for years."

"That's not true," Lachlan said. "We would've known that."

"No, you wouldn't have. Not even I knew it. How would you know if I didn't?"

"Seems fake. If you didn't know it how can you be sure you're not just rewriting things for yourself? Doesn't sound super legitimate to me," Lachlan said.

"All I wanted with Elizabeth was to have fun," Brody said. "But I also knew that I was going to be getting into a complicated situation, given that she had a kid. I still couldn't stay away from her. That's not just attraction. That's something bigger. Maybe it isn't love, not at that stage, but it's the seed of it. That's the thing. When there's a woman you want, and you can't deny it, you can't keep away from her no matter how much you should…"

Tag and Hunter raised their hands. Yeah. He knew that was true about them. Given that Hunter had gotten together with his best friend's much younger sister, and Tag had ended up with a very sweet town librarian. That was definitely undeniable and not something planned.

But still, he didn't see why he couldn't manufacture a little bit of that domestic bliss the way that he was planning. They were overcomplicating it. And it was because they had this…singular experience. But he didn't think that it took that singular experience to make it. That was what he wondered. That his parents thought that they were in love? That was the thing that got him. He didn't ever want to take that chance. Going into something led by emotion.

He wanted to go about this, but in a more rational way.

"So you're considering marrying my sister-in-law," Gus said. "I don't see how that could go wrong. Definitely not going to make my life a living hell."

"You chose to marry Alaina. Whether or not your life is a living hell is on you, bro," Lachlan said.

"Watch it," Gus said, eyes narrowed. "I saved your life. I can go ahead and rescind that if you want. It's not murder, then. It's just balancing the scales."

They eyed each other for a moment. "I'm teasing you. But anyway. I like Fia. She's a nice woman, and she cares about the ranch. She's also pretty." Gus shrugged. "I don't see how it could go wrong."

"Why do you have to say things like that?" Hunter said. "That's like daring the universe to drop a bomb on you. You know that, right?"

"It's just a date," Lachlan said. "And given my vow of celibacy and my vow of no alcohol—" He raised his beer bottle when he said that, then quickly lowered it.

"Good job on the no alcohol, chief," Hunter said.

"It doesn't count. Because Fia isn't here to see it, and neither is Charity."

"What does Charity have to do with this?"

"I told you. I went to her and asked what exactly I needed to do to become… I don't know. Reformed. Ready for marriage. And she gave me a list of things."

Every single one of his brothers laughed. Even Gus, who notoriously didn't laugh much.

"That's rich. She going to turn you into a choir boy?" Gus asked.

"No. She's just helping me out with the whole thing. Anyway. Be at my house for the poker game if you can be, and bring some food."

"I can't miss this," Tag said. "Nelly and I will be there."

"Count me and Elsie in," said Hunter.

"I would, but we're taking Benny to his dad's tomorrow, and we decided to stay over in Portland for a couple of days rather than drive back," Brody said. "Going to spend a little quality time with my wife in the big city."

"Wow. Sounds fun," Lachlan said.

"It will be. Because we'll be in the hotel the whole time."

Lachlan grimaced. "All right. I'll see some of you tomorrow. And you'll see. It'll all be just fine."

Lachlan wasn't a big one for plans, but once he set his mind to something, he accomplished it. And this would be no different.

## CHAPTER EIGHT

HER INVITATION TO Lachlan's poker game came over text, and she decided to whip up some cookie dough, since they had demolished all of it the night before. She also decided to bake some crescent roll appetizers, and collected some chips and dip. She liked to have a lot of snacks, and she found that Lachlan was often woefully under snacked. She hummed happily while she put everything in her car and got into the driver's seat, ignoring the band of tension that seemed to stretch in her chest.

It had been a strange few days.

She was only human, she supposed, and the fancy restaurant, lovely meal and good company had made things feel a little bit more…genuine than they should have. It felt like something out of the ordinary, something that their friendship didn't normally encompass.

And tea…

That moment where his beauty had felt specific. Not like a factual truth for anyone to observe, but something that lived deep within her.

But seeing him would make it better. Seeing him at a poker game, this very normal thing they'd done so many times.

There were a lot of trucks parked in front of Lachlan's cabin. It was a pretty small space, but they had gotten good at cramming in when he hosted a poker night. She recognized Tag and Nelly's truck, and Hunter and Elsie's. But there was a golden, newer truck that she couldn't place.

She got out of her car, her bowls of snacks stacked in her arms.

She walked up the front porch, and to the door, tapping it with her foot, since she didn't have any free hands. The door jerked open, and Lachlan was standing there. "For heaven's sake." He reached out and unburdened her completely. "Don't try to carry everything in one trip," he scolded.

"But if I do two trips, I lose the game."

"What game?"

"The one-trip game. Which I'm playing only against myself."

"Wow."

She shrugged that off and walked in, and when she saw the spread of people there, she froze. Because there was Fia Sullivan. Sitting in a chair at the table, with a deck of cards in front of her, her red hair swept up into an effortlessly messy bun. She was pretty. Incredibly pretty.

"Hi, Charity," Fia said, completely oblivious to the momentary pang of… Well, she wasn't actually certain what it was, but it was intense. And very real. And it made her feel about like she needed to double over to catch her breath.

"Hi," she said.

She went straight to the kitchen where her bowl of cookie dough was and preheated the oven, then went hunting for a cookie sheet. She was just going to keep busy.

"Go ahead and do the first round without me," she said. "I'll just… I have the cookies."

She listened as everybody negotiated and haggled over the first hand—what the game would be, who would deal, what was wild and what the minimum and maximum would be for betting.

They had done this so many times over the years, that even Charity had her own poke full of change that was reserved just for this pretty low-dollar poker. A quarter was the highest you could go. So really, the most anybody ever made was a good twenty-dollar pot if they went in for a long time. She kept her focus firmly on each scoop of cookie dough that she put onto the cookie sheet. She didn't know what was wrong with her. Except that it was just the surprise of all this. She knew that he had been considering Fia, but he must've asked her out, and he hadn't told her, which seemed strange, because she had been included in this entire thing. For him to actually make a move, but not tell her he was making a move, seemed off-brand to the whole endeavor.

"Read them and weep!" Fia had won the first round, and she was laughing gleefully over taking what was probably a five-dollar pot.

Charity bristled.

She was new. She shouldn't take that much obvi-ous joy in beating everybody. It just wasn't done. Not a good look. In her opinion.

"Come on, Charity," Lachlan said. "Next game."

"I'm waiting for the cookies to be done."

"You probably have ten minutes. Come on."

The only seat available was on the other side of Lachlan. Fia was in the one to his right.

So Charity took the one on his left and felt like a weird accessory. Lachlan was the dealer and declared that it would be five-card draw, which was a game Charity was familiar enough with.

Her dad had once told her that she should be careful getting overly involved in vices like gambling. That it was one thing to enjoy the odd game with the McClouds, but she had to be careful about going any further with it.

She had always thought it was charming that he was so concerned about things. It just made her miss him now, especially with the strangeness of the situation making her own saliva feel like ash in her mouth.

She wasn't used to feeling dramatic.

There had just been a preponderance of dramatic feelings lately, and she did not like it.

It felt like this was crashing in with Byron coming in a couple of days, and she felt overwhelmed.

Her father had taught her to handle everything as it came. He was one of the calmest men she had ever known. Quiet and measured and just utterly relaxed with each and every change that life brought.

Even when his health had declined and the doctors had put him on hospice he'd been at peace. Accepting of the cycle, wherever he was at in it.

It was one of the things that made him such a great veterinarian. One of the things that made him such a wonderful and accomplished member of his field. Such a good dad.

But this was… She wasn't able to accomplish that. Not right now. She was losing hold on something that she hadn't even known was slipping, and she didn't know what to do about it.

And what could she do when she felt like Lachlan was suddenly the source of some of her upset? When she felt like some of what was going on inside her was related to whatever was happening with him. To the way that he had involved her in this quest.

It didn't make any sense. *She* didn't make any sense, and she wasn't used to it.

She went through the motions of the game, folding midway through, and getting up to babysit the cookies. Then she got them out and pretended to watch them cool.

After one more game, she decided that she couldn't stay anymore.

"I'm not feeling very well," she said. "I think I'm going to go."

"What?" Lachlan looked at her. "Are you okay?"

"It's just…my stomach. I'll… I'll talk to you later."

She got up, leaving all of her things—her bowls and food—and heading quickly out the front door toward her car.

She heard footsteps behind her and the door close firmly, and honestly, she should've known that Lachlan wasn't going to let her get away with a sudden exit.

She turned around and there he was, backlit by the porch light.

"What's going on?"

"Nothing. Nothing. I just… I don't feel well, and I realized that Byron is going to be here in two days, and I don't have everything prepared for him. Maybe I'm actually anxious about that. I think that's it. I don't know. There was just something about… I just… There's a lot of stuff." At least that was honest.

"Yeah."

He walked slowly down the steps, his eyes never leaving hers.

"Should I leave? Should I go with you? I don't want you at home by yourself not feeling well." He frowned. "I don't like that you live by yourself."

"It's probably just a stomach bug. I don't need tending."

"I'm glad that you don't think you do, but I'm not entirely convinced of that."

"Stay. You invited Fia over and I think it's going well. She seems to like you."

"Maybe. Or maybe she's just polite, and she's enjoying the free food and the money she's winning from us."

"Well. You're going to have to make sure that Elsie doesn't kill her for winning too many times in a row. You know how she gets."

"I do. But I'm sure that Fia can handle her own, given that Alaina is her younger sister, and you know how *she* is."

"Yeah." She just stood there for a moment, beset by the strange cloud of awkwardness that had settled over her. One that she had never experienced before. It was upsetting, to say the least.

"I need to call Byron. I'll feel better."

Lachlan drew back, one brow lifted. "Oh. Yeah. Of course."

"Right. Okay. I'll see you tomorrow probably."

"Yeah." She turned away. "So," Lachlan said. "You think he's going to get you a ring?"

"Do I… I haven't thought of it."

"You've been engaged for a long time. With no ring. And no wedding date. That's all I'm saying."

"Are you questioning his commitment to me?"

"No. Not at all."

"Because it doesn't matter to me. I don't care. And if I did care I would say something."

"I know. So I guess I'm not really questioning his commitment to you. I'm more questioning your commitment to him."

Anger fired through her veins, because how dare he? What had she done to become the focus of his nonsense? And what did he know about anything? He was having one group date with a woman, and he felt like he had the right to comment on her years-long association with a man who fully intended to marry her?

"I don't want to get in a fight with you," she said.

"We've never had a fight ever," Lachlan said.

"Well, you're edging very close into fight territory, Lachlan McCloud. Because you're being... You are being... An *asshole*."

He started. Probably because he had never heard her say such a thing. And in truth, *she* was a little surprised that she had.

"How?" he asked.

"You don't have any right to comment on my relationship. None at all. I didn't ask for your input, and it's not fair of you to undermine that. Especially not now. I lost my dad, and everything feels awful, and scary and sad. And you're supposed to be my friend, and you are one of the good things in my life. Picking at the other good thing in my life is just... Well, it makes me question your usefulness."

"Well," Lachlan said. "God forbid my usefulness be called into question. I do live to be useful to you, Charity."

"You infuriate me," she said, and she got into her car, breathing heavily.

He took a couple of steps toward her; then she decided to pull out anyway and drive toward home.

As she did, the silence in the car seemed to settle heavy around her, and she had no idea what in the hell was happening. Why was she this upset? Why had he made her so angry? Because normally he could make whatever comments he wanted and it wouldn't matter. She would just sit comfortable in the knowledge that she knew the truth about her life, and he could merrily go about not understanding Byron all he wanted.

But it was because… Because she wasn't sure. That was the problem.

She wasn't sure.

Not about herself, not about him, not about anything. And it just felt… It felt extra awful to have her friend doubt her in the middle of all that.

Or maybe it just felt extra awful to know that she was losing him.

Because that was the stark truth of it. If Fia Sullivan ended up with him, if she sat at his right side for all the rest of the poker games ever, then Charity didn't really have her place anymore.

*You aren't supposed to. You're also getting married. You're doing your thing. He's doing his. It's good.*

But it didn't feel good. When she pulled into the driveway, she realized she hadn't left the porch light on again. And she leaned her head against the steering wheel and cried.

# CHAPTER NINE

LACHLAN FELT PLENTY bad the next day, and he decided that he needed to lead an expedition to find out how Charity was. Because he had made kind of a hash of that whole thing last night. He didn't know why he felt the need to say what he had about Byron.

Except…it was true.

If you were madly in love with somebody, wouldn't you want to pin down a wedding date? Wouldn't you want to wear their ring?

Not that he knew definitively about things like that, but it just seemed like what had happened with his brothers. None of them had wasted any time getting married when they had found their women.

Hell, Brody had gotten married so fast he practically set a land speed record, even though Lachlan knew that was partly because Elizabeth didn't like the idea of shacking up because she had a child. And Brody most definitely wanted to be shacking up.

So yeah. He questioned it. It was reasonable enough.

But he probably shouldn't have, given she hadn't felt well, and he had been pushing at a bad time. But he had felt like there was something else going on with her, and he wanted to figure out what it was. It had kept him from enjoying the rest of the evening all that much.

Fia was lovely. Funny and kind of mean, which he

personally liked. She was also very pretty. It was easy to imagine what kind of life he could have with her. Maybe they would even live at Sullivan's Point, in the farmhouse. Because she probably needed more help over there than his family needed at McCloud's. But he would of course continue to work both places.

He could see how it would go. How it would even give him a chance to do more with Four Corners, and he liked that.

So yeah. He could see all that working pretty damn well. It made logical sense. But until he patched things up with Charity, he didn't think he would be able to evaluate that very well.

So he came to her place with a peace offering. In the dusky morning hours. Cinnamon rolls. He had pilfered them out of the grocery store early—one of the things the Sullivans sold over at John's until they got their own place up and running—and he figured that he could probably get at least a little bit of a smile out of her by bringing pastries.

He parked the truck in front of her place and walked up to the door. He knocked.

She didn't appear.

That was weird. Because Charity was an early riser. His heart started to pump a little faster. Because normally, she would be up and about by now.

He knocked again.

She didn't come to the door.

She could be in the shower, granted. But…

He knew that she had a spare key, and he knew where it was, so he decided to lift up the fake rock in the front garden and make use of it. If the shower was on, then he could leave, but he just needed to know that she was okay. She hadn't felt well. What if it was something terrible like appendicitis, and she had left and gone home by herself, got really sick and…

He jammed the key into the lock and opened the door up wide. "Charity?"

He didn't hear her or the water.

He charged back toward her bedroom just as the door jerked open.

And there she was, standing there wearing nothing but a white T-shirt that just barely grazed the tops of her thighs. In fact, it was so short that he could see the flowered panties that she had on underneath. Just barely.

He looked up, and her wide eyes met his.

"Sorry," he said. He looked down again, just for a moment, and could see the dusky outline of her nipples through the thin fabric of the shirt.

"Dammit. I brought…cinnamon rolls." He turned around and walked toward the kitchen. And suddenly, in a flurry of movement she scampered back, slamming the door shut.

"What are you doing?" she shouted through the door.

"You weren't answering the door, and I got worried. So I decided to see if you were…okay? Because you didn't feel well last night."

"I was sad! Not sick."

"You said that you were sick."

"Well. It felt like sick. But I was just sad. So I cried about it and I went to sleep, that's all."

"I brought you cinnamon rolls." He went into the kitchen and set them down on the counter and tried to take a breath. That had happened. He wished that it hadn't. Because that moment had shattered something. Compromised a deal that he had made with himself a long time ago.

Charity Wyatt wasn't a sex object.

He'd decided that way back when. A protection for both of them. There had been some moments, sure, when he had thought to himself… What would it be like to kiss her? To see her lips swollen from passion, and the wonder in her eyes, because he knew that she'd never experienced it before.

He had, for a moment in time, obsessed about it, truth be told. Her innocence, and what it would be like to be the one to teach her about life's more carnal delights.

But that was when he'd felt that darker part of himself taking hold. The thing he wanted to keep at bay more than anything. He'd put a stop to it.

Plus, he wasn't the kind of person who should be introducing anyone to passion, because he didn't have the necessary emotional tools to deal with the potential fallout of it. That was when he had decided that he had to stop thinking about her that way. Ever. Stop thinking about what she had done with men, what she hadn't done, what she might look like when she was aroused.

It had been a good thing. Because he really didn't know women in a context other than a sexual one. He had thrown himself headlong into the joy of physical pleasure when he was fifteen, and he had been consumed by that. Charity was more. She was his friend. And he had made sure that he saw her that way to the best of his ability.

That T-shirt had undone a lot of good intentions.

He heard soft footsteps behind him and she appeared, dressed in her usual long floral dress, with thick woolen tights underneath.

"Thank you," she said. "For the cinnamon rolls."

He could see that her face was swollen; could see that she had been crying.

He wanted to take her into his arms and hold her. It was a strange, foreign feeling, but one that was incredibly strong. He couldn't say that he was used to having those kinds of feelings. Wanting to comfort in that way. And he couldn't. Not now. It was too dangerous. At the moment it was just too damned dangerous.

"Did I make you cry?"

The thought made his chest feel like it had been run through with rebar.

"No," she said stubbornly, rubbing at her red nose.

"What did?"

"My dad died, Lachlan. I cry about it sometimes. I didn't feel well last night because… I dunno. Just some things caught up with me. That's all."

"Sweetheart…"

"I already told you not to call me that."

"Sorry. Doc."

"That's better." She went over to the coffeemaker, and he put his arm out. "I'll do it."

"You don't need to do that."

"I want to. Let me do this for you. Let me make some coffee for you. Get a cinnamon roll and have a seat."

"I need to get going. I have appointments in an hour…"

"I know. That's fine. But let's get you fueled up and ready to go."

"You've been doing this a lot lately."

He got the ground coffee out of the cupboard and

started to pour a measure of it into the coffee filter. "Well. You need it. And maybe I need it. Because... Because I worry about you. Because I worry about you losing your dad, and this makes me feel better. Okay?"

She sniffed. "Okay."

"It wasn't as much fun after you left."

"Really?" She laughed. "Because I wasn't actually any fun last night."

He thought about that for a moment, because it was true. But he still felt like he had suffered for the loss of her. "All right. You've been friendlier. But... I missed you."

She shifted on the couch. "Well. Thanks."

"It's just true."

He got the coffee brewing and grabbed a cinnamon roll for himself, then sat in the chair opposite her on the couch.

"So how did things go last night? With Fia."

"Oh. She's nice."

"Do you think you'll see her again?"

"If she wants to."

"You didn't, like, make any declarations or... Kiss her or anything?"

He raised a brow. "I'm under strict orders to be chaste."

"Kissing is acceptably chaste."

He nearly choked on his laugh. "Not the way I do it."

He could feel her staring at him, her eyes wide and earnest, color mounting in her cheeks. He wished he hadn't noticed that. Wished he hadn't seen it. He wished a hell of a lot of things right then. He really did.

"Anyway. That's um..." She cleared her throat. "I'm glad that it went well. I'm glad that...she seems compatible for you. I mean, what you were looking for. The values and all of that. The ranch. It makes sense."

"Oh yeah. A hell of a lot of sense. Plus, we already have to combine families at Christmas. And true, we already combine with the Garretts, too, but Wolf and Sawyer are already married so I don't really have a shot there."

She laughed softly, taking a bite of cinnamon roll. "Yes. That is the barrier to you being with Wolf or Sawyer."

"There might be a couple others. What are you doing today?"

"I have a medic check on all the horses down at Windemere stables on the coast. It's a bit of a drive."

"You all right to go alone?"

"Yes. It's my job. I'm okay to do it alone."

"I can go with you."

"None of your brothers need you today?"

"There's so many of us."

"Well. Maybe you should… I don't know. Make a follow-up date with Fia…"

"No. I don't think that's necessary right now. I mean… I was thinking I'd give it a couple of days. You've got Byron coming in to visit and then you'll be busy. I might work on it then."

"Oh."

"I can go with you today."

His body was tight, and everything in him was telling him that he should give her some space. Give them some space.

He really wanted to get the image of her opening that bedroom door out of his mind. Floral panties and tight nipples and all. Because he didn't need to think of her that way. Ever. Not ever ever.

Yet here he was, thinking about it double time.

"Yeah," she said. "That would actually be great. I'm very tired. What if that means that I'm not as good as my dad? He didn't spend a whole bunch of time crying in his bed and then wake up late and need help on the job."

He wasn't used to seeing Charity at a loss. This was totally new territory.

"You don't know what he did when he was in his thirties. He didn't have you until he was fifty."

"I know. I do. It's just… I feel… I feel inadequate right now."

"Hey. I'm not doing a very good job of giving you confidence, then, am I?" In spite of himself, he reached out, leaning across the space, and gripped her chin between his thumb and forefinger. He didn't know what the hell had possessed him to do that, but it had been a mistake.

She was soft. So soft. The other night when he had grabbed her arm to keep her from falling, and he had noticed that, he hadn't given himself a reason for noticing. He had just gone ahead and ignored the observation. Because it was easier that way.

But right now? He knew why. Because it had to do with floral cotton panties. He knew.

"Listen to me, Doc. You are phenomenal. In every damned way. You're not just the person I'd want working on my horses. You're the person I want working on me. Who cares what those motherfuckers think?"

"Well, I do, because there might…"

"Say it."

"Oh no. I can't say that."

"Say it for me," he said, his eyes never leaving hers. And he ignored the danger signals flashing in his gut; he ignored everything that he shouldn't and kept on holding her chin. "Say it for me."

"Who cares what those…motherfuckers think."

She turned bright red. And something inside him ignited.

He let go of her face and sat back in his chair. "There you go. Some people find that gives them power, you know. Saying words like that."

"Really?"

"They've done psychological studies on it. You don't need to go saying it in front of anyone else. But maybe shouting it when you're all by yourself will hype you up sometimes."

He wasn't sure he could handle ever hearing her say it again. Because it had done something to him. If nothing else, it definitely indicated there was something the hell wrong with him.

He got up and took a thermos out of the cupboard and poured all the newly brewed coffee into it. "Come on, Doc. I'll drive. You need to get caffeinated."

She got up, and they headed out the door and she paused to fish another cinnamon roll out of the box and stick it on her plate, which she brought to the car along with the coffee.

She got into the passenger seat of the mobile veterinary unit, and he got into the driver's seat.

"You sure you can handle this thing?"

"Don't impugn my driving skills, Doc. I can do an extended cab pickup with a horse trailer. I think I've got this."

Of course, the veterinary vehicle was old school and didn't have much in the way of bells or whistles. No alarms to let you know if you were about to run into something; just an alarm to let people know to get out of your way. It was a little bit hairy getting it out of the driveway, but once they were on the highway it was all good. She was sitting next to him, happily drinking coffee and eating her cinnamon roll. Every so often she would pause to lick her fingers, and just once he looked over and saw her pink tongue gliding over her skin, and had to adjust his position.

"So how far is this place?"

He needed to get his shit together. He was getting turned on by his best friend, and really, it was probably some weird psychological thing because she was the one who had told him that he needed to be celibate for the next six months, so he was attaching sex to her in a way that was unhealthy, completely inappropriate and utterly outrageous.

But that was all. It would go away. It had to. There really wasn't another option.

She sighed happily when she finished up the cinnamon roll, setting the plate on the bench seat between them and clutching the thermos against her chest as she sniffed the contents. "I love the smell of coffee."

"You're a creature of many vices," he said.

And sensual.

Maybe in a way he hadn't fully noticed before. Because he had endeavored to make her wholly nonsexual. So it was really something to realize that she was so in tune with her body. With smells and tastes...

"I expect that by next week Byron will be the one

assisting you on calls like this." He said that as a reminder to himself as much as anything.

"Remember," she said. "I said I didn't need assistance. I just like it today. I like that you're driving."

"I was just observing. We probably won't see each other much when he's around."

"I don't see why not. I'd like it if you got to know him a little better. He's a good guy, Lachlan."

That rankled. "I'm sure he is."

"You don't sound overly certain."

"No. I'm certain." He just didn't care. It didn't fundamentally change the way that he felt about the guy, or about her attachment to him, or any of that. That was all. He could be as charming as could be. Hell, he could be the Pope. Well, except he couldn't be the Pope, because then he couldn't be married to Charity.

He would prefer that.

Right. *So what is it you want exactly?*

He didn't want to answer that question; that was for damn sure.

They drove through the little town of Copper Ridge, then continued on down the coastline, out a ways to the seaside equine facility called Windemere.

It had a pretty damned uppity-looking sign—in his opinion. Clearly people who were hugely impressed with themselves. But he had to admit that it was awfully pretty. Rolling green lawns and a view of the ocean. Pristine white stables and a matching house with green corrugated metal roofs.

"You're just doing…"

"The horsey equivalent of yearly physicals. They have about twenty animals. It's an all-day job."

He got a full appreciation for the physicality of her

work that day. She attacked it all with ferocity, even feeling not all that great.

He could tell that she was still kind of low ebb, even though she had rebounded a bit.

By the time they finished up, it was nearly dark.

"You want to stop and get some food?"

"That's okay." But then he heard her stomach growl.

"Come on. We'll stop in Copper Ridge."

"I'm really all right."

"Why are you being ridiculous?"

"Because I'm okay. You keep fussing over me like a hen, and I don't need you to fuss over me. We're friends, Lachlan. You're not my father. You're not my fiancé."

He gritted his teeth. "I'm aware. But that doesn't mean… You know what. I'm hungry. I'm stopping somewhere, and if you don't want to eat, you can sit in the truck and pout about it."

She practically hissed, the wretched creature. How had they gone from not having a fight ever to things being this touchy between them? He didn't know.

Or maybe he did, and he didn't want to identify it.

They decided to stop over at the little crab shack on the beach that served hot crab sandwiches with lemon on the side. It was right next to a little stand that served fish and chips.

The crab was on cheap white bread that didn't really need to be there, but it was all good in his estimation. Charity angrily tucked into hers, her expression while eating fresh seafood so fiercely angry that it was almost hilarious.

"Smile, Charity. We're sitting by the fucking ocean."

"Sorry," she said. She set her sandwich down for a

second and seemed to force her shoulders down away from her ears, trying to make herself relax, it looked like.

"No problem, sweetheart. But you can definitely take it down a peg."

"I suppose."

"What's got you so riled?"

"I found our... The dinner that we had the other night was a little bit... I don't know. It made me sad. So I didn't really want to eat with you again."

Of all the answers he had expected, it hadn't been that.

He frowned. "It made you sad?"

"I don't know."

"I'm sorry."

"It was probably the dessert. The tribute to my dad. My feelings just are very...raw right now. It's like some of what happened when he died got delayed. Or maybe it's the fact that Byron is coming, and things are changing. Every little shift in the world around me is starting to feel like a loss, and I don't know what to do about it. I just... I feel like this crab," she said, gesturing to her sandwich. "Forced out of my shell. Boiled. Shredded."

"That's intense."

"It is. And I'm sorry that I took it out on you. You don't deserve that."

"Well. I might deserve a little bit."

A reluctant smile curved one side of her mouth. "Yeah. Maybe a little bit. But not quite to the degree that I was dealing it out."

"I don't know anything about this kind of grief. But I know what it's like to lose someone you love. When my mom left... Everything was so quiet, in the scariest way. It was like the one thing that made the world feel safe was gone. I thought… I thought for sure she might as well have signed my death certificate on the way out. I thought for sure there's…no way that he's going to let me live another year. Because he just… I *infuriated* him. Everything that I was. I think losing somebody always feels like losing a safety net."

"I'm safe, though."

"It doesn't matter. The world feels scary when the person that you felt like stood between you and whatever is out there is gone. You have to make all your own choices, and you have to… You have to do all of it yourself. It's scary as hell, Charity. It's not easy. You just do your best, but that doesn't make it simple. And it doesn't make it a straight line, or something that gets progressively better. There's just some days that are worse than others."

It was a fine thing for him to give out advice, like he had it all together, when he didn't. But she deserved to be reassured, and he was the one who was here.

"Yes. That's exactly it. I'm sorry, Lachlan. I only knew you for a couple of years before your dad… Before he left."

"Before Gus ran him off."

"Yeah. But I remember vividly all the times you came to me bloody and broken."

"I remember you asking what you could do. And the terrible thing was there wasn't anything. My dad was friends with the sheriff. Thank God that guy is gone."

"It wasn't fair. It wasn't fair that there were no safety nets in place to protect you."

"That's life, though, isn't it? That's why I felt so lost when my mom was gone. Because she had felt like the safety net. Your dad was your safety net. You oriented your world around him, and now he's gone. I'm not surprised that it's been tough."

She took a bite of her sandwich and chewed thoughtfully, looking out at the ocean. The wind ruffled her hair, and she shivered slightly. He remembered how he had given her his coat when they'd had dinner together.

"Cold?"

"No," she said. She *lied*.

"Okay."

He let her lie.

They finished quickly after that, then piled into the vehicle, heading back toward Four Corners.

He was glad he had spent the day with her. Because if this morning had been his dominant memory of her, her half-naked, he didn't think he would've gotten back on equal footing with her quite as quickly.

But they had spent the whole day together. And while there had been a little bit of conflict, everything felt more normal on the drive back.

Things were just a particular kind of hard right now. He understood that. He understood that it was just a moment of change, in the world in general, not between the two of them.

That was the thing to remember.

There were other things happening. And his reacting to seeing her in her underwear wasn't really about her, but about the changes. Yeah. That seemed about right.

They drove back to Four Corners, and for the first time Charity got into the driver's seat.

"Bye," she said.

"Yeah. See you."

She nodded. "See you."

His eyes dropped to her lips.

And time got slower.

He didn't do that. Didn't pause to look at her mouth. He just looked at her face. Her familiar face. Then right then he was zeroed in on that mouth.

He raised his eyes back to hers. "Bye, Charity."

He turned and walked into the house, went straight down the hall and turned on the shower. He made sure to keep it ice-cold while he stood under the spray.

And when he got into bed, he did it frozen. For a damned good reason.

# CHAPTER TEN

BYRON WAS HERE. She was so grateful that he was finally here, rather than living in anticipation of it.

She had decided that some of her issue was being in this sort of middle ground with him and their relationship. He was almost here, but he wasn't here yet. She had decisions to make about what she was going to do, whether or not she was going to move. Whether or not he was going to decide that they should be here. Yeah. There was just a lot of stuff. And she was feeling very grateful that at least something was moving itself into the done column. He was here. So there wasn't simply anticipation.

He texted to let her know that his plane had landed and that he would be driving out to her place soon.

She had decided to cook dinner for the two of them for the evening, because she knew already that he didn't particularly like the atmosphere of Smokey's. They could go to the café, but that wasn't the nicest, either. So she thought maybe he would like a roast chicken dinner.

When the rental car pulled into the driveway, she fixed a smile on her face. She was excited that he was here. She was.

She opened up the front door and stepped out of the house and for some reason he gave her a strange sense of déjà vu. When Lachlan had driven up for their dinner last week—the way that anticipation had filled her. The way that she had smiled without trying. She frowned.

She didn't need to go thinking of that. It had nothing to do with this.

Byron unfolded his lanky frame from the driver's seat and pushed his brown hair off his forehead. He was wearing tan trousers and a pale blue button-up shirt tucked in.

"I'm so glad to see you," she said as relief burst through her chest. She had said it. And it was true enough. And that was good.

She crossed the drive and opened up her arms, and he did the same, accepting a quick, gentle hug.

"It's been too long," he said, his smile kind and reassuring and familiar—in spite of the time that had passed since they'd been together in person.

"It has."

She didn't know what it should feel like to be in person with the man she was supposed to marry, and she wondered if it was this.

"Come on inside," she said. "I made chicken. I thought we might enjoy dinner together."

"That was very thoughtful of you," he said.

She knew he meant it. He was old-fashioned and charming and in some ways he reminded her of her dad. It wasn't just the tweed.

"If you want to go out instead this will save."

"No, not at all. I'd rather stay in."

She smiled. "Oh. Good."

"I brought Ticket to Ride. The game we talked about."

"Oh! Great. We can eat and then play."

She could feel herself finding her footing with him. It was strange to have him here. He didn't quite fill up her house the way that Lachlan did. Lachlan's broad shoulders and height made her kitchen look tiny. Byron seemed to fit in it perfectly.

"Dinner smells delicious," he said, washing his hands in such a way that she could almost hear him humming "Twinkle Twinkle Little Star" to himself.

She smiled.

Then he dried his hands on the tea towel that hung over the stove and came to sit at the table. He looked at her, his brown eyes deeply sympathetic all of a sudden. "How have you been coping?"

Her heart squeezed tight. "It depends on the day."

"Your dad was a wonderful man, Charity. I'm so sorry that you lost him."

"Me, too."

"I wish I could've come for his funeral. I'm sorry that I was unable to get away from the practice."

"It's okay. I had…" For some reason she was reluctant to say Lachlan's name and she shouldn't be. Byron knew full well that Lachlan was her best friend. That they had a very close relationship, and it was one that was important to her. "Lachlan has done a very good job of taking care of me."

She wondered if she had been right the first time. Thinking that maybe she shouldn't mention it. Because his expression did something strange.

"I'm glad to hear it."

Except she wasn't sure that he was. The words were tight, and so was his mouth.

The timer dinged, and she got the chicken out of the oven. She had also made some rolls—well, she had opened up a can of dough and baked them quickly—and some green beans.

She had made gravy for the chicken, which was rich and all very simple and homestyle, which was something she knew Byron appreciated.

She eyed him expectantly as he took his first bite of chicken.

"Delicious," he said.

This was the kind of thing they would do when they were husband and wife. She would make dinner. He would eat it. Maybe sometimes he would make dinner. She didn't really know how marriage worked. She had never seen one up close. She'd seen them on TV, of course. But they were either idealized, or ridiculously dysfunctional, and she wasn't silly enough to believe in the idealized version, or masochistic enough to want the disaster. "So you said Lachlan has been taking care of you?"

"Yes," she said. "You know…he knew my dad very well. And we've been friends for so long… He's just making sure that I'm not alone. Making sure to help when I'm feeling sort of low…"

"That's very nice of him." The way that he said it, again, and that tone, made her think that he didn't actually feel that way. Was he jealous? She'd been certain that they had the kind of relationship that didn't include jealousy. But she was questioning that now.

"Lachlan is getting married," she said.

"Really?" That seemed to make Byron a little bit happier.

"Yes. Well. He hasn't…exactly settled on a person yet. But he is intent on settling down. Reforming."

"Reforming?"

"You know. He has a… He's… You've met him. He's quite…"

"What are you saying?"

"He and I are very different," Charity said. "I thought you kind of knew that. He likes to go out and… He treats relationships quite casually."

His brows lifted. "You're telling me that he engages in casual sex?"

"He used to," she said, feeling awkward now. "But he doesn't anymore. He's trying to be serious. I'm… helping him."

Byron's expression became very careful. "Well, that's very kind of you."

"He asked me because you and I have such a great, compatible relationship. He thought that I might be able to give him some insight into what a marriage-minded woman is looking for in a husband."

Byron smiled then. "Well. That is indeed you living right up to your name. Charitable."

Charity laughed. "I want him to be happy. Anyway, when we get married I'll feel better to know he's taken care of."

But for some reason it made her heart feel sore.

"We all want that for our friends," he said. "Have you thought any more about whether or not you want to move to Virginia?"

She winced. "I was hoping that you might like it here enough to want to stay."

"Maybe," he said. "I have a feeling I'm going to try to convince you to come with me."

Her stomach shook slightly. "I guess we'll see what happens."

After dinner she made tea and took some scones

out of the pantry. She hunted down her lemon curd and extremely hard-won clotted cream—she'd had to order it online—while Byron set up the board game.

They battled it out for train routes and talked about all the late nights their group had spent playing elaborate board games back at school.

"The Risk game that wouldn't end was something," he said.

"If by *something* you mean *nearly violent*, yes."

He won all three rounds of Ticket to Ride, but she was sure she'd figured out the strategy by the last game and was confident she'd get him next time.

"I won't stay too late," he said, helping her clear the dishes from the table.

She reached across the space and hugged him, lingering this time. He smelled familiar and he reminded her of a happier time. When she'd been at school and she'd been carefree. When her dad had been home waiting for her with the porch light on.

"It's so good to see you," she said.

He patted her back and then he did something he hadn't done before. He dropped a kiss on her head. "It's good to see you, too."

After he was gone she sat still, analyzing the evening. It was so good to see Byron. He made her feel... happy. But it was a simple feeling. Comfort, warmth, familiarity. And it brought her back to the jagged, complicated things she'd been feeling with Lachlan over the past few days. How different it was when she parted from him. The past few days she had felt a lot. Sad. Jittery. Sick.

And she did her best not to think about him walking in and finding her in that T-shirt, which wasn't even pajamas, but nobody was supposed to be there.

*You should feel more for your fiancé. Surely.*

What was more? She felt for Byron. She cared for him. She wanted cozy dinners and game nights with someone who reminded her of brighter days.

She didn't want sharp, jittery and sad.

She wanted Byron. It was that simple.

It was okay for life to be simple.

## CHAPTER ELEVEN

THE VISIT WAS going well. It was. Dinner the night before had been so nice with Byron, and she wasn't exactly sure why there had been a weird gnawing sensation inside her ever since.

She wanted to press her fists into her eyes and make it all go away. Except she shouldn't want that. She should be happy. This was the problem. She couldn't quite sort out where her happiness was supposed to be in all of this. Right now it all just felt like change. And it made her want to retreat to what was normal.

Because what if at the end of the week Byron still wanted her to move to Virginia?

His family was there, and her dad was gone. It made sense. That was the problem. She didn't want to move, but she understood why he wanted her to.

That was why she had asked Lachlan to come over and have breakfast with her. Because it felt like it might be a normal thing. Eating at the café with him.

She drove in her mobile veterinary unit so she could leave straight from there to go to her appointments for the day, and he drove up in his rugged pickup. They ordered coffee, and each got the large traditional breakfast with eggs, bacon, hash browns and she got a biscuit, while he opted for a short stack of pancakes.

She poured ketchup all over everything but the bacon and biscuits.

"Little philistine," he said.

"You're not going to put ketchup on your potatoes?" she asked.

"Sure. But not on my eggs."

"Ketchup is wonderful on eggs," she said.

He snorted. But this felt good. It felt right. Normal. It did something to dispel the strangeness that had been there between her and Lachlan for the last little bit, and it eased that sense of the unknown that she was currently grappling with in ways she didn't want to.

"So how are things?" he asked. "I'm surprised you're not having breakfast with the fiancé."

"I wanted to see you," she said.

The corner of his mouth turned up, and he looked unreasonably satisfied. He took a bite of his non-ketchup eggs.

"Can't say as I blame you."

"Well. How are you? Have you gone out with Fia again?"

"I have not. Though I'm thinking I ought to. Soon. We didn't really go out, though. She came to my house."

"Yeah. I guess that's different."

"This is going out," he said, gesturing between the two of them, and she didn't know why he had said that.

"Well, on a technicality, then, I don't suppose I've been out with Byron since he's been here, either."

"This is practically illicit, in that case," he said.

She wrinkled her nose against that teasing. Because it was skimming against something raw inside her that she didn't want to examine. *He* was clearly not raw.

"So are you in love with Fia?" she asked.

"Oh, hell no," he said. "But I do think she might be a great candidate for marriage."

"You say that like it's...obvious that you wouldn't be in love with her?"

"How can you be in love with somebody after one poker game?"

She shrugged. "I don't know. I don't think you can be. But I think it's funny that you're so set on marrying her, when you aren't in love with her. When you actually sound pretty dismissive about love. Why exactly do you want to get married, Lachlan?"

"I want the stability. I want something normal. I look at the things that it's done in my brothers' lives..."

"You don't think it's the love?"

"No, Charity, I don't. I think it's more than that. I'm just saying I prize companionship over that. That's what I'm looking for. Friendship."

She looked up, and her eyes locked with his and held. An uncomfortable sensation wound through her body.

*Friendship.*

She suddenly felt like there was a magnet somewhere down beneath the floor that was pulling her sharply to the chair, but down farther. Like she was being dragged down beneath the surface. She didn't know what that was. But it made her dizzy.

"Friendship," she repeated.

"Well. Yeah. Companionship. Someone to have kids with."

"Kids."

"Yeah. I might have some kids."

"I want kids," she said, feeling wistful. It was one reason she had decided that she and Byron really needed to hurry up and get married. Because she was thirty, and the logistics of pregnancy and fertility became a little bit more thorny after thirty, and she wanted to have a couple of children.

She didn't want to have one child that was lonely the way that she had been. She didn't want to be single. She didn't want her child to have one parent. She wanted something different than what she'd grown up with. Listening to Lachlan, she could see that it was much the same for him.

Neither of them seemed to be all that bothered about a great passionate love. If pressed, she would say that she loved Byron. Except…

There was a strange sort of lightness in her chest when she thought of him. No gravity. No weight. No magnet.

And they had never said it to each other. They were more careful than that. They said things like that they were looking forward to seeing each other. That they enjoyed each other's company. But they had never said they loved each other.

She couldn't even imagine it. That was wrong, wasn't it? Except, there Lachlan was, being utterly dismissive of love, acting like it had practically nothing to do with marriage. So maybe she was the one who was wrong about it. Maybe Lachlan had the right idea, and there was actually nothing to be worried about.

Friendship.

She was friends with Byron.

The word echoed inside her. "I just think that getting involved in all that passion and stuff, it's not good for some people," he said.

"It's not?"

He shook his head. "No. I think there's a good, logical way to go about this. Find somebody who shares my values. Find somebody that wants the same things I do and make a life. That will go a long way to… I don't know. It just feels like it'll fix some things."

"Yeah. It does. I understand that. I was really lonely when I was a kid. And the idea of fixing it by creating a family on purpose feels right."

"Yeah," he said. "It does."

She grabbed the ketchup bottle and poured more on her eggs.

"Disgusting," he said, lightly salting and peppering his.

"It's zesty," she responded, taking a bite.

"Zesty. Probably about the zestiest thing you've done recently."

That little mocking grin twisted up the corner of his mouth and there was an answering pull in her stomach that she didn't care for.

The kind of pull in her stomach she never felt when she was around Byron.

What would she do without Lachlan? What would she do if he married someone else and she moved away? She hadn't told him about the potential move, and she did need to.

"Just let me enjoy my zesty eggs in peace."

"Of course, my lady doc."

And at the end of breakfast, by the time she got into her car, she wasn't sure if the breakfast had made things better, or a little bit worse.

# CHAPTER TWELVE

"So how are things with the fiancé?"

He was surprised he'd seen Charity without Byron at all, let alone yesterday for breakfast and today.

"Oh, good," she said. She had come out to the ranch to do a checkup on two new horses that had come in.

"I'm glad to hear that."

"Yes. He's very… I dunno. He's very easy. Though… I think he might have some concerns about you."

Lachlan's brows shot up. "Me?" Not because he couldn't understand why a man wouldn't want another man to be extremely close to his fiancée, just because it was something that he and Charity had never touched on or acknowledged. They had always treated each other like friends of the same gender, his own reaction to her the past few days notwithstanding. They had never really treated each other differently. So they would never have talked about a significant other being bothered by the other's presence. Of course, she'd only had Byron, and he never had anyone.

"He knows we've been friends forever."

"Yes. But… I don't know. Not concerns, really, it's… I don't know. He seemed maybe like he was jealous of you at one point when we were talking."

"Of me?"

"He wants me to move to Virginia with him."

"He *what*?"

Move to Virginia. His Charity, leaving him. Moving to Virginia.

"You've got to be kidding."

"No. I'm not. I'm not kidding. I…"

"Charity," he said. "You've lived here your whole life. Why should you leave this place? You love it. It's your home."

"Yeah, I know. But also, you're right. I have lived here my whole life. And it's part of the problem with getting taken seriously and…all of it. Maybe it would be easier… What if it was easier if I just left?"

"You can't leave." He was in absolute disbelief. Complete and total.

"I might have to," she said. "Because that's what you do when you decide you're going to make a life with somebody. You compromise."

"What exactly is he compromising? Because as far as I can tell, he's going to get you to move where he wants you to. He's staying at a room across the street because of his personal feelings on the matter of cohabitation…"

"Why do you care so much? You're going to move on. Make a different life. You know things are going to change. It's inevitable."

"Yeah. I knew that it was inevitable things would change because you were going to marry the guy. I didn't know you were going to move across the country."

He felt…betrayed. She was an integral part of his life. An integral part of his…his happiness. His sanity. She had been for a very long time. From the time he had been a teenage boy, cut and bleeding in a forest, Charity had been the bright spot. His angel. Something rare and beautiful and so far above anything or anyone. And she was going to leave him.

Just like that.

"I can't believe you're leaving me."

"I'm not leaving *you*, Lachlan. I'm leaving Oregon. And still, only maybe."

She was leaving *him*. She could call it whatever she wanted, but she was leaving him.

"I don't even know for sure if it's happening," she said. "So settle down. This week I'm trying to show him that it might be all right if we stay here. I'm just letting you know that I'm considering it. That I'm really thinking about whether or not it might be a good idea. Practically. Given my current situation."

"Well, you haven't really given me a chance to boost your confidence."

"Just… Forget about it. Nothing is settled. I was just trying to… I just wanted you to know. I didn't want you to be blindsided by anything if at the end of the week the decision is that…we're going to end up living in Virginia."

*We.* He didn't like that, either. Because she meant her and Byron.

And usually when she said *we* she meant the two of them.

*Yeah. Aren't you some kind of bastard. Because you intend to marry somebody else, and then who do you think* we *will be to you? You just want to keep her.*

It was true. He wanted to keep Charity all to himself. He wanted her to stay in that little house on the property adjacent to his; his sweet, innocent angel. His woodland fairy. For forever. That was reasonable, right? He didn't want anything to disrupt it. He didn't want anything to change it. He had resented her years away at veterinary school. He had resented the appearance of Byron in her life and had been thankful that the guy had never been local.

That he had only come out to visit a couple of times, and that in general he didn't impact on Lachlan's daily life. He was all right with Charity having an attachment as long as it didn't hinder the one that he had with her.

So there. There was that.

"Fine. What are your plans with him this week?" he asked, knowing he sounded sullen. Not caring.

"I don't know. I don't have… I don't have firm plans."

"You want to show him Oregon? Let's go on a trail ride."

"Oh. That might be fun."

"We can all go. Fia can come."

He wasn't quite sure what he was doing. Except… Maybe if she could find a way to make all this fit together, it wouldn't feel quite so…enraging. Because that was what it was. Enraging. He felt like she was doing things without his permission.

*She needs your permission?*

No. Not like that. But they were…halves of a whole. And they had been for a very long time. The idea that she was just going to take herself away from him was such a… It was something he couldn't even fathom. So yeah. He wanted to see what it would look like. This future where they had partners and tried to maintain everything that they were. He wanted a sneak peek of that. He wanted to control it. Well. He had never said that he wasn't invested in controlling his life.

He knew what it was like to be out of control. He had spent his entire childhood that way.

Charity was stability. And he didn't think he had ever fully realized that until now. She represented something safe and sane. Her house had become a touchstone for good feelings. Her father had been an adult he could trust. And she had always been there for him. He couldn't lose Albert and then have her leave. It was absolutely unfathomable. It was like wave after wave of emotional indignity. And he didn't handle regular emotions all that well, so the intensity of these was… Well, he was damn well over it.

"That sounds nice," she said.

"Super nice. What if we do it tomorrow?"

"Isn't it supposed to rain tomorrow?"

"Not till the late afternoon. We can go in the morning. It should be pretty sunny up until the clouds roll in around two."

He was making a lot of proclamations based on a brief scroll through his phone's weather app. But he knew the area well enough to say that it sounded about right.

"Yeah. Well, I'll talk to him about it."

"Do you have appointments that you need to take into consideration?"

"I'm actually pretty free tomorrow. I left the week fairly sparse because Byron was going to be here, so I didn't make any new appointments after talking to him about his exact dates."

"Perfect. So unless there are some unforeseen piglet emergencies…"

"In which case the piglets will have to take priority," she said seriously.

"Obviously." He said that with equal seriousness.

"Okay. Well, I guess… Let's do that."

She finished up with the horses and smiled at him, a tentative smile that looked like the facial equivalent of an olive branch.

"See you later," he said.

"Yes."

She hightailed it out of there, and he looked down at his phone. He decided to call Fia rather than text her, because that seemed to indicate more serious intent.

"Hello?"

"Hi," he said. "Lachlan."

"Oh. Hi."

"I was wondering if you wanted to go on a trail ride tomorrow. Charity's fiancé is in town, and he's from Virginia. I want to show him the area. Thought we might make it a double date."

"Sure," she said, something unreadable creeping into her tone. "That sounds fun."

"It's funny that you say it like that, because your voice doesn't indicate that you think it sounds all that fun."

"It isn't that," she said quickly. "I didn't realize Charity was engaged."

"Yeah. She has been. For a long time."

"Weird."

"Why is that weird?" he asked, feeling defensive. If that was a crack about the fact that Charity was a little bit conservative-looking, that she didn't get flashy or done up or anything like that, well, he didn't like that at all.

"I just… Lachlan, I kind of thought that it was weird you asked me out because I always thought that you and Charity were… I always thought you were sleeping with her."

"I'm *not*," he said, realizing he sounded like a scandalized maiden.

"Okay."

She didn't sound convinced.

"Never have. Wouldn't. She's… You've met her."

"Yes. She's very pretty. And very sweet. I just kind of always thought she was your long-term…whatever."

"She's my *best friend*," he said, the words dragged from deep within him, the conviction in them real and raw.

"I'm sorry. That's really sweet. I didn't know that. I guess that kind of shows my own… I don't know."

"What about Landry King? Do I have to worry about him?"

She laughed, hard and bitter. "No. You do not have to worry about me and Landry. Rumors of us are greatly exaggerated. Fabricated, even. He's a pain in the ass. That's it."

"Well, there you go. Everybody's wrong about us, I guess."

"One thing's for sure. The two of us… That will give people something to talk about."

He chuckled. Because she was right. He hadn't realized that there was a prevailing thought—or maybe it wasn't a prevailing thought that he and Charity were more than friends. But clearly…

Also, if she was to be believed, she and Landry weren't quite what other people thought. Maybe people were just wrong altogether. Assumptions, he supposed, really did just make an ass out of you and me.

"Great. See you Wednesday."

"I can pack a picnic lunch for everybody," she said.

"Well, that would be lovely," he said.

"Lovely. You know, Lachlan, you're not quite how I thought you were."

"I'm trying to be a little bit better than people think I am. At least, that's the goal."

She huffed a laugh on the other end of the line. "Well. Aren't we all."

"Not all of us. I think Gus is basically the same asshole. He just loves your sister."

"I guess that works, too."

"I guess."

"See you tomorrow."

"See you tomorrow. Eleven o'clock?"

"Yeah. Eleven o'clock."

# *CHAPTER THIRTEEN*

SHE AND BYRON had shared dinner at Becky's that night, and he had been amenable to the trail ride idea, even though she could tell he wasn't all that thrilled about the idea of spending the day with Lachlan. Lachlan was her best friend, so he just had to get used to it. And by the time the next day rolled around, he showed up dressed in tweed pants, a sweater and scarf, with a plaid cap pulled down low over his head.

He always reminded her of a man in a British TV show. Which she kind of liked and frankly, found rather soothing. Because it was something she had spent so much time watching as a kid.

"We're going to drive over to McCloud's Landing," she said. "We're meeting Lachlan and his date."

"Oh. He has a date?" That seemed to please Byron.

"Yes. I told you he has intentions to get married in the next…bit. He's seeing one of the women that works at the ranch just across from his." *Seeing* might be a strong word. He had her over for one poker game. But she knew what Lachlan's intentions were right now, so it seemed pretty significant to her.

"Well, that's great," Byron said. He was visibly happy with this development. And she had to wonder… *Was* he jealous of Lachlan?

They got his rental car and drove over to McCloud's,

and when they got out Fia and Lachlan were already there. Fia was wearing a pair of tight breeches and tall boots. She had a cream-colored button-up shirt tucked in at the waist, and it emphasized the fullness of her figure. She looked…stunning. She was an incredibly beautiful woman. Charity had never really spent any time thinking about her looks, except… When she saw her standing next to Lachlan… They fit each other. She could see that. They looked like they should be together.

Right then she could understand why Byron was jealous of Lachlan. Lachlan stood at least five inches taller, his chest and shoulders much broader. He wore a tight long-sleeved shirt that stretched over that chest of his and clung to his narrow waist. His cowboy hat looked much more…roguish. More dangerous than the cap that Byron wore on his head. And she had just been thinking that Byron looked exceptionally cozy and safe.

Lachlan, *her* Lachlan, that she had known for years, suddenly looked dangerous by contrast.

She stood there, feeling dumbfounded by that observation. How could Lachlan be dangerous? Lachlan was her best friend.

She watched as he smoothed his large hand over his horse's neck, a smile curving his lips. He hadn't shaved today. He had whiskers covering his jaw and chin. And her fingers suddenly itched, like they were trying to guess what it might feel like if she touched them.

*Touched them?*

Suddenly, Lachlan looked up, and his eyes met hers. And it was like a clash of electric blue.

She felt pinned to the spot. She felt caught. Like she

had been trying to sneak cookies out of the jar, and she'd been made.

Except, she didn't know what the cookies were, and she didn't really understand what was happening. But her heart gave a great jump and hit her breastbone. And she felt...

"We got all the horses ready," Lachlan said. "All you need to do is saddle up."

Fia grinned and put her foot in the stirrup, swinging herself up onto the back of the horse elegantly. Charity was a good enough rider, but she wasn't like that.

Fia looked utterly at home on the back of a horse. Charity just rode on occasion. She knew everything about horses, about their anatomy, about ailments, but she didn't spend a ton of time riding them. She spent most of her time treating them. So it wasn't that she didn't have familiarity; it was just that she didn't have as much practical physical experience.

Lachlan led the horse that she was supposed to ride over to her, a big black beauty, and she patted his neck before hefting herself up onto his back, feeling more like a sack of potatoes than the elegant picture that Fia had made.

Byron mounted easily enough, and Lachlan led the way past the barn down a trail that went around the base of the mountain.

It was beautiful. The pine trees that rose up on either side of the closed-in trail were deep green majestic sentries, standing guard over them. The wedge of blue sky between looked nearly artificially bright. The way the sun filtered down across the pines made them glimmer, a gold and shadow patchwork all around them.

"So," Lachlan said. "Byron. What do you think so far?"

"It's been a very nice trip," Byron called over the top of Charity and Fia. He was bringing up the rear. Lachlan, Fia, Charity, Byron. All in a single file line on this narrow trail.

"Glad to hear it," Lachlan said. "Of course, I wouldn't want you to miss any of the majesty of my home state. It's beautiful. And you can get any kind of scenery you might want without ever leaving the state. Go east and you get high desert. Go up north and it gets even greener, rainier. Down south you can get more sun, heat. Head west and you get the ocean. It's amazing."

"Very impressive," Byron said as if he was being polite. "I'm fond of the rolling hills in Virginia. The way that the leaves change. Though Evergreen is certainly its own kind of beauty."

"Its own kind of beauty," Lachlan said, snorting. "I don't think there's anything prettier. And these mountains. I love a mountain."

"Do you?" Charity asked, unable to help herself.

"It's a noted fact, Charity. I am a longtime lover of a mountain range."

"Indeed."

"I've probably written a sonnet or two about them." He shot her a wicked look. "I'm also a great lover of poetry."

Fia laughed. "I would like to hear your mountain sonnet, Lachlan. I didn't take you for a composer of verses."

"I have hidden depths. But you have to go on at least four dates with me before you get a sonnet."

Fia laughed again, and Charity was irritated, because they were flirting, and it was going well. Very well. Fia was clearly charmed.

"When we get to the top of this trail, there's a great view. You'll all be writing sonnets of your own. You won't need mine."

"You might be writing sonnets about my food," Fia said, and Charity knew that it was for Lachlan alone.

"Oh, I'm sure. I've already enjoyed your cooking many times at the town halls. You have to come to a town hall sometime, Byron. It's the way that we manage business on the ranch."

"Oh. I… Perhaps."

Byron couldn't have sounded less interested if he tried. And that actually kind of annoyed Charity. She knew that Lachlan was goading him, but Byron didn't know that. So she felt that Byron should be more polite. She didn't know quite why Lachlan was goading him. But she did know it.

He wanted Byron to like Oregon, but there was this additional thing that he was doing that Charity couldn't quite understand.

And still, she was being a little bit harder on Byron, which she didn't think was all that fair, and she couldn't quite understand.

She chose not to think too deeply about it as they pressed the horses on up the trail.

"So Charity," Fia called back. "How are things going now that you've taken over the veterinary practice?"

"Oh, great," she said, feeling the need to sound relentlessly cheerful. "Everything is just fine. The people here are so…wonderful. And it is a very rewarding thing to feel like I'm continuing on in my father's work."

"Of course," Fia said. "There's nothing quite like a family business. There's nothing quite like how important it feels. I completely understand. Sullivan's Point is the most important thing to me. Keeping everybody together. I'm afraid I was a little hard on Alaina about leaving. I didn't mean to be, but I just… With the way my family splintered… I'm not carrying on the legacy for my parents. Not after the way they abandoned us. But… It's for…my sisters. It's what keeps me connected to them. To everything. So I completely get the reward there. The legacy."

Something stirred in her chest. *The legacy.* And if she left with Byron she would be leaving the legacy behind. Except… Her being a veterinarian was actually a huge part of her father's legacy. That in so many ways she had chosen to be like him. She realized right then that she was sort of his female counterpart. Conservative dress, a quiet manner, a love of animals.

She hadn't really intended to be her father's mirror, but she was.

She was wholly and completely dedicated to being someone who made him proud. She always had been. Because she had always felt like he had done so much when it came to dedicating his life to her. And it felt so utterly important.

Now she just felt…turmoil. Because leaving had seemed so possible, and now she wondered if that was really the tribute that she wanted to give her dad.

*Should your whole life be a tribute?*

It seemed like it should be, in a way. Like you lived on for the person who came before.

Especially when they had been so utterly good.

"Yes. The legacy. It's really important to me."

She had been trying to project utter confidence to Fia, to find some way to bring herself up to equal footing with the more beautiful, much more elegant, woman. And instead, she had found herself drowning in doubt.

Great. That had backfired spectacularly.

They kept going, and she noticed when the first, very fluffy, full-looking cloud rolled in. They were white at first, and then there were more with rims of gray around the edges. The swollen undersides dark, as if they had been brushed with charcoal, fading upward into a paler white still.

"I think that rain might be coming sooner rather than later," she said.

"We just need to get to the top. Then we can have lunch," Lachlan said.

They pressed on, and when they arrived at the top of the ridge, the reward was obvious. The dark cloud still had the sun spilling through gaps in that woven mist, pouring it down into the valley below, highlighting the trees in the fields, a glorious golden green that almost glowed. There were vineyards and rows of corn, the different fields bisected by roads. You could make out the shape of cows grazing down there, and the little tiny main street of Pyrite Falls, which looked out of time and place from all the way up here.

"It's beautiful," she whispered.

"I told you," he said.

They dismounted, the horses standing by, well trained and docile, used primarily for the equine therapy and therefore not really flight risks.

Lachlan took blankets from saddlebags on the horses, and Fia gathered up the two picnic baskets that her horse had been carrying. They sat down at the edge of the ridge, looking down at the view below.

Lachlan was sitting next to Fia, a big gap between them and where Charity sat next to Byron. Couples.

Charity looked across the space to Lachlan and he offered her a smile.

She looked away, opening up the basket and digging inside. "This looks beautiful," Charity said, taking out a sandwich wrapped in cellophane.

"Thank you," Fia said, looking pleased. "I think I'm going to sell all of this kind of thing in the farm store. I'm getting really excited about it. We're closer and closer to actually having the building in a reasonable state. And definitely closer to figuring out the logistics of the permits on the roads."

"It really is such a complicated business," Byron said. "Arranging all of that. When we opened the clinic in Virginia, it was a new construction, and the bureaucracy was a bit stunning."

She laughed. "Yes. Definitely stunning bureaucracy. But here it's more been trying to arrange things with other ranchers. A little bit bracing. But it's fine. We've got it more or less sorted out. I'm not terribly worried."

"That's good," Lachlan said.

She ate her turkey sandwich and enjoyed it far more than she would even like to admit. It had cream cheese and cranberry sauce and was on a croissant, and was so good she wanted to weep. Then there were little mini pies filled with tart berries that made her want to moan with pleasure. But of course, she wouldn't let herself. A compliment was one thing, but she didn't need to go falling all over herself over the other woman's food. Charity herself made very good cookies, and if she had brought some, everyone would've liked those just as much.

*They wouldn't have. Your basic chocolate chip cookie is not this incredible pie, and you know it.*

No.

Charity was a chocolate chip cookie. Fia was a beautiful pie.

Maybe that was a terrible and ridiculous metaphor, and she didn't know why she was marinating on it, or why she felt quite so keenly. Only that she did. And it was really annoying.

They had just finished the last bite of their pie when a fat raindrop fell from the swollen clouds.

"Dammit," Lachlan said. "We might've overstayed our welcome."

"I did tell you," Charity grumbled.

"Well, was the view worth it or not?"

"You know it was. But now we're going to have to ride back in the rain."

"Are you made of sugar, Charity?"

"No," she said, wrinkling her nose.

"Then you aren't going to melt."

He inched a little closer to her when he said that, and she found herself wanting to go a bit closer, too. But she didn't.

She took a breath, looking behind her at Byron, wondering if he had sensed the same weird electricity in the moment. But he seemed rather oblivious, adjusting his cap and looking up worriedly at the sky.

"Better get going," Lachlan said.

They got back on the horses and started down the trail, this time at an increased clip, trying to get ahead of the weather. But it was no use, because halfway down, the sky utterly broke open and began to dump on top of them. The rain a fury, the day suddenly as miserable as it had been gorgeous.

The drops were fat and cold, and there were so many of them there was no way to dodge them. It was a deluge. By the time they got back to McCloud's Landing, they were soaked.

They got off the horses and Byron shook his arms out, water falling straight from them. "Do you need help with anything?"

Byron knew about horses, but he wasn't a horseman per se. He was also soaked and clearly freezing. "Go get some dry clothes," she said. "We can handle this. Dinner later?"

"Yes. Thank you. I'll go grab some dry clothes. You don't need a ride back?"

She shook her head. "I'm fine."

Fia laughed, shaking out her hair, her smile like the sun. Which was handy, since the sun was now completely obscured by the clouds. And she somehow looked even more beautiful drenched in rain.

Charity was confident that she herself looked like a drowned kitten.

"I'm going to head back, too. Nice to meet you, Byron. Good to see you, Charity. Give me a call, Lachlan."

"I will."

"Bye," Charity said, rain rolling down her face, her nose.

"I'll help you get the horses put away," she said.

"You can go get changed, too. It's kind of my fault that everybody's drenched. It was the timing. Should've gone earlier."

"No. It's not your fault. We'll just… Go get every-body put away."

She followed him into the barn, painfully aware of the fact that her hair was hanging like a limp curtain in her face, down her back, that she was damp and stringy and her dress was sticking to her skin.

"So you really like him?" Lachlan asked, a restless energy overtaking him.

She frowned. "Yeah. Why?"

"I don't know. I've been in situations with him a few times now, and I have to say… I don't get it."

"What do you mean…you don't get it?"

"He seems nice, Charity. But there's nothing special about him."

"How can you say that? I don't know anybody else like him. He dresses quirky and he loves board games and animals, and I love those things, too. He's into Star Trek and gardening, and I think it's a delightfully strange combination of things for a person to like, and *I like him.*"

"Okay, great. Fine. But he's not really funny. Not like you. He's not…really anything. He fits neatly and quietly into a line of people, and makes innocuous con-versation and comments. And I guess that's something, but I just don't… I don't get how it's what you want. I don't get how it's good enough for you."

"I met him at veterinary school. I have things in common with him that you don't understand. And what was that whole performance earlier anyway? A *sonnet.* You, Lachlan McCloud, have never written a sonnet in your life. I don't even think you know what one is."

"I fucking do," he said. "I went to school. And, we occasionally had required writing times, and maybe I did write poetry about mountains. I find your view on me to hold limited scope."

"Limited scope," she scoffed. "You're going to act like you know my fiancé better than I do, then claim I have limited scope in regards to you? I know you better than just about anybody else."

They took the tack off the horses, and she began to help towel them dry.

"I just think that you… I just think…" she sputtered.

"What do you think?"

"I think you don't like him because you don't want to like him. You're acting like you're my big brother and no man is going to be good enough for me. But Byron and I have things in common that you don't get. I can talk to him about medicine, about his experiences at school. I have things in common with him that you and I will never have in common. You will never understand those things about me. So… So there. It could be argued, Lachlan McCloud, that you and I have nothing in common, and yet we seem to spend a whole lot of time together. So… So."

"What's your argument, Charity? It is better to have something in common, or no?"

"You need to have something in common with the person that you're going to marry. It's all fine and good to have a friend who's…who's different from you. But he and I understand each other."

"Okay. Great. Do you want to fuck him?"

The words took her off guard. She felt… She felt like he had scalded her.

"I *beg your pardon*."

"Do you want to fuck him?" He repeated the question, this time with more purpose.

She tried to speak, but she couldn't make her mouth work. Or her voice box, which seemed to be emitting a helpless string of start-stop-sounding noises. "I don't think of him that way," she finally managed.

"Hell and damn, Charity. You are supposed to think of the person you want to marry that way."

"No. I mean… What I mean is… It's not the driving factor in our relationship. And even then, I wouldn't think of it in those terms. I want companionship. What I want is something companionable and…"

"Get a golden retriever, babe."

"Don't call me babe." She found herself moving toward him.

"Why not?"

"Because it's what you call every woman. And I'm not every woman, and I never have been. When you call me sweetheart and babe it's like you're dismissing me. Putting me in that category. I'm Doc. That's what I am, and I'm the only one that's that. And that's what I want."

"You want to be special?"

"Yes," she whispered. "And I don't like when you do that thing where you try to make me the same. Because it makes me feel small, and I hate it. And you're doing it now, and you're doing it because… I don't even know why."

She looked up at him, and her heart was pounding, her chest aching. And she didn't think that wrinkling her nose was going to make the feeling go away. Which was confronting and annoying, and she hated it. And why did he have to keep saying things like this to her?

Like when he had mentioned sex and virginity. And now he had said… He had said that. And he had jarred her brain into this territory that she didn't know how to navigate. That she didn't understand.

She had never once in her life thought about…that word that he had used as a verb. She had thought in warm, sweet terms. That they would get married, and things would be sort of nice and soft and special. Then they would have that magical connection that she didn't share with anyone else. It was the thing that would make them married. It was the thing that would make her feel that way about him. And once they were a married couple, they would have it. It made sense to her. Except, standing there looking at Lachlan with her heart threatening to burst its way out the front of her chest, it didn't make sense anymore, and that made her angry. Outraged, in fact, because how dare he? How dare he take something that she had so carefully defined for herself and try to impose his own rules on it?

She was just different than him. That was all. He was trying to measure what she wanted with his own yardstick, and it just wasn't fair, and it didn't work.

She was still wet. Miserably so, and somehow warm with it, and she didn't like it.

"Doc," he said, his voice suddenly low, rough. "You might want to take a step back."

She shivered, painfully aware of the fact that her dress was wet and cold, clinging to her skin. She was breathing hard, because she was angry. His own shirt was plastered to his body from that rain, and she could see the outline of his every muscle.

Muscles that she had gone out of her way not to look at, for all the time that she spent with him.

She remembered that moment again, when he had walked into the house and stripped his shirt off and she had looked away, because it was a practiced habit. Because she could remember clearly a time when he'd done that when she had been sixteen, and they had been down at the creek. A memory that she worked hard not to dwell on or really have at all.

Right then she did.

The sun shining on him, he grabbed his shirt and stripped it off, and she had been thrown into a world of heat, lust and other things she didn't understand. She had been incapable of looking away from him. Mesmerized by how muscular his body was, even at seventeen.

She had done her level best to never really look at him again when he had taken his clothes off. Which he did, with fairly alarming frequency, because that sort of thing just didn't matter to him. And her seeing it didn't much matter to him. So she had endeavored to make it not a thing.

But she was looking now. Even with his skin covered by the shirt. Not only did her heart hurt, but something began to hurt a little bit between her legs, and she wanted to turn away from it and him, and she found that she couldn't. She became unbearably conscious of her mouth. She slipped her tongue out to lick her lips.

She noticed his eyes lower quickly, then look back up at hers. He took a step toward her and she scrambled backward, tripping over the feed bucket and starting to go down. He reached out, grabbed her arm and pulled her up, which brought her hard up against his body.

And she was sure that he could feel her heart beating against his chest as well as hers. She was sure that he could read her mind, and it made her angry, because *she* couldn't even read her mind right now.

*Can you not? Or is this the thing that you try so hard to never name?*

*Is this the thing that made you feel sad after your date? That made you feel insecure about what you were wearing?*

*Is this the thing that you decided you didn't want to understand all the way back when you were sixteen because you knew that it would destroy every good thing?*

"Doc," he said, his voice husky. And he put his hand on her face. His hand.

Big and rough and on her cheek, his thumb sliding across her lips, all rough and calloused. His fingertips moved along the line of her jaw down to the center of her chin, and she found herself closing her eyes. And the sound escaped her mouth. A harsh, needy sound that wasn't quite like anything she'd ever heard in her life, much less heard come out of her.

But it felt so good. This moment. This touch. It wasn't like anything. He wasn't like anything.

She could feel his breath on her face, and she would've said that that was…something she wouldn't want. Because who would want it? Except, sharing air with him was like something special she had never known you could do with another person, and she wanted to lean into it. Into him. To explore the inevitability of what was closer than that. There was only one thing she could think of.

Her eyes snapped open. He was right there. His blue eyes intense as he looked at her.

He was the most beautiful man in the world.

She felt that then. With a certainty, deep down in the pit of her stomach. She had avoided ever acknowledging that.

She had always felt proud of him. Like he was something special. But she had gone out of her way not to acknowledge that he was attractive.

She had deliberately put blinders on herself. Had created spaces in moments where she automatically looked away, because looking at him would make it undeniable. And she had never wanted that.

The hell of living in a world where she knew that Lachlan McCloud was beautiful. She had never wanted to subject herself to that. Because she had him. And he was her best friend in the entire world. They had each other, in that sense.

And she had always been happy to have him be the sort of opposite, wonderful, external expression of the wildness that she was always too afraid to tap into herself. But she had been happy to leave the concept of that wildness as gauzy. The past few weeks, he kept making it specific. Bracing.

The words that he chose to use scraped up against a sensuality in her that she had always tried to ignore.

She knew the mechanics.

She knew the mechanics, but she had gone out of her way to not understand what drove people to have sex with each other, even when it wasn't a good idea. Even when they weren't in a relationship. Even when it might ruin something. Yes. She had gone out of her way to never know that.

And standing there with him, she thought she might know. Because if the moment was a grenade, she was very close to pulling the pin out and seeing what would happen.

*You aren't brave enough to pull the pin out. You aren't strong enough. You don't know what you're doing.*

No. She didn't.

So she put out her own hand and touched his face, just like she had imagined doing earlier. His whiskers were rough underneath her skin, and she mimicked the move he had just made, dragging her thumb over his mouth. The answering response in her body was a shock. The piercing arrow that shot itself up between her thighs, a pang of need that she had never experienced before in all of her life.

*Danger.*

Only earlier today had she seen the danger.

And now she felt like she was being swallowed whole by it.

His lips were warm and like velvet. Hot still, in spite of the water droplets. And she felt frozen just then. In this moment. She didn't want to move. She didn't want to breathe. She wanted to stand there with her hand on him and let her body acclimate to the feeling. To the moment.

To the new, utterly wild sensations that were rioting through her body.

This was desire. And she knew that it must've existed inside her for a very long time.

*Do you want to fuck him?*

That word was like someone had reached down deep inside her and grabbed on. Pulled. Squeezed. Taken everything that she thought she knew about herself and inverted it. Twisted it. And she could scarcely breathe.

No. She didn't.

She didn't want to do that with Byron.

But she had figured that it would never factor into her life. Not in *those* terms. That was this kind of rough, crude thing that other people did. That other people needed. She had retreated to the realm of the cerebral. She was rational and reasonable, like her father.

*Except he wasn't always that way. Or you wouldn't exist.*

No. But she had decided that she would live her life the way that she had always seen him behave. She had decided that she would avoid the heartbreak, avoid the loneliness. That she would do whatever she needed to do in order to have more.

She could see a future with Byron. Steady and sweet. A home and a family.

And she had never thought about…the sex. Not in detail.

It was easy to do that when you decided that you were a person who didn't really need it. When you decided that you were a person who wasn't in need of such things.

She had kept that blank. She had kept her desire in check. She had minimized it. Made it the smallest part of herself. So small it had nearly disappeared. Yes, she acknowledged that it would be part of marriage. But again, every time her mind went that direction, she just told herself that she knew the mechanics.

But this wasn't mechanics, the feeling of her hand on his face. The feel of his lips.

*It isn't sex, either. You are standing in a barn with your hand on your best friend's face, and he might think that you're crazy.*

She dropped her hand quickly and began to pull away, and he held her firm. "Do you want to?"

"Do I want to what?" she asked, the words coming out strangled.

"Do you want to kiss me?"

She wiggled, her face bursting into flame.

"Lachlan…"

"Do you want to?"

Did she want to? If she did, she couldn't take it back. This was like standing in front of the tree of the knowledge of good and evil. He was Adam and the serpent all rolled into one. Offering her knowledge. And she knew that when she had this knowledge, she couldn't go back. Couldn't break away. Couldn't not know. She had spent her life outrageously innocent for a reason. It wasn't because of morals. It was fear. Fear of this very thing. Of something bigger than she was. Of something that superseded logic. Something that belied her claims that what she wanted was a quiet, simple, easy life. She did not wish to belie her own claims. But maybe one fight. Maybe one bite.

Wasn't that always the way?

She could see herself walking toward her own ruination. She could see it clear as day. Why the hell was she doing it?

Maybe it had been a slow chipping away over the course of years. He'd gotten her saying swearwords multiple times over the past few weeks. Maybe that was the first step down the road to hedonism. She had never really considered it. She had always thought it was somewhat arbitrary, but had always decided to defer to her father when it came to matters of language. Because he didn't like certain words, and she thought that was fair enough. People were entitled to their opinions on such things. She had never found them important enough to fight for the cause of saying any.

She had never thought it made someone better or worse, and even though she had found Lachlan's language shocking in the beginning of knowing him, she had never felt like she needed to change him. Or scold him. Not at all.

But now she wondered. Yeah. Now she wondered if it was like a gateway drug.

"I want to kiss you," he said, those blue eyes leveled to hers. "Doc, I really want to kiss *you*."

And it was that; that was her undoing. Like a thread had been pulled and everything inside her had released.

Gloriously.

"Okay," she said, nodding. "Okay."

He moved his hand so that he was holding her chin between his thumb and forefinger, as he had done on her couch that day.

Then he leaned in and pressed his mouth to hers.

## CHAPTER FOURTEEN

WHAT THE HELL was he doing? He had seen the question in her eyes, and he hadn't been able to leave it unanswered.

He'd decided that he wouldn't do this. Years ago he'd decided that.

But here he was.

Losing control.

Losing everything.

She was terrified. Shivering and shaking in his arms as he covered her mouth with his own.

But he had *wanted* to do it. It was like every defense he'd ever had, every single one he'd built up since he was a teenage boy, had crumbled. And left behind had been the puerile fantasies that had possessed him back then.

The desire to be the one who showed her. The desire to be the one who made her lose it.

His Charity had so much control. She seemed so soft that people often interpreted it as her being inconsequential. But that wasn't it. Everything about her was a consequence; every single damn thing. She was a storm wrapped in a flower petal, and woe to anyone who didn't understand how deep she was. How hard. How strong.

He did. He understood.

And now he was kissing her. Slow and gentle. He coaxed her lips apart with the tip of his tongue, and she jerked against him when he breached her lips.

Then she softened, parting for him. He slid his tongue against hers, his whole body shuddering at the movement.

He was tasting her. *His girl*. This woman who had been a fixture in his life for all these years. Whose mouth had been a mystery to him all this time. He had tasted her.

He was shaken. It wasn't his first kiss. He wasn't totally sure if it was hers. But he wondered. And that teenage boy inside him wanted to roar in triumph. Because he had always wanted that, hadn't he?

Her hands came up and gripped his damp shirt, and he wasn't sure if she was holding him to her, or holding herself up.

He supposed that functionally, it didn't make much difference.

He tilted his head, taking the kiss deeper, tasting her deeper, and she whimpered. She didn't move much; in fact, it was like she was frozen, letting him lead, letting him charge the path forward on this exploration.

That was okay. For now. But he wanted more. He wanted her passion. He wanted…

*What in the hell are you doing?*

He lifted his head, pulling away from her. She was looking up at him, her lips swollen, her eyes wild. He had fantasized about those swollen lips. But not about the terror in her blue eyes. No. Not about that. He felt bad about that.

"Charity…"

"Is that what it's like?" she whispered.

"What?"

"To be you. You want to do something, so you just do it? Damn the torpedoes?"

"Oh." He laughed. Because it was kind of an absurd thing to say. "No. I… Is that what you think? That I just do whatever the hell I want whenever the hell I want to do it?"

"Yes."

"If I had done that I would have kissed you when you were sixteen."

She blinked. "You would have?"

"Yes."

"There's no way that you… You haven't… You haven't wanted to kiss me ever since I was sixteen."

"I first wanted to kiss you when you were sixteen, and I made a decision to just not want to do that afterward. Because you've always meant more to me than that. Always. Look, I messed up. Just now. I'd… I couldn't help it. I saw the way that you… I could see that you were…begging for it."

"That's horrible," she said, frowning deeply. "I don't want to hear about how you pity kissed me because I looked like I was pleading for it." She shoved his chest and pushed herself backward. "That's offensive."

"It's not what I meant," he said, grabbing hold of her arm and stopping her from getting too far away. "You wanted to kiss me."

"I don't know what I wanted. You said you wanted to kiss me. So why are you trying to make it… Why are you trying to make it my fault now?"

"I'm sorry. I didn't handle that well. I didn't like what you said. About me…just doing whatever the hell

I want. Because I stopped kissing you, didn't I? I didn't want to. I just knew that I *needed* to."

She shivered violently, and he felt a whole load of guilt dump down over the top of him. Dammit.

"I'm sorry," he said. "About everything. But most of all about all of this. Every single thing that I've said since I stopped kissing you."

"You're supposed to be dating Fia. And I'm engaged to Byron. And this would never have been a good idea, not ever, but it's a worse idea now."

He growled out a breath. "It happened. Okay? I wanted to do it. I did it. You're right. I didn't think it through." That was a lie, though. He had thought it through. He had thought about this so many times over the past few years. He had thought about kissing her. He had tried to make himself stop. He had. For the most part. But more and more, he noticed how pretty she was. And…

"Don't worry about it. It won't happen again. I'm not going to get in the way of you and Byron," he said.

"Well, I'm not going to get in the middle of you and Fia."

He couldn't care less about Fia.

That made him feel terrible. Made him feel guilty, because he had convinced her to go out with him, and she was an extremely nice woman.

There was absolutely nothing wrong with her. She was beautiful, she was funny, she cooked like a dream. On paper she was everything that he should want, but there was just no spark. He could happily go six months without sex as long as he was dating Fia. Because he wasn't desperate for her. Not even a little bit. He was… He was… *Hell.*

"I need to go," she said. "I'm wet."

He gritted his teeth and groaned.

"What?" she asked, looking angry.

"You should go," he said. "Because you're soaking from the rain, and I can't listen to you say things like that without… We need to reset. Just go home. I'll see you later."

"Okay," she said, turning and beating a hasty retreat from the barn before realizing that she hadn't driven.

He walked out after her. "You don't need to walk all the way home," he said.

"Yes, I do. It's fine. I'll just walk."

"Don't be stubborn."

"It's not even raining anymore," she said. "It doesn't bother me."

"Dammit, Charity, let me give you a ride home."

Charity didn't push him away. They were friends. They were each other's person. The only person who wasn't family who was always there for him and now she was pushing him away.

"I don't want to be in the cab of the truck with you," she said. "I don't want to be next to you right now. I need space."

He took a step back, because you couldn't say it any stronger than that, that was for damn sure. "Okay. Text me when you get home and let me know you're okay."

"Fine."

And then she turned and walked away from him, and he knew that… Well, he'd messed it up. Big time.

## CHAPTER FIFTEEN

SHE LET HERSELF CRY. All the way back to her house.

She was tired, and she probably should've let him give her a ride, but she couldn't stand... She didn't know what was happening to her. She thought that she might be going crazy. *You do know what's happening to you. You do know.*

That kiss.

She had never been kissed before.

She found her hand drifting up to her mouth.

It was shaking, her hand. She was shaking. From the inside out. Everything was a mess. Especially her.

She was an absolute disaster.

And she couldn't stop replaying the moment over and over in her head. The velvet glide of his tongue against hers. She had never thought that she would want another person's tongue in her mouth. There were just things that she had known would be an inevitability of marriage, and she had gone ahead and decided that everything would be fine when she was in that position. That it would all work itself out. Because it was the natural order of things. It had made as much sense to her as anything. But now the problem was...

She had felt the way his body fitted against hers. Big and hard and hot.

And he had...tasted her. It had been deep, unflinch-

ing and sexual. She had no idea what she was supposed to do with the feelings that it left behind. With
the scorched earth that it left in her wake.

She'd had no idea.

She was so grateful when she got to her house, and
she fumbled with the doorknob with numb fingers and
locked it behind her, going down the hall to the shower.
She turned it on and waited for it to get hot while she
peeled her clothes away from her body.

She looked at herself in the mirror, but this time she
knew why she was being critical. This time she knew
why she was worried about how she looked.

When you slept with someone, they saw you naked.

She should be thinking about what Byron would see
when she took her clothes off, but instead she found
herself wondering about Lachlan. She could imagine,
far too easily, those intense blue eyes staring at her.
Her small breasts and her pale nipples. At her rather
slim hips and the pale golden triangle there at the junc-
ture of her thighs.

What would he think about that?

He'd seen so many women naked. And she had
never seen a naked man. It was all well and good to talk
about how you knew mechanics because you had engaged in many aspects of the facts of life with animals.

It was almost hilarious. Because it went right back to
her and Lachlan's little snippy fight when she stitched
him up.

Animals were more complicated because there were
more of them. Because there was more to know. More
to do. People were just people.

But what people did was entirely different than what

animals did. It was entirely different than the where and the why.

It wasn't for procreation. It was for desire.

People did things that were bad for them. People did things that could hurt them. They did things because they felt good in the moment, but had desperate and drastic consequences for the rest of their lives.

Yes. People were unreliable. And complicated. And...

She could feel steam begin to pour over the top of the shower, and she stepped inside. She soaped up her body and couldn't ignore how sensitive the dips and hollows on her skin felt. She avoided her breasts, because her nipples were tight, and she had thought it was from the cold, but the fact that the warm shower did nothing to ease it proved otherwise.

There was an uncomfortable slickness between her legs.

*I'm wet.*

His reaction came slamming back into her like a freight train.

*This* was why. This was why he had reacted that way. Because he had been thinking about her...

She leaned against the shower wall. He had been thinking about her body. In that way. Again, she wasn't stupid. She knew what the female body did to ready itself for intercourse.

It was just dealing with the fact that a kiss from Lachlan had made her body prepare for *that*.

She wanted to cry. She wanted to curl up under a blanket and cry.

She suddenly felt desperately, utterly alone. Because Lachlan was the person she talked to. About everything. Everything that she hadn't talked to him about, she had talked to her dad about, but they hadn't talked about this.

He hadn't been comfortable with it as a topic. He had been a veterinarian. He had been able to speak about things in clinical terms. He had handled her getting her period better than she had. She had felt embarrassed, and he had said it was simply a biological function and there was nothing to worry about. But he had talked about sex as if it were simply a biological function as well. He had never acted like there was any more to it. Anything more to consider.

Right now she felt buried by the *more*. All that she didn't understand. All that she had never fully allowed herself to comprehend. She felt undone by that.

And if there was one thing Charity wasn't used to, it was feeling undone. Because she had been taught to be practically minded about things. And there was no way that she could outthink this. There was no way that she could make this…practical.

Byron was here visiting, and she had just kissed another man.

She had just kissed Lachlan.

She shivered, because even though she was upset about it, her body still craved more.

Bodies were apparently very stupid. That wasn't really all that surprising. She felt like most of human history seemed to back that up. She had just assumed that she was exempt from it.

That made her want to laugh. Because it was pretty much ridiculous.

Except, she didn't think she could laugh. She wasn't sure she would ever laugh again.

Maybe that was a touch overdramatic, but maybe not.

How had she found herself in this position?

She had been unfaithful to Byron. Because knowing she had kissed someone else would hurt him. It would probably be a deal breaker.

She shut the water off and wrapped her towel around herself, looking in the mirror. Trying to figure out who that girl was standing there.

Then her phone started buzzing.

It was Lachlan. Which enraged her, but she answered it all the same.

"What?" she grumped.

"You said you would text me when you got home. I wanted to make sure you made it there okay."

"I'm fine. I'm sorry that you weren't my priority the minute that I walked through the door."

"You don't sound sorry," he growled.

"I just got out of the shower. I was cold."

There was a heavy pause on the other end. And it made her feel flushed that she was standing there, naked except for her towel. Talking on the phone to him suddenly felt intimate in a way that it wouldn't have… Well, a while ago. There had been things that were shifting between them, and she did know that. It had been snarling and tangling and complicating for a little while now. But the kiss had blown it to pieces.

"I was thinking," he said.

"I don't know that I like the sound of that."

"I know I don't like the sound of it," he said. "I want to come over."

Her stomach went tight. "I don't think you should come over."

"Why?" he asked, his voice ragged.

He had to know why. He had to know why he

shouldn't come over. It was… It was hardly ambiguous at this point.

"Are you afraid that you're going to lose control? Because I would never do anything that you didn't want to do. So if something was going to happen…"

"I don't know what's going on," she said, her voice practically a whisper. "I don't know what I would do, Lachlan. I really like to know exactly who I am, and what I want, and what I'm going to do. Right now, I don't."

"I want to come talk to you. I messed that up. I messed up really bad, and I'm sorry."

"Why do you want to talk to me?"

"I want to see you in person." He paused for a moment. "I might kiss you again."

"You shouldn't kiss me."

"If you don't want me to, say the word and I won't do it."

It wasn't that simple, though, and she knew it now. She bet he did, too.

"You can come over. But only for a little bit."

"I'll be there in a minute."

She rushed to get ready, throwing on clothing as quickly as she possibly could and resigning herself to the fact that she was just going to look like a drowned rat still, because she didn't have time to blow-dry her hair.

What was he thinking? What did he want? He hadn't wanted to tell her over the phone, and she couldn't get a read on why.

There was a heavy knock on the door only a moment later, and she swallowed hard. "Come in."

"It's locked."

"You know where the hide-a-key is," she said, grumbling. But she went to the door and unlocked it, opened it.

The impact of him took her breath away.

This was what she had been worried about. This very thing. Because she couldn't... She couldn't see him the way that she had before. She couldn't put the blinders back on.

It was simply terrifying. Well, maybe *terrifying* was overstating it. But then, maybe not.

He stepped into the living room and he had been here any number of times. Countless times. She had watched him step into this room as a broken, bleeding teenager, a wiry young man, a muscular man in his thirties. But this felt different. Singular. It felt like something unprecedented. It was scary. Because they should know each other too well for things to be unprecedented, except now she knew they didn't.

After that kiss, she knew they didn't.

"So what are you..."

And suddenly, she found herself being pulled into his arms. Her heart gave one wild thump before he lowered his head and pressed his mouth to hers. Before he started to kiss her again, this time deeper, hungrier than before.

She put her hand on his chest, because she intended to push him away. But then she just didn't. Then she found her fingers curling around the fabric of his shirt. Found herself holding her body to his.

She found herself doing everything she said she wouldn't.

He wrapped his arms around her, not simply holding her chin this time, but enveloping her in the muscular warmth of his frame.

He was so much bigger than she was. Stronger. He made her feel fragile. All of this did.

Because this wasn't like anything she had ever experienced, and when he parted her lips and took the kiss deeper, impossibly so, she found herself nearly melting into a puddle.

It was like he knew. He held her upright, walking her back to the couch and sitting them both down on it. He kissed her. Kissed her until he pressed her down into the soft cushions, laid her across that narrow space, kissed her like he was dying of thirst and she contained what he needed to survive.

She hadn't known it was this.

She didn't know what she thought. It had always sounded hard and sharp and carnal and dirty. Maybe distasteful, even.

But this wasn't distasteful. She couldn't explain it. She didn't want to. Didn't need to. She just needed to feel it. To be in it. She just wanted to live in this moment, no matter where it took her. Because of all the things she had ever experienced in her life, she had never experienced anything like this. The sense of being both wholly present in her body and transported somewhere else.

Of being so aware of what she was doing and at the same time, carried away.

It was magical. Beautiful. Dangerous.

His body was hard and hot above hers, and when she shifted her hips slightly, he settled between her legs, the hard length of his arousal suddenly undeniable, pressing right against the most intimate part of her. She gasped, pulling her mouth away from his and arching her back.

"Charity," he whispered, his voice rough.

*"Yes,"* she said.

She didn't know if she was answering him, or answering a deeper question between them. A deeper question in her body.

Somehow it didn't surprise her. That she was ready to give him everything, to peel off what lay between them and explore the furthest extent of these feelings that had been called up inside her. She was thirty years old. The only reason she'd never done it was that she hadn't known how it could make her feel. It wasn't because of morals, or fear, or anything like that.

*Are you sure?*

She banished that thought.

Utterly. Completely. She wasn't afraid now.

She shivered, as if to contradict herself.

"I want you," he said, those blue eyes looking directly into hers. He wasn't afraid. Of course, he wouldn't be. This wasn't new for him. He'd had sex any number of times.

Were they really going to do *that*?

Nerves rattled her, but she didn't want to stop.

"Keep kissing me," she said.

She would have time to figure this out. Time to decide. If he would only keep kissing her.

He growled, cupping her cheek as he kept on kissing her. Taking it deeper, pressing her more firmly into the couch. He rocked his hips against hers, and an electric throb radiated through her body.

She found herself parting her legs a little bit wider,

trying to accommodate him, allowing him to press his body more fully against hers.

He kissed her and kissed her, until her mouth was swollen, until her body was tingling. Until she felt like she had maybe made up for all the years that she hadn't been kissed up until now.

His whiskers made her cheeks sting, and she didn't mind. Not at all.

Then he moved his hand down to cup her breast, his thumb drifting over her nipple. She wasn't wearing a bra.

She yelped, a completely undignified sound as pleasure arrowed between her legs. And she rocked harder against him. Trying to soothe the ache that was growing and expanding there, moving deeper, making her so conscious of the fact that she was hollow. Desperate to be filled by him. Utterly and totally needy for the center of his desire, which grew larger and harder between them with each passing moment.

She knew the mechanics.

With grasping, greedy hands that she didn't even recognize as her own, she found herself pulling at his shirt. Pulling at it, so that she could look at him. So that she could see what lay beneath. All that glory that she had schooled herself into ignoring. The tawny skin and glorious muscle, the dark chest hair.

He helped her get it off, and she felt like her breath had frozen in her lungs. Felt like she couldn't do anything but simply gawk at him. Stare at all that masculine beauty.

Then she moved her hand out, pressed it to his bare chest, ran her fingertips over the crisp hair there and found herself shuddering with desire.

Her hands skimmed over his chest, his back, as he licked deeper and deeper into her mouth, as she grew accustomed to that, as it became not enough. Not enough at all.

He pushed his hands beneath her shirt and then his thumbs skimmed her bare breasts, her tightened nipples. So overly sensitized by what had already risen up between them.

All she could do was whimper. Whimper and arch her back, a silent entreaty for more.

He pulled her shirt up over her head and his eyes were like blue fire as he gazed over her curves. He cursed. Short and sharp and harsh, shocking. The need inside her expanding. Growing. Until she thought she might expire of it.

He lowered his head, sucking one tightened bud deep into his mouth, and the sight of him, his dark head lowered over her breasts like that, the feel of his tongue, his lips…

She exploded.

Pleasure moved through her like a wave, and she continued to move her hips against his as she rode it out, desperate cries exiting her lips.

She was shaking. Trembling. When it passed, it left her weak.

"Oh, Charity," he said, looking at her. "We're fucked."

And then he picked her up off the couch and started to carry her back toward her bedroom. She didn't have the strength to protest. Or the desire.

She clung to him as he made the short trek back there, and when he set her down on the bed, there was one sliver of fear that worked its way beneath her skin.

She could see him. Hard and insistent beneath his

jeans. And she knew that there was no going back. If they did this, they would never go back.

*You already can't. You know that.*

She wondered if maybe their fate had been sealed that night that Fia had come over for poker, and jealousy had invaded her to such a poisonous degree that she had been shocked and embarrassed. Hadn't wanted to admit that was what it was.

She had gone out of her way to pretend it couldn't be that.

All these times she'd had feelings that she refused to name. From the dinner where she had desperately wanted to be the girl he was there for, to the comparison. The relentless comparison between herself and the beautiful Fia Sullivan.

Yeah. She could pretend that she didn't know why. But she did.

She had been eaten alive with the idea that another woman was going to get to have him for the rest of his life.

That another woman would be the most important one to him. Because that was the thing.

They had never touched each other. They had never done anything like this. But he was singular in her life. She was singular in his. Nobody else commanded his attention on a daily basis the way that she did, and what she had known was that the minute he took a wife, she would be his priority. The most important thing to him, and it shouldn't bother her. She should be happy. Because she should have been glad that he would be taken care of when she got married, and maybe moved away. But she wasn't. Because she had wanted to marry Byron, settle into a comfortable, placid existence with him… Keep Lachlan all to herself. Because that was who she was. She was selfish. Utterly and completely selfish, and she was rather ashamed of it now.

Because it was unreasonable. Unfair. Because it was…

Because it was childish. These games that they were playing. *She* had been childish. If she didn't look at him without a shirt she could pretend that she didn't want to see him. If she wrinkled her nose she could make the tension in her stomach disappear, and pretend that it wasn't the tension they'd been avoiding naming all these years.

She could love him without it being futile.

It wasn't what happened after this that would ruin them.

It had already happened.

She didn't want to stop.

Charity Wyatt had never been a sensual creature. But right now she felt entirely made of need. Entirely composed of her desire, and it was playing her like a symphony. She didn't have it in her to turn away.

So she wouldn't. So she didn't.

She had a choice to make. So she went with the one that scared her the least. She grabbed hold of her own sweatpants and underwear and slipped them down her body, leaving her naked to his gaze.

She would rather he see her and have an informed decision on whether or not he wanted to go forward.

She was slightly intimidated, to be honest. To see his entire body. If she saw him, and then he saw her, and he decided that she really wasn't beautiful enough, well, then she might die.

She didn't want this to be fatal. Of all the things.

He let out a long, unsteady breath and brought himself down onto the bed, over her, propped up on his hands. "You're beautiful," he said, his eyes never leaving hers.

It was the honesty there. That was what undid her. Absolutely and completely.

"So are you," she said, wishing that her voice sounded stronger. Wishing that she felt stronger. But she was painfully aware of the gulf in their experience. Of the fact that what lay ahead for her was unknown. When this was a dance that he knew the steps to, and well.

It was his smile that eased her fears. Because it was the smile of her friend. Not someone different. Not the dangerous man she had only recently identified him to be. He was both, in the moment. Because this was certainly dangerous, and he was certainly far beyond her imagination. But he was also Lachlan. Her Lachlan.

It was just nice to know that he could be both.

He kissed her again. She loved when he did that. And this time he put his hand between her thighs, where she was wet with the evidence of her desire for him, but she wasn't embarrassed by it. It felt so good. The way that he rubbed his thumb over that sensitized bundle of nerves there. It was like a flame, white-hot, and scorchingly pleasurable. She found herself moving her hips in time with his touch as he continued to kiss her.

She really liked to be kissed.

Her whole body was alive with sensation that she had done her best to ignore for all of her life, and it was like she was now a starving person at a feast. She loved it all. Was obsessed with it all. Wanted it all.

She let him tease her, touch her, until she was on the verge again. On the verge of that wonderful, glorious feeling that had burst through her only a few minutes before.

Her inhibition was gone. Lost. And when he kissed his way down her neck, over her breasts, down her stomach into the center of her thighs, she couldn't even protest. Couldn't even muster up a moment of shock, as his tongue replaced his wicked finger and the warm, slick glide shattered her. She clutched his shoulders as she gave in to another release. She was almost embarrassed by that. That it was so easy for him to do this to her.

But she had a lot of need built up.

So she supposed there was really nothing to be ashamed about.

He kissed his way back up her body, putting his hands between her legs again, and this time he put a finger inside her. The invasion was foreign, unfamiliar, and she shifted, acclimating to it. It was what she wanted, what her body was hungry for, but at the same time it was untested. Untried.

He added a second finger, stretching her gently, and she knew that he was doing his best to prepare her for what was to come.

Though judging by the aggressive outline in his jeans, this wasn't going to ease all of the discomfort that would come with her first time.

*First time.*

*Virgin.*

She'd really never thought of herself that way.

But she did now. A virgin in the arms of her best friend.

She was about to let him change that.

She wanted him to change that.

This was her decision. Though it felt like something much deeper than a simple choice.

It was beyond that. More elemental. More of a *need*.

An inevitability, even. Something she couldn't turn back from, even if she wanted to.

He pushed himself away from her, unbuckled his jeans as he kicked his boots off, pushed his pants and underwear down, and she saw him fully for the first time.

The ache at the center of her thighs intensified. He was so beautiful. A work of art. She had nothing to compare him to, but she didn't need to. Because she wanted him. Lachlan.

She knew beyond a shadow of a doubt this wasn't just about wanting sex, because if it had been... She had been engaged to the same man for a long time, and she had never been sorry over his desire for them to remain celibate. She had respected his convictions. She still did.

It was just he had nothing to do with this. With this moment.

She didn't want him. That was the crystal-clear lesson to take away from this very minute.

There was a difference between being fond of someone and wanting them.

Because you had to have something more, something deeper, to want this.

To be naked with another person, to let them inside your body. To let them taste you, touch you, in the way that Lachlan had done.

Well. *She* needed more.

It was clear now.

He brought himself back to her, kissing her gently as he positioned himself at the entrance of her body. As he slowly began to push inside her. He pressed his forehead against hers, and she could see that his teeth were gritted, that the cords in his neck were strained.

"Sorry," he said as he thrust all the way inside her, a tearing pain accompanying the moment he buried himself to the hilt.

She clung to his shoulders, dug her fingernails into his skin. "It's okay," she said, whispering. "It's okay, Lachlan."

"Charity."

And he began to move. The thrust of his body into hers creating a slick rhythm of desire that overtook any pain she had momentarily experienced. Oh, she wanted him. She wanted this. She wanted all of it. Everything.

She was lost. In the maelstrom of need, a storm of desire that overrode common sense, that overrode a lifetime of inhibition.

She wrapped her legs around his hips and urged him deeper, arched her back against him with every thrust. The sounds he made were animal, and she made her own in kind.

She kept her eyes open, watching him. His gaze was intense, and he was… He was him. But not in any way she had ever seen him before. She knew so much about her best friend. But she hadn't known this part of him.

This was how he looked when he made love to a woman.

That thought made her incredibly sad, so she took it and she reconstructed it.

This was how he looked when he made love to *her*.

And she shivered. Clung to him even harder, allowed her desire to build up in her to a point where she thought it might destroy her.

"Lachlan," she said, repeating his name like a mantra, a prayer, a plea to keep her from falling apart.

Except then he thrust into her hard, grinding his hips against hers, and she couldn't hold back. She shattered. Like a thin pane of glass, into millions of pieces that could never be reconstructed. Not in the same form they once had been.

What had once been clear and straight, easy, was now shards of crystal, glittering and more beautiful, but nothing that could be seen through clearly.

A metaphor for their relationship. For what they had been. For what they had become.

His hips pistoned hard as he lost his control, as his thrusts became erratic. He grabbed her hips, his hold bruising as he froze above her, his arousal pulsing inside her as he gave himself over to his desire, utterly and completely.

Then he collapsed against her, kissing her, resting his forehead on hers.

"That was better than I imagined," he said.

"What do you mean?"

"I wanted to be your first. I am such a bastard. I wanted that when I was eighteen. I wanted to be your first. I was sure no man had ever touched you. And I was…preoccupied by that. I fantasized about it. About this." He rubbed his thumb over her lips. "I thought about how they'd look, swollen from kissing me. I thought about your face. When you came. When you discovered how good it could feel. I wanted that. For me. Only for me. It was for me, wasn't it?"

His words were suddenly so intense, so filled with need, and she couldn't deny him. Not in that moment. Not ever.

"Yes," she said. "Only for you. Only ever for you."

"Charity," he growled.

And she kissed him back. Hard and with ever-expanding need.

It should be done. Shouldn't it? After all that? She shouldn't be able to want him again.

But she did.

She started to shake, uncontrollably, because suddenly… It was terrifying. The ferocity with which she wanted him. The desperate depth of this desire that hadn't seemed to exist before today.

What would she do? If it took over everything? What would she do if this remade version of herself wasn't something she could control?

She'd always had control.

She started to cry. Tears sliding down her cheeks, and she was mortified by her weakness. Except, Lachlan was the only person she would ever cry on. Ever cry with. He reversed their positions, rolling onto his back, letting her weep against his broad, bare chest. They were naked. And perhaps that was fitting. Naked as she cried, limp and spent and terrified.

"I'm an awful person," she said. "Byron is a good man, and he never did anything to me and…"

"Charity," he said, his voice level, his eyes never wavering from hers. "I want you to marry me."

THIS HAD BEEN his purpose in coming here. Because he had realized with stunning clarity after their lips had met earlier today, that this was the right thing.

This was what he wanted. Charity was the woman that he wanted to marry. He couldn't imagine spending the rest of his life with anyone else, partly because he couldn't imagine rearranging his life so that she took a secondary role in it. He couldn't imagine putting another woman in front of her. And the simple truth was he wanted her. He always had.

All it had taken was one moment to let that desire loose, to let it free, and it had been clear. Everything had been.

She was already his best friend. She made him feel soothed.

Yeah, there was…stuff about him, about his life, that he'd always tried to protect her from, but he could do that. She made him better.

She was what he wanted.

"This is why you want to marry me?" she asked.

"Yes."

"Lachlan…we…"

"Why not? It makes perfect sense. Why were we going to marry people that we liked less than we like each other?"

As soon as he said it, it all seemed so ridiculous. Because really. *Really.* Why the hell had either of them been thinking of that? Why had they thought for one second that they would be happier with anyone else? She was his best friend, and wasn't that the thing? You married your best friend?

"I…"

"I'm changed. I'm reformed. You saw to that," he said.

"You did *not* go six months without sex," she said, trying to sound reproving.

"No. But you went thirty years without it, so I figure that balances out the scales for both of us, doesn't it?"

"It does not work like that," she said, her tone frosty, her eyes looking evil all of a sudden.

"Charity," he said. "I want you. You. Not anyone else."

"You've known me an awfully long time, Lachlan, and you have wanted plenty of other women in between."

"You got engaged to someone else. You went away to college, you left me and you got engaged to another man."

"Were you about to get down on one knee back then?"

He huffed a laugh and settled back on the bed. Charity's bed.

"We should marry each other because we don't actually want other people. I don't want to spend my life with another woman. And you don't want to sleep with him."

"How do you know that?"

"Because you're passionate. That was why I came over here. I figured if I came over here and I kissed you, and you told me to leave…then I would let you marry him. I would back off. I would…"

"You would *let* me marry him?"

"Yes, Charity. I figured if you rejected my kiss I wouldn't kidnap you, carry you out of whatever church you decided to say your vows in, sling you over my shoulders like a sack of potatoes, and spirit you off to a cabin up in the middle of the mountains where he couldn't find us. I would've done that. I will do that. If, after all this, you still think that he's the one you want to be with. After being with me, if you still want to marry him…"

"You would really do that?"

"Look at me," he said, and she did.

"You mean it."

"I fucking do," he said, as deep of a vow as any could be. "I will not let him have you. You're mine. Do you understand me?" The words scraped his throat raw and they were not...

This was what he *didn't* want.

But he had to get her to marry him. Then things would be fine. Byron would go away, and things would feel normal.

They would feel normal.

He'd be able to get a handle on the more untamed feelings inside of him and they would be them again.

Once she said yes.

Once she said she'd be his.

"That is the most unenlightened thing that anyone has ever said to me."

"Really? Even with all the sexist assholes you have to deal with for your job?"

"Yes. Because they might be dismissive, but they certainly never tried to claim ownership of me."

"How about this. I'm yours, too. I want the same life that you want. Here. I live in this house with you. If that's what you want. I don't need to keep my cabin. I'll move here with you. I'll... I'll work McCloud's Landing and you'll keep on doing your veterinary work. We can have kids." A slow, dawning realization hit him. "You could be pregnant now."

Her eyes flew wide. "Oh my gosh."

"I'm sorry. I never forget condoms. I don't. I'm very careful. But I couldn't think. I just... I just wanted you." Awe spread through him. "It doesn't make me upset. To think about having a baby with you."

This was everything he'd wanted. And it was all in a much neater package than he had anticipated. One he hadn't fathomed he could have. As far as he was concerned…this was perfection.

"Lachlan, I don't…"

"What is there to think about?"

"Byron…"

"Do you want him the way that you want me?"

She shook her head.

"I didn't think so. Do you love him the way that you love me?"

He hadn't meant to ask her that; the question was like a knife wound through his own chest. But he made sure to look at her and never look away while he said it.

She did love him. He knew that. There was a difference between the love they felt for each other and the kind of toxic love his parents had. The love they had for each other and the tumultuous romantic love other people had, but it was love all the same.

"That's not fair," she said.

"Answer the question."

She looked away. "No. I don't. I don't."

"If we could have everything with each other, why shouldn't we?"

"I don't know. But I've spent all these years trying not to have a crush on you, because I couldn't think of anything more ridiculous. I never let myself look at you when you didn't have your shirt on. I never… It would be too humiliating. I…"

"Look at us," he said, cupping her face. "Look at me. It's the same for me. I want you. It's not embarrassing."

"I'm not pretty. Not like Fia."

"What the hell are you talking about?"

"She's beautiful."

"Charity, from the first moment I saw you I thought you were an angel on earth. And that was why I decided I couldn't touch you. You know what my life was like."

"So why can you touch me now, Lachlan?"

The question tore at something inside him. Because all the reasons he'd turned away from this for years were as valid now as they'd been then.

*Why now?*

"Because I didn't want him to have you."

That answer was torn from him. He hated it. As much as he hated himself in that moment. Because it was a shitty thing to say. It was a shitty thing to *feel*.

But he felt it.

It was the kind of thing he'd never wanted to feel.

The idea of Byron's hands on Charity enraged him. Or the fact that the guy could embrace celibacy when he had her all these years… That almost made him madder. Because Lachlan wouldn't exercise any restraint with her. As he'd proven.

That meant he wanted her more. So there.

Removing Byron would remove this feeling.

"Say yes," he said. "Say yes to me. Because you can't… You can't marry somebody else now. Please."

He was not above begging. It was real. Sincere. This wasn't some halfhearted attempt at getting his way. It was suddenly the only thing he wanted. An all-consuming need. He was going to have a wife; it needed to be her.

"Yes," she said. "Yes, Lachlan. I'll marry you."

He growled, pulling her into his arms and kissing her.

"We don't have to live here," she said between kisses.

"We can," he said.

"No, I think… I think I need something new. I think I want something new. With you."

"Okay," he said. "But you know you're gonna have to help me. I have it on good authority my house is not suitable for wives."

"Oh no," she said.

"What?"

"I gave you the beetles. And now they're just mine again."

He laughed. "Feels symbolic."

"Don't go there. I might start the bad idea."

"Better not," he said.

"What am I going to do about…"

"Tomorrow's problem," he said. "You can tell him whatever you want, it doesn't have to be the whole truth. Relationships end."

"I knew something was wrong. When he came I… He walked up to the door, and it reminded me of when you had come to pick me up for the date. But I was more excited to see you. And I see you every day. I knew something was wrong."

"This just showed you. Why you couldn't marry him."

She nodded. "You're not wrong."

"Do you need some tea?"

A soft smile that would've been a whisper if it was spoken out loud. Then she shook her head. "I'll just lie here with you."

"Can I stay the night?"

He didn't do that. Didn't sleep with women.

Sometimes he didn't sleep at all.

She clung to him then. "You have to. You can't leave me."

A lead weight settled in his chest. "I won't. I promise."

He'd handle it.

He realized that was more than just a promise for tonight. It was a vow. One he damn well had to keep. Because she deserved everything. She deserved… He wondered if he was capable of giving her everything she deserved. But it kind of didn't matter. Because this was what he wanted. And this was what he would have.

## CHAPTER SIXTEEN

SHE WOKE UP with a start. Lachlan wasn't in bed with her. She was very aware that he should be, which was funny because he never had been before. But she woke up marked by her time with him, and she didn't forget, even for a moment. Even with the last vestiges of sleep still clinging to her.

He hadn't stayed.

*He'd promised.*

The pain of that was like a knife, and she fought against the panic it brought on.

She sat up and suddenly, there he was, in the doorway. Wearing nothing but a pair of jeans, which he quickly discarded as he moved toward the bed. He walked over to her and got onto the bed, caging her between his arms. "Good morning."

"Lachlan." But he kissed her. He kissed her, and everything melted away. Most especially her resistance. And then he got beneath the covers… He was making love with her. Her pleasure crescendoed so quickly she could hardly believe it. His own followed just as quickly, their cries mingling together.

He let out a ragged breath and kissed her shoulder. "That's a quickie," he said.

"Efficient," she panted, her body humming with satisfaction and need.

"Just a preview. For later. But I figure… I figure we've got some things to get done today."

"I guess so," she said.

She was resentful of that. Of Byron being here. Of having work to do.

Thankfully, his flight was scheduled to leave tomorrow. But she could not put off breaking up with him. She had to do it now. She just had to.

With a heaviness in her chest, she pushed herself out of bed.

She felt momentarily self-conscious that she stood, feeling his gaze roaming over her naked body.

"Don't," she said, scampering over to the closet. She threw the doors open and grabbed a dress, holding it over her body.

"What? It's nothing I haven't seen. And tasted."

"Yes. But I'm embarrassed now."

"You don't ever have to be embarrassed in front of me."

He threw the covers off and made a rather blatant display of masculinity as he stood up, stretching, each and every muscle shifting and bunching with the movement.

"Can I use your shower?"

"Yes," she said.

"Can I use it with you?"

She blinked. "Together?"

"Showering with another person is one of life's great joys."

She bristled. "I don't like that."

"What? The idea of showering with me?"

"No. The reminder that you've done all this with other people."

He frowned. "I'm sorry. That's not what I meant by that. At all. I was trying to put you at ease. I wasn't trying…"

"I know."

"Can I show you?"

She bit her lip and then nodded.

He walked into the bathroom and she couldn't help herself. She took a leisurely visual tour of the musculature of his back and the perfect firm roundness of his butt. Along with his thick, muscular thighs.

He was glorious.

The epitome of male beauty. He made every classical sculpture ashamed to exist. He turned the water on and she crept into the bathroom, the tiny space suddenly feeling wholly inadequate as she stood there staring at him.

He grinned, wrapped his arm around her waist and pulled her against him. He kissed her until the water heated up, and then he dragged her inside beneath the spray. Their skin was slick like yesterday, but there was nothing between them, and they weren't freezing. He lathered her with soap until she was in a near sexual frenzy.

Then he rinsed her off and kissed her firmly when they stepped out of the shower. "You have places to be."

She smacked his shoulder. "That's not fair. You turned me into a…a horny ferret."

"A horny ferret?" He laughed.

"I work with ferrets. Believe me, it is an apt description."

"Well, get along, little weasel. We have forever."

The words almost stunned her. Because yes. She'd said that she was going to marry him. So they did have forever, she supposed. It was wild. Wonderful. Intense. She didn't quite know what to do with it. Didn't quite know what to make of it.

But she didn't make an issue of it. Instead, she simply began to dress, and couldn't take her eyes off him while he did the same.

"Let's have dinner with my brothers tonight."

"You're assuming that I'm going to get this breakup with Byron done very quickly."

"Yes, I am. Because I want you to be mine. All mine. And I want him to know it." The possession in his eyes undid her. She liked it, heaven help her.

"Well, I want to get it done quickly because I don't want to hurt him anymore… I don't want to be…cheating. That is a terrible thing for a woman who has literally never touched a man in her life. To suddenly be…a vixen."

He *laughed*. She hit him again. "What's so funny?"

"You. You are adorable."

"I don't really like being adorable when I'm in distress. It's insulting."

Once dressed, she texted Byron and asked if he could meet her for breakfast.

He was of course up and had already been for a lovely walk, as he'd put it.

"I'm going to breakfast with Byron," she said. "I'll… I'll call you."

"Okay."

She got in her car and drove over to Pyrite Falls, pressing her fists against her eyes as she sat there in the parking lot of Becky's, waiting for Byron to arrive.

"Hi," she said when she saw him. She got out of the car and just sort of stood there, as he did.

"Is something wrong?" he asked. His voice was tender and full of concern. He really was a very nice person, but now she couldn't understand how she had been so deluded as to think that finding someone a *nice person* meant that you could be married to them.

She wasn't exactly sure what she was doing with Lachlan. Because he hadn't said that he loved her. But he had asked her if she loved him.

There was only one answer. She did. She loved him more than any other person on the planet. There was a lot she didn't know, but what she did know was that you shouldn't marry a man when you loved someone else more.

Was she *in* love with Lachlan? She wasn't sure what the difference was. Not when you introduced sex. Maybe that turned love to *in* love.

What she knew, with her newfound knowledge of sex and desire, was that she didn't want the man standing in front of her. And she didn't love him.

"Let's go inside," she said.

They were seated immediately, and she looked at the menu, which was extensive. Biscuits and gravy, eggs fixed any kind of way and a myriad of other things.

"We need to talk," she said once the coffee had been set in front of them.

"I agree."

"We can't get married," she said.

"I don't think this is going to work," he said at exactly the same time.

Well, maybe they would only get coffee. Maybe there would be no breakfast.

It turned out, breaking up with somebody really was kind of a short endeavor.

"We can't?" he asked.

As she said, "It won't?"

"You first," Byron said, but then followed with, "It's him, isn't it?"

He asked that without any venom in his voice.

"Yes. He and I have really been just friends for a lot of years, but when it came right down to it… When I realized what it would mean to be married to somebody else, when I realized what that would mean for our relationship, I realized that I wasn't prepared for that. And he… He was going to marry somebody else. And when all of that came up, it was just kind of clarifying and…he asked me to marry him. And I really want to." Her voice broke. "I'm sorry. It's not fair. I thought that I wanted to marry you. I really did. It has been such a stabilizing, lovely thing in my life, this relationship. You have been such a good friend to me."

"But it turned out I was more *just* your friend than he was."

"It's complicated. Our history. Our life."

Byron was silent for a long moment.

"I've always known that you loved him," Byron said. "I thought you had your reasons for not being with him."

That hurt. That he'd seen something about herself she hadn't. But maybe it took someone who was outside of it to really see. She and Lachlan had called each other friends, just friends, for so many years. It had never been *just* anything.

"I guess I did," she said softly. "I didn't mean to lie to you or lead you on."

"I know you didn't. I realized something seeing you here. You love your life. You love your friends here.

You love him. I thought I could move here with you and leave my family, but after your dad died I thought… I wouldn't have to. I don't think it's fair for either of us to leave the lives we love so much. At least, that's what I was going to say."

"We can just go," she said.

He shook his head. "I'd like to order breakfast."

"You're not mad? About Lachlan?"

He sat back in his chair. "No. If I had any doubts about my own reasons for ending this, it clears it up. We could have been happy. But one of us would have had to leave a place, and people, that were more important to us than each other. I think that's the biggest, clearest evidence that we weren't meant to be married."

"I've been afraid of this. I just didn't want another change. But part of me thought there was a reason we didn't hurry up and set a date. That there was a reason I didn't have a ring." She paused. "If you thought I loved him, why were you willing to be with me anyway? Why were you willing to take…not the best or first? You're a good guy, and you really didn't deserve that."

He was quiet for a moment. "I really did care for you. I thought you would make a good wife, the kind I'd always wanted. And I always try to be who I was raised to be. Good and moral and willing to be last. Willing to be second."

"Don't do that, Byron. Be with someone who puts you first. Put yourself first."

That made him look lost. "I don't know how to do that."

"Maybe… Maybe being without me will help. Maybe this was the first step to better."

He forced a smile. "I really do like you a whole lot."

"Me, too," she said, tears welling in her eyes. "You know, you kind of remind me of my dad."

"I can't think of a better compliment. I'll see if I can get a flight change. I'm happy to have breakfast with you, but it's probably time for me to go back to Virginia. You can get on with things here, and maybe I can...figure out what I want."

"I want that for you."

She knew that their friendship would fade. Because the break wasn't hard enough or painful enough for them to hang on to anything.

She tried to remember what had connected them back in college. Why they had thought it was romantic. Maybe just because they didn't have a romance with other people. Because no one else was as much alike. Maybe that was all it had ever been.

She was grateful now, for the ease of it. But the ease itself spoke volumes.

She was learning an awful lot these past weeks. She wasn't sure how to feel about it.

It was grief, maybe, that had accelerated the process. That had made her reach down and touch on feelings that she'd never had before.

It made sense. Even if she didn't want to admit that.

It made a terrible kind of sense.

They ate their eggs and bacon and talked about memories of veterinary school. Their friend group, times spent at the ice cream shop down the street. Board game nights that got so competitive there was nearly bloodshed. What they'd had since then was a shadow of that college experience. Maybe they'd both been clinging to that. The memories were happy, joyful. More so than their present had been. He gave her a hug goodbye out in the parking lot.

When he let go, she knew he'd really let go.

"Be well," he said.

"You, too. Please, Byron. Be so happy."

"Are you happy?"

"I have feelings that are too big to be neatly categorized right now. It's a weird experience. But... I'm not fighting it."

He nodded slowly. "Good. We'll talk soon."

She knew they wouldn't. Maybe they would someday. She hoped so. When he found someone who loved him wildly. Someone he loved in return. Maybe when he loved *himself* wildly enough for it.

But she wasn't heartbroken. She didn't think he was, either. It was a comfort, at least.

When she finished, she texted Lachlan.

It's done. Now I have to go back and get the mobile unit. I'll see you tonight.

See you tonight.

It was a rare day when Lachlan, Brody and Gus were all out riding the range rather than being tethered to equine therapy for the day.

It was Lachlan's favorite thing to do. Spend these moments with his brothers, surrounded by all the wild. They reminded him why he loved this land. This place. Because of them. Because of his commitment to them, and theirs to him.

Because of everything that they'd done for him.

"I have news," Lachlan said, his gut going tight.

"What's that?" Gus asked.

"I'm getting married."

Gus and Brody both gawked at him like he had grown a second head. "You're what?"

"Getting married."

He had called Fia this morning and told her the news. She had laughed.

*"I knew it."*

*"I didn't want to hurt you."*

*"Don't worry about it, Lachlan. No offense but... I've been through enough that a guy breaking it off after a couple of group dates doesn't have the power to leave a dent."*

They hadn't held hands or kissed or anything.

The fact they hadn't even had a brush with any of those things had to mean the disinterest was pretty mutual.

"To *who*?" Brody asked.

"Charity."

"Really?" Gus asked. *"Really?"*

"Yes."

"After all this time?" Brody asked.

"What do you mean by that?" Lachlan asked.

"I just figured... This many years of being in each other's pockets and you weren't sleeping together...it was never going to happen. And isn't she engaged?"

"Not as of this morning."

"Wow. What happened?" Gus asked.

"We slept together."

Brody laughed, crossing his arms over his chest and sitting up straight on the horse, tilting his head back. "That's *funny*."

Lachlan's stomach hitched with umbrage. "Why is it funny?"

"I don't know. It's just… Look, I know what it's like to give in to temptation after knowing somebody for a couple of days," he said. "The idea of *suddenly* wanting somebody after all that time… I don't get it, man, but that's something."

"It wasn't *really* sudden," Lachlan said, not sure why he was giving any of that information away.

"Now, that surprises me," Gus said. "Seeing as you genuinely seemed platonic to me."

"We were," he said. "But I met her when I was a horny teenage boy. You know I thought about it."

Gus grunted. "Fair. I mean, I was platonic with Alaina, but definitely for a few years there I didn't feel platonic."

"Well, I've been attracted to her for a long time. What you should all get is that sometimes taking that risk doesn't feel worth the cost. It's always been there. She's my person, right? And that's the point of this, isn't it?"

"So you're in love with her?" Gus asked.

"I *love* her. There's no question about that. Apart from family, there's nobody on the earth that I care more about. So…she's the person to marry."

"I guess. But marriage isn't just getting a roommate that you have sex with," Gus said. "Believe me. Having navigated that particular wrong assumption, I'm speaking from experience."

"I'm sure you are, Angus," Lachlan said. "But it's different. You weren't friends with Alaina before you married her. Not like Charity and I are."

"Every relationship is different," Gus said, his tone

placating. "But I'm just saying… When you marry somebody, you get into a lot of *stuff*."

"Charity's my best friend. We talk about all kinds of things. Honestly, I think it's a great foundation."

"You guys thinking of having kids?"

A smile curved his lips, and he lapsed off slightly. "I mean. We might already be having one. Not that I'd rush to do it. You know, when we're thinking more clearly."

"Famous last words, man. *Thinking clearly.* You never think clearly again." That came from Brody.

"That can't be true. You're all happier than you've ever been."

"Absolutely," Gus said. "Happy as a beaver."

"Are beavers happy, Gus?" Brody asked.

"Well, they aren't sad, are they?"

"I guess not."

"So if you never think clearly, then how are you happy?" Lachlan asked.

"Because I wouldn't trade my life for anything. I'm happy in a way that makes all the other stuff feel like gravy."

"Not lava, Gus?" Brody asked, gesturing to Gus's scars.

"Fine. Real hot gravy. The point is, the past pain matters less. It's just different, Lachlan," Gus said. "And you have to trust us on that. Being married is *different*."

"It sure as hell is," Brody said.

"But neither of you ever had relationships before you got married. Charity is my longest term relationship. It just didn't include sex until last night."

"Still not the same," Brody said.

"Whatever. I'm not the last man standing anymore."

"Hell," Gus said. "I'm happy for you. Really. I just hope that it ends up being everything that you wanted."

"Why wouldn't it be? We don't have any secrets from each other."

"You've never lived with her. You've never lived with anybody."

"I practically do. Anyway, she's coming over for dinner tonight. Preferably at your place, Gus, since you have the big kitchen table and your wife makes great food."

"I will be sure to notify her," Gus said. "Because she's going to think this is a hoot."

"Yeah. Well. Hopefully, her sister didn't call to say that I broke her heart or anything."

"You didn't sleep with her, did you?"

"No," he said. "Give me a little credit, please."

"Well, good. Look, I'm happy for you, Lachlan. I just don't want you to make any messes in my life," Gus said.

"No messes made," Lachlan said. "Trust me. Everything is good. No worries at all."

"Well, congratulations. We'll have to find something extra unpleasant for you to do today," Gus said.

"Yeah, buddy," said Brody.

"I hate you both."

## CHAPTER SEVENTEEN

CHARITY DIDN'T KNOW what she should wear to her big family engagement dinner. She felt like she should've talked to Lachlan just a little more about it. It was good. She was happy they were having it. A get-together with the whole family. She loved Lachlan's family. And that made her feel even more resolute in her decision to marry him. Because…it was good. Of course it was. Marrying him. It was wonderful. She would have not only Lachlan, but his whole family, too.

She wore the black dress again, because it was pretty, and it had done its job on their date night, after all.

She drove over to Gus's house and parked next to all the trucks in the driveway. She was joining this family. The thought made her heart flutter rapidly. Would she go to bed with Lachlan tonight? She probably would. They probably would always.

That thought made her want to jump out of her skin a little bit. She had gone from *never* going to bed with someone even once in her whole life, to the prospect of doing it every night.

She understood that was what she had always been committing herself to when it came to marriage, but they had jumped into this head first, and without a lot of thought, so it just seemed…different.

And it was Lachlan.

So there was that.

What had happened between them last night—and this morning—wasn't companionable. It wasn't soft or easy. It had pulled her apart. Wrecked her. Made her a new creation.

She was still not sure what she thought about it or felt about it.

When she walked in, everyone was there and they let out a huge *whoop*.

All the women raced toward her. She had never really been…involved in their lives. The marriages were fairly recent, but still, she was Lachlan's friend. But now she would be their sister-in-law. A wife, not a friend, and she wondered if that shifted things slightly. If she would be expected to hang out with them at family gatherings. It stood to reason, she supposed. It was often when she and Lachlan saw each other on a given day, when there was a family event, so of course they hung out with each other, and not along gender lines. But now she would be living with him. Well. Soon. So maybe it would be her chance for a reprieve from him. Which was something she had never imagined wanting or needing. She still couldn't.

"Congratulations," Elsie said, beaming.

Alaina flung her arms around her.

"Thank you," she said, trying to force a smile.

"I had no idea," Nelly said. "None at all."

"Yeah," she said. "Me either, to be honest."

And Nelly laughed. "Oh. Well. I know all about that."

"Same," Elsie said.

"Same, to be honest," Alaina said.

"Not me," Elizabeth said. "It was Brody the minute I laid eyes on him. And I *knew*. It was very inconvenient. Extremely off-putting."

"Why?" Charity asked, genuinely interested.

"I had sworn off men."

She couldn't quite imagine that. But then, she knew Elizabeth had a very different life experience than she did.

"I thought I hated Tag," Nelly said.

"I thought Gus was old."

Elsie shrugged. "I just thought Hunter was an asshole."

"In fairness," Alaina said, "Gus is still old, and Hunter is an asshole."

Elsie nodded. "True."

She knew that Elsie and Alaina had been best friends for a long time, until they had nearly imploded over an incident with a guy who worked on the ranch, but it all worked out. The guy in question was a loser, and they had both ended up with the far superior McCloud boys.

That was the thing. The McClouds... They were good men. Good people. They had been through so much, and they had come out of it just the best.

Really, no one could fault them.

And here they were, all married and happy. Having children. Now she and Lachlan were doing the same.

She felt compelled then to look around the knot of women and find Lachlan.

As soon as she saw him, her anxiety ebbed. Her heart turned over and expanded in her chest. He was beautiful. And she let herself be hit with the full impact of that beauty. She wasn't trying to deny it anymore. Wasn't trying to ignore it. She let it hit her. Fully and absolutely.

"Hey," he said.

He rushed across the space over to her, and she found herself moving to him. He pulled her into his arms and he kissed her. Right in front of everybody.

Everyone *cheered*.

"Yeah," Hunter said. "That's what I'm talking about."

"It's about damn time," Tag said.

"No kidding," Brody commented.

"You know," Charity said. "Men and women really *can* just be friends."

"Sure," Hunter said. "Sure."

She felt the need to defend their platonic relationship that no longer was. Just because it seemed right and proper.

Alaina had made delicious roast and rolls, and also a giant cake. Charity felt almost guilty to be the center of such a fuss.

Especially when... Well, if they knew how it had happened. That it was more like they had kissed and lost control than fallen in love...

Her heart squeezed. It didn't matter. The end result was the same. And she was *happy*.

She was so happy.

They ate and laughed, and the cake was delicious. By the time it was all done, she was exhausted.

"Spend the night with me?" he whispered in her ear.

"Yes," she said. Mostly because she was afraid if she went back to her house it would feel like it had been a dream. And even if it was, she wanted to keep having it. She didn't want to lose this. Suddenly, it felt fragile and precarious.

If she separated from him, this magical golden thread that had spun itself between them would snap.

She didn't want that.

She didn't want to be Cinderella. She didn't want to lose her shoe and have her car turn into a pumpkin. Have the prince go back to thinking she was just his friend.

She didn't want to go back to thinking it, either.

No. She wanted the magic.

Change had felt so scary for a while. Like she couldn't handle even one more. But not this.

Not this magic.

She drove back to his place closely behind him and parked out in front of the porch. He got out of his truck quickly and walked over to her car, opening the door for her and extending his hand.

"What are you doing?" she whispered.

"You'll see."

She took his hand then, so rough in hers.

He held her hand all the way up the porch steps and into the house. It was the casual contact that underlined how much things had changed in the past twenty-four hours. Because walking into Lachlan's house was so not in and of itself a strange thing. But holding his hand was. And what lay ahead was.

She was suddenly terrified that everything they had been was going to be erased by this. That what they were building over the top of it was going to destroy what they *were*.

She didn't want that. No. She didn't want that. She didn't want to lose their friendship to this desire.

She didn't know what she wanted.

She felt overwhelmed by new sensations and new discoveries. By change.

"Come here."

He led her down the hallway and pushed open the door to his bedroom.

Her lips parted and she looked around, awe filling her.

He had… He had changed everything.

"I went to Mapleton today. Picked up some new stuff."

The bedspread was a lovely plush white, and there were fluffy pillows strewn all over it. There was a lounge in the corner that looked perfect for her to stretch out on and read a book.

He had created space for her in his masculine sanctuary. Had given her something soft and wonderful.

"How did you choose this?"

"I had help," he said. "I asked a woman in the store what she would like, and went from there. But she mostly said that if I went with soft I was going to be doing pretty good."

"Definitely," she said. "This is so much more than I expected."

"I want you to be happy here. With me. I want this to be a life that you want to live."

"It is. I do."

Whatever her other reservations were, she knew that much was true. She wanted that. She wanted him.

And suddenly, she was desperate for him. For what she knew awaited them when they lay down in that fluffy bed. They kissed, but it was different than last night. It wasn't an inferno. It was a slowly building flame. A cozy fire in a wood stove that gradually heated everything all over.

The kind that you could rest in front of for a long time. Not the kind that chased you down and consumed you.

She stripped his clothes off slowly, deliberately, and let the flame of her desire stoke her boldness. She pressed her lips against his chest. Kissed her way down his body as he had done to her. She dropped to her knees in front of him, wrapping her hand around his arousal, squeezing him tight.

"Charity," he said, his voice a warning. "You don't…"

But she wanted to. "I know the mechanics."

He huffed a laugh, his head falling back as she leaned in to flick her tongue over the head of him.

She did not know the mechanics. But she knew she wanted him, and that was going to have to be enough. It was going to have to be her map.

She licked him from base to tip, then took him deep into her mouth, reveling in the feeling of power that it gave her as he began to come apart beneath the pleasure she gave him.

This made the playing field feel so much more equal. She was so much less conscious of the greater depth of his experience.

When he trembled beneath her, it made her feel like a queen.

"Enough," he said, dragging her to her feet.

He opened up his nightstand and took out a box of condoms. "Also got these when I went to town," he said.

She appreciated that. Appreciated knowing that they hadn't been there already for other women.

He had opened the box already, obviously to make things easier in the moment, and he quickly took out a packet. She knew a moment of anxiety, afraid that this was something she had to figure out. But he opened the protection and put it on with practiced ease. *That* was a moment when she was grateful for his experience.

He pressed her into the softness of the bed and hooked her leg up over his hip, sliding inside her, never looking away as he filled her completely.

Their desire for each other was a storm, and she was more than happy to stand out in the rain.

They found their release together, clinging to one another as they rode out the cataclysm.

Her lips curved into a smile, and she rested her head against his shoulder.

"Just one minute," he said.

He rolled out of bed and disappeared into the bathroom. He returned a moment later and then opened up the nightstand drawer again.

This time he pulled out a different sort of box. A black velvet one. "I have something for you."

He got back into bed with her and lay alongside her, opening up the box.

Inside was a beautiful diamond ring.

"Lachlan," she said. "When…"

"I told you. I went shopping today. I wanted to make sure that I got a ring on your finger as quickly as possible. I want to set a date for the wedding."

"Okay."

"I want you to have whatever you want. A church wedding, a wedding by the lake, whatever wedding dress you want. So we'll find out how much time we need for whatever venue, and how long it'll take for you to get your dress…"

"I don't care," she said.

"What?"

"Let's just get married. As quickly as possible."

He frowned. "Do you really not care?"

"I really don't. I never dreamed about the details of my wedding with Byron, mostly I think because I couldn't imagine it. With you, the details don't seem to matter either because the only thing that matters is the groom. I finally have the right one. Definitely for sure, this time you're the right one."

"Well, I'll be damned."

He slid the ring onto her finger, and she felt dazed by the glory of it.

"Next week. Let's get married next week. It'll give us time to let everybody on the ranch know and to get all the paperwork."

"That sounds good."

"We can get married at Sullivan's Lake, or we can use the barn if you want," he said.

"I guess it'll depend on what the weather's doing."

"Yeah. But either way, we'll get married."

"Yes. That's all that matters."

It really was all that mattered. Looking around at everything he'd done… This was real. She didn't need to be insecure. She didn't need to be worried about losing their friendship.

Lachlan was the same person. They had just opened up a new dimension to their relationship. That was all. That was all.

"Good. Let's get some sleep. We've got a big week ahead."

## CHAPTER EIGHTEEN

THEY KICKED OFF preparations for the wedding and getting Charity moved into his house as quickly as possible. He decided to leave the wedding planning up to her, while carrying all the heavy stuff was his job. Well, his and his brothers'. They had everything packed up and ready to move, and then a cleaning crew was going to come in and get it ready for them to put it out to rent, which would be another source of income for Charity. Not that she needed it. Not really. Now not only did she have her veterinary practice, she had him to contribute, too.

He was overcome with the responsibility that came with that. Not in a bad way. But she was his. He had to take care of her. He felt that keenly, down to his soul.

"That should be the last of it," Gus said, coming out of the house holding a large box, which he hefted easily into the back of the truck.

"Some of the stuff will go in storage," Lachlan said. They had a lot of her dad's things, and they definitely didn't want to get rid of it, but they had finite space in his little cabin, and they had a big barn that they used for storing anything excess they had between them at McCloud's Landing, so they could set up a little section where her things would be safe, and she could still get to them if need be, but they wouldn't be underfoot.

But of course, a few of the things would come to the house, including the afghan. He wasn't sure about what he should do with the bug collection. She had been slightly distressed that it was going to be back with her for the foreseeable future.

He chuckled.

"Well, that's a good sign," Hunter said, slapping him on the back.

"What?"

"You laughing for no reason."

"I told you. I'm happy. Charity is wonderful. This is exactly what I wanted."

She was his friend. And yes, the whole thing with Byron had produced some weird, dark feelings, but now that was solved. This was going to be perfect.

The only reason he hadn't thought of it in the first place was because of Byron.

If she'd been single she always would have been the first woman he thought of.

Because he *did* love her. She was his friend.

What was better than that?

He already knew how his life was with her.

She was tea and cookies, and the best moments. She was good conversation and companionable silence.

She was his deepest sexual fantasy come to life.

She was everything great that he could imagine would be in a marriage.

He also hadn't managed to spend the whole night in bed with her yet. But he was an early riser and she hadn't noticed. There was a weird closeness to sleeping with someone. He didn't like the idea of it at all.

But that was fine. It was good. Hell, it was almost

all good and he couldn't think of a damn thing that came close to being half as sweet.

"Yeah, welcome," Brody said. "To the ball and chain club, which I have to say, we have all willingly gotten ourselves into."

"Same," Lachlan said. "I didn't want to be alone." And really, it was the perfect mix of worlds. Because he had her in every way now. And it was… She was a revelation.

She was inexperienced. This was all new to her, and that was pretty clear, but he found that delightful.

He had been so dedicated to his life of womanizing, drinking. It was the strangest thing how suddenly all the things that he used to enjoy had been just…nothing.

When he had seen what his brothers had, the ways that it had changed them, his life had felt like nothing.

Now it felt like something again. Now he could see a way forward. Not just a way to keep sitting in the same stagnant pond he'd been in since he was a teenager.

Redemption.

That was what he was after.

He ignored the slightly uncomfortable twinge that entered his heart when he pinged in on that word. On what he'd told himself early on about Charity, and what he would never, ever use her for.

It was different now. She was thirty, not fifteen. She had her own money, her own career. She had gone away for a while and gotten an education. She had been engaged. Had fully had the opportunity to be with another man and hadn't taken it. He wasn't taking advantage of her.

Back when they were teenagers, he would've felt like he was. But this was different. It was different now.

She'd seen some of the world. She knew what choices she had available to her. She'd chosen *him*. So there.

"I guess all it took was seeing some functional marriages?" Tag asked.

"It didn't hurt," Lachlan said. "Think about it. None of us ever saw anything functional growing up."

"Yeah," Tag said. "You're welcome. I'm the one that decided to break that damn cycle."

"Yes, Taggart. Everybody thinks you're the best," Gus said.

"Actually, Nelly is the best," Tag said. "That's a fact. She took a pretty messed up cowboy and made him into husband material. That is no mean feat."

"Amen," Hunter said. "Though I'm not sure Elsie did any taming. Hell, I would have to tame *her*, and I'm not interested in that."

"Personally, I like a hellcat," Gus said, smiling smugly.

Charity was not a hellcat. He was glad that Hunter and Gus enjoyed their fiery-tempered wives. Elsie and Alaina made them happy. Tag and Brody's wives were sweeter natured.

They seemed no less satisfied.

"Well, let's get all the stuff moved over. There's tons of it. I want to have it done before she gets back from work. I don't want her to have to do a damn thing. Anyway, she's already putting together the wedding shindig. Did you ask Alaina if we can use the barn at Sullivan's? The weather is probably a little bit too iffy to get married out by the lake."

"Alaina wants to know how much you're willing to pay, since you were trying to date Fia just five seconds ago, and now you want to get married in her barn."

"I'll pay anything," he said.

"Obviously, she's kidding," Gus said.

"I don't know that she is," Lachlan said.

"Yeah," Hunter agreed. "Have you *met* your wife, Gus?"

"It's true. She's a pretty vindictive little shrew." Except when he said that, he smiled and looked lost in some kind of fantasy that Lachlan felt for sure he didn't need to be privy to.

He was just glad to get to join in this… This whole thing. The McClouds were paired off. They were settled. They were marked safe from being their damned parents.

Life had changed. He didn't have partners in crime anymore. They wanted to stay home, play poker, eat family dinners.

It was new for them. This kind of warm feeling in that house that Gus lived in now. It was like they had taken all these demons and cast them out.

*Too bad it hasn't done anything inside you.*

He was realizing there were some things he hadn't considered when it came to blending his life with someone else's, because the woman had been theoretical. Even when he'd been thinking it might be Fia Sullivan, it had been different.

But he knew Charity's life.

Her little house.

Her habits.

They were going to share a room. Share a bed. Not just for sex.

Right now he couldn't imagine it.

But he also felt a growing intensity in him. A need to have her with him all the time.

None of that was what he'd imagined.

"How many Christmas lights do you suppose we have between us?" Lachlan asked.

"I've been told that Wolf's wife loves Christmas, and has more Christmas decorations than any ten people should have," Hunter said.

"Okay. And everybody else?"

Gus shrugged. "I'm sure there's thousands between all the families here."

"We should do Christmas lights all over the barn. White ones. She'd love that."

"I thought you were leaving the wedding up to her?" Brody said.

"I am, more or less. But… I know she'd like that."

Another point for marrying a woman he liked so much. A woman he knew so well. Tonight she would be in his house, not going between houses. Tonight she would be his *totally*. Then in four days' time they were getting married. It was good. It was all good.

"Well, I guess that's our next project," Hunter said.

"Great. I didn't want to work today anyway," Brody said.

But first, they had to get all the stuff moved in, because Lachlan was anxious to get this locked down.

This was the first step.

# CHAPTER NINETEEN

SHE FELT SELF-CONSCIOUS, because she had gone straight from work to Gold Valley to meet the sisters-in-law for wedding dress shopping.

Elsie was dressed similarly casually to Charity, being a fan of nothing more decorous than jeans and a T-shirt herself. But Alaina was effortlessly feminine, and Nelly was slightly less flashy, but very pretty. Then there was Elizabeth, who exuded sophistication, a much slicker sort of beauty than anyone else in the group.

The little wedding boutique at the end of the street in Gold Valley was adorable. There were samples of wedding cake at the door, and several rows of beautiful gowns, and the dressing room area was luxuriously appointed. Some of her self-consciousness about her jeans and sweatshirts faded when Elsie took a seat on the plush chair like she was the queen in residence and smiled.

"Well, this is fabulous," Elsie said.

The woman attending the shop took her through information on different wedding gown styles and told her that she should try one of everything, no matter what she thought she would like. Charity didn't know how to tell her that she had no earthly idea what she liked and had never once thought of it before. She hadn't given any thought to the wedding dress aspect of marriage.

It just hadn't featured.

The sisters were happily eating cake, and Charity went and started perusing the aisles.

"Probably not something like this," she said, gesturing to one of the wedding gowns. It looked tight, with a very formfitting sort of shape, and a lace overlay that was completely sheer and wouldn't conceal the bodice beneath.

"You should try it," the woman said.

"I'm not…sexy," Charity said, wrinkling her nose. "It's not really my thing."

"What you wear on your wedding day is entirely up to you," the woman said. "But if you want to be sexy, you get to be. It's your day. Nobody gets to tell you who you are on your day. It's all up to you. Completely."

"I'll try it. But I might not be brave enough to come out of the dressing room."

The woman started taking different dresses back to the room for Charity, and Charity was beginning to feel a little bit like a princess.

She couldn't say she had ever really felt like that before. It was kind of an amazing thing. In the past few days she had felt so taken care of. By Lachlan. By the sisters-in-law. By this random woman at the shop. She had lost so much when she had lost her father, but it was amazing to see all these people in her life fill in these deep gaps. Not that they were replacing him; nothing ever could. Just the ways that people around her knitted together this network of care that made her feel loved in spite of the loss, that made life feel full in spite of the places where there was emptiness.

It was amazing how this fullness could exist alongside emptiness. And she could only marvel at it. It was something of a miracle.

At first, she was embarrassed to have somebody assist her with getting dressed, but there would've been no earthly way she could've squeezed herself into these dresses without help, so she had to simply grit her teeth and deal with it.

She tried on so many that made her feel like a cake topper, and she was beginning to get discouraged that nothing would feel quite right. Then she looked at the one she had scoffed at initially.

She decided to try it.

It fit her perfectly. That was the first sign. Skimmed over her curves like a second skin and made her...well, actually look like she had curves. She stepped out of the dressing room, and the attendant fanned out the train, which was completely see-through, made entirely of delicate lace. The sun came through the window and shone across the beads, cast light through that part of the dress and highlighted her figure.

Normally, she would be just...so uncomfortable with that. But now she pictured Lachlan's face. Because now she knew the effect her body had on him.

It felt incredibly exposing to think of that, standing there in front of the other women. But...it was a part of her now. A part of her that was changing.

She had spent so long pushing down this part of herself. Ignoring it. Denying it. And now here she was... Proud of it. Thinking about accentuating it. Because it didn't matter what anybody else thought; when she thought of coming out in this dress, she saw Lachlan's face. Saw the way that his blue eyes would glint with electricity and the way that it would ignite an answering heat in her.

Yes, other people would be at the wedding. But it was about them. About this newly formed connection and the vows they were taking to make yet another one.

"Oh yes," Alaina said, breaking the silence. "That is hot."

"Agreed," Elsie said.

"I don't know," Charity said, feeling a sudden rise of insecurity.

"He'll love it," Elizabeth said. "The perfect amount sexy and sophisticated. He won't know what hit him."

Well, she liked the sound of that. She liked the idea of being a surprise. Of being sexy and sophisticated when she had never felt anything of the sort even once in her entire life.

"Okay," she said. "This is it. This is the one."

"This is why sometimes you have to step outside of your comfort zone," the woman said.

Charity had been existing entirely outside her comfort zone lately. This was another lesson on how that was a good thing sometimes. A necessary thing. Her comfort zone would have taken her into the wrong marriage with the wrong man. Her comfort zone would have kept her and Lachlan where they'd always been, and they never would have had this.

But she was ready for a break. Ready to go back to the familiar for a little bit. Too much growth was exhausting.

She and the sisters got dinner at an Italian restaurant in Gold Valley, and then piled into their separate vehicles. She was grateful for the silence. For the alone time. She loved the network of people, but…she still needed time on her own. Especially after…so much had happened.

She felt thrust into the feminine in a way she had never been before. Surrounded by all these women who were now family, and therefore determined to be better friends. They had known each other for years, obviously, and had been around each other quite a bit, especially since they had married into the McCloud family. Last Christmas Charity and her father had even gone to Elizabeth's place for the holiday. It had been lovely.

But still, this was different. She was getting to know them on a different level. Just like she was getting to know Lachlan on a different level.

She lapsed into a blank sort of silence as she drove on the darkened highway. She was grateful for the endless stretch of trees. For the twinkle of the stars high above. Even the lack of streetlights.

Grateful that the only sound on the road was her tires on the asphalt, and that there hadn't been any oncoming traffic to blind her with headlights. Because she didn't have words left. Not inside her whole soul. She was just *feeling*.

Marinating in the changes that had come her way in the past weeks. Months. Losing her dad, losing Byron—because it was a loss, even if it was one she had chosen. *Losing* so much. Again and again. Then gaining. The sisters. Lachlan, as her lover, as her future husband. The McClouds as her actual family.

She had spent so many years not changing, that this metamorphosis felt sudden and intense. Bordering on painful. She drove on without the radio. Nothing but her feelings. And when she pulled in to her house, the porch light was on.

She got out and walked up to the front door and put the key in the lock, and opened the door to a completely empty living room.

"What?"

She looked around, and she saw that none of her things were here. None of them. She went from room to room and saw that nothing was there.

"Lachlan," she whispered.

She went back outside and got into her car, driving straight over to McCloud's Landing trying not to feel… She didn't know what she felt.

Skinned? Like she had been exposed and hadn't had any time to rebuild up her shield. Now her little moment in her familiar surroundings had been taken from her, because Lachlan had… He'd done her a favor, she was certain that had been his intent.

When she arrived at his place she was already torn between being angry, irritated and just plain understanding. She had agreed to move in, so why would he think this would be upsetting?

She walked into the house without knocking, because if he had taken all the things out of her house, then surely, this was her house now, and she didn't have to knock.

"Hi," he said, turning around from his position at the stove in the kitchen. "I made chili."

"I ate," she said. "Why didn't you talk to me about moving all of my stuff?"

Well, so much for just saying thank you.

"I thought that you would appreciate it," he said, frowning. "I wanted to surprise you."

"I thought that's probably what you wanted," she said. "But… Lachlan, I… I was expecting to be able to go home tonight and be in the house, and have something feel normal. We're going to get married in a few days and…"

"You're not in a hurry? Because I'm in a hurry. I don't want things to go back to how they were. I don't want to be away from you."

"I don't want to be away from you," she said. "I was just… So many things in my life changed. There's something really sad about leaving the house behind. Really closing the door on that life I shared with my dad. It isn't about you. It's about me. It's about wishing I could be in my dad's house because he won't be here for the wedding. I wish he was. If we'd been engaged before he died, I would have rushed the wedding for him to be there." She hadn't cared about that with Byron. It should have been another sign. It hadn't been. "I wanted to spend a little bit of time back there. That's all. Surely, you can understand that."

He frowned. "I mean, I can, but I can't say that I really want to."

"Don't be like that. I'm marrying you. I got a wedding dress today. I… Lachlan, I'd never even had sex before and now… I don't know. It's like I spent so much time by myself, and now I'm even sharing a bed with you and…"

"Charity," he said. "I'd never had sex with you. It doesn't matter that I'd been with other people. It wasn't the same. It isn't the same. And it isn't going to be. You and me… That's its own thing. Nothing is that. Nothing is us. Do you think this is easy for me because I had experience? I've never spent the night with a woman before."

"You… You haven't?"

"No, ma'am. Hit it and quit it was my thing."

"That's kind of awful," she said.

He looked at her, his expression grave. "Charity, I have at times in my life been kind of awful. I have at times in my life felt like my pain was a hell of a lot more important than anyone else's could be. I'm trying to be different. I'm trying to be better. It makes sense that you be the person I marry. Because you're the only one that I ever had an easy time with as far as… I do care about your feelings. About your comfort. About your pain. I know mine is not more important. Yeah, it's a lot for me, too, but I'm ready to jump in with both feet." He put his hand on her cheek. "As deep as my feet go."

"I'm sorry. I guess I'm just kind of freaking out. Because a week ago I was engaged to Byron, and now I'm marrying you in a couple of days. And…sometimes it's difficult to reconcile the change in our relationship, too. To figure out what it means. And I wonder a little bit if what we were is gone. Because now there's…all the sex stuff."

"The sex stuff didn't erase our friendship," he said. "It's just…another way we get to spend time together."

Somehow, she knew that was wrong. That it wasn't quite it. That it skimmed over the surface of the change that had occurred inside her when she had first been with him. Because it had been a change. A deep one.

He was saying all the right things, but somehow it was still skirting around what she felt. She felt filleted. Opened up. He obviously felt something, but she wasn't sure it was that. And maybe it was just the ways that it was all different for men. She didn't know.

But she had heard about it, of course. Because people talked about such things.

That love and sex and all manner of those things were different if you had testosterone.

She sat down at the little kitchen table, and he sat across from her with his bowl of chili.

"I should've told you I guess that I was going out to eat."

"Well, I guess I didn't tell you where you would be sleeping tonight. So I suppose all is fair in love and surprises."

That word stuck in her chest.

"Lachlan," she said. "I love you."

She did. She had been toying with that for a few days. Because she had always known that she loved him, but what made a person in love. Was it sex?

She was certain she'd been in love with him since way before he had ever touched her. He was the most important person in her life, and the idea of putting another man above him really never would've worked, because he was the one. He was the only one who could ever occupy that position. The only one she ever wanted to do it.

"I love you, too," he said.

Her stomach swooped, her heart hitting her breastbone.

"You said you didn't want love with marriage," she said.

"I didn't need it, no. But I've loved you the whole time. Like I said, sex didn't erase our friendship."

Just like that. So easy. But yet again, she wondered

if he meant something different. And she didn't quite know how to ask.

If it was that easy, then why had both of them been planning to marry other people? She could attribute her own idiocy to inexperience. But then…maybe that was the same with him, too. He'd slept with people, but he didn't know anything about emotional intimacy.

There was something about that that stuck in her chest, too. *Emotional intimacy.*

"I guess it's good we're marrying each other, then."

"It was stupid to think that we shouldn't," he said. "Stupid to think that there was someone else that we would be happier with. There isn't."

"No," she said.

Except right then she had the fleeting feeling that Byron would've felt *easier.* Would have felt…like less of a risk. Even with that simple *I love you* that had come off his lips, she somehow felt more exposed than he did. She still felt peeled. Like there were bits of her that were exposed that had never been meant to be.

She didn't have the vocabulary to ask why. Why when she said she loved him it felt like more, deeper than when he'd said it back.

"Did you find a wedding dress?" he asked.

"Yes."

"Can I see?"

"No." She frowned. "It's against the rules."

"I feel certain the best friend of the bride is allowed to see the wedding dress."

"But you're also the groom."

"Damn loopholes."

"Really," she said.

"All right," he said when he finished his chili. "Let's go to bed."

She didn't have the heart to refuse him. Or maybe more accurately, she didn't have the heart to refuse herself.

SHE WOKE UP at around three o'clock and realized he wasn't in bed. She drifted back to sleep, assuming he had gone to the bathroom. But she woke up again at four, and he still wasn't there.

She crept out into the living room and saw him sitting there on the couch, wide-awake. There was a bottle of alcohol on the table in front of him, and the glass half-full.

"Lachlan?"

"Oh hey," he said, his voice gruff. "Did I wake you?"

"Not really."

"Just couldn't sleep. Don't worry about it. Go back to bed."

"Okay."

She was still groggy, not even half-awake, so she didn't have the capacity to argue with him, or question him too deeply.

But even while she tried to go back to sleep, it was the look on his face that kept flashing back before her eyes. One of utter hopelessness.

She had never seen him look like that before.

The next morning he acted like nothing had happened, and he was back to being completely himself, to the point where she was almost certain she had imagined it. It had just been a sleepless couple of hours. Nobody looked *happy* when they couldn't sleep. It sucked. So she let it go and focused on the last-minute details of the wedding. Because in just two days she was going to marry Lachlan McCloud.

And in spite of feeling frightened of change, and feeling a bit overwhelmed by it all, she knew that it was the right decision. She knew that it was the best thing.

She knew that it was going to be the happiest day of her life.

# CHAPTER TWENTY

IT WAS HIS wedding day. Damn.

He hadn't gotten a tux, but had decided to wear a black suit, a black hat and a black pair of cowboy boots. Which he felt was pretty damn fancy. Especially considering his brothers—with the exception of Brody—had worn jeans at their weddings, he was a damn sight ahead of them.

He was behind the barn where all the lights were strung and set up, and there were different cakes provided by different members of Four Corners, all mismatched and perfect, and the Kings would be bringing barbecue, and the sides would be done potluck style. It was, without a doubt, one of the fancier weddings they'd had at the ranch.

He was glad of that. Because he wanted to give Charity that little extra.

"You ready?"

Gus came around the side of the barn to where he stood, the sunlight hitting his brother's scarred face and making the pockets there look a little bit deeper. But it didn't make him look less happy. Ever since marrying Alaina, Gus had looked happier than ever.

It was always hard for Lachlan to look at those scars. Because what he saw was sacrifice. What he saw was a whole bunch of pain that had been meant for *him*, but had been meted out to his brother. Their father hadn't done anything with efficiency. He had done it with rage. Messy, overwrought rage that caused utter destruction.

Gus had taken the rage for him that day.

"Yeah. I'm ready," he said.

"I'm proud of you, Lachlan. I really am. You and I went through shit. Everybody did. Everybody. They all had to live around the violence. But you and I got the worst of it. He used you like a damn punching bag."

"Great. This is just the best man speech that I wanted to get right before I got married, how did you know?"

"Well, it's the best man speech you're gonna get. I know what you went through. I mean I *really* know."

"Yeah. I know. We both should be dead, really."

"Yeah."

Gus had deflected the rage that their father had directed at Lachlan. During that fire. Gus had taken that rage on himself.

He'd had the worst of their father's violence.

But Lachlan had his *hatred*. Their father had accused their mother of having an affair. Of Lachlan not being Seamus's. How Lachlan wished that were true. But he looked like his dad. They had the same blue eyes. Sometimes he worried the same mean streak. Though Lachlan had spent his life finding ways to not express it. Not ever. To not give it oxygen.

Their father had tried to kill Gus. But only because Gus had made him angry. He tried to kill Lachlan because he hated him. Just for being born. Just for existing. Hated the idea so much that his blood ran in Lachlan's veins that he refused to believe it. And what the hell was that? What the ever-loving hell was that?

Everyone else had *seen* it. But Gus was the one that really knew how it looked when that hatred was unmasked entirely.

"I just think it's… It's a good thing that you're letting yourself have this. That you're letting yourself have her."

"I thought you were a big proponent of our platonic friendship," Lachlan said.

"Yeah, because in a lot of ways I thought it was a nice way you were letting yourself be happy. Having a friend. But I think it's even better if you can love her."

He'd told her that he loved her yesterday. She'd said it to him.

It had triggered a whole bunch of shit. Shit he definitely didn't want to think about now, because he had to go get married. And he didn't want any of it hanging over him tonight. Didn't want to spend tonight contending with demons. That forced him into a space of wakefulness that either demanded he drown it with alcohol, or sit there in a fight with that urge to drink, because he knew it was what his dad would do.

He used to get kind of a perverse pleasure out of the fact that for him alcohol primarily fueled his happiness. His sex drive. That it could banish demons rather than call them up. But on those endless nights when sleep eluded him, he questioned the difference. It was all just a lack of control. A willingness to surrender himself to something that got to dictate who he was and what he did. Yeah. Sometimes he wondered if he was winning that game, or just losing it a different way.

He wasn't an alcoholic. It was just about his relationship to it. What he used it for. That defiance he had as a cocky young guy who thought he was so different than his dad just because of how he worshipped at that particular altar.

He said he loved her.

He *did* love her. That, he supposed, was the final victory against his dad. He could love somebody, and it could be this. It could be healthy. At least as healthy as he could be. So there.

"You don't need to worry about me," Lachlan said. "You did enough of that. I'm fine."

"I hope so," Gus said.

"Why wouldn't I be?"

"Because *I'm* not always fine, Lachlan. Even with everything being the way that it is. Even with Alaina, and Cameron, I… I'm not always okay. That's part of marriage. She's there for me. There are some difficult things that come up when you have kids. I'm a *father* now. And when I think of how Dad treated us… When I look at Cameron, and I think… The one job I have as a father is to protect that kid with my life. And I would. I wouldn't just kill for him, I'd die for him. In a heartbeat. I would cut off my own arm before I let anything happen to him. Dad *hurt* us. Suddenly when you look at your own child you realize what that means. How young you were. How helpless. It's hard. I'm not always okay. Being married to Alaina doesn't mean I'm always okay. But she gets me. And she's there. She loves me anyway. Because of it, in spite of it, I don't know. I just know that I'm lucky. Because I might've had a terrible childhood. I might've had a shit time of it, but I have a wife that loves me. I have a son. It's just waves of love. But it's waves of grief sometimes, too. And that's okay. Sometimes I envy my kid. My own kid. Because he's got two parents who love him more than anything. And we didn't even have one. It's hard. It doesn't make things perfect to get married. But it does make them better. I guarantee you that."

He didn't know what he felt about that. Because he thought… He thought that Gus was *fine*. That he had somehow overcome all that stuff. He didn't think he was…still actively dealing with it.

Maybe that wasn't realistic, but hell. It wasn't like he had any examples of reasonable healing in his life. It wasn't like he was all that familiar with how functional adults did relationships. Or anything.

But things would be better with Charity. They had to be.

"Thanks, Gus," he said.

It wasn't for the talk. He was thanking him for saving his life. They had a hard time talking about it. He had a hard time with his own guilt. There were different kinds of hell. There was a hell of remembering his father's fists connecting with his face. But that was just pain. Pain was only a feeling, and it passed. Hell, if there was too much pain, your body wouldn't let you feel it. So it went away. Went away, because your body protected you from it. From the reality.

That was fine. But, then there was the memory of Gus. Of Gus and the shed and Lachlan running away because he'd been too scared.

The memories of the long months that it had taken for Gus to recover. Of being terrified his big brother was going to die. And when he hadn't died…there was the suffering. That lived with him. Rightly so. It ought to. It ought to live with him because it was the fate he'd been spared. On the back of his brother. The *face* of his brother.

He hoped that he could carry it so that Gus carried a little less. He knew that was a foolish thing to hope. But…he did all the same.

"You better go inside so you can get married," Gus said.

"I guess so."

The barn was done up amazing. And for one second he just stood there. Unable to believe that this was his life. That this was happening.

He was going to have a wife and a child someday. He was getting married underneath the canopy of Christmas lights, and friends had made cakes to celebrate.

The lonely kid he'd been could never have imagined this.

Could never have imagined that this moment could exist for him.

Emotion swelled and expanded in his chest, so big he nearly couldn't breathe around it. It almost hurt. Because it wasn't something he ever thought… It wasn't anything he'd ever dreamed about. Because how the hell… How could you ever imagine your way out of the kind of hell you've lived through? You couldn't. You couldn't imagine love when you'd never been given it.

Except he thought of his brothers. The love he'd experienced had been from them every time. Gus had nearly sacrificed himself to save Lachlan. What was that if not love at the highest level?

He was humbled by it then. *Overwhelmed* with it.

Overwhelmed with the realization that his life had led to this moment. *This* moment.

Women were supposed to get emotional about weddings. Not men.

He cleared his throat and watched as people filtered into the barn and sat down, like there was nothing they wanted more than to watch Lachlan McCloud marry Charity Wyatt. Even if that wasn't true, it was what it felt like.

He gritted his teeth against the swell of emotion that kept on coming. He remembered looking at Charity and thinking that her grief was like that. Waves and waves. Ebb and flow. That was what he experienced now. Swells that kept coming. That kept increasing. Growing and building like a tide.

He took his position at the front and waited.

A few of the guys who worked on the ranch had banded together to play music, and while they normally did fiddles, the sweet country renditions of love songs they played now filled the barn and tangled with the Christmas lights to make magic.

He hoped she thought it was magic.

He really did.

He wanted to be enough for her.

That was a feeling he hadn't expected. Hadn't seen coming. He thought a lot about what he was going to get out of marriage. But not a whole lot about what he was supposed to give back. He wanted to be enough for her. More than anything, he wanted that.

The double doors to the barn opened and suddenly, there she was. Floating toward him like an angel wrapped in lace. The gown clung to her curves, her breasts rising up over the swell of the white silk, shocking him. Because he had never seen Charity display that much of her body in public, and he both wanted to beat his chest with pride over how incredible she looked, and run up to her and cover her with his jacket so that nobody else could enjoy it.

She was breathtaking. There had never been a more beautiful woman, her blond hair loose and curling over her shoulders.

She was a vision. A vision of a future he'd never known could be his. A vision of the future he wanted now more than just about anything on earth.

Charity. His Charity.

His.

His woman.

His friend.

His wife.

She was carrying a bright bouquet of flowers that he recognized from the garden here at Sullivan's Point. Brilliant early spring blooms that ran the gamut from red to pink to purple. An explosion of the beauty they enjoyed here, held right in the palms of her hands.

Somehow it was just so apt.

And when she arrived to where he stood, he took her hand and drew her to him. "You're beautiful."

She looked up at him, her blue eyes glittering. "So are you."

They didn't have anyone standing up with them and yet, he felt like everyone was standing up with them. Everyone who had brought them to this place. Everyone who had helped him get here so that he'd *lived*. So that he didn't become the same raging asshole his father was.

He didn't know the pastor who was doing the service. Because he couldn't remember the last time he'd ever been in a church, and even when he had, it had been Catholic, and at the behest of his mother, so it certainly hadn't been a casual event. *This* pastor was wearing sandals like it wasn't fifty-eight degrees outside.

But the service was nice and short. Sweet, without being a full-on sermon. There was something about that moment. About the tradition of it that filled in cracks in his soul he didn't know were there.

They'd had nothing traditional growing up. Their holidays had been scattered, angry affairs. Their mother had left one year right around Christmas.

They hadn't had birthday parties.

Their house hadn't been safe.

It had been a minefield. One wrong step and they detonated their father's rage.

Tradition wasn't something they were allowed.

Their legacy was pain. Violence.

But they were making a new one. In this simple moment in the barn, where he and Charity spoke words to each other that people had said back and forth over an altar for hundreds of years... That felt like something real. It felt like something good. Like something infinitely possible to build a life from. Something bigger than they were.

And he damn well needed something bigger than he was.

"For richer or poorer," he said. "In sickness and in health. Till death do us part. With this ring I take you as my wife." He slid the wedding band onto her finger, the companion to the sparkly rock he'd given her just last week.

It was his turn to be surprised when she produced a wedding band for him.

"With this ring, I take you as my husband." That heavy gold band sat there on his left hand, unfamiliar, and altering in a way he hadn't imagined it could be.

That was a married man's hand.

They were married.

They could be the damned Cleavers if they wanted to. She had grown up without a mother. But their kids would have one. He had grown up without either parent, functionally. One gone, one a danger.

But their kids would have him.

They would have each other.

She wouldn't have to be lonely, like the way she'd said her dad was.

And he wouldn't have to be afraid.

He shoved that thought aside. He wasn't afraid. He was a grown-ass man who had survived death for the first time at age six. He wasn't afraid.

But life, and the path forward seemed a little bit clearer now. A little bit brighter.

There was that.

"You may now kiss the bride."

He did. Full on the mouth and with all the passion that he had inside him. A promise, not only of tonight, their wedding night, but of their shared future together, which would contain all this. The family around them, and the passion between them. The tradition, old as time, but new for them.

They might not have had examples around them. But people did this. This family thing, this marriage thing. They did it; they had done it. They continued to do it. And hell, they could do it, too. They could.

They were doing it.

"May I present to you, Mr. and Mrs. McCloud."

They turned and everyone in the barn cheered. All the McCloud men had gotten married.

Not a single one of them had turned into their dad.

Everybody here probably considered it an earthly

miracle. One they couldn't explain. But he was glad of it. Lordy, he was glad of it. He felt like he had escaped something. A boulder that he hadn't even been aware was rolling behind him. One he'd now successfully sidestepped. With this.

This had saved him.

She'd saved him.

Afterward, they cleared the chairs and set them off to the sides so the people had a place to sit and eat their barbecue and cake. Outside, a big bonfire was roaring, so those who weren't concerned about the spring chill could enjoy their place out there.

And people began to pair off and dance. He and Charity never danced together. But he figured they ought to now. It was one of those things that was different about them. Husband and wife ought to dance together at their wedding.

He pulled her into his arms and spun her in a circle.

She laughed. "Are you happy?" he asked.

"Yes. I wish… I wish my dad were here. I wish he could have given me away. Because I think he would've liked to give me to you, Lachlan."

"Sweetheart," he said, "don't you know he already did?"

"What?"

His chest squeezed. "Right before he passed, I had a conversation with Albert. And he said… He said 'don't you let anything happen to my baby girl, Lachlan Mc-Cloud. Or I'll tan your hide.'"

"He did not."

"He did. I believe it was a threat to tan my hide quite literally from beyond the grave."

"And what did you tell him?"

"I told him that I would always be there for you. And I will be. I promise you that, Charity. Nothing is ever going to come between us. You're mine. You're my girl."

"Thank you. That was just the perfect thing to say."

"I think he's here. Because I think he gives his blessing on this. He loves you. Still."

"And *you* love me," she said.

"I always have," he said, a strange emotion welling up in his chest. One he couldn't readily define.

They quit talking. And just danced. And they cut the biggest cake together after the song was over, and he fed her a bite and watched as she blushed.

It was such a traditional wedding. For having been thrown together in just a few days, it was perfect.

People took countless pictures on their phones, and he knew that they'd get all of them sent to them. Evidence that this day actually had happened, because as the evening wore on it was starting to feel surreal.

When they came out of the barn, his truck was decorated.

"What in the hell…"

His brothers held their arms out, gesturing toward the truck, looking proud of their handiwork. There were streamers and beer cans, writing on the window.

"You crazy asses," he said. "I am driving two miles away back to McCloud's Landing."

"Yes," Gus said, shrugging. "But we figured you deserved a big sendoff."

"Son of a bitch," he said.

But there was no venom behind it.

Charity laughed. "Just married. Well. It's true."

He went around to the driver's side and scowled. One of them had written Minute Man on his window.

"I'm *not*," he muttered.

"What?"

"They're just assholes," he said.

Charity rounded to his side of the truck and read the window. "Minute Man. What does… Oh. He's not!" she said, and he howled with laughter, because he knew that cost Charity to say. To joke with them like that about something so private. She'd done it anyway. To defend his honor. He appreciated it.

They got into the truck and she started laughing.

"What's so funny?" he asked.

"I can't believe that happened."

She rolled the window down and leaned halfway out, waving as he started the engine and they began driving back toward their place.

Their place. Their life.

This was happening. It was damn well happening.

He could hear the rustle of the cans behind the truck, and also a couple of balloons popping as they hit the gravel.

"I'm glad," she said. "That we did it. And also… That was the most beautiful wedding I've ever seen. I never thought that I'd have anything like that."

"Me either," he said, his voice coming out rougher than he'd intended it to.

"Did you ever think about your wedding?"

"No. I never really thought about my future. Not until my brothers started…changing things. It's weird to be left behind. To look around you and see people who are just as messed up as you…decide not to be messed up. I… Well, I figured that I had to take a chance on it. It made me start planning. Thinking. Because what the hell else was I going to do? Just sit there and... sit there and waste away? I was going to be some old guy in the bar, picking up women. That's just sad. That's what I was going to become. It was going to happen without me even realizing it. Because I wasn't *thinking*. Because you know, when you live under constant threat of danger you just learn not to wonder about tomorrow."

He hadn't meant to say that.

"Lachlan," she said, her voice soft. She put her hand on his forearm. "Did you really never try to think about tomorrow?"

"Ever," he said. "Because the next day might bring more rage, and that time you might not be so lucky. You might not dodge the blow that could take you out. You might get hit so hard that this time you don't wake up."

"Your dad hit you that hard?" Her voice was small. Sad.

"Yeah. He got a particular amount of joy out of hitting *me*."

He hadn't meant to say that, either.

He had promised himself that he wouldn't corrupt Charity. For all these years, that had meant not telling her everything about his home life, either. It was something that he had sworn to himself.

It was why he had banished all his fantasies of kissing her. Because not only would he corrupt her with that, but eventually it would lead to this. Somehow when he'd decided to marry her he hadn't let himself think about the fact it might include this. Because they'd gone their whole friendship, all their lives, without ever really getting into the details of this. Not by accident. So why the hell he was doing it now, he didn't know.

*She's your wife.*

*It's different.*

But he shouldn't. He shouldn't do it.

He was anyway.

"I don't know why, but when my mom had me, he thought it was suspicious. He didn't trust the timing. Whatever. But he didn't think that I was his son. That was our secret, of course. His, mine and Mom's. I *am* his son, just to be clear. Not only have I done those ancestry DNA things with my brothers, which, we are very Scottish, and I am very much their full brother, but he's definitely my dad. You can tell by the look of me. You can tell. But *he* couldn't. He hated me. Hated me on sight. So the smallest things, the littlest things, they would just get him in a total rage. He used to throw beer bottles at me. Kick me like a wounded dog if I was in his way. Sorry. You don't need to hear about this."

"I do need to hear about it," she said. "I didn't realize that he abused you worse than he did the others."

"I mean, in the end, Gus got the worst of it. Let's be perfectly real. And everybody—except Brody—dealt with physical abuse. It wasn't just me."

"He didn't hit Brody?"

"No. Trust me, that's a mind game all on its own that Brody has had to deal with. Nobody came out of that house unscathed. We were all a mess by the time we were adults. There was no coming out of it without scars. So it doesn't matter what happened to me, not when you compare it to what happened to Gus, or even to the emotional manipulation that happened to

Brody. I'm not unique. It's just the same effect of living in the house with a psychopath."

"But he hit you the most."

"Like he breathed. He hit me like it was on his to-do list. That's why you had to patch me up so many times. They weren't even big blowups. They were just…casual. I think that's the worst part. When he hit me and he wasn't even visibly angry. He just did it because I was there."

He gritted his teeth. He didn't want to think about this now. Not on the heels of what had been really kind of a wonderful day.

"So yeah. I didn't think about the future. And I really didn't think there was something good waiting for me. Much less a wedding. Where the bride wore a white wedding dress, and there was cake, and my friends were there and my family was there. It feels like a minor miracle, all things considered."

"Why were you up the other night?"

Something like fear made his stomach jump. "I told you. I couldn't sleep."

She didn't need to hear about all of his issues. Not all at once.

"Lachlan…"

"Tonight's our wedding night," he said. "I want it to be about us. The two of us together. I want it to be about how much I care about you. I don't want it to be about anything else. It's you and me. Together."

"Okay."

When they pulled up to the cabin it felt momentous. He wondered if he should've taken her to a hotel. The wedding had ended up so traditional that he wondered if he was messing up here. He should've done something grander, more spectacular.

Like she could read his mind, she put her hand over his. "I'm glad that we came back home," she said. "I really am."

"Good."

They got out of the truck, and for a moment he just stood there, staring at her, the moonlight illuminating her and her gown. He went over to her and took her hand, drew her to him and spun her like they'd done in the barn. There was no music, but they started to sway back and forth.

His bride.

His wife.

Charity was his wife.

Charity McCloud.

"You know, that day when I went into the woods… I was hiding. My dad was looking for me. This was after Gus had been burned, of course. But it didn't stop things. And my dad… He just got worse and worse. Gus got rid of him soon after that. That's why you never had to know how bad it was. But… I went into the forest hoping to hide, and I found an angel. I think you're still saving me, Doc. I really do."

"I think you saved me," she said, reaching up and touching his face. "I was so lonely. And so strange. I didn't know any other kids. I didn't have friends. You taught me how to laugh. *Really* laugh. You taught me sarcasm, which my dad was fundamentally incapable of. He was far too sincere and literal. Always. I would stitch you up a thousand times, and still not even come close to doing for your outsides what you did for my insides."

"Darling, you could stitch me up a thousand times and not come close to doing to my outsides what you did to my insides. You showed me that there was something soft in me. Something good. You showed me how to care about someone that wasn't one of my brothers. And that was kind of a big deal. A revelation. And you really gave me someone to protect. I wanted to protect you, all the time. I guess I'm doing a pretty bad job of it now."

There were things that needed to stay behind those stitches. Locked away tight. Ugliness that he'd never visit on her. There was love, and then there was…

He could still remember it. The way he'd heard his father crying after hitting his mother, accusing her of infidelity.

*I just love you so much.*

It made him want to vomit.

Never that. He would never feel that.

It was the same word. But it meant something else.

"What are you talking about? You only protected me from marrying the wrong man. Protected me from a life of not knowing what pleasure was. Protected me from being alone."

"You were going to marry somebody else. You weren't going to be alone."

"No. I would've been alone. Because Byron and I had so much in common. But we didn't complete anything in each other. We didn't fix anything in each other, and you and I have been doing that for a long time now. We fix each other. We really do."

"Yeah. We do."

"Let's keep on doing it."

They danced under the stars without music and he

twirled her again, dipped her and reveled in her laughter. He spun her around under that diamond-scattered sky and when he brought her back to him, he kissed her. Kissed her till they were both dizzy.

They went up the steps into the house. It felt different. Because she lived here now. Because it was hers. And so was he.

He led her down the hall, back to the bedroom that he had turned into their bedroom. And he looked at her, wrapped in that white wedding gown. His virgin bride. Well, she'd been a virgin until last week. And he'd been the one to take it, so it counted. It counted.

He lowered the zipper on her dress, letting it fall down to her waist. And his body roared in approval at the undergarments that were beneath the gown. A sheer, white lace corset, her breasts spilling over the top of it.

He couldn't tear his eyes off her.

He put his hands on her hips and pushed the dress down the rest of the way and found that what he'd taken for a corset was actually one piece. See-through lace all the way down, the triangle between her thighs accentuated more than covered by the white lace.

She was still wearing the high heels she'd had on beneath the dress, and he felt like his world was caving in.

His sweet, beautiful friend. His wife.

Demure Charity. Standing in front of him in *that*.

She turned around, and his blood pressure skyrocketed. The back was a thong, and it showed the perfect pale globes of her ass, and he could hardly take it. He'd seen her naked any number of times in the past week. But this deliberate provocation was something else altogether.

"Do you like it?" she asked.

"If I liked it any more I would've died of a heart attack right here. I'm not kidding. I think my soul left my body."

"Good." She looked shy for a moment.

"I would like you in anything, and in nothing. Just because I didn't act on this for all these years… It doesn't mean it wasn't a strong feeling. It doesn't mean it wasn't there."

"I used to go out of my way not to look at you," she said.

"What?"

"It's true. Remember before we went to the bar, just a couple weeks back, and you came in and took your shirt off…"

"Not really. I never thought about taking my shirt off in front of you."

"I know. You did it all the time. I never looked. Not ever. Not once. Because I trained myself not to look at you that way. I trained myself not to see you that way. It was the best thing I could do. Because I never… Lachlan, I never wanted to want you all alone. I never wanted to… To *love* you alone."

He swallowed hard, the lump in his throat impossible to shift.

"Here we are now. And you're not alone."

"I know. I know."

He reached out and cupped her cheek, dragged his fingertips down her jawline and brushed his thumb over her lips. It was a wonder to touch her. This woman. This woman who had been off-limits to him for so long, when he had pretended to himself that he'd given himself permission to indulge in any and every vice. He hadn't. He hadn't indulged in her. Not ever. Because he had decided that she was the one thing he couldn't have, and he wondered just then if the truth of it was, he had kept Charity from himself, because what he really liked to do was punish himself.

That was why the wedding today had felt like such an extreme break with reality. He had never thought he could have anything good.

She had definitely been on that list.

He let his fingertips trail down to the top of the lace cups on those widow-making undergarments she had on, let his fingertips graze the plush flesh there.

He groaned.

"I've never wanted a woman more," he said.

He'd never wanted a woman. Not specifically. He wanted *sex*. He would take it with any feminine form he could get.

It had never mattered.

They just had to be there. Be willing. The kind of woman who showed up and let her enthusiasm do most of the work. Yeah. He liked that.

He liked *women*. But they'd never *specifically* mattered.

Charity mattered.

She mattered so much he couldn't breathe around it. She mattered so much, he thought he might choke to death on it.

This was the problem with good things. Standing next to something quite this miraculous. Quite this pure. He could only find himself lacking.

He didn't want to think. He pulled down the top of the garment, roughly, inverting the cups and exposing her breasts. Pert and lovely, with tight pink nipples that were begging for his attention.

He was more than willing to accommodate. He wanted to worship her. So he did, lowering his head and flicking his tongue over the tightened bud there, drawing her deep into his mouth and reveling in all her sweetness.

He moved his attention to the other breast, her whole body shuddering as he teased her first with his mouth, and then moved his hand to the neglected breast to continue teasing her there, too. A rough, raw cry escaped her lips and she arched against him.

"You were such a good girl for so long," he said. "But that was all a lie. Wasn't it? You were just afraid. But you don't have to be afraid with me."

It was the first time that he thought maybe, maybe he had done something decent. That maybe his presence in her life really was a good thing. Because she was beautiful, and bold and she deserved to have the freedom to express that. He had to wonder if living that small, quiet life of hers had made her feel like she couldn't do this. Couldn't be bold.

But she could be. With him.

She could do anything with him. Be anything with him, and he would live to accommodate her. To encourage her.

He kissed down the center of her breasts, slowly drawing the lace bodysuit down with each millimeter he moved. She was glorious. Perfect. His.

He continued his path down, until he had lowered the garment down midway past her thighs, until he had exposed the heart of her to his hungry gaze. He leaned in, pressing his face to her, giving a slow lick down her molten core.

She jerked, a short, sharp sound rising up within her.

"Yeah," he said. "That's right. How did you think you didn't want this? How did you think this didn't matter to you?"

She wrapped her arms around his head, cupping him, holding him to her.

And she was shaking.

"Answer me," he said, licking her again.

She jerked and shuddered. "Lachlan…"

"I said answer me, dammit. How did you think you could live your whole life without passion like this?"

"Because it didn't matter." The words came out a sob. "It didn't matter until you."

He growled and propelled her backward, to the edge of the bed, jerking the lace down completely off and spreading her thighs, using his shoulders to hold her wide for him as he gripped her ass and ate at her ravenously.

*It didn't matter until you.*

He mattered.

*Him.*

He was the reason she wanted this. He was the reason she was this way. It could never have been another man.

It was improbable, and he didn't deserve it. But he hadn't deserved to be born a boy whom his father hated on sight.

So if there was any kind of magic, anything at all, that made a person look at him and just feel something, this seemed fair. Because he had been hated. Just for breathing.

To be wanted all the same, just for *being*, to be wanted by her... It was magic. A damned miracle.

And he was going to claim it. For all that it was. All that it could be.

She wanted him. Just because.

They had met each other, and it had been inevitable. In that forest they had seen each other, and they had mattered to each other.

In this whole shit show that was life, that was the closest thing to magic that existed.

It amazed him. That she was his wife. That he was here. That yeah, all this shit had happened in his life, but there was this glittering gold piece of perfection, and it was her.

Hell, yeah, it was her.

He tasted her, gorging himself on her until she screamed. Until she was writhing against his mouth, bucking up off the mattress, her fingers threading through his hair.

"Want me," he growled. He kissed her hip bone and moved up her body, looking into her eyes. "Want me."

"I do," she said.

"Only me."

"I said that. Only you. It's only you."

"Good," he said.

He growled, thrusting deep inside her, his desire blocking out everything else.

There was nothing but them. This moment. They might as well have been the same flesh. The same person. Where they melded into one another and nothing mattered but that moment. Not the past. Not the future. It was just them. Lachlan and Charity.

Husband and wife.

He shuddered, his need rising up inside him like a tide. But no. He wouldn't let this end that quick. He wanted to make her come again.

He growled as much, against her mouth, her neck, desperate for release. Desperate for her.

"Lachlan," she said, the words broken.

"Charity." His thrusts became wild. "Please," he ground out, whether to her or himself, he didn't know.

Then she rocked her hips against his, and all was lost. He put his hand between them, rubbing his thumb over her sensitized bundle of nerves there, as she cried out her release, permission for him to give in to his own.

He roared, control completely beyond him in the moment.

"Mine," he said, kissing her shoulder.

She looked up at him, and there were so many questions in those blue eyes, and he feared he didn't know the answer to them.

"How did this happen?"

He knew exactly what she meant. Only weeks ago they'd never touched each other. Now it was like this need was air.

"I think it was always going to," he said. "I think it was fate. I haven't given a lot of thought to that sort of thing. But I was born into pain beyond my control. The way my old man saw me, I didn't choose that." He gritted his teeth together. "So maybe this is beyond our control, too. Maybe the good and the bad. Maybe they just come to you."

Her lips curved up. "You're sort of a romantic."

"I am?"

She adjusted their position, put her hand on his

chest. "Yes. The way that you believe my father is here watching. The way that you believe in the miraculous. The good, and not just the bad. I think it's incredible."

"Well. Not too much," he said. "I just can't believe it's random. It doesn't make any sense to me."

"I like it," she said.

He wasn't sure if he did. Not always. Because that meant he had been fated for a certain amount of suffering, and that wasn't the nicest thought. But then there had to be a reason.

He liked for the world to run in order. To have a purpose to different things. To make some sense. But it didn't really matter now, not one way or the other. Because if it was more about karmic debt, and she was the thing that he got in return, he'd take it. He'd take it every day.

"As long as you like it. That's all that matters."

"Is it?"

"It matters a hell of a lot." He let his hand drift over her shoulder, down her arm. Over her bare skin. "Tell me this. Really, why didn't you think much about sex?"

"You can't imagine not thinking about sex?"

"Not really."

"Well, that makes it feel like it's more special for me than it is for you." She looked insecure.

He gripped her chin and tilted her face so that she was looking up at him. "No. Don't think that. I used sex as a method of blocking out the things that hurt me. I used it to fill this gaping hole in my soul." This was about as deep as he got. About the darkest he went. He felt… Dammit, he just felt a whole lot of things.

"It was so dark," he said. "For a while I could feel good. Feeling good seemed like a gift. So I used it. But I used it the way people use drugs. It wasn't to strengthen anything in me. It wasn't anything good. Anything that fixed the broken places in me. It just distracted me for a while. Made it so I didn't think so much about it. I had a sex drive, but it wasn't about anybody."

He cleared his throat. "Until you. You're the only woman that's ever mattered. It's about *you*. It's not about sex. And that's different."

She was silent for a moment. "I suppose it's a bit of the same thing for me. It was to protect myself. I felt like it would be easy… On some level, to want you. Because you were beautiful. And so I just…let all your glory blur out around the edges."

He snorted. "My *glory*?"

"You're beautiful. You know that. You have to."

"It doesn't mean anything, though. I've always felt a little bit like a snake. They flash their shiny scales, but they're not up to any good, are they? Their looks are just a trap."

"You're not a trap," she said. "Or a snake."

"I might be a little bit. Remember. Apples. Original sin."

"That isn't what I mean," she said, hitting his shoulder.

He grabbed her wrist and bit her fingertips. "You hit me a lot, Charity."

"Sorry. I…when I think about your past I realize that's not an okay thing for me to do."

"*No.* I like it. Because you know that I can handle it. Because you know you don't mean to hurt me. It's all touch, and from you, that's only a good thing."

"We're married," she said.

"We are."

"It won't really be different."

He stared at her, and he didn't quite know what to say. "I don't know. Maybe not. I expect… Well, hell. I kind of expect it *could* be. What do you think?"

"Change scares me so much. Because there's been so much of it. I don't know. I had so much of my life be the same."

"How did you handle college?"

"Oh. Well."

"Specifically, how did you make it out of college as innocent as you are?" he pressed.

"Well, I hung out with girls who mostly wore turtlenecks and cross necklaces."

He laughed. A great guffaw that shook the bed. "Okay. Fair enough."

"Also, again, I'm just very good at ignoring things that I don't want to deal with."

"I remember you were lonely. I remember you calling home and talking to me. I was afraid, you know. That you were going to go there and discover the joy of sex without me."

"You already knew about the joy of sex."

"You know what I mean, young lady."

"Fine. I do. I *didn't*, though."

"No. Anyway, you did something worse. You came back with the guy that you got engaged to. Man, I was pissed about that."

"You were?"

He let out a hard breath. "Yes. I was."

"So you were attracted to me, when we first met."

He nodded slowly. "I told you. I worked myself into a little bit of a fixation and decided that those fantasies were of a perverse nature, and I couldn't do that to you. So there's that. But I still felt possessive of you. Protective." She didn't know. Not really. And he didn't want her to. He wanted to keep on protecting her, while having her at the same time. "I wasn't happy when you went away to college, like I said. I was glad you kept on calling me. I was mad you didn't tell me about Byron. Not until you came back. Why didn't you tell me?"

"I don't know. It didn't feel right. It felt like he might come between us. He didn't. Because we had a long-distance relationship. But it felt… In the end, the thing that felt the most wrong was that I could not have another man in my life that mattered more than you. I think that's when I knew."

"Knew what?"

"That I love you."

"I really love hearing that."

He leaned back against his pillow and closed his eyes. His brothers had probably said it to him. Hell, Gus had said it at the wedding. But… He didn't take the love of another person for granted. Not ever. You couldn't. Not when you had parents who you should be able to expect love from, but didn't get it.

That was the thing. There wasn't a single thing in Lachlan McCloud's life that he took for granted. Least of all Charity, and her caring about him.

"I'm glad." She reached out and touched his face. And he put his hand over hers. She was never going to say good night to him and go home again. Because this was her home. Her place was with him. And he was… He was pretty damn thrilled with that.

Right now it felt like it might work. As long as he did what he'd done with her from the beginning.

As long as he kept the right boundaries in place.

# CHAPTER TWENTY-ONE

SHE WOKE UP the next morning and looked at the ring on her finger. Then got up, and decided to make some breakfast.

Lachlan wasn't in bed, but she assumed that he was out working on the ranch.

She shot him a text and asked him if he was coming back for breakfast, but she didn't hear anything.

So she just made herself some eggs and got ready to go to work.

She went to Ed Forsyth's and checked in on his horse. To her annoyance, he was nicer to her. She had to wonder if that was Lachlan's influence. Either the talking-to he had given the man, or the fact that she was now his *wife*.

She supposed she shouldn't be defensive about that. That people might treat her a certain way because she had married Lachlan. Or because she was married at all.

But she did resent the fact that attachment to a man, whether it be her father or her husband, seemed to affect the way that some people treated her.

It was difficult not to let it feel insulting.

She supposed because it *was* insulting. But she did the work anyway, and she did the best job she could, because if there was one arena it wasn't worth being

petty in, it was most definitely her job. Where her pa-
tients didn't have anything to do with the cruddy behavior of their owners. It wasn't their fault.

By the time she got back home it was getting dark,
and she was exhausted. Lachlan's truck was in the
driveway, and all the lights in the house were on.

She walked in and he smiled. "How was your day?"

"It was good. Good. I guess maybe we are a little
bit unexciting considering we worked the day after we
got married."

"I don't know. I think we're pretty exciting."

Silence stretched between them.

She wasn't quite sure why she felt…like there was
more. Especially after last night.

What he'd said to her had been deep. Honest.

But she had the sense that there were walls all
around his heart still and she didn't quite know why.

It made her feel this need to do…something. He was
trying. She knew that.

He'd taught her so much about life. Sarcasm and
swearing and sex.

She wanted to find a way to lead him here, but she
didn't know how. She wanted to give to him the way
he had to her.

This didn't quite feel like their friendship, but it
didn't quite feel like… Like what she was looking for,
either. Last night she said again that she loved him. He
hadn't said it back. But he had said it before.

He'd said that he did.

But she was still turning over the concept. Because
she had loved him all her life. At least, all her life that
she'd known him, and that was real. But it had changed.

It wasn't just sex. Wasn't just saying vows to him.

There was something that grabbed hold of the deep part of her soul and took anchor there.

It had happened before they'd ever kissed. There was something about Lachlan McCloud that held her to the earth.

Something about him that made her a better version of herself, and that she thought might be where love met *in* love. Plus, there were butterflies.

And sex, of course.

But she felt like there was more. She wondered what. Because past the barriers of love, sex and marriage, what else was there?

*Intimacy.*

She didn't even know what that meant.

Not functionally.

"Tell me about your thirteenth birthday," she said, sitting down at the table.

He looked over at her, his expression blank. "Why?"

"Let's pretend we're on a date. Or maybe let's really be on one. Because all we ever did was pretend to date, and then we got married."

"I think you and I have been dating for a long time."

"Not really," she said. "We met, and we got to know each other. We meshed into each other's lives. The first day that I met you, you had been beaten up by your father. But you didn't tell me that for a while. It was something I kind of figured out. Didn't I? I figured out because you made some comments, and my dad had heard rumors about him. Finally, I asked you. But we haven't done a lot of actual getting to know each other. We just sort of…formed a friendship. Then we lived so many years of each other's lives just being together, that we didn't ask each other these kinds of questions.

Kinds of questions we would've asked if we'd gone on a date. So I want to know. What happened on your thirteenth birthday?"

"You already know I didn't get birthday parties. So it's a shitty question. And a leading one."

She bit her lip. "Okay. Sorry. I'm hungry."

"I can open up a big can of stew?"

"Sure." She felt like he was being deliberately difficult and she wasn't really sure why. It was those walls.

"Canned stew all around."

He got up. Went over to the cupboard and opened it up, pulled out a big black label can of what she knew to be very cheap stew.

"I'll put it on the stovetop."

She sat there staring at him, feeling like this was a very surreal version of that magical night when they'd gone out to the restaurant. But instead of a gourmet meal, it was stew, a bit of resentment and a whole lot of uncertainty on her part.

She had married the man. This should all be less confusing. Not *more* confusing.

"Are there at least corn chips?" she asked.

He grimaced. "Corn chips."

"Yes," she said.

*"Saltines,"* he said.

"Oh," she said.

"Saltines for chili and stew," he said.

She pulled a face. "Corn chips for both."

"I should've asked you about this before we got married," he muttered. "The ketchup eggs were a red flag and I ignored them."

He dumped the big, block-shaped bit of stew out

into the pan and started to smash it down with a big wooden spoon.

Then he took a box of saltines and a bag of corn chips out of another cupboard and dumped them on the table between them.

He started to stir the stew, adding a bit of water to the condensed mixture.

It only took a few minutes, and he had served up a couple bowls of steaming hot... Well, it reminded her a little bit of puppy chow. But she wasn't going to complain. It actually smelled decent, anyway.

And he was being scratchy but it was because...

She couldn't figure out why.

She had to...lead by example, she supposed. Because she didn't know why this was hard for him, but she knew it was. And that was all that mattered.

"On my thirteenth birthday," she said, "I started my period. And I was really embarrassed. I didn't want to tell my dad. He had made me a cake and got me a stuffed animal and I thought it was really sad, because it was all stuff that looked like it was for a little girl, and I felt like maybe I was betraying him by growing up. But he was very matter-of-fact about it all. He said it was just biology, and I didn't have anything to be embarrassed about. He also didn't know how to tell me how to use pads. He ended up looking everything up on the internet. What to buy and all of that. He took me over to Mapleton, and we went to the grocery store and bought about five different types. Since he said apparently a lot of it came down to preference. Then we went to get pizza and I wanted to cry, and I didn't know why. I wondered about my mom, and how it would've been different if she were there. I've always done my best not to wonder about her, but it really is hard."

"Wow," he said. "That's pretty intense."

"Now tell me about yours."

"Gus stole a pie cooling on the windowsill at Sullivan's Point. I'm not kidding. He took it out to the woods, where we used to play. We built forts. We ate the pie out of the tin with plastic forks that he lifted from John's. He paid it back later. When he actually started making his own money. He kept a running tally of all the things that us boys used to take. So that we could pay them back someday. We were desperate sometimes."

His throat bobbed up and down. "John knew. You know. He told Gus that later. He said…that we didn't owe him anything. That he knew that our parents didn't take care of us. And he knew that we only took things when we were desperate. We weren't in there stealing beer or anything like that. Not causing trouble like some of the local kids did. No. We were in there taking food, or bait. Little things for each other. Forks, so we could eat a pie. And you know what I liked about my thirteenth birthday? There was only five years left of being a kid. I hated being a kid. It wasn't fun. You see all this shit in movies. About the magic of childhood. And about how when you grow up you quit believing. I believe in more miraculous things now that I'm an adult. When I was a kid, I didn't believe in anything. How could I? I only believed in what I could see. What I can feel. I knew what it felt like to take a punch from a grown man. I knew that I could see my own blood running down my face. I knew what it tasted like. All metallic can like shame. So yeah, thirteen marked getting closer. Freedom. To the end of it all.

"But then Gus ended it. Gus ended it good. He just beat the shit out of him. Not very many people know what happened. But I do. Gus finally had enough, and he told him to leave. And when he said he didn't have to go, Gus beat him within an inch of his life. I saw it."

"You did?"

"I watched. Hidden. And it felt so good. It felt so good to watch him take hits, like he'd been dishing out all of our lives. It turned out I didn't have to wait till I was eighteen to be rid of him. We got the ranch. We weren't the ones that had to go. The monster had to go. That was a whole thing. A whole hell of a thing. I just… Yeah."

"What about your sixteenth birthday?"

"We didn't steal pie. But I seem to recall going to the woods and meeting a beautiful girl. I seem to recall that she stitched me up."

"He hit you on your birthday?"

"Yes. Because he didn't care. I bet he didn't know. He would've liked to have known, but he didn't know. He didn't care. But you did. And that made all the difference in the world. It always has to me."

"You were there for my sixteenth birthday," she said. "Remember. Dad made a chocolate cake, and he got me a stuffed animal. Just like he always did. And you were there. And I felt like a princess. I think because of you."

"There. How's that for conversation?"

"Pretty good."

The momentary tension between them eased. And she didn't mind that it was a date with cheap stew rather than a fancy gourmet dinner. It didn't really seem to matter.

"You've never been tempted to get in touch with your mother?"

Charity shook her head. "I don't know where she is. And you know she'll never use one of those DNA sites, not if she doesn't want me to find her."

"Fair point."

"She's the woman who gave birth to me. She isn't my mother. I'm not saying that to be cruel. But she made the choice to not have to carry that. And I can't... I can't make a relationship out of something just because of genetics. My dad was the one that was there for me. He's the one that raised me. He's the important person in my life. Yeah, it's kind of tempting...to search around wildly for her now that he's gone, but she's not a replacement for him. She couldn't be. He... Well, he bought me stuffed animals every year for my birthday like I was still a kid. And he bought me pads. With or without wings. And bras. With and without underwire. Sports bras, front clip, back hook. Because it came down to preference, and he couldn't dictate what mine would be, of course. He was practical like that. He's the one who raised me. He was both. Because he had to be. Except he didn't have to be either. He didn't have to keep me. He didn't have to want me. He didn't have to raise me. And he did."

"It must be nice," Lachlan said.

"It is. I'm grateful for him, and I don't take it for granted. Especially given what I know about your life. Especially."

"Always good to be the cautionary tale," he said.

"You're not really a cautionary tale."

"Kind of."

By the time they finished their bowl of stew, she did feel like maybe they had gotten a little bit closer to each other. Like maybe they were closer to that all-elusive concept of intimacy.

They did the dishes together. Then it wasn't time to go home, because she was home. So he took her to bed, and he made her feel beautiful.

He wasn't ready for more.

She was, though.

But if she was asked to write a list of what *more* was, she wouldn't have been able to say. It was a feeling. Just a feeling.

She was going to have to find a way to show him the feeling.

## CHAPTER TWENTY-TWO

IT WAS LACHLAN'S BIRTHDAY, and it seemed like no one had planned anything. Over the years he had always told her that he did birthday celebrations with his family. She had accepted that. For all these years. Now she wondered if he just deliberately avoided birthdays.

She was starting to realize he *never* slept with her. It was adding to all her uncertainty. She'd been so sure she knew him. Everything about him.

Making love with him should have shown her that… no, she didn't.

She knew him, but not what kind of lover he was. That was the tip of a very large iceberg of all she didn't know, and she was overwhelmed with it now.

He wasn't sleeping with her on purpose. He never did. Not the whole night. She'd thought he was just getting up early, but she wasn't sure he ever really slept with her at all. It hurt her. She was bothered by the fact that there seemed to be a deliberate distance between the two of them, but that awful story about what his father had done to him had begun to solidify her understanding of him in ways that she hadn't understood him before.

It was a strange thing, this marriage business. But she had never known how he slept or didn't sleep before. His sleep was always interrupted. She hadn't realized that. He didn't like birthdays. She hadn't realized that, either.

She wanted to give him a party. And while she was tempted to rope the whole family and to make something spectacular out of it, she had a feeling that he wasn't quite there yet. She got home early and started the process of baking a cake. She had gone to the outdoor store over in Mapleton when she had been there for an appointment and had gotten him a couple of things. Some new work gloves, because she had noticed that his were worn. A new belt, simply because she had liked the look of it, and the cowboy hat, for the same reason.

A nice mix of practical and something that she would just enjoy. And she hoped he would, too.

She was rudimentary in her cake-decorating skills, but she did her very best to pipe Happy Birthday Lachlan onto the top of the cake, and she had gotten candles so she was committed to putting thirty-two on the top of the cake, which was no mean feat, but she managed to position them all around the letters. When she heard his truck pull up, she stood quickly in front of the cake so that he couldn't see it when he came in.

"Hey," he said.

"Hey," she responded. "Why don't you wash up for supper?"

"You cooked for me," he said.

"I did," she said, beaming. She made a roast. Potatoes and carrots, everything that she knew he liked. Because it was his birthday.

He went into the bathroom, and while he was in there she quickly lit the candles. They would have dinner first, but she wanted to surprise him with the lit-up cake.

And when he came out of the bathroom, she held it out. "Happy birthday."

His face cycled through several extreme emotions all at once, and she suddenly felt like... Like maybe she had gotten it wrong.

But she wanted to make a new memory. With the two of them. That was the point of this marriage. Wasn't it? That was the point of them.

"Thanks," he said, his face looking like it was made of stone.

"Lachlan, I just wanted..."

"I get it. I told you about all the times I didn't have a birthday party. You felt bad for me."

"I understand that it's a little bit of a thing..."

"Charity... It's not your fault. None of this is your fault. It's just I'm... I don't like birthdays."

He looked tortured.

"I'm so sorry. I..."

"No," he said. "It's not a big deal."

She watched him put a lid down on all his emotions. She knew now that this was what he did. If stuff came up, and it was hard or heavy, he found a way to dampen it. Mute it. But he never felt it. Not all the way. Maybe that was why he had wanted a marriage like theirs. Friendship. Because it was a lot like love, but dampened.

He'd said that he loved her, but it wasn't...

It wasn't the same as the way she loved him. Because she didn't know how to dampen it. She didn't know how to soften it. She didn't know how to do anything but feel it. And it was such a whole mess, she just had no idea what she was supposed to do with it.

She loved him. She'd known him half of her life.

She didn't know him.

She'd made a mistake because she needed to get to know these parts of him better.

"I'm sorry."

"No. Don't be sorry." He leaned in and blew the candles out. "Happy birthday to me. When I tell the story later I'll have one for my thirty-third."

"Yeah."

She set the cake down on the counter. They both sat down at the table, and she realized she hadn't gotten the food. She got back up and grabbed plates and the roast pan and everything. She was blinking back tears. She felt just…so silly.

"Hey," he said, grabbing her wrist and looking at her. "You didn't do anything wrong."

Except she had. She had done something wrong, or maybe it was just not enough. She didn't know how to fix what they were. She was starting to love him in a way that felt uncontainable. It didn't feel like friendship with sex layered over the top of it. She wanted all these things that he kept hidden away. And she didn't know how to ask for them. She was just…scared of it.

Scared to dig deeper. Scared to be denied.

How could you ask for something you didn't have words for?

Scared of being lonely for the rest of her life while living with her best friend. What was that all about? What was this?

They ate dinner in relative silence.

"I'd love a slice of cake," he said when he was finished.

But his face was grim almost the whole time he ate, and he forced a smile. "Great. Thank you."

"I got you some presents."

He made a show of opening them, but she could see that he never quite got his facade back into place. She wondered how often that carefree persona was just that. A facade. She had no real way of knowing. Because she hadn't been so conscious of it before they had gotten married.

She hadn't been aware of it at all.

"Thanks, Doc," he said, gesturing to all the stuff. "I can honestly tell you it was the best damn birthday I've ever had."

She didn't know how to take that heaviness out of his eyes. How to ease up the corner of his mouth. She knew how to make love to him, though. So she took his hand and drew him up out of the chair. Kissed him. Then led him back to the bedroom.

Because in the absence of everything else, they had this. That, at least, she understood.

"I'm sorry," she said, sounding choked. "I'm sorry that I did that. The birthday party. I didn't know. I thought you just hadn't gotten birthdays. I didn't realize..."

"It's not your fault," he said, the words scraping his throat raw. "It isn't. None of this bullshit is your fault, Charity. But... You have to... There are lines that you can't cross, okay?"

Even in the dim light of the room, he could see how sad that made her.

"What if I don't want lines?"

"I don't know any other way to be. Anyway. You've got your own. We all do. It's fine."

"I don't want to have any."

He said nothing, not for a long time, and the pain that stretched between them was both shared and all their own. She didn't know what to do with it. Didn't know how to find a way to what she wanted. If she couldn't find it, how could she help him?

It just hurt. Loving him like she did. Seeing him hurt. Seeing him close himself off.

"Go back to sleep," he said.

"You won't come to bed."

"Not just yet."

## CHAPTER TWENTY-THREE

HE'D NEVER SPENT the night with anyone before. Hazard of his lifestyle. He had never had a romantic relationship, and he always split once the sex had ended.

He hadn't realized it would be a thing.

But it was. Whenever he thought of sleeping beside Charity he...couldn't.

He controlled himself, all during the day. He kept his walls up. But thinking about holding her while she slept, sleeping next to her...

He felt like it was a step too far down a road he wouldn't be able to come back from. Marrying her might have been the first step. But he was with her now.

He could feel it changing him.

He'd cared for her for years. And it had been good. Easy. Why wasn't it like that now?

She'd gone to bed, but he could tell that she was unhappy. And of all the things he hated the most about his decisions over the past couple of months, the fact that he made Charity Wyatt unhappy was the biggest one.

*This was why you were never supposed to touch her, dumbass.*

Because he needed this. A carefully controlled, friendship kind of marriage. And he could see her beginning to be hungry for something else.

It was something that he simply couldn't risk.

It was his birthday anyway.

The hours blurred together in an alcohol haze, and he didn't realize it was past two until Charity came out.

"Lachlan?"

He looked up and saw her standing in the doorway. Her arms were wrapped tightly around herself, and she looked so sad.

Why the hell was she sad?

The angry thought came up from nowhere and shocked him, but that didn't banish it.

It was his damn birthday and he had every right to be sad about birthdays.

Angry.

"You know what birthday you've never asked me about?" he asked.

"What?" she asked, her voice hoarse.

"My ninth birthday." He poured himself more whiskey. "You're so obsessed with the damn birthdays, you should know about that one."

"What happened on your ninth birthday?" she asked.

"On my ninth birthday, my mom insisted on giving me a party. The trouble was my dad wanted her attention. She had baked me a cake and done decorations and she hadn't... I don't know. She hadn't done something he wanted. He came in and he picked up the cake and dumped it on the ground. Then he grabbed me by the back of the shirt and dragged me outside. He had a wooden switch that he used to spank us. And when he got tired of using that on me, he went ahead and used his hands. All the way up and down my back. He punished me. Because she wanted my attention. He punished me, because she cared about me. Because that was how they were."

"Lachlan…"

He shook his head and took a sip of the drink in front of him.

"There's no use pitying me about it. It just is what it is." He felt a blackness spread through him. "And then you know a few months later it was Christmas. And then she left."

"You poor boys."

"Yeah. Poor boys. But that's just the way of it."

"But it was wrong."

"Sure it was. Sure it was wrong. But…it happened. So what can you do?"

There was no use crying over it. Not any of it. So he wouldn't. He never had. He never did. He wouldn't start now.

"He just got worse and worse, you know. He couldn't stand losing her. It made him crazy. It made him—" He looked up at Charity and the feeling of possessiveness that gripped him was near paralyzing. "Go back to bed."

"No," she said. "I'm not going away. What did your dad do? What happened?"

"No," he said. "I don't… I don't want to talk about it."

"Lachlan…"

"I don't want to talk about it, Charity. I've known you a hell of a long time, and we never talked about this shit. I'm sitting here drinking because of your damn birthday party. Because of all this openness you claim to want." That wasn't fair. He had these often enough without ever talking about his father, and blaming her was petty in the extreme. But he didn't want to tell her.

He didn't want to expose the poison that had run through his father's veins. A poison he'd spent all his life being afraid was in him, too. He had his wedding, and he had changed his life and he was supposed to be fixed. It was just supposed to be fixed.

"Lachlan," she said softly. "You can talk to me. I want to know everything about you…"

"That's not how it works. You didn't know it before. It's not… It doesn't matter. This isn't a part of us. You understand? It never has been."

"But…"

"No," he said.

"I want to help you."

"You can't, Doc. Not with this."

Because when he looked at Charity he felt a dark, spiraling need to pull her to him. Hold her to him forever. It was the thing that compelled him when they were in bed together. The thing that made him get out of that bed every night and sleep on the couch.

The dark thing he'd been sure banishing Byron would get rid of.

It made him feel ashamed. Made him feel like he was…

Like he was his father.

He suddenly saw the wedding in a whole new light.

Had he been happy because it felt normal?

Or happy because she was bound to him.

"Lachlan, I don't understand…"

"Then you're not going to understand."

"Maybe we should have set some boundaries before we actually did this marriage thing. Because I don't understand how parts of you can still be off-limits to me after I have…put my mouth on almost every single place on your body."

"That's sex," he said.

"You know… You're right. It's sex. I thought that it changed things. I thought that it really changed them. That it changed you and me. But it didn't. Not really. We're friends, and we have sex. We're friends, and we said the marriage vows to each other. But if you won't share this with me…then what are we?"

"Go to bed."

"Do you love me, Lachlan?"

"I love you more than I've ever loved anybody else."

And hell if he knew what that meant. Hell if he did. If it was a lot, or if it was barely a thimbleful of what a normal person could feel.

He just didn't know.

## CHAPTER TWENTY-FOUR

CHARITY HAD GONE back to bed alone. Lachlan had never come back to bed, and then he was gone when she got up.

She'd wanted to do something nice for him by giving him the birthday party. She'd had no idea he had that much trauma associated with it all.

She did just always think they knew each other. Now she felt suddenly like she married not her best friend, but a stranger.

Marriage was hard, and it had only been two days.

They were invited to family dinner that night, and she supposed neither of them felt there was really a way they could say no, in spite of the fact that they were both still twitchy with each other.

It was at Gus's house, and Gus, Elizabeth and Brody were there, along with Alaina, of course.

Charity took solace in spending time holding Gus and Alaina's baby, Cameron, because that was at least a bright spot in the middle of all this. They ate, and everything was fine. But…the frost between her and Lachlan just wouldn't fade.

After dinner Gus took his brothers out to the shop to show them something, and that left Alaina, Elizabeth and Charity in the kitchen.

"So how are things?" Elizabeth asked, smiling.

"Um…difficult?"

"Really?" Alaina asked.

She shouldn't have said that. She shouldn't have said anything about the situation with her husband. It wasn't loyal. Back when she and Lachlan had been *just friends* she never would've done that. But back when they had been *just friends* he would've been the one she would've gone to when she was upset, and now he was the one that had upset her, so what was she supposed to do? That made things a whole lot more complicated, and she didn't really know how to navigate them.

"But you two are best friends," Alaina said. "I would've thought that the adjustment for you guys was easier than it was for just about anybody. I mean, you know each other so well. Gus and I didn't know each other at all when we got married."

"I know that," Charity said. "I thought the same thing. Foolishly, it turns out. That it would just be the same relationship that we had before, except that we lived together and slept together and…" She felt her cheeks getting warm.

"But it isn't the same," Alaina said, gently.

"No," she said. "It's not. Not at all."

"Well, what's different?"

"I want… I want to *know* him. In a way that I didn't before. And there are things that he doesn't want to tell me."

*"Men,"* Elizabeth said. "They really don't like the emotion part of all this."

"Even Brody?"

*"Especially Brody,"* Elizabeth said. "He's got such an easy facade, you would think that he's this easygoing guy, but he is one hundred percent not."

Alaina's expression turned to one of barely suppressed amusement. "It won't surprise you at all to learn that Gus is extremely difficult, and it is nearly impossible to get down to the bottom of his feelings."

"That doesn't surprise me at all," Charity said. "Gus doesn't seem forthcoming on that subject."

"No," Alaina said. "He's learning. But it isn't exactly second nature for him. You know, in that he would definitely rather eat a handful of bees than actually tell me about his innermost heart."

"I just thought that I *knew* Lachlan's. But I don't think I do. And that's made me feel…a little bit wobbly."

"Understandable."

"It's understandable, I guess, but I don't know what to do about it. And he outright refused to tell me what was going on with him last night."

"What happened?" Alaina asked.

Charity shook her head and looked down at the baby. "I can't say. I mean, I could. It's his secret, though. He doesn't even want to talk to me about it. So I can't talk to anyone else about it."

"I understand that," Elizabeth said softly. "But if there's anything we can do to help…"

"I know. I know you want to help. I wish I knew how to ask for help. I wish I knew better. I wish I knew how to be what he needed. I did when I was his friend. But now I'm his wife, and I feel like I need to give him more, in the same way that I feel I need to get more. I don't really know what to do about this. It's just scary. I don't think that I can be what he needs me to be. And what if I can't?"

"I don't think he would've married you if he didn't think that you could be that thing. I mean it. Not that you have to be everything to him. He's gonna have to be some things, too." Alaina said that with deep ferocity. "He's the one that wanted to get married so badly, badly enough that he was sniffing around my sister. He really should be more open. To you. To everything."

"Well, I think he wanted to be. I just think that he's having difficulty with it."

"Understandable. But he has to get it together."

"Seriously. He needs to get it together," Elizabeth said.

"I appreciate that. But I wonder if there are some things I need to get together," Charity said.

"In what way?"

"I just wonder. I wonder what more there is to all this."

"I guess it must be difficult. To figure out what changes when you go from a relationship as deep as yours to one that's different. Still deep, but very different," Elizabeth said.

"Maybe the mistake is just thinking it's the same. People always say that—I married my best friend. But they mean something more. Something different."

"Yeah. They do," Elizabeth said. "I've been married twice. I thought I was in love with my first husband. I thought we were friends. I thought it was everything. But I realized that I was contorting myself to be something that *he* wanted me to be, and I wasn't happy. I was never going to be. I didn't realize that until a lot later. Till I was with Brody, and it was different. I couldn't breathe with my first husband, and I couldn't just be myself."

"I can be myself with Lachlan. I've always been able to be."

"Your whole self? Because you guys didn't start sleeping together until recently. That's another dimension of who you are. Desire. Now you guys have all that together. I know it's physical, but it's more than that. It's spiritual."

"Well, you're right about that."

"So now there's so much that he knows about you that he didn't before. And you about him."

She nodded. She felt a little bit embarrassed by the direction of the conversation, but she also knew that it was true.

It gave her a new perspective.

"But it isn't making him want to tell me about his past."

"Maybe not. But maybe there's a way for you to push down his walls by breaking down more of yours."

"I don't know that I have any more to break down. I've already done more and been more with him than I ever have another human being. I'm afraid that anything else might break me apart."

"If there's one thing I learned," Alaina said softly, "it's that there are times when love does break you apart a little bit. Oh, it shouldn't be like that always. And they need to break apart for you, too. It can't be in the sacrifice on one side. But it can't be tit-for-tat, either. You can't keep score. And you have to be willing to go through the hard things to get where you need to be. Gus and I had a very difficult time. He married me with this idea that he wanted to protect me, but in the end, it turned out that he loved me, but that didn't actually make things easier. I do wonder a bit if that's what's happening with Lachlan. Gus was afraid to love me."

"Did he tell you that he loved you?"

She shook her head. "No. It took him a long time to say the words. Even when he almost lost me, he had a hard time actually saying the words."

"Well, Lachlan has told me that he loves me."

"That's good," she said. "But I do still wonder if he's maybe protecting something inside of himself, and he doesn't even realize it."

"Definitely possible."

"I just think this is all complicated for them. Because of what they went through growing up. I don't think that love is a simple, happy thing that they can simply look forward to. I think it cuts them really deep. And I think the fear of losing it is only equal to the fear of having it."

"*That* I think is true."

"How do I reach him?"

"Sex," Alaina and Elizabeth said at the same time.

"We have that. All the time." Her cheeks went pink.

"I mean, good for you. But I just wonder…"

She didn't have a whole lot of inhibition when it came to him. But she had an idea. Suddenly. She knew what she wanted.

"Thank you," she said.

She stroked the baby's velvety head, and she felt a deep longing well up inside her. She needed to fix this. To the best of her ability, she needed to fix this.

Because she wanted what Alaina and Elizabeth had. And she could see easily that she and Lachlan weren't there yet.

Gus didn't have secrets from Alaina. Brody knew Elizabeth.

They needed to know each other.

It was more than asking about birthday parties, though that was a start. She wasn't wrong totally about the way that she needed to know him.

But it was also more. More complicated. "I think I have an idea."

It would require breaking through the thought, even though he didn't deserve it. It would require changing things between them even though he hadn't asked her to.

She just had to. Because it was the right thing to do. She couldn't wait.

Because it wasn't about keeping score. That resonated with her. That meant something. She was going to cling to that. Remember it.

"I never saw a marriage," she said. "I just have no idea at all what I'm doing."

"I saw a few," Elizabeth said. "I grew up in foster care. I saw good marriages, okay marriages, bad ones, great ones. I had the opportunity to see the way that a lot of people were with each other, but I didn't necessarily learn from it. Not consciously. But it's something that I think about now."

"Wow," Charity said. "I would never have guessed that you grew up in foster care."

"It looks a lot of different ways," Elizabeth said. "I was very lucky. I was with some really good families. They treated me well. It helped me feel like I had a concept of family. I felt that I got a lot of concepts of family. That gave me something kind of special and unique."

"I saw a marriage that imploded," Alaina said. "But it was happy for a long time before. It gave me a lot of anxiety when it came to love and relationships. And you know, I chose badly with the first guy I hopped into bed with. But Gus has shown me every day what love looks like. He always loved me. That's the thing. He was good at doing the things to *show* me that. But he wasn't good at opening himself up in ways that would let me feel the *closeness*. In ways that would let me feel that love. I think that's maybe what's going on with Lachlan. It's clear that he loves you. I would've said that years ago. Just as a casual observer of your relationship. I don't think that's the problem. But love is action. And there are a lot of ways to act it out. There are a lot of ways to feel close to someone. And when one is missing…it doesn't feel right."

She nodded slowly. Lachlan had always been there for her; it wasn't that she felt insecure, not anything like that. It was just that she wanted more from their relationship than feeling like she was living with a stranger.

She had lived a quiet life.

And she had loved her dad. But she realized, suddenly, just sitting there, that she had always felt a little bit timid. To be louder than he was. To be something different than he was.

Because he had sacrificed to raise her, she had felt like she owed him something. So she had always acted with a certain amount of caution.

She didn't want to be cautious. Not anymore. This whole thing with Lachlan had been a process of stripping away, finding her boldness. Finding who she was. Absolutely and completely. She had to keep going. No matter what that looked like. No matter what that meant.

LACHLAN DIDN'T TALK to his brothers about the state of things. He told them everything was great and drank three extra beers, and when he and Charity went home, he made sure to fall asleep immediately.

He wasn't actually asleep. He could hear her tossing and turning next to him; could tell that she was upset that they hadn't had sex, because it was really the first time since they'd started cohabitating together that they'd skipped a night.

Of course, they were married, so skipping nights would eventually become normal…he assumed. He never had a relationship before. So there was really nothing to compare it to. He imagined stretches like this were normal enough, also. Times when you were just kind of mad at each other.

He realized he didn't actually have the right to be mad at her.

He wasn't even sure she was mad at him. She was hurt. And he was the one being kind of petulant.

But oh, well.

His sleep was bad, and he avoided Charity the next morning by getting up at 5:30 and heading out to work as soon as possible.

He was out on the range, repairing fences with Gus and Brody, when he got the text.

I need you.

Where are you at?

The woods.

A twinge of fear spiked in his chest. Why was she in the woods, and why did she need help?

Where are you?

I told you. You know where I am. Our spot.

The light was pale, but a little bit more effective than it had been. They were advancing through May now, and it was beginning to warm up, if slowly. Some years May was hot as summer, others winter hung out. You got a lot of sunny days, and then the sun would disappear for a while. Or you'd get a bright, clear day that was still so damned cold it seemed like an unfair tease.

Yeah. He was accustomed enough to that.

But today was actually beautiful, and he looked across the green field, illuminated by the sun, the purple flowers starting to bloom. And some of the fog of last night's memories faded a bit.

"Charity needs something," he said.

"Heh," Brody said.

"Kiss my ass," Lachlan said.

Especially after the other night, he was certain that Charity didn't want to *Heh*.

But he was headed over to find her regardless.

He decided to walk, because his truck wasn't around, and he knew exactly where she meant. She meant their spot.

Their spot.

He walked into the woods and followed the path that led from McCloud's Landing down to Charity's old place. No one was renting it still, so there was no one around in the area. It was isolated.

You okay? He posed the question quickly and texted, because he was beginning to get a little bit worried.

Just fine.

He kept on walking, looking around, the sunlight through the trees reminding him of the fairyland, which was an odd thing, because he walked through this place all the time, so getting weirdly sentimental about it was kind of an odd thing to do.

He was caught between two worlds. The one where he had married Charity, and she was his wife, and the one where that darker part of him pressed down on him. He didn't like that it had spilled over onto her; he didn't like that she knew about it.

He should apologize to her. Flat out. Just tell her that they needed to forget that it happened. That would be the best thing to do.

Suddenly, he came to that spot. The sun shone across the pathway, around the big tree where he had first seen her. All those years ago. And then suddenly, she was there. Her blond hair was loose, and she was wearing a floral dress, demure as ever, demure as she had once been.

"What are you doing?"

"I was thinking. I was thinking that I can't demand total honesty from you unless I give you total honesty back." He didn't like that. He didn't want it. Because it would compromise what he was working to protect. But she went on anyway. "All of me. I've been working on it. But in some ways I didn't even know what that was. I'm still figuring out who I am, Lachlan. Because for so many years I just… My dad was such a good dad, so when I say this I don't want you to think that I'm saying he wasn't. I just think that even the best of parents give us issues. He loved me. He sacrificed for me. And I internalized that. I wanted to be like him. Whether I actually was like him or not. Does that make sense?"

Yes, it did. Because he knew the flipside of that.

He wanted to be nothing like his dad, even though he knew that he might be.

So yeah. He understood.

"There are a lot of reasons that I suppress certain parts of myself. To not get hurt is really the primary one. But some of that was to not hurt Dad, to not get hurt by him, to not have him be disappointed in me in any way. Some of it was to avoid having a crush on you that was impossible, believe me. But even down to choosing Byron. I wanted Dad to be proud of the man that I chose. So I chose one that was like him. That was staid and steady, but I realize that that wasn't all there was to my dad. He was a whole person. He had a whole life. A relationship with my mother. And if he hadn't, then I wouldn't even exist. So the idea that he somehow... I didn't really ever want to think about it. But of course he had a sex life. As horrifying as I find that. What he chose to do or not do with that once he had me is another story entirely. But he was a real person. With all those aspects to him. Why I thought I wasn't allowed to be, I don't know. I just wanted to be perfect. I wanted to be the girl that he got stuffed animals for. I wanted to be easy. I wanted to be something he understood, because I knew that he had difficulty with people."

"You're everything," Lachlan said. Before he could even think about what it meant. "And you can be anything."

"You make me feel that way. I don't need to be the kind of good that I always thought I had to be. I don't need to be embarrassed for wanting to do this."

She reached behind her and pulled down the zipper

on her dress, letting it drop there in the woods. Leaving her body exposed to him, under that golden sun.

She had on a white bra and a pair of white cotton panties, and a less provocative set of underwear didn't exist, but it fired his blood like nobody's business.

He didn't deserve to touch her. He was supposed to protect her. From the world, from himself. But he wanted to touch her all the same. And there she was, offering herself to him. Not in exchange for anything. Not in exchange for a resolution to their fight. For a resolution to the things that he said he wouldn't tell her. It wasn't a trade. It was just a gift. It was so far beyond anything he had ever dared hope for he didn't quite know what to do with it.

She was so beautiful and lovely and giving, his Charity. He didn't deserve her.

He didn't deserve her, and that made this moment feel fraught. Because he wanted to receive it with fully open arms. Wanted to receive it with all that he was, and he felt like a part of him still had a door slammed firmly shut. Because what else could he do? What else could he do when he didn't know if that part of himself was even redeemable.

He wanted her. He knew that much. And he wasn't strong enough to turn her away.

She reached behind her back and undid her bra, letting it fall down to her feet, and then she slipped out of her panties. She was like everything he had fantasized about then, and everything he wanted now. She encompassed every dream, every hope. The moment of their wedding; the moment of their first kiss. The moment of their first meeting. The woman who had stitched him back together in so many ways.

He didn't have the strength to refuse her. To refuse this. He just wanted. Utterly and completely. He couldn't deny either of them.

But he let her come to him. And she did. Her feet were bare, and she took dainty steps across the forest floor toward him. She reached up, her breasts rising with the motion as she gripped his face and brought his head down for a kiss. "I'm yours," he said.

Whatever she wanted from him, he would do that. He would be that. He just needed to keep that door closed. He needed her to never know. He needed her to never change the way that she looked at him. Because she had always looked at him like he was something special. She was the first person ever to do that. She didn't know. She couldn't know. What it meant to him. How it had changed him. How it had taken all the things inside him and made him new, in that moment when she had first laid eyes on him. She might've stitched him together after, but she had looked at him and healed him in that very first moment.

He had loved her then.

He truly had.

He had done his best to keep himself back from her. To keep himself from hurting her, but he had wanted her all the same. He had loved her all the same.

He had never been strong enough to leave her life. He wasn't now, either.

So he kissed her. With everything he had. With everything he was. She took him by the hand then, and led him behind the tree. She had laid out a blanket there, in the small patch of grass that was bathed in the sun, and she laid him down and took off his clothes as if he were a picnic that she was putting before her as a treat.

She stood above him, and he took in the sight, the way the sun made her golden hair seem to catch fire, the way it highlighted the rosy crests of her breasts.

The way the air kissed her bare skin. She was naked out in the full light of day for him. And that felt like something.

A gift.

She lowered herself down slowly, the slick heat of her coming over the top of his aching shaft. She rubbed herself over him, her lips parting as she pleasured herself using his body. She let her head fall back, her hair a shining curtain of gold.

"Lachlan," she said. She said his name like that with ease, and it had become his favorite sound. She had said his name so many times over the years, but this was new. Different. The way that she said it as he pleasured her… That was a gift. She was a gift.

She leaned forward, and he arched up, taking one nipple between his teeth and tugging.

She let out a cry, uncaring that they were out in the open. Uncaring that anyone might hear.

He didn't care, either. All that mattered was this. Them.

He wanted to build a fortress around them. Protect them from the outside. But who would protect her from him? That was the question. It was the one he didn't have an answer to.

She moved herself back and forth, teasing them both, before tilting her hips and nearly taking him inside, the near penetration sending off a firestorm of need through his system.

But she denied them. Over and over, she denied them, until he grabbed her hips and seated her fully on his arousal. "I need you," he growled, and she let out a hoarse cry, her internal muscles tightening around him, pulsing with desire. Her climax was sudden, raw and needy, and he wanted more of it. He wanted everything. It wasn't fair. Because he couldn't give her everything, but he wanted every last shred of her. Down to her soul. He wasn't disciplined enough to deny himself that.

He was so greedy. He wanted everything.

Everything that she was willing to give.

She rode him, and he watched the show, watched as the sunlight slid over her pale skin, as the breeze kicked up and made the leaves move, shifting the shadows over her beautiful skin. Her breasts moving gently in a sensuous rhythm, as she set a pace for them that threatened to drive him insane.

Finally, he grabbed her hips and forced her down hard as he thrust up, drove them both to the edge again, made her scream out his name before he lost himself. Or maybe he found himself. He didn't quite know which.

And he didn't know which he actually wanted.

Except her. Except this moment. Beyond it, he didn't have a clue. But right now he wanted her. Right now he had her.

"I definitely never thought I would do that…outside."

"Well, you're very good at it," he said.

"Thank you. I don't know if I ever expected to take a compliment on my skills, either."

"What was that about?"

"I just want for us to be us. Lachlan and Charity, but more. Everything. Now you know me. Naked inside and outside and in the dark and in the sun. You know how much I want you. You know that you take all of my inhibitions and turn them into nothing. You're my everything."

He wrapped his arms around her, held her close. "You're mine, too," he said. "Don't doubt that."

Except, he wondered if a person could be everything when the other was still guarding a piece of themselves. *Could you have everything if you couldn't give everything?*

What he had to give had to be enough. Because there was just no way he could ever expose her to the rest of him. It would have to be enough.

They went back to the house and had dinner together. Then they went to their room and made love again.

*Stay.*

Something in him wanted it. Demanded it.

Suddenly, he was exhausted. In a deep way he'd never felt before. It wasn't about needing sleep. It was needing to stop the war.

The one that demanded he draw closer to her and pull away.

He couldn't pull away. Not anymore.

He didn't have the strength.

So he pulled her into his arms and held her close, listened to her heartbeat.

Peace. This was peace. It didn't have to be war.

He could have this.

And Lachlan had never slept better than he did sharing a bed with Charity.

## *CHAPTER TWENTY-FIVE*

SHE WAS FEELING sort of wretched and awful, and she felt like she ought to feel triumphant. Things had been going better with Lachlan.

There were still nights that she woke up sometimes and he wasn't there. But he wasn't ready to talk about whatever was going on with him, and she was trying to find a way to deal with that. In many ways she was the one who had changed the terms of their relationship. She was the one who had decided she wanted something more. Something different. She was the one who had decided she needed something more than sex and friendship to call it love.

So she had done the work to expose herself to him, and the fact that he wasn't ready to do it for her was something she was just going to have to suck up and deal with.

She wasn't that silly girl she'd been.

She'd lost her dad. She had endured pain. She had faced the fact that she was ignoring parts of herself that needed to be tended to. She had been honest enough to realize that what she had been doing with Byron had been a replacement tactic.

Had been a relationship that didn't challenge her.

Lachlan challenged her.

When they had been friends, only friends, it had

been different. They hadn't challenged each other in quite the same way that they did as a married couple. Or rather, he challenged her. He was resistant to her doing the same back.

But it would be okay.

She could be patient.

After all, their relationship was more than fifteen years in the making. What was a little more time? They could keep building this. It wasn't finished.

That was the thing. Happily-ever-after was a process.

They'd said they loved each other. They'd slept together. They'd gotten married.

There was still a lot of work to do.

She was beginning to understand that, to accept it. She hadn't seen enough marriage to really have a concept of that before then. She had thought maybe people just had happy marriages or unhappy ones. She and Lachlan had so much happiness. She loved to be with him. He was her favorite person. She liked his humor and his warmth. She always had. But now she also loved his touch, the way that he made her body feel. The way that she felt like they were changing one another every time they came together. Becoming a part of each other. More and more, she felt like they were being woven together into something that could not be easily separated.

She loved that.

But there were also isolated moments. Sad moments. Times when she could feel him shutting her out.

Times when she wanted something from him she didn't have words for, so she had to swallow her anger, even though she just wanted to lash out.

It was a weird thing. More and more, she was feeling a bit vulnerable and touchy. To go along with a sense of lagging energy. She wasn't really enjoying that.

She mentioned that to Alaina one afternoon when she came by McCloud's Landing to check in on a horse.

"Are you pregnant?" the younger woman asked, her green eyes flashing with excitement.

"I… Oh." She didn't feel like she knew Alaina well enough for that, but clearly Alaina didn't care about that. Charity had a hard time caring, because now she was way too bowled over by the realization Alaina had just forced on her.

She had spent so many years knowing that she was categorically not pregnant, and she felt extremely stupid for not immediately wondering that now. But it had never mattered much other than for convenience's sake if she tracked her cycle, because of course, having never slept with a man, there was never a risk that she could be carrying a baby. Not so now.

"I… I guess I could be."

She knew she could be. She and Lachlan had been haphazard with birth control at best. She was thirty years old, so there was certainly nothing unwelcome about the fact that she might be having a baby. They were ready. Or at least, they were certainly old enough.

But it felt like a shock. Because while children had definitely been an implied part of this arrangement, they hadn't talked about it all that much.

She had never had an experience of a mother. He had a terrible father. She knew that both of them wanted to do something to heal those absences in their lives, but very suddenly it felt monumental. Knowing the mechanics, having assisted with many animal births, did nothing to make her feel better now.

"I could be."

"I have pregnancy tests," Alaina said.

She must have given Alaina a shocked look.

"What? I already had one unplanned pregnancy, and even with Cameron being tiny, I'm a little bit paranoid. I don't trust anything. I got pregnant my first time having sex. You go through that, and every twinge makes you a little bit nervous and, as much as I want to have more kids, I just can't stand the idea of having to wait to find out if I suspect, so I have a little bit of a stock."

That's how Charity found herself following Alaina back to the main house. Where thankfully, nobody else was.

Gus had taken Cameron out with him in a front pack, taking a cue off Sawyer Garrett, who had always had his daughter out with him on the ranch, for as long as she'd been able to stand.

Charity liked that. The way that the men on the ranch naturally took care of their children, even though they did have wives that were also present and invested.

She wondered if Lachlan would be the same kind of father.

The thought made her stomach feel tight.

All of this made her stomach feel tight.

She took the offered pink box from Alaina and went into the bathroom.

After following the instructions, the evidence was undeniable. She was two pink lines' worth pregnant.

Emotions swamped her. She hadn't been prepared for this.

Her dad would've been a wonderful grandfather.

That was the first thought she had, the realization piercing her soul.

She buried her face in her hands and cried. He wasn't here for this. And he *should* be.

He would've been so happy. So very, very happy.

A big part of it would have been his happiness for *her*.

That she was making a life for herself, and she did know that.

So she had to… She had to be okay. She had to see the joy in this moment, because her dad would want to, and he wouldn't want her to be robbed of it on his account. Not at all. Not in the least.

He would never, ever want that for her.

She took a breath and came out of the bathroom. She hadn't even let herself think about her. Or Lachlan.

"Well?" Alaina asked.

"Definitely pregnant."

Alaina squealed and threw her arms around her. "You'll be a great mom. You're so good with Cameron. I love that. I'm so excited to have a niece or nephew. I love babies so much."

"I thought you were just telling me you were terrified to have another one."

"Oh. I'm terrified to be *pregnant* again. Because I felt so gross. Like a beached whale at the end. But I love being a mom. And other people's babies are great."

"I… It's so funny. Because I didn't really think that I would feel afraid of it. I know the mechanics." She realized how often she had told herself that mattered more than it did. Knowing the mechanics did nothing to prepare her for the real-life version of anything. The fact that she was all too aware of that now contributed to her anxiety.

"The only thing you need to know is that in the end, love is enough. It carries you through. There are parts of it that are hard—the pregnancy, the labor and the delivery—but so much of it is a joy. Once they're here it's all worth it. And there's nothing better than watching the man you love soften like that. It's just a wonderful thing."

"Well, I'll be interested to see how Lachlan handles it."

"Lachlan is a great guy. He'll handle it well. Because they all do. Look at how Brody became an instant dad. I don't want to make a big deal out of the fact that Gus isn't the biological father of our baby, because you know, we're a family, and that doesn't matter. But the way that Gus stepped up for me was so admirable, and I bring it up sometimes just to highlight the fact that he's a caregiver down to his soul, in spite of what happened to him. Or maybe *because* of what happened to him. I don't think Lachlan will be any different."

Charity clung to that. She clung to it hard on the drive back to her and Lachlan's place. She canceled the rest of her appointments for the day, since none of them were emergencies, and she felt a little bit guilty about it, but she needed to have a nap.

She lay there on her side, her hand pressed to her stomach, which was still flat, and tried to imagine that there was something happening in there.

She felt gross, but she didn't feel any sense of miraculous at all. She couldn't feel a change or a connection. She didn't feel particularly like a sacred vessel.

Her mouth just tasted like the inside of a van.

Was that a problem? Did that mean there was something wrong with her? Did it mean she wouldn't be good at this?

Those questions all swirled around her head when she heard the front door close. Lachlan was here.

"Charity?"

"I'm in here," she said.

She rolled over onto her back and pulled the covers up to her chin.

"I wasn't expecting you back until quite a bit later."

"I didn't feel well, so I canceled my appointments," she said.

"Oh, sweetheart. What's wrong?"

"I feel nauseous."

"Sorry, Doc."

They were doing so well. Things were going better. This was going to change things again and she was... She was so scared of this new change. But she couldn't keep it from him, either. That was the problem with being married to her best friend.

She couldn't keep things from him. Especially not this.

"No. It's only that... I'm pregnant."

She clung to the edge of the covers, her fingers spearing the soft fabric like they were claws.

He looked like he'd been hit with a brick. "You're what?"

"It's funny that I was surprised. Because there's really no reason to be surprised. We had a lot of unprotected sex."

"We had protected sex, too," he said, sounding defensive.

"Yeah. But not a ton of it."

He nodded, his expression slightly sheepish.

"Anyway, I wasn't feeling well today, and I mentioned it to Alaina, who immediately guessed what might be wrong, and she dragged me back to the house for a test. And, well, here I am. Maybe I'm not so much sick as I am overwhelmed."

Lachlan's expression was almost completely neutral. Like he didn't quite know what to do or say.

"This is a good thing," he said.

"I think so," she said. "I'm just a little bit shocked. It's another change. A lot of changes."

"Sorry. I should've been more careful about this."

"No. I wasn't careful, either. All I wanted was to be with you. I didn't particularly want to think about practicalities. This is how the species propagates. All people can think about is pleasure, and not the consequences of the pleasure."

He chuckled. He leaned in and rubbed his thumb over her cheekbone. "You're going to be a great mother."

There was something about those words that hit her deep. Touched her down all the way in the bottom of her soul, and she smiled. "I want to be. I want to be a good wife to you. I want to be a good mother to our... Our baby. *Our baby*, Lachlan."

It felt like an explosion happened in her chest. The joy that she hadn't been able to feel for the past few hours suddenly burst there like a firework.

*Their* baby. They were having a baby. A baby that was hers and his, and she thought of those lonely children they had been when they'd met each other, and wished that those kids could've known. What they would make together. Because it was a deep, extravagant joy that she had never once truly thought would be for her. Yes, she had planned on getting married. Yes, she had planned on having children, but she hadn't imagined anything half as wonderful as this.

"I love you," she said.

He leaned in and he kissed her, and the only thing that she noticed, the only thing that made her joy feel a little bit more tentative, was the fact that he didn't say it back. He had said it less and less. She noticed that.

But he had said it. So it must still be true. The way that he kissed her seemed to suggest that it was, and she was just going to go ahead and take that as her evidence. It was the only real evidence she needed.

They were going to have a baby. And it was going to be wonderful. Because he had been the most wonderful thing in her life for all these years, and it wasn't going to change now. Now that he was everything. It would only get better. It had to.

# CHAPTER TWENTY-SIX

THEY WERE HAVING a baby. A baby. He'd wanted that. He wanted that all this time. He was thrilled. He really was.

And he'd invited his brothers out to tell them the news.

Because he was determined to tell them all the way they'd told each other. To react the way they all had.

So maybe he was supposed to be reformed. Maybe he was going to be a dad, but he felt like he was allowed to go out and have a drink in celebration. Anyway, Charity had cleared him to do so. He had left her with a bowl of soup and a packet of saltines, and she had seemed sleepy and happy when he'd left. His heart felt raw. A bit bruised.

But it was okay.

He shoved aside his reservations.

He didn't know what the hell was wrong with him anyway. There wasn't really anything.

Nothing he could put a finger on. Nothing he had words for. Just the general kind of issues that he always had.

He tried to imagine holding a tiny baby. He held his nephew, of course, but that was different. It wasn't his. This one... It was going to be his responsibility. This one was *his*.

When he thought of the word *father*, he saw a madman in his mind, and what the hell was he supposed to do with that?

*Just think of Albert. Albert was a good dad. And you saw him. You saw him be a good dad to Charity. You can figure it out.*

Except when he thought of it like that he couldn't help but think that what she really needed was to be with a guy like Byron, because Byron had basically been Albert but younger. And maybe that was the thing that he really should have been. The thing that her partner really should've been.

But he had been too selfish, too possessive of her to let her be with anyone else.

*Well, now she's having your baby. So buck up.*

"I'm buying a round," he said, when they were all seated at the table.

"Great. Why?" Brody asked.

"Wait till you have the beer."

The bartender passed the beers around the table, and Lachlan raised his. "I'm having a baby."

The table erupted with no small amount of whooping and hollering.

"So toast to me, stepping into adult life."

"Congrats," Gus said, clanking the beer bottle against his.

"It's a good life," Brody said. "It's a good life."

"Don't take this the wrong way, Brody," Gus said. "But you only have the kid half the time."

"More than half," Brody said. "But anyway. We're going to have some of our own full-time kids eventually. We were just waiting for Benny to feel totally settled with all the other changes."

"I know that it's good," Lachlan said. "Because you've all gone from being the most interminable assholes to being functional people. I give your wives credit for that, and it's why I went and found one of my own. And those of you that have kids…even better. So I look forward to my own transformation."

"You think it's magic?" Gus asked.

"Seems like it to me."

They laughed at him. All of them.

And he just stared at them. While they laughed.

"It's blood, sweat and tears, little brother," Hunter had said. "Elsie and I have all kinds of things we're still working out. Crap that our parents did to us."

"Yeah," Brody said. "Hate to break it to you. But you come into your marriage with baggage, and you spend a lot of time unpacking it."

He couldn't process that. "But you're all happy."

"Yeah," Brody said. "Deliriously happy. That's kind of the miracle. You learn to be happy, even while you bring all that with you. Because what you decide is that your love is bigger than all that stuff. That's the key. That's the secret."

He felt rocked by that. A little bit duped.

Because they were his goal. His dream for himself. His proof he could be normal. That there was a different kind of love out there and maybe if he did all the right things, he could have that, and not the monster.

"But…"

"But nothing. It's all good. You're going to be a great dad."

"Why do you think that?" Lachlan asked.

"Because you're a good person. So you're going

to figure out how to do this, just like you figured out how to love her."

Except he wasn't sure he *had* figured out how to love her. That day in the forest she had stripped off another layer for him, and he had gone ahead and reinforced his own guard inside him. Because he decided that he didn't want her getting too close to the parts of him that were disastrous. He still felt that way. Because she was too good to be exposed to all of his bullshit.

Well, what the hell was he supposed to do with a kid? He wondered if he'd been lying to himself.

If it didn't just fix you...

She had said to him one time that she thought it was amazing he had *hope*. That he believed in the way things were meant to be. And he wondered if he was actually kind of an idiotic optimist, all things considered. Life had never given him a reason to be. He just sort of was one. *Because.* Because being a pessimist had felt like a long, dark road to hell, and he hadn't been able to live with that. So he decided that things would work out. Maybe there was a mistake in that. What if there was?

What if there was no fix for him? For this growing need in him that he feared pointed to a deeper, darker part of him that he had successfully kept covered all this time.

*What if.*

It was a pretty damn sobering thought. He lifted his beer bottle to his mouth, but suddenly it felt acid.

He set it down on the table.

"What's going on in your head?" Gus asked.

"Nothing. Just thinking about how expensive diapers are."

"Good thing your wife is a vet. And has a rental. She brought a lot to that marriage."

"*I* bring a lot," Lachlan muttered.

"You're the one whining about diapers."

"I'm not whining."

"Okay," Gus said.

But he did his best to cover up what was really going on. Did his best to ignore what felt like a boulder building in his chest.

He shoved it off. This was what he'd wanted. He wanted it. And Charity… Charity felt like his salvation.

When he got home he took her to bed and held her in his arms all night long.

He might not be able to feel that light, that hope, for himself. But she was a golden forest afternoon, and he could cling to that. Cling to her.

And he would.

# CHAPTER TWENTY-SEVEN

EVERYTHING HAD CHANGED in the past week. That day in the forest. Something had fractured between them. Certainly, his barriers had been demolished.

He slept with her every night. Thought of her all the time.

They'd been starving for each other since the revelation about the baby. Like they were trying to affirm something between them. He'd had her against the wall right next to the front door in the cabin. The floor. He couldn't seem to stop staring at her. Touching her. He'd spent the night in bed with her. Holding her close all night. It had been a revelation. It had done something to demolish all these barriers inside him, and the intensity of it was addictive.

He never felt anything like it. He couldn't remember why the hell he'd resisted it. Because it was just so damned... It was just so damned good.

And then she'd told him she was having a baby. And it was like a heady cocktail he'd never even dreamed of before.

*His.*

*His.*

She was his.

She was giving vaccinations in the barn at Mc-Cloud's Landing, and he happened to track her phone to that location and see that she was there. The perks of now being on the same plan. He saw her, and immediately pulled her into his arms. He kissed her. And she kissed him back.

"What are you doing?" she asked.

"I can't stay away from you," he said. He deepened the kiss, angling his head and growling as he did so. He could feel when she went limp against him. When she surrendered. He wanted to push her up against the wall and make love to her that way, which was something they had both discovered she enjoyed just the other day. He wanted it all. Everything. All the time. And it was starting to feel almost unmanageable. That was the problem. It was starting to feel...

Like a burden. A heavy one. It was starting to feel like obsession.

The word sliced into him, cut beneath his skin.

And echoed in his soul.

*Obsession.*

Yeah. He was far too familiar with that. He cupped her face and surrendered. To her. Then he did back her against the wall, feeling the press of her breasts against his chest. He groaned. He moved his hands down and took hold of her backside.

"Get a room." They stopped, and he looked up as Gus walked in, crossing his arms over his chest. "Seriously. Actually. You have a room. So this shouldn't even be happening."

"Did you need something, Gus?" he asked.

"The use of my barn. Thank you."

"It wasn't going to go any further than that," he said, his voice rough.

"Clearly," Gus said, looking more than a little bit amused. Charity was beet-red.

He felt kind of guilty.

"Hey. We're all going out to Smokey's tonight. You two want to come?" he asked.

"Sure," Lachlan said. "Though it begs the question why you all had already decided to do this before talking to us."

"Well, because we were just talking outside the barn, and you two were inside the barn making out. Nothing wrong with that. If I wasn't doing my job, I would rather be making out with my wife, too."

Gus seemed so…happy. Lachlan didn't feel happy. He felt…ragged. At loose ends. He felt… Honest to God, like something was breaking apart inside him. Like all these carefully built structures that he had erected around his soul were beginning to give way, and he didn't know how the hell to grapple with that. Didn't know what to do.

"Yeah. We'll go."

"Great. See you both there."

"I have to go," she said. "I have other jobs."

"Well, that's just inconvenient for me," he said, moving nearer to her, the possessiveness that rose up inside him like a thing with teeth.

He wondered what had happened for his easy feelings for his friend. Those nice, simple friendship feelings. Yeah. He wondered what the hell had happened to those. "See you in a few hours," he said.

She smiled sweetly. "See you."

He felt like he was coming apart, and the way she looked at him only became more and more dreamy. That almost didn't seem fair.

He was counting down the hours until he saw her again. This girl was messing with his head. In an extreme way.

Finally, it was dinnertime, and he had his brothers drive him over to Smokey's, where he had already planned to meet Charity.

He didn't think he was imagining it, but she looked... sexier than usual. Not to him. He thought she was sexy in her little white socks. He always would. But sexy in the way that other men might notice. She was wearing a pale pink top that conformed to her curves, and a pair of pants made out of some light fabric that seemed to hug her rear a lot more than what she wore normally did.

It made him want to put his hands all over her so that everybody there would understand who she was there with.

Instead, he sat down at the table with his family and made a good show of behaving himself.

Drinks got passed all around, followed by burger baskets, and he and Charity mostly just sat in silence listening to the others talk. He wasn't sure why he didn't much feel like talking. But he supposed it was the same reason she didn't.

"Let's dance," Alaina said.

Her sisters were babysitting, so she and Gus were there baby free.

"In a minute," Gus said, taking a sip of his beer.

"I'll meet you out there."

Alaina went off onto the dance floor, and Elsie and Elizabeth followed.

"You can go," he said, even though everything in him tensed up.

"Really?"

"Yes. If you want to go dance with the girls, go dance with them."

She grinned and kissed him on the cheek before heading out to the dance floor.

"So things are pretty hot and heavy with you and Charity," Gus said.

"She *is* my wife."

"Sure."

"She's also pregnant."

"I'm aware. I just didn't think that meant…you have it that bad."

"You didn't think we were attracted to each other?"

"It's just that no one's been able to tell about the two of you," Hunter said. "For a lot of years."

"Well, there was nothing going on. Then there was. As soon as there was, things became pretty clear."

"Naturally."

It was Tag who said that, as if that sort of thing was just logical. Everybody else nodded along.

"So what I'm thinking in terms of expanding the ranch," Gus said, and Lachlan just fell into listening as Gus spun out his plans for where to take the equine therapy program over the next couple of years. He should have known that Gus wouldn't be satisfied with what he'd already built. And it was going to cause drama, because the Sullivans were fighting for their share of expansion money.

But hey, it was Gus's fight. If he wanted to be in it, well, he was married to a Sullivan sister. So he could go right ahead and pick that fight if he felt like it.

"The girls are attracting attention," Brody commented.

Lachlan looked over his shoulder and he saw a pack

of men walk in with boots that were too clean, belt buckles that were too shiny and eyebrows that were far too groomed.

City Slickers.

Looking to pick up on horse girls. No doubt. His hackles rose.

There was one man chatting up Alaina, and all Gus did was roll his eyes. Elizabeth was determinedly ignoring a man to her left, and there was a man who reached out and touched Charity on the arm.

Before Lachlan could make a decision, he had launched out of his chair. He watched Charity draw away from the guy, and the guy take another step toward her. "No, thank you," Charity said.

"Come on, kitten. You're not going to get a better offer than this all night."

Lachlan walked up to the other man and looked down at him. "Beg to differ, son."

The guy was probably older than Lachlan, but he was a few inches shorter. So there.

"Are you serious, man? There's a lot of women in here."

"But only one of them's my wife. My *pregnant* wife. Notice the wedding rings. You made a miscalculation."

"Hey, man," the guy said. "I don't want any trouble."

"You walked in here looking for trouble. She told you no, and you kept moving in on her. And you better give me one good reason why I shouldn't cave your face in."

"I'm not picking a fight with you, dude."

Lachlan reached out and grabbed him by the front of his shirt. "My guy," Lachlan said. "Call me dude one more time and I will make it physically impossible for you to enunciate the word."

Rage was pouring through him. Blinding and hot. He had never wanted to be violent quite so badly as he did in this moment.

What would've happened if he wasn't here? Would the guy have kept pushing? Was he the kind of guy who would put something in her drink? The kind of guy who reacted badly when a woman told him no? Lachlan wanted to destroy him. Utterly. Completely.

Lachlan wanted blood.

"Fine, she's not that hot anyway."

And that just *did it*. Lachlan punched him. Right in the face. Which brought every other guy in the group right on top of them. He heard Gus sigh. "Well, damn."

Then, all the McCloud boys were out on the dance floor. Doing a whole different kind of tango with the city assholes who had shown up.

Sheena hurled a beer bottle at the wall behind them, hollering at them to take the fight the hell out of her bar and you could still hear Taylor Swift telling them all to *shake it off* from the jukebox. It was a melee, and the city boys were outmatched. There was one more of them than there was of the McClouds. But Gus was a whole freight train in human form, and the rest of them weren't slouches. "I ought to call the cops," the one guy said, holding his face.

"Go ahead. This is a small town. The cops are my kin."

They were not kin. But hey, Daughtry King was close to kin, in fashion.

"Let's go," one of the guys said. And they all slunk right out of the bar.

He looked over at Charity, whose eyes were wide, fear radiating from them.

"Honey," he said. "It's okay."

"I know," she said. "I was fine, though."

"It wasn't fine."

Suddenly, it all started to hit him. They had just been in a huge bar fight. Because he had gotten jealous. Because he was… He was *obsessed* with his wife. In such a toxic way. It had just been getting more and more intense. And he had no idea where to go from here. This was what he had been afraid of. That it would do this to him. That he would be like his father.

It turned out he was way more of a chip off the old block than he'd like to believe.

The McClouds all went back to the ranch with minor cuts and bruises, but really, you should see the other guys. His brothers were amused by the whole thing, but Lachlan felt suffocated by his own darkness.

It didn't get better when he got home. He avoided going to bed when Charity did, and joined her long after, but he couldn't stand lying next to her.

Horror was still pounding through him after the fight. He couldn't believe that he had done that. That he'd gone after that guy, and he left no choice but for his brothers to get involved. They were damn well lucky that the cops hadn't come out. It was only because they were local, and they were the McCloud boys, that they weren't getting dragged straight into the sheriff station like they probably should've been.

But it was the rage that he recognized in himself that had fractured everything. Ruined every damn thing.

Because he'd been convinced. He'd been convinced that he could do this. That he could have a baby with

Charity. Be her husband. He had been convinced that the friendship love that they had would be enough. That it would insulate him from this kind of insanity. But it hadn't.

He'd been unhinged. And he didn't know where that would end.

He damn well didn't know. He was going deep into uncharted territory with her.

And it killed him.

He tore the covers off him and got out of bed. He went outside, ignoring the frigid weather.

"What am I supposed to do?" Maybe he was asking Albert. Maybe he was asking whoever was in charge. "How am I supposed to… How am I supposed to do this?"

He couldn't. That was it. That was the answer. He had already taken Charity and ruined her life. He had married her. He had gotten her pregnant, and now, here in the last moments of it, he wasn't sure if he could do it.

He had to leave.

He had to get some distance. He had to get his head on straight. He put his jeans and a T-shirt on and stumbled outside. And on his way out to the truck he fell to his knees. Because he felt too weak for all of this.

Too weak to go and too weak to stay, and he hated himself for that. Because hadn't that been what his dad had always told him? That he was weak.

"You didn't hate me because I'm weak, Dad. You hated me because you saw yourself in me. That's the truth of it. It's the Goddamn truth." The words, the truth, it was all torn from him.

He knew it was true.

Because it was why he hated his dad. He was the one who really got it. He was the one who knew.

It wasn't hatred that drove that man.

It was love set on fire so that it burned to ash, so that it wasn't recognizable as what it had been. Nothing but destruction.

"Lachlan?"

He didn't say anything.

"Lachlan McCloud. I swear if you run from me, if you run from your best friend, if you run from your wife, I am going to be very mad at you."

He heard her footsteps, and she came close to where he was. "I'm here," he said.

"What are you doing?" she asked, her voice trembling.

"I can't do it. I can't give you what you want and stay…the person that you need me to be. I'm sorry. I thought that I could do this. I wanted to do it. I wanted to do it when I thought that it would… When I thought I could control it," he said, the words scraping raw out of his throat. "I thought that if I picked my best friend to be my wife I wouldn't be in any danger of being like my dad, but look how I was tonight. Look at that. It was supposed to be a good night. We were supposed to go out and celebrate the baby, and I started a fight. I lost my fucking shit. How can you want to be married to me? How can you want to be married to this guy who treats you like this?" The words felt torn from him, like a part of him being ripped away. Walls torn apart inside him until there was nothing left.

"Lachlan," she said. "Tonight was a mess. It was. You're not wrong. But… *We* don't have to be. We can do this."

"You don't know what you're saying. You don't know. The thing that haunts me is that I know my father loved my mother. I know that love can tip over into obsession, and I don't know the difference."

"It's not love," she said. "It's not love when you would hurt the person that you're supposed to protect. And you never would. You never would. I know that about you."

"How? How can you know it? I don't even know that about myself. Charity, I'm afraid. I'm afraid of what I could become… I can't sleep with you. Because it makes me… I just… I want you so much. I don't have any control over it. I don't have any control over myself. And you're right. It's not love. My brothers, they love their wives. And it's… Look what it does for them. But look at me."

"I am," she said. "I'm looking at you. I have been looking at you, Lachlan McCloud, since you were sixteen years old. And if you can't know these things about yourself, then you need to let me know them. For you."

"You just don't… I know. I know, because I saw the way it made my dad hate me. The way my mom loved me. What if… What if I'm jealous of our own kid?"

"Then you'll do something about it. We'll talk to somebody. You'll get help. Because you don't want to be that bastard. I know you don't."

"I didn't want any of this," he said. "I didn't want to feel this. I feel like… I feel like I can't breathe. I have to go."

"You can't leave me."

"I just need to leave. For a little bit. Charity, whatever happens, I'll make sure that you're taken care of. You know that."

"I do know that," she said. "I do know that. That's why I'm not afraid. I don't understand why you are."

"You didn't see it," he said. "You didn't see it. He wanted to kill me. He wanted to kill her. He locked Gus in a shed and set him on fire. And I remember... I remember standing outside that shed and watching it burn. And feeling so helpless. That's how I feel. I can't save us. I couldn't save him when he was in there being burned alive. And this just still... It's the same. I was broken from the time I was born. I was born with my dad hating me. I don't know how to be anything else. I wanted to. I wanted to. I believed this could save me. But I just can't."

"Lachlan."

And then he turned and walked away from her.

"Lachlan!"

He stopped, just for a moment. "You promised me," she said. "You promised me that you would never leave me. You promised me that you were my friend."

"I'm trying to give you what you deserve. My dad couldn't let go when he needed to. I'm going to let go before it gets there. I owe you that. And I can give it to you. So I will."

"You said you loved me."

"I know I did. I said that I loved you, and now I'm not sure that I even had a right to say it. I do... I care for you. But I don't know if I can be with you."

"I'm fine," she said. "You have to trust that I'm strong. You have to trust me that I'm not scared."

"I know you're not scared. Because I told you that you could trust me."

"No. You showed me that I could trust you. For the last fifteen years. How are you going to turn around and act like now I can't? It's ridiculous. I know that I can trust you."

"I don't trust myself."

"So what? Because of some existential fear that you might not be as good as you want to be, because you think there might be something wrong with you, you would leave me?"

"I wouldn't abandon you. I'm just wondering if things worked better before. Because I didn't have all this stuff coming up."

"I think it's unavoidable. When I found out I was pregnant I missed my dad. Now more and more I'm thinking about how my mother wasn't with me. How she didn't want me. I think that it starts to become more and more difficult because these changes in our lives force us to confront what we are and where we've been. But I spent a lot of my life hiding, Lachlan. And I'm not doing it anymore. I've found the thing that makes me happy. And it's you. It's worth it. It's worth all the pain. It's worth the suffering.

"It's worth whatever we have to go through to make this forever. To make it real. To make it ours. It's worth all that. So I'm willing to fight for it. I'm willing to go through this with you. To figure out what it means. You're not a violent person."

"You can't say that. You know how much I enjoyed watching Gus beat my father up?"

"That was different. It was revenge. For what he did to you. And the fact that he is still in your head, that's not fair. He doesn't deserve to be there. You're a good guy, Lachlan. You are not your father. And you won't magically turn into him just because you have a wife and a child. How can you believe that it would magically fix you, and now not, but still believe it might magically ruin you?"

"Not *it*," he said. "You. You're going to ruin me. You're going to ruin me... Hell, Charity, I can't handle this. I was supposed to marry somebody, and it was supposed to be easy. I was supposed to choose, and it was going to be companionable. And that was how it was supposed to be with you. Because you're my best friend. And it's always been easy with us. But it's changing. It's changing, and now it's changing again, and I don't trust myself. I cannot trust myself with a kid."

"But you did."

"I know that I did. But I can't. Not now."

"I don't understand."

"I know you don't. I'm sorry. I wish there was something I could say to make you. I wish there was something that I could do. I can't. I can't... You can stay here. I'll make sure that you're looked after. Taken care of."

"Lachlan," she said, panic edging into her tone. And he felt it. He felt an answering panic rising up inside him, but there was no other choice. This was what had to happen. He had to do this. It was for her. It was for their baby.

Because he was just like his father. Obsessed with her. That was what his brothers didn't understand. Their father hadn't hated their mother. He had *loved* her. Obsessively. He had used Lachlan as bait to get to her, because he had known... He had known it would work. And that terrified him. The idea that a man would use his own child, hurt his own child, to try to get back at his wife. To try to get her to come.

He had gone after her relentlessly. And the one thing his brothers didn't know about… When his father had used Lachlan to draw their mother out. After stalking her relentlessly. It was the only reason he knew about it. Because his father had used him. As a bargaining chip to try and draw his mother out, and then when he'd finally been with her he… He kissed her. And then he hit her. Over and over again, and she'd run. Hadn't even looked back.

And he couldn't blame her.

She should've run.

But that… That lived with him. The fire in his father's eyes then.

It was the same kind of fire he felt inside him when he looked at Charity.

He couldn't ignore the fact that the capacity for violence seemed to be in his soul. That he could feel his control slipping more and more as his obsession with her grew. Because it wasn't just that she was his friend and he'd married her. No. It was more than that. So much more intense than that. She was his friend, and he'd married her.

She had become everything to him. Maybe on some level that was what he had always known would happen, and that was why he had kept her as his friend. Only his friend. Because anything more than that was dangerous. This was a dangerous game.

What had happened tonight was evidence of that.

He needed to get her away from him. That was the bottom line.

"I will make sure that you're taken care of," he said. "My brothers will help take care of you. And the baby."

"Don't," she said.

"I have to. I didn't know. I am so, so sorry."

"Lachlan, you said that you loved me."

"I thought I could make a different love. A better love. I thought I could save us, save me. But I don't know what anything healthy feels like. I wanted to. I wanted to. You have any idea how much I loved our wedding? Because it looked like something that a normal person could have. But that isn't me. I'm not normal. I'm… I'm toxic, and I'm obsessive and I can't deal with all of this. All of these feelings."

"I would rather go through this with you than try to…" He felt like she was coming undone, listening to her sound like this. So filled with sorrow he'd caused. "Lachlan, I don't want to be without you. Doesn't that matter for anything? Doesn't what I want matter for anything?"

"My mom wanted my dad at one point, too." He laughed, bitter and hard. "They had five kids. They wanted each other. But the cost… I've already changed. What happened tonight… This is poison. For me, what we have is poison."

"So you're going to give our kid what we had? A parent who didn't care enough to stick around even when it was hard?" she asked, all that sorrow fury now.

"My mom was running for her life. That was different. It was a damn sight different. And I'm having the decency to do what my dad didn't. I'm choosing this. I'm choosing it because anything else isn't fair. I'm not my mother."

"The *baby*, Lachlan."

Her eyes shone with so much hurt, so much betrayal, and it killed him. But he knew. He knew what it was like to have this in a father. "Charity, he hurt us. His kids. I don't trust myself."

"Is this about what happened at the bar?"

"Of course it's about what happened at the bar. Do you see how I get? I was crazy. Jealous. Possessive."

"If a woman came up to you and talked to you like that I would feel possessive, too. We aren't used to looking at each other that way. We are learning. You have to stop acting like this is it. Like this is all we'll be, and we won't figure it out."

"I've seen the progression of it. That's the problem. It scares the hell out of me."

"I'm not afraid."

"But you should be. You really should be."

# CHAPTER TWENTY-EIGHT

CHARITY LOOKED AT LACHLAN. She had never seen him like this. He was talking about leaving her like it wasn't going to be so painful he was doing harm to her. He was acting like it would be doing her a favor, and she could see that he believed it. He was broken in a way that she hadn't witnessed, all these years, and she knew there wasn't a stitch that she could put in his body to shore this up. To make it right.

He was going to have to see himself completely differently, and he couldn't do that. It was like he had been completely unprepared for the reality of love and what it really meant.

So had she. It heightened your emotions. It made everything feel so much more terrifying. Love *did* border on obsession, and they had become a kind of all-consuming force in each other's lives. She understood why it scared him.

But the bottom line was… The bottom line was that she loved him. Through this. All of it. But she was terrified of him leaving and not coming back, because her dad had left her and not come back. She knew that he had died, but still. Why did she have to keep losing people? She didn't want to be left. And she had given herself. Her true, real self, and he was leaving. It was her worst nightmare.

And it was Lachlan. And it *wasn't fair*.

Leaving her and her child, a rejection that cut so deep she could scarcely breathe through it. It was so painful. So ridiculously hurtful.

She knew that he was actually cutting himself open. She knew that he was bleeding out, right there in front of her. As much as she was.

Why was he doing this? Only because he thought he had to. Because of fear. She knew him well enough to know that. He would never hurt her on purpose. And he was hurting her. He was destroying her.

But he thought he had to.

"Don't leave me," she said.

"I'm saving you," he said.

He stood and walked back into the house. And she just stood and watched him go. He returned a moment later, carrying a small bag, and he got into his truck.

"No," she said. "What are you doing?"

"I'll get in touch in a couple of days."

"No, Lachlan. You can't do this. You can't do this to me. You can't do this to us. I am begging you. Please."

"I'm doing this for you."

He got into the truck and started to drive away.

She grabbed a rock out of the driveway and threw it. It hit the tailgate with a violent sound, and she knew it left a dent there. But she didn't care.

She could be the same way. She could be violent, too. And angry. *So angry*.

And right now she could hate him as much as she had ever loved him. In fact, she could feel both things right at the same time. It wasn't even hard. It just felt like dying. That was all. She went back into the house, and she paced around for a second.

Then she picked up the phone and called Gus.

HE WAS A mile down the highway when the truck came up on his bumper. Flashing its lights and just about butting up against his tail end. What the hell? It was weird enough that it just about undid his focus on the bloody pain that he was in. And it *was* bloody. Nearly unendurable. The worst thing he'd ever experienced in his damned life.

But right now he had a madman on his ass.

The truck behind him crept up and nearly tapped his bumper, he was coming so close. Lachlan swerved off to the side of the road, and the truck did the same.

His muscles tensed. And he braced himself. He got out of the driver's side, ready for whatever fight this guy wanted to be in. Boy, was he ready. For some real violence.

Then he realized it was his brother. Gus.

"And what in the *ever-loving fuck* are you doing?" Gus roared.

"Gus?"

"Your wife called me and told me that you're being a little bitch."

"I'm not," he said. "I'm protecting her."

"I'm sorry, from what?"

"You don't understand."

"The hell I don't, Lachlan. For God's sake. The hell I don't. Look at me." He grabbed Lachlan by the arm and pointed to his face. "Do you remember that day?"

"Yes. I do. Dad was obsessed with Mom, and that

whole obsession put me at the center because of her attachment to me. And it just… I feel so aware of that. That toxic part of who they were, who he was. I have always been afraid it was part of me."

"With all the love in my scarred-ass body that is some of the worst bullshit I've ever heard."

"Excuse me?"

"You're a good guy, Lachlan. You have never been anything but a good guy. You've taken care of Charity and loved her since she was fifteen. Why would you do anything to hurt her now?"

"Gus, there's something wrong with me."

"I didn't save your ass so that you could be an idiot."

"You don't know. Dad went after her. He used me. Used me to get to her because he was obsessed with her. And I think… I think that's how I feel about her. I'm obsessed with her."

"Yeah. Well, you probably should be. She's your new wife. It isn't bad to want someone. It isn't wrong to feel something strong."

"Dad…"

"Was broken. But we don't have to be. That doesn't mean we aren't allowed to feel things. It doesn't mean you aren't allowed to be in love."

"This can't be love. It's terrible."

"Yeah. No kidding. It's awful. It's like my heart has been carved out of my chest and it's out there…walking around. Alaina. Cameron. I'm not mine anymore. I'm theirs. But I also can't imagine living any other way. I wouldn't want to." His brother stared right into his eyes then. "But this idea that you're dangerous? You know that isn't true. You have to know that."

"I… I… Why, then? Why did he hate me, Gus?"

The words were torn from him, like shards of glass getting torn from his throat. "If he saw himself in me that makes sense, I guess. But if there's nothing…if there's no reason… When you're just a little kid that gets treated like garbage, how do you… How? Because I always tried to believe that there was a reason for it, but I can't see it. I can't see it. And if I can't see it… what's going to stop Charity from…seeing the same thing he did? To just stop loving me."

"Oh. You sad bastard." Gus rubbed his hands over his face. "Lachlan, there's nothing wrong with you. It's him. It was him. It was never you. He got to define what love was for you, and that isn't fair. He made you feel worthless, and that wasn't fair. It was never you."

"How do I…"

"The only thing I know is that we had a bad hand, Lach. A bad dad. We didn't get to choose that. But we can choose something better now. You care enough about her to do anything. But can you care enough about yourself to want more?"

"How? I don't get how. I've always tried to believe that there was a reason for anything, for everything, because it made it feel like maybe our childhood wasn't so desperately random. Like there was a purpose. But I can't find it now. I was just a kid that got treated like garbage. And how the hell are you supposed to…"

"Not by her. Never by her. The thing you can't see, she does see it. And at some point you have to love her enough to trust that."

"I don't even know what it is."

"What?"

"Love."

Gus laughed, hard and humorless. "This is it, dip-shit. Congratulations."

"It *can't* be."

"It is. You feel like garbage, you're running away, you're terrified for your very soul. Sounds like love to me."

"But…"

"There's no *but*. It just is what it is. It's terrible, hor-rible and awful. But it's the best damn thing you'll ever do. It's also the hardest. You turn your ass back around, and you go tell her that you're gonna work it out."

"But why does it feel like this for me? I don't feel… healed or easy or at peace. I feel…like I'm breaking apart."

"Because it's hard to change. And you've spent a long time telling yourself there was something wrong with you. I'm sorry I didn't tell you you were all right. I was too busy…you know." He gestured to his scars.

"It isn't your fault…"

"Yeah, I know," Gus said. "None of this is our fault, is it? And nothing is wrong with you."

"Gus…"

"The only thing wrong with you would be if you left behind a woman who loved you, a child who needed you. This is your moment. Decide who you're going to be. Not who Dad made you feel like you were."

Lachlan stood there. Then he looked back toward his truck, back toward the dark road he was driving down.

He didn't know who he was. His mind went back to that moment when he had first seen Charity in the woods. She was his anchor. That was when he had known. Who he was. What he could be. What he wanted. It had only ever been clear with her.

She was the only thing that could ever stitch him back together. And here he was, torn apart and bleeding. And he needed her.

He was afraid. Gus was right. He was a coward and a jackass. And he wasn't protecting her. He was trying to protect him. And he had been, from the beginning.

He had never kissed Charity when he was younger, because if he had she would have been everything. And what if she saw that thing in him that made him unlovable? That made him so wrong?

He didn't know what it would take to shake that feeling. But he did know he had to be willing to risk himself for her.

Because she was worth it.

They were worth it.

"You're right," he said. "I have to go back."

"Damn right you do."

He got into the car, and drove. His foot almost all the way down on the gas. He passed Smokey's. That place where he had spent so many of his nights. So many nights chasing oblivion. Running away from real, deep feelings.

Now he was running to them. All the way.

He just had to hope that he hadn't broken things irreparably between them.

SHE HAD KNELT down on the living room floor, and she hadn't gotten up. She was in too much pain. Everything hurt. Without Lachlan…everything felt dark.

Around her. Over her. In her.

Then suddenly, she heard tires on the gravel driveway. A door slammed.

Footsteps on the front porch.

The door flung open. "Charity?"

She pushed herself up into a seated position, horrified that she had been discovered this way.

"Are you okay?" He ran across the room and knelt down beside her. Lachlan. He had come back. He had only been gone for an hour. He hadn't left her.

"I'm okay," she said. "I mean, physically. You hurt me."

"I know," he said, his voice rough. "I hurt myself. Gus came after me, and basically told me that I'm a dumbass."

"Well… You are."

"I know. Charity, I couldn't control the feelings I had for you. And I told myself I was afraid of me. But I was afraid for me."

"Lachlan?"

He knelt down on the floor beside her. "My dad hated me. From the time I was a kid. He made me the source of all the bad things in his life, his marriage. He didn't think I was his son. And I spent years scrabbling around in the dark trying to figure out why. And it was easiest to think maybe it was because there was something bad in me. Because if I don't know… Charity, if I don't know why, if I'm good, if I've been good…why did he hate me so much? What's going to stop someone else from…from seeing the same unlovable thing he did?"

"Lachlan," she breathed, pain rushing through her chest. She'd been so hurt, so angry at him, and now she was just hurt for them both. "There is nothing unlovable in you. You have been there for me for all these years, and I've loved you for every single one of them.

As a friend, as my lover, as my husband. Every year I love you more. Better. Different."

A hard sound that might have been a sob in a softer man, shook his frame. "Gus told me that you believed in me, and I needed to believe in me, too. It's hard."

"I know it is. I mean… Lach, I don't know. I don't know what this costs you. But I want to love you through it. I do."

"I love you. I mean, I'm deeply in love with you." It looked like it pained him to say that. It almost would've been funny if it didn't hurt so much.

"You don't have to say that like it's torture."

"I know. I don't mean to. It's just that it's really pushing up against things in me that… I'm scared. And I would rather punch things than be afraid of them. I would have rather convinced myself I was dangerous than admit I'm just scared." He shook his head. "I never saw functional love. I saw love that was twisted and weaponized. Given then taken back as punishment. I look around me, and I see it. So I know that it's possible. I'm just so afraid that isn't going to be possible for me."

"It's not magic," she said. "It never was. I believe that things happen for a reason, too. But I don't believe that it's all just fate. We have choices that we have to make, Lachlan. I chose to hide for a long time, and I'm not hiding anymore. I can't, not if I want to love you the way that I know that I can. And you can't hide from me, either. We have to be brave. We have to choose this. We have to choose how we'll love each other. Because we chose a lot of years loving each other as friends, a key part of ourselves guarded. So now we have to choose radical love. Huge love. The kind that changes things. I won't hide from it. You don't hide from it, either."

It was amazing. How much they changed. How much their lives had changed in the space of just a couple of months. But it was time to grab on. It was time to quit running.

"I love you," he said again. "I love you." Like it was a spell. An incantation. A promise.

"I love you, too. I always have."

"I know that, Doc. I think you really did reform me. It just took a lot longer than I anticipated. Because it's not about not drinking, or not having sex. Both of which I have failed at miserably. It's about changing something inside of me. It's about taking all those stitches and using them to put me back together inside."

"You've done that for me, too. You made me more me. You helped me find things out about myself that I would never have known were there. I certainly never would've been brave enough to explore it on my own. This is the life that I want to live. This one. With you. And I'm not afraid of you. I'm not afraid of how big the feelings are between us. I'm not afraid of any of it."

He pulled her into his arms and kissed her. "I love you."

"You keep saying that."

"I know. But I said it a bunch of times without really getting to the bottom of it. Without getting to the depth of it. Now I have. And when I say it, I mean it. With all the fear, all the trauma, all the hope that I have in my body. I want you to love me that same way."

"I do."

"I'm so glad that we're married. That we're having a baby."

"I can't even believe that," she said. "But I guess we have all the time in the world to get used to it."

"And all the time to keep on loving each other."

She leaned in and she kissed him. And then she pulled away and looked at him. He was the very image of a man in love. Backlit by the kitchen light, on the floor beside her, sitting there in that place where she'd been broken, working now to mend the pain. Lachlan McCloud was the epitome of a cowboy. And she was proud to call him her husband. And the love of her life.

\* \* \* \* \*

# SECOND CHANCE COWBOY

# CHAPTER ONE

THE FIRST TIME Jude James caught a glimpse of salvation, she was wearing overalls. Her blond hair was in disheveled pigtails, dirt smeared on her cherubic cheeks.

The second time he saw salvation was in the produce section of the grocery store. He stopped and stared as she leaned over to pick up a peach. Her slender fingers closed around the fruit, her blond hair—not in pigtails—falling forward. It was like a golden halo shone about her. She wasn't in overalls. She was wearing a dress that came just above her knees, showing off very shapely legs.

Penny Case. *Penelope.* The one woman he had never been able to forget. Strange, because mostly, he had known her when she was a girl. They'd both been kids, really. With no say over the lives they'd lived and no way to control the chaos around them.

But he'd been sure he loved her.

He'd kissed her one night under the stars and had wanted to have everything, but they were too young and he would never take the risk that she might get pregnant. Not when his own mother had spent her whole life dealing with the fallout of her teen pregnancy and raising him alone.

Then everything had gone to hell and the Kings had come to take her away...

He had wanted nothing more than to let her escape.

That life they lived, that awful, unstable upbringing they'd had... He had missed her. Always. But he had been glad that she had gotten away. Now, there she was. And him, with a basket in his hand containing only beer while she was selecting healthy food. Felt apt. It wasn't that he hadn't done okay for himself. In fact, he'd just come back to town. He did decent work and had cultivated land that supported him. It was a far cry from the petty criminal acts his father had committed.

But still, standing in front of her was like standing before an angel. Walking on holy ground.

He had always felt that.

He had always known it.

And then she turned, and her blue eyes went wide.

PENNY FELT FROZEN in place. As if she had been spotted by a predator. And in many ways, she had been.

What a strange thought to have about her childhood best friend. Her first love.

Her first kiss.

Jude.

She hadn't seen him since...since she was fifteen, and she had gone to live with the King family. Since Denver had taken her in, trying to make up for the things that his dad had gotten her dad involved in.

It was his own damned fault in her opinion. The only person responsible for Walter Case's actions was him. But she couldn't exactly be salty about the care that she had received from Denver in the intervening years. He had given her a nice place to grow up.

A stable environment. Family. But before them, Jude had been her family.

And now he was…

She would recognize him anywhere. His black hair cut close to his head, his cheekbones still sharp. His eyes were an arresting shade of blue that contrasted intensely with that dark hair. He was tall, broad-shouldered, his muscles rangy. He had tattoos entirely covering both arms, extending down to his hands. The sight of that did something to her. It called to an old thing that rested low in her stomach. Recognition. The sort of person who lived a rough life.

She had tried to get away from rough.

Her favorite thing about living with the Kings was that it had given her the opportunity to be soft. They'd let her have chickens. A kitten. She had finally been able to rest. She wasn't existing in a state of hyper-vigilance trying to deal with her father's temper, with the unpredictability of the kind of life he had thrust her into.

Danger whispered along every nerve ending of her body, the hair on her arm standing on end. But she didn't run. She was holding a peach, anyway. She couldn't run away while holding a peach.

"Penny," he said.

Of course he must know who she was, because he was staring at her. There was nothing strange about that. Except it did feel strange. Singular.

"Jude," she said, because once he had acknowledged her, she couldn't do anything less for him. She…

She felt stunned by his presence. Overawed by him. And yet, there was an ache there. A familiarity.

"It's been a long time," he said.

"Yes," she said. "It has. I… What have you been up to?"

He lifted the basket in his hand. "Buying beer."

"Every day? For the last seven years?"

He chuckled. "No, I guess not. I just moved back. I have a mechanic shop. Got my own place. Little ranch."

"Really?"

That made her happy. It made her feel good. Good to know that he had gotten out. That the tattoos on his arms weren't simply telling the story that he had joined up and become one of those same men that had worked with the Kings. Running drugs and all manner of other things like engaging in money laundering or illegal gambling.

They were part of the rough-and-tumble action in Huckleberry County.

Small towns like Pyrite Falls could be idyllic, but small towns also had a lot of poverty. And with poverty often came desperation. She knew because she had lived it.

In that desperation, people sometimes did terrible things. Particularly when they were exploited by those who had more than they did.

Elias King had been a great exploiter. He had the means to wrap desperate men around his finger, and he had done it without a shred of guilt. And while she really did blame her father for his own actions, she also felt…some pity.

Because life was difficult. And it had been especially difficult for those who lived in the trailer park nestled up against the side of the mountain, and the trailer park had been better than a lot of the houses scattered at the hillside. A community of people who had been doing their best in a very hard situation. If you were lucky, you could get hired on as a ranch hand at Four Corners, the biggest ranching outfit in the state, a collective run by four families, including the Kings.

But then, that was the problem with Elias King. He would promise something like that, and then do a bait and switch.

Of course, when the next generation had taken over Four Corners, everything had changed. As soon as Denver had been in charge of King's Crest, the King family quadrant of the ranch, he had put an end to any shady activity that had been happening there. And he had set about making restitution for what his father had taken from the community. She admired Denver for that. He had given so many people a new life. She wondered if he had helped Jude.

"Did Denver King…"

His lip curled. "I've never had anything to do with the Kings."

She looked down, her cheeks feeling warm. "I have. Substantially. They have nothing to do with their father. They're nothing like him. I only wondered because Denver has done his best to make amends—"

"I didn't take his offer," said Jude. "I refuse to take a chance on trusting a King."

"I've been living with them. For most of this time. Well, I went to college."

"No kidding. Listen, Penny. I'm glad. I'm glad that you took what they had to offer. I'm glad that it benefitted you. I had to make my own path. It's no commentary on you. You got out. Stayed out."

"It seems that you got out too."

The corner of his mouth lifted. "Sure. But I'm back, aren't I?"

"When did you move back?"

"Last week. I was living in Portland for a while, working at a mechanic shop. Got my skills on the job. The city was never going to be my home. Not for me."

"No." She frowned. "Why did you come back?"

There was a lost sort of expression on his face. "I don't know."

## CHAPTER TWO

THIS WASN'T THE conversation they ought to be having in the grocery store. And it was a lie anyway. Because the truth was something he was trying to keep hidden, even from himself. But Penny Case was the one thing he couldn't quite let go of. The one piece of the past that he just didn't want to be rid of. Because he would be in jail or dead if it wasn't for her. That was just the truth. It was hard to explain how her kindness back then had changed everything, made it all different. But it had.

"Do you want to come out and see the place?"

"Oh," she said, squeezing the peach in her hand. "I… I do. Denver and everybody are expecting me back for dinner."

"Well. It's only two o'clock. I won't keep you."

"All right. I'm happy to follow you out to the place if you want."

"Yeah."

He felt compelled to show her. To show her that he had at least done something with himself. And he wanted to try to explain. Explain the ways in which she had been important to him. He knew it might not make sense to her. But he wanted to try. He hadn't expected to see her this quickly. But he could no longer lie to himself and tell himself that he had hoped he didn't. He had been curious about her for a long time, hoping she was doing well. He hadn't heard anything through the grapevine, so it had seemed like she was probably doing all right.

Sheena Patrick checked in on him every now and again. She had been like the mother hen to so many of the kids over by the mountain. She had worried about them. Cared for them, even as she cared for her own younger siblings. If something bad had happened to Penny, Sheena would've told him. As it was, he never asked about her, and Sheena never offered.

But he had always wondered.

"I'll just… I'll…" Then she put the peach back. "I don't have enough to go through checkout."

"I don't need the beer."

They walked through the store and he deposited the beer back on the display case he had grabbed it from when he had come in. They both walked out empty-handed.

When they walked outside, her eyes widened. "That's not your motorcycle."

"It is."

"You have any idea how dangerous those are?" She moved toward the sedate-looking sedan parked a couple of spots away.

"And that's yours?" he asked.

"Yes," she said crisply.

Yeah. She had left that life behind. She was safe now. Conventional. He was glad for her. He had done well enough. Well enough for a kid who had been put on the path he had from such a young age.

But Penny had transcended.

She deserved that. She had always deserved the world.

"You should ride on the back of it sometime," he said.

"No, thank you," she said.

Then she got into her car, and he watched as she positioned herself inside the vehicle. He got on the back of his bike and put his helmet on. Then he revved it up, making sure that she was following him as he headed out to the main highway. His homestead was out a ways from town, and that was how he liked it. He hadn't been lying when he'd said Portland had been claustrophobic for him. He couldn't stand living that close to other people. It reminded him, in many ways, of the trailer park. Of being in the middle of all the drama, no matter whether you wanted to be or not. Hearing the disputes of the neighbors and all of that. Yeah. He could do without.

As the wind whipped over his body, he felt that semblance of peace he had only ever gotten from riding a horse, riding his bike, or being around Penny.

She had always been sweet. And it was an extraordinary thing to meet a sweet person in their circumstances. Their parents had both left them at home alone for extended periods of time. She only had a dad, he only had a mom. In a fashion, he thought they had both tried. He wasn't as angry at either of them as he maybe should be. But as kids they had been left to their own devices, and there was little but trouble to be had in that environment. He'd started sneaking beers when he was only eight. There was nothing else to do.

She had made him want to do a better job than that. Maybe be a better person. Penny Case didn't sneak beers. She didn't get in fights. She wasn't… She wasn't angry. Not in the way he had always been. She taught him another way to be. And for that he would always be grateful.

As he drove the road home, he thought about the fact that he wouldn't have this place, wouldn't have this life, if not for Penny. He was glad he got to show it to her.

He was… He was just glad.

The farmhouse was modest, probably nothing like what she was used to living in with the Kings, and so was his shop. He was proud of them. They were things he'd worked for. Things he'd worked up to.

He couldn't fault Denver King for what he was doing, not really, but the simple truth was, the man still made money by gambling. At least that was the rumor. That he did big on poker tournament circuits. That he had taken his father's ill-gotten cash and multiplied it. And sure, he had done a fair bit of giving it all back out, but even so.

Jude had opinions about it.

Penny's sensible car pulled up beside his motorcycle, and he got off the bike as she stepped out of the sedan.

He took his helmet off as she shook her gold curls.

"This is really nice," she said, looking around, a smile on her face. Of course she was as sweet as she had ever been.

"So tell me, what have you been doing all this time?" he asked. "Not just the overview."

He looked at her, and he felt tension stretched tight in his gut.

She'd been fifteen and he was sixteen last time they'd seen each other, but he had never forgotten the way that she made him feel. When he'd been a teenager and the endless ache for her had been consuming. He had stayed awake at night dreaming about kissing her, knowing that he shouldn't. That he couldn't.

He'd given in the night everything had gone to hell. Elias King had been out of the picture for a few years. After a job gone wrong had gotten Sheena's dad killed, he'd gone to jail and Denver had taken over King's Crest. But on his release, he'd come sniffing around to get his old gang back together, and together they'd gotten.

And back into running drugs in a big way.

That was when Penny's dad had gotten arrested.

Penny had been beside herself.

He'd only meant to hug her but he hadn't been able to resist.

Then the Kings had come to collect her, and at first, he had been angry. Terrified.

It was Denver who had knelt down, hat in hand, and said he owed her a place to stay. He'd told her even though Elias had gotten out of jail, even though he'd managed to dodge the cops this time, he wasn't welcome back at Four Corners and never would be. It was a safe space.

"How did you… What made you decide to go with them?"

He had never gotten a chance to ask that question before.

"With the Kings?" she asked.

"Yeah. You didn't know them, and what you did know about them wasn't any good."

"I didn't really have another choice. The trailer wasn't mine. I would've been thrown out of it."

"You could've come to live with me."

He knew that wasn't fair. Offering her a chance to

live with him and his mother… It was no kind of life. His mom had her struggles, and she worked long hours in Mapleton as a waitress. She had gotten involved with Elias King because it meant a kickback of some of his supply. And his mom needed a little chemical help to feel good. She had been a good woman. But life hadn't been kind to her.

He knew it wasn't a fair thing to ask Penny. Hell, he wouldn't have invited her, even then. Because it wouldn't have been a soft place to land, and Penny really did deserve soft.

"I wanted something different," she said, the words honest but painful all the same.

"You figured it was worth the risk?"

"He told me he would pay for my college. You know that's the only way… It was the only way I was ever going to be able to make my own life."

"And what is it you do with your college degree?"

"I started my own graphic design business. I know. It doesn't look like that's what I do."

"Is there a look?"

She shrugged. "I don't know. I feel like I don't look like someone who spends a lot of the day on the computer. The business start-up has been pretty successful. Most of my clients aren't local. But I came back to King's Crest until I could get money for a deposit on a house. Plus, I like being with them. They really have become my family."

"I guess I have a hard time understanding that."

He turned and began to walk toward the front door. She followed quickly.

"That's a fine thing to say when it isn't like you were there for me."

"I would've been there for you," he said, turning to her.

"But *Denver* was," she said. "You left."

"Not right away. You're the one who left, Penny. You're the one who quit going to school in Mapleton. I never saw you after you went with him."

His voice got rough, his heart beat even rougher.

"I know," she said. "I…" She closed her eyes and turned away from him. "I didn't think I could keep one foot in that life. I didn't think it would work. I felt like I had to start over."

"So don't go accusing me of anything. I *did* leave, but not until you did. And I'm back now."

"Why did you want me to see this? If you're angry at me."

"Penny, you of all people should know that being angry with somebody doesn't mean you don't care about them. There's not another person in the whole world I want to see my house more than you. Maybe to show you that I was too good to leave behind. Maybe just because I'm happy to see you. You can feel all those things. I would think that you of all people would understand that."

Because they knew what it was like to love extremely imperfect parents. To have good memories wound through a bad childhood.

"I don't know…"

"Answer me this. If somebody offered you beanie weenies instead of a gourmet meal, don't tell me you wouldn't be tempted to take the beanie weenies."

She laughed. "Okay. Why do I suddenly want beanie weenies when I haven't had them since I was a kid?"

"Because it's crappy food. It really is. But if you

grew up on it, you still kinda want it. I figure that's like everything else. You can have nostalgia for the rough parts of your life too. For the times when powdered orange drink was the only kind of juice you had. For drinking out of the hose. For being allowed to run wild because you were being neglected, but you made an adventure out of it. So yeah, I can be a little angry and also happier to see you than I've ever been to see anyone in my whole life."

"Let's go inside."

# CHAPTER THREE

PENNY FELT A host of complicated feelings as she stepped through the front door of Jude's home. This place was new. Not anything like what she associated with him and their friendship. But he was familiar. Even as the tattoos on his skin were unfamiliar.

She wanted to stop and study him. That ink on his arms. He was beautiful. He made her stomach feel tight.

Oh, that was very bad.

She'd had a couple of boyfriends in college. Really starched-shirt guys. Polo shirts. Khaki shorts. Very safe. Safer than any man she had grown up around.

But she had always told herself that there would be no bad boys for her. Because bad boys could often be very, very bad, and not in a fun, sexy way. So she'd never let herself see the appeal of tattoos, leather jackets and motorcycles.

It was just so disturbing that those things happened to be painted over the top of her childhood best friend. And if she was honest, the first man she had ever really fallen in love with.

All right, he'd been a boy then. But she had… She had loved him. He had been beautiful then, too. But he hadn't had this edge. There had been more of a feral element to him. He had already been drinking when she'd met him when they were small children. She'd convinced him to stop. Had tried to distract him, keep him from getting himself killed.

At first, he had felt like a pet. She had thought sometimes she was the same for him. A novelty that had been as entertaining as they were companionable.

But their friendship had only grown more fierce with time.

They had ridden next to each other on the school bus and ridden back home on one too. They had also eaten lunch together in the cafeteria or outside on the stone benches. If anybody had ever made fun of her clothes for being secondhand, Jude defended her.

He had gotten into fist fights for her.

How could she not have loved him?

Her beautiful warrior, who fought for her in a way that nobody else in her life ever had.

Ever would.

And now he had a kitchen. Like a real grown man.

He was a real grown man. Only twenty-three and his muscles were already sculpted. Probably from the kind of work that he did.

He made her heart flutter.

"This is beautiful," she said.

It was an old kitchen but meticulously cleaned. She imagined him doing that himself. The trailer that he had grown up in had been a mess.

His mother had never had time to clean. It didn't surprise Penny that his own space was meticulous.

"Thanks," he said. "It's serviceable. Of course, I haven't lived here very long."

"You were living in Portland," she said.

He nodded. "It was the best place to find job opportunities. I had to go to so many garages to try and get them to take me on as a kid who didn't know anything. I dropped out of high school after my mom died."

Her chest went cold. "When did your mom die?"

"When I was seventeen."

"Why didn't I hear about it?"

"I don't know if you realize this or not, but Four Corners is its own world."

She did realize it. In fact, she had relished it. For a long time. The Kings had become her family. Arizona had been like the sister she never had, even though she was prickly. Denver, Daughtry, Justice and Landry had been like brothers.

She had been welcomed into the fold, welcomed to the one-room schoolhouse. She blinked back tears. Because she realized then that what he said was true. She had left him. She really had. She had been so desperate to escape all that turmoil that when she had been given an out, she had taken it. Grabbed onto it with both hands and never looked back.

"I'm sorry," she said. "I really am. I was just so tired. I was so tired of that life. Of being hungry. Of being ignored. Of not knowing what a real family was like."

Looking at him, she had the sudden realization that perhaps she'd had a family in a different way all along. And she hadn't appreciated it. Hadn't fully realized it.

"Like I said, you had to do what you had to do. Hell, sticking it out with me certainly wouldn't have gotten you a degree."

"There's more to life than degrees, though, isn't there?"

"Not if you want to start a business and need the

degree to have the know-how. You did what you had to do."

She sat in that knowledge. That what he said was true, even if it was kind of hard. Even if she did feel guilty. She did what she had to do. She had been happy with the Kings. They had given her security like she'd never known before.

"So you went and learned how to be a motorcycle mechanic," she said. "Started from the bottom and worked your way up to where you can own a business?"

"Yep. And of course, it seemed important that I not be competition for the guy who helped me get here. Clyde is a good man. He did a lot to restore my faith in humanity. He helped the scrappy kid just because it seemed like a decent thing to do. He had know-how that he could pass on. He's not a saint. Drinks too much, has some run-ins with the law here and there."

"What about you?"

He chuckled. "Oh I manage to keep my head down. I had no interest in ever getting involved in the kind of things we saw back then."

"Well, that's good."

Tension hummed between them. She didn't think she was imagining it. He looked at her, his blue eyes roaming over her curves. She wasn't overly vain, but she had certainly never had trouble attracting a man when she wanted to. Of course, she was always very circumspect. She didn't get physical with just anybody.

She had all these rules. Rules that she lived by, rules that made her worthy of the kind of help the Kings had given her.

She knew that Denver particularly was making up for the sins of his father. But she saw a helping hand that he didn't have to give. He did more for her than he had to.

She had never wanted to waste that. She had never wanted to be unworthy of it. So she got good grades, and she never drank to excess.

She only dated good men who had decent prospects, and she never had sex just for the sake of it.

Just thinking the word *sex* fired something deep inside of her as she looked at Jude.

He was every bad boy fantasy she'd never allowed herself to have.

She hadn't expected this. They had been teenagers when they'd seen each other last, and she was certain that they had wanted each other. But with an innocence.

Sure, they hadn't lived an innocent life. The adults around them did nothing to shield them from the rougher parts of the world, but they had shielded each other. So there had still been a bit of innocence in them.

She had wanted to kiss him then.

Twenty-two-year-old Penny wanted to tear his clothes off. She felt her own breathing become ragged.

"We haven't seen each other a long time," he said.

"No, we haven't," she said, becoming breathless.

"You shouldn't look at me that way. Because I think you're a nice girl, aren't you?"

"Historically," she said, her eyes lingering on his muscular forearm.

"How good?"

"Mostly," she said, her eyes flicking up to meet his. "I'm not a nun."

"Good to know. I'm not a monk. But then, I also never claimed to be good."

She could imagine him cutting a swath through a raft of cheap motels, one-night stands with girls in painted-on tank tops and short shorts. It should've made her angry to think of it. Instead, she found herself getting aroused. He was the kind of man who probably knew his way around a woman's body. More than she could say for some of those good boys at school. That was the other thing. She had tried—so hard—to be an emblem of something sweet and lovely, sophisticated and demure when she had been away at school. She had tried to fit in with the people around her. With the group that she was trying to cultivate so that she could wiggle herself into that different life she was trying to achieve.

But none of it was her. Her college friends didn't really know her. Even the Kings didn't really know her. Because she had come to them and she had made sure that she was only sweet. Only ever demure and out of the way because she had never wanted to cause them any trouble. Not when they had done so much for her.

Jude was different. He knew where she was from. He knew who she was. Maybe they hadn't seen each other in years, but in some ways, Jude was the only person who really knew her. Before she had cultivated a mask of any kind. He had always been her wildness. He had always been the rougher part of her. And suddenly, she missed it.

"Do you know how badly I wanted you back then?"

She felt like her stomach had balled itself up into a fist. "I don't know," she said. "Was it as badly as I wanted you?"

"Oh don't tell me that. Not if you want to walk out of here chaste."

"Whoever said that I was chaste?" she asked.

"You have that look about you."

"I said I *wasn't* a nun. I thought the lack of chastity was implied."

"Let me guess. You like a guy to take you out. A few dinners, some conversation. Gestures toward the future. Am I right?"

"Usually." *Always*.

"That's not what you're going to get from me. I..."

She knew what he was trying to say. Maybe if they had never separated things would've been different. Hell, they probably would've been married.

He probably would've been her first time.

They would've moved in together. They might've had a baby way too early.

They would've been stuck in the same cycle they had come out of.

She would never have gone to school. He would never have learned a trade. She would wait tables at the bar, maybe he would work at the mill.

No shame in it. None whatsoever. Part of her actually ached for it. For the future that wasn't. The possibility that never would be. But she couldn't regret where she was now.

And now... What he was saying was there was no way back to that place. And anyway, she wasn't supposed to want. She had walked away for a reason.

*This is hardly the same place you came from.*

Yeah. It wasn't. But all Jude James was, was unfinished business. The promise of something. The possibility of something that could never really be now. But maybe that didn't matter. If there was one person who could make her play the part of bad girl just for an afternoon, it was him.

He was practically a stranger. Except he wasn't. And that added an edge to the whole thing. A bit of excitement that fired in her veins.

"You said you had dinner plans," he said.

"I'll send a text and let them know that I got busy."

"I hope you know exactly what kind of busy you're acting like you want to get."

"I know," she said. "But you're right. We wanted each other back then. We were just too young to do anything about it. But we aren't now. You're not a virgin and neither am I. We both know what this is. We ran into each other today. I think about you. I think about you a lot. And I… You're the exact opposite of everything I go for now in a guy. Do you have any idea how exciting I find that?"

"Really. I think it's a little insulting." He took a step toward her, a dangerous light in his blue eyes. "You are the opposite of what I go for in a woman. You definitely don't look like the kind of girl who's out to have a good time. You look like exactly what you are. A girl out to buy some peaches and go home and have a family dinner."

"I might surprise you."

And right then, she decided to surprise them both. Before she could think it through, she took a step forward, wrapped her arm around his neck, and stretched up on her toes for a kiss.

And her world turned to flames.

## CHAPTER FOUR

HER LIPS WERE so soft, her hand gentle on the back of his neck, and when she arched forward, pressing her lush breasts to his chest, he let out a groan of desire.

He hadn't expected this. It wasn't why he'd invited her over.

*But you wanted it.*

Well. Hell yeah, he had. He had hoped. That was the thing. That someday…

What he wanted to do someday was hold her in his arms. Indulge in the molten heat that had flared up inside of him when he was a teenager, wanting what he knew he wasn't good enough to take.

He still wasn't. She was… She was sweetness and light. Except, she wasn't. There was an edge to her kiss that he hadn't expected. Sugar tinged with a little bit of heat. When her lips parted his and their tongues met, he felt a shudder of desire roll through the both of them.

And that was when he found himself wrapping one arm hard around her waist and crushing her body to his.

He intensified the kiss, claiming her mouth.

She moaned, and he felt her hips walk forward, making contact with the rock-hard jut of his arousal.

He wanted her.

This was crazy. Even for him, a guy who really was

not overly picky about taking lovers, this was pretty over the top. He had seen her in a grocery store less than an hour ago, and he was ready to tear her clothes off of her body.

Of course, it wasn't that simple. It wasn't just running into her in the grocery store. It was everything.

All the years of longing. All the time apart. When he had never forgotten her. Not ever.

How could he?

He could only give thanks that he had the presence of mind to make his bedroom look nice. Because in the time since he came to Four Corners, it wasn't like he had hooked up with anybody. That wasn't his priority.

Or maybe the issue was she had been all he could think about. All he really wanted.

Damn.

She was like liquid silk beneath his fingers.

He found himself gripping the skirt of her dress and pulling it up, inch by inch, exposing her thighs. He moved his hands down and found her ass bare. He growled. "You're running around in a demure little dress like that and you have a thong on?"

"I told you. I'm not… I'm still me."

"You always seemed pretty sweet to me."

"But not too sweet. I wouldn't have been palling around with *you* now, would I? I'm afraid to be this person. But it's what I want. You. I want…" Her eyes met his, and he could see everything she was looking for there.

She wanted hot sex in the middle of the day. She wanted to not have to play a part. He could give her that. Hell, it was about all he could give her.

So he gripped that dress and yanked it up all the

way, taking it off her body, and leaving her standing there in a cute little pair of sandals, a lacy bra and underwear.

He pulled away from her. "Turn around," he growled.

She looked up at him, those innocent eyes doing something to him as she turned slowly, showing him just how brief the underwear was.

"Dammit," he gritted out. "That's the hottest thing I've ever seen."

"Surely you've seen sluttier underwear," she said.

"It's the combo of things. I definitely didn't have any idea that's what you have on underneath that. You have someone who was expecting to see it?"

She shook her head. "No. I steer clear of the local guys. There hasn't been anyone since college. It just feels too messy."

As soon as she said that, he felt a tug in his stomach. Because this was the epitome of messy. Maybe it should be simple. Because they could just walk away and not see each other. Hell, they hadn't seen each other for years. They certainly didn't need to see each other now.

But it just felt messy. Complicated. A tangled-up string that was all snarled around his insides. But instead of responding to that heaviness, he stripped his shirt off. And was gratified by the way her jaw dropped just slightly.

Then he moved his hands to his belt and was surprised that they were shaking.

But she was Penelope Case.

Salvation.

And he was about to drag her down right to hell with him.

## CHAPTER FIVE

PENNY COULDN'T BELIEVE her boldness. This was not like her. For all her daring talk with him, she had really only slept with a couple of guys, and it certainly hadn't been like this. It had all been much more planned. Jude was right. Dinners and talks of the future. And certainly not this.

And then…

There was his body. He didn't just have ink on his arms. It swirled over his chest, his pectoral muscles, there was even a tattoo low on his ridged torso, emerging just up from the waistband of his jeans. He began to undo his belt, and her mouth went dry. She could see by the aggressive outline in his jeans that he was a hell of a lot more man than she was accustomed to. It made her giddy. She had been shopping for groceries not that long ago. And now she was about to do the wildest thing she'd ever done. Take a trip down the road completely not traveled. She felt alive.

As she stood there in her underwear, completely unashamed.

He stripped off his jeans, then his underwear, leaving his whole, masculine body exposed to her gaze. He was perfection. More than she'd ever taken, certainly, but everything she wanted.

She moved toward him and pressed her body against

his, kissing him again. The heat and fire of his mouth was almost unbearably good. She was wet and slick between her legs, her breasts heavy.

He reached behind her back and undid her bra, letting it fall down her arms, her breasts now bare against his chest. Her nipples were so tight it was painful. She moaned, letting her head fall back, and he kissed her down her neck, his teeth scraping her skin, before moving down to the plump part of her breast, then down farther to her nipple, where he took her deep in his mouth, sucking hard. The sensation creating a pull of desire between her legs.

She could hardly wait. Usually, she needed a little bit of foreplay to get going, but she was there. The only thing was, she didn't want it to end. She almost wanted this torture to go on forever.

It was like he sensed it.

"Let's go upstairs," he said.

"Okay…"

"You can walk in front of me. I'm happy to watch."

She was very aware of the way the thong framed her rear end as she walked ahead of him and up the stairs, certain she was giving him quite the show.

"That's good," he said, his voice like gravel.

She could see the door cracked in the hallway, and when she looked inside, correctly identified it as the master bedroom. The bed was big, with dark, masculine blankets.

But she didn't care about his blankets. She just cared about the fact that she was going to be in bed with him soon. With all that hard, powerful length moving inside of her.

She would love to be shocked at herself. But she was too pleased with herself.

Because this was her embracing another side of herself when she never had before. And she never would have if it wasn't for him. But then, that had always been true. Jude had always been the wildness. While she had been the softness. But she was done with that.

They got into the bedroom, and he continued to kiss her, consume her. He laid her down on the bed, then took her panties down and cast them off to the side. She was desperate for him. Completely beyond herself.

She couldn't understand how they had ended up here, and yet in other ways, she couldn't understand how she hadn't thought that someday, someday she would end up here. That he would find her someday.

It simultaneously felt like the most romantic and heartbreaking thing. And she was alight with it.

Because the truth was, she had built a life that had no room for a man like him. Her life was built around polo shirt boys. Her life was... Built around fear, maybe. But not right now.

Not in this moment.

In this moment, she had him. All that ink. All that sin. And she wouldn't let there be anything else.

She ran her hands down the fine musculature of his back. Arched herself against that hot, hard length. He put his hands between her legs and began to tease her there. Finding her wet and ready. She had never been so wet in her life. She had never been so close to the edge just from this. From this teasing. He kissed her neck, down her body, paused to take a nipple deep into his mouth. And then continued his journey down her stomach, to that sensitive place between her legs.

And she should've known. He was everything that a bad boy ought to be. Including voracious. He didn't hesitate. He grabbed her thighs and spread them roughly, putting his mouth over that wet, needy place. Licking her, sucking her. Before pushing a finger deep inside of her, and then another.

She arched against him, her body strung tight like a bow. She was drowning in it. Drowning in him.

He moved his hands down to cup her butt and lifted her up off the bed, bringing her into more firm contact with his mouth, setting her off.

Her orgasm rolled through her like a wave. On and on and on, the sound of it crashing within her echoing on and on.

She gripped his strong shoulders and urged him up her body. He kissed her mouth, and then reached over to his nightstand, thankfully having a presence of mind to take a condom out and apply it quickly, before moving back to her. He kissed her, letting her taste her own pleasure on his lips, as he pressed the blunt head of his arousal to the entrance of her body and thrust home.

She wrapped her legs around his hips, and for a moment, she was immobilized.

He met her gaze.

All that familiar blue looking down into her. It wasn't solid. It was crystalline. Fractured. Like shattered ice. And in those shards she saw everything. Adventure. Danger. Safety. Comfort. Home.

She resisted that. Pulled away from it. He was a stranger to her. A virtual stranger. A man she had been friends with seven years ago couldn't be all those things. She had no idea who he was now.

*You know where he came from.*

*You know how he built himself.*

*You know the content of who he is. Really.*

But then he began to move and she couldn't think anymore. Couldn't breathe. Her world was reduced to him. The feeling of him thrusting in and out, the slow glide of friction as he claimed her, over and over again.

He was perfect. And they were endless. She couldn't tell anymore if they were two different people.

It made her think back. Made her think back to all those times they had spent together as children. Where they had been stronger together than they were apart.

She was afraid. Knowing that she could feel so deeply when she barely knew him now. At least as the man he'd become.

But she let all that go. All her thoughts, all her fears. She let go of it all. Let go of everything. So that she could simply be. In the moment, with him.

It was everything. Like being barefoot and free, running through a field without a care in the world.

He kissed her and she felt pleasure building inside of her again, higher and higher. She clung to his shoulders and let herself go. Let herself shatter.

And when she came back to herself, she was safe. Because she was in Jude James's arms.

# CHAPTER SIX

JUDE WAS ENTIRELY BROKEN. That had been the best sex of his life, but even thinking of it that way cheapened it. Reduced it. Because there was so much more to it than that. So much more to her. It was like being healed, and he couldn't fully articulate why. He didn't think he would ever be able to.

Because she was Penny. Just like she always had been.

And she had always been more than that. She had always been everything. It was still light outside. The sun was streaming through the window, and she was lying beside him, the golden beams highlighting the beauty of her naked body. The brilliance of her golden hair. She was an angel. Even if a fallen one.

*She's fallen because of you.*

Yeah. Well. That was the thing he had always worried about with her.

But maybe it was in a permanent state. Because this was just a moment out of time.

This was just a moment.

She put her hand on his forearm. "Don't leave me," she said.

"What?"

"You just had that look on your face. You used to get it all the time when you were a kid. Like you wanted to run away. But also like you wanted to stay. Like something was torturing you. And whenever you looked like that, I couldn't quite reach you."

"Just thoughts," he said. It was weird, though, the way that she had honed in on that. Because those had been his constant thoughts when he had been young: How could he get out of there? How could he take her with him?

He felt like he was too tangled up in all that they had been. In all that their community was.

He hadn't known how to take care of a family. How to take care of a girl like Penny. He'd had a hard time imagining them grown, even though he had wanted to. He had wanted to figure out how to become a man. A good man, but he didn't have a waypoint. He didn't have any idea of how to change himself. There were no examples around him. Not really. And so, he knew exactly what she meant.

Because there had been moments when he had lost himself. When he let himself imagine what a future with the two of them could look like. But only if they were different. Only if they were somehow more than Penny and Jude, raised by dysfunctional people who had instilled dysfunction deep within them.

He had wanted to imagine them in a two-story house. With a big backyard.

A strange trickle of fear slid into his stomach as he realized that he lived in the exact kind of house he used to imagine being in with her. Oh, he had imagined it being more in a neighborhood. A little more like houses he had seen on TV, because that was the only way he could fully picture that life. But he had gone and bought it, and here she was in it, a few days later.

What did that mean?

"Did I lose you again?"

"No," he said. "Just thinking. Thinking."

"About what?"

"What do you dream of?"

She wrinkled her nose. "That's an interesting question."

"I want to know. Because when we were kids, we used to lie down underneath that tree, and we used to make damn sure we didn't talk about the future. We both know we couldn't picture one that wasn't just the same as what we had been. But you went to live with the Kings. And that brought you something new. So now that you can imagine a different life, what do you want?"

A small smile crossed her lips. "I want my business to be successful. I want to get a house of my own. I want Denver to feel like he did a good job. Because… He's not really a father figure. More of an older brother. They all are. I want them to feel like what they gave me matters. I want them to feel like I was worth the effort. Worth the money."

"That's all stuff. What about…"

"Oh, do I want to get married? Maybe. I mean I always thought I would. Or I guess it just kind of existed in the back of my mind. It's why I dated the men that I did when I was in college."

"That's what you want to have," he said decisively. More to himself than to her. "One of those college boys."

"Why?"

"For all the reasons you just said. Except I know you're worth it. So you should have that."

"And you?"

"I haven't figured it out yet. I came back here because I'm trying to. I came back here maybe because I needed to bring all these new things I learned and touch the grass where we used to run barefoot."

"I never go back there," she said.

His heart began to pound harder. "I think we should go."

"Really?"

"Yeah. I think you should take a ride on my motorcycle with me."

## CHAPTER SEVEN

IT WAS BEAUTIFUL OUTSIDE, the golden hour beginning to descend. Penny got dressed and let him lead her outside. "I have an extra helmet," he said, moving into a shop that was detached from the house. She followed after him.

"Is it for your girlfriend?"

"No," he said. "But I run a mechanic shop. Motorcycles are kind of my thing. I have a lot of extra parts lying around." He picked up a helmet off of one of the workbenches. She looked around the space. It was clean, perfectly organized like the rest of his house, nothing like she would imagine a little shop out in the middle of nowhere might be. She could see all his effort. All his effort put into being the best version of himself that he could possibly be. But he still didn't think he was enough.

Maybe he just really didn't want to get married. Maybe it wasn't the life he wanted. But it was weird. Hearing him say that she ought to be with one of those college guys when... When they had been lying in bed naked together. When the only thing she could actually imagine wanting was him.

That made her stomach twist with anxiety. She didn't say anything. She just held the helmet closer to her stomach. "You'll go slow, right?"

"I'll go as fast as I think you need to."

That was how she found herself on the back of his bike, clinging to him tightly as they whizzed down the familiar winding road. She had never driven back this way. She just didn't. The dirt road that took them to Boulder City was a road she'd deleted from her personal map.

The trailer park dotted with a few old stick-built homes hadn't changed at all since she had left. There were plastic toys in people's yards. A big trampoline that she imagined everybody shared.

Clothes hung out on a clothesline, bed sheets functioning as curtains in the window. One window was covered by a brightly colored blanket with a smiling Thomas the Tank Engine printed onto it. There was something deeply comforting about it. Also something that made her feel a kick of anxiety.

It was hard to explain. The feeling of homecoming. The feeling of wishing she wasn't there.

The feeling of wanting beanie weenies sometimes when there was a steak already prepared. She got off the bike, and he gripped her hand. They walked down the road, all the way to the field where they used to sit. She bent down and started to take off her shoes.

"What are you doing?"

"I just want to run."

HE STOOD THERE for a moment and watched her, her blond hair flying behind her as she took off and went barreling through the field. And then he kicked his own shoes off and ran after her.

By the time he caught up to her, his heart was pounding.

She spread her arms wide and turned in a circle. And then she turned to face him.

"I can't believe it."

"What?"

"I can't believe I'm here with you. I can't believe I'm here. After being afraid of it for so long."

"What were you afraid of?"

"That I would somehow become part of it again. I don't know. But it's not all bad here, is it? What was bad was the things my dad did. I let it all become kind of shameful. I let myself be afraid that I was only doing okay because I had put so much distance between myself and this place. Myself and…"

"Me?"

She shook her head. "No. You were never the bad part. You were never the thing I was ashamed of. I just didn't know how to take the good and leave the bad. I didn't know how to deal with the shame of my drug dealer father who hurt people to collect money, who worked with Elias King and hurt people in our own community. I just want to remember you. Remember that this place is beautiful." He looked around, at the trees that surrounded the field, at the brilliant blue sky.

It was beautiful. The kind of way that reached down deep into his soul. The kind of way that punched him in the gut. Left him gasping for air.

The kind of beautiful that made a new foundation inside of him. That had set the standard. That made everything else pale in comparison.

Just like her.

"I'm sorry," she said. "I'm sorry that I didn't come back for you."

"And I'm sorry that I didn't come after you."

It was like seeing everything brand-new again. It was like finding hope.

Or maybe it was just what he thought when he'd seen her in the store. Salvation.

"It's okay. I get why you didn't."

There was more to be said, but it was lodged in his chest, stuck there like a boulder. And he couldn't quite figure out how to shift it.

"It's getting late," she said. "We probably want to head back before it gets dark."

"Why is that?"

"I'm new to the motorcycle riding thing. It's still a little bit scary."

"Okay."

She clung to him while they rode back, and he relished the feel of her warm weight against him. Maybe this was what he was looking for. He hadn't had an answer for her. But now he wondered.

He really did. But instead of saying that, when she got off his bike and started to walk toward her car, he just waved.

"I need to go home," she said. "So that they don't worry."

"All right."

She bit her bottom lip, and looked up at him, her eyes glistening.

"What?"

"Ask me to stay, Jude."

His throat went tight, his words like gravel. "Stay."

And she did.

## CHAPTER EIGHT

WHEN PENNY DROVE back to King's Crest the next morning, she knew that there were going to be questions. She was braced for it. For an interrogation. Denver did like an interrogation.

She had sent him a text to let him know that she wouldn't be home, but she hadn't offered an explanation. He hadn't asked.

But she knew that there would be questions.

She pulled up to the beautiful farmhouse. The place that had represented stability to her for so long. She had cried like a baby when she had left to go to college, even though it had been a dream.

Even though it had been good. To be away for a while. To be someone new.

It had felt like a death back then.

And now it felt…beautiful. Happy. But like something was missing.

She parked her car and got out, and her chickens ran toward her, gathering around her ankles.

"Cluckerella," she said, bending down and picking up a little black banty hen. She held her close. And she felt a yawning ache in her chest. A familiar need. It had been like going to college. When she had felt this expansive desire for more. For something bigger.

Something complete. When she looked up, Denver was standing on the front porch, his arms crossed.

"Welcome home, prodigal daughter."

Her guardian was a big, imposing brute of a man. Women described him as handsome. He was, there was no denying it. Though it made her want to punch them in the face for saying so, because he was like her brother to her.

He was safety, as far as she was concerned. And it was an odd thing. Looking at a man's face, a man who had a similar collection of features to her father and see someone safe.

"Hi," she said, tossing the chicken into the air, and letting her flutter down.

"Do I need to go rustle some polecat out of the bush?"

"What does that mean?"

"Just wondering if I need to go lay down the law or something. Some guy I need to meet and scare."

"No," she said. "You don't need to scare him."

"I sent you out for groceries."

"You did. I didn't get groceries."

"What did you get?"

She lifted a brow. "Laid?"

"I deserved that," he said, wincing. "Come on in. Everybody else is here. I'm sure they want to hear about it."

"Absolutely not, Denver King. That's a bridge too far, even for you."

He smiled, and it didn't quite reach his eyes. Not Denver. He tried so hard to make up for everything that his father had done. He had brought the family close together, but sometimes she wondered if anybody was actually close to him.

It was like there was always distance there. Between him and everybody. He cared about all of them. Teased them. Treated them just... The best.

"I do want to hear about it."

She looked behind Denver and saw Arizona leaning in the doorway.

"I'll give you details," Penny said.

"Excellent," Arizona said grinning. "I might be old and married, but I want to hear the juicy details."

"I'm out," Denver said, walking into the house.

"So what you just...met some guy at the store?"

"I knew him," she said to Arizona, suddenly feeling bashful. "He was an old friend. And...he wanted to show me the place that he just bought, and one thing led to another. I've never done anything like that before."

"Good for you. You deserve a little bit of a wild time."

"Yeah."

"Why do you look sad? Was his dick disappointing?"

"Oh no," she said. "Not at all. It was great. It was amazing. I just... You can't be in love with somebody after one time. But... I've known him for half my life. We just got so out of touch. And I missed him. And I really didn't realize how much."

"Where do you know him from?"

"From before. My old life. The one I tried so hard to leave behind. He was my best friend."

"I actually think you can be in love like that," Arizona said. "It was like that for me. I fell in love with Micah that summer he was here at the ranch. We didn't even kiss. And still, all those years later, he was the only man that I could ever imagine being with. The only man that I really loved."

"That's how I feel. It was supposed to just be for

the afternoon, and then I stayed the night. I just kind of want to stay forever."

"What's stopping you?"

"Well, he has his own opinions. I don't know for sure if he actually wants to be with me like that. It's probably a little bit sudden."

"You haven't seen the guy in how long?"

"Seven years."

"Seven years. And you saw him and it was like nothing had changed."

"Sort of. But also everything had changed. I thought he was cute back then. But I was desperate for him today. I love him. I… I think I always have."

"You need to go to him then. And you don't have to tell them that you love him yet. You can't say that."

"Yeah. I guess I can't."

Except she felt like those kids that ran barefoot through the grass would never have held it back. She wanted that. With him.

She had gotten his number before she left. And she picked up the phone and texted him.

Meet me at our spot.

"I actually have to go."

"You weren't going to come inside and tell everybody about his wonderful dick?"

"No," she said. "I'm just going to go off and tell the man that I love him."

"Well, okay."

She got in her car, and drove toward her past. And hopefully, toward her future.

## CHAPTER NINE

HE GOT HER TEXT. And without thinking, he jumped on his motorcycle. He knew exactly where she was going. And he'd been thinking. All day. He had the answer now. The one he hadn't given yesterday.

The one he'd been afraid to give.

But this was too big to hold back.

He'd lived a whole lot of lonely years since he'd lost Penelope Case.

He was determined not to live any more loneliness.

By the time he got to the field, she was already there. Standing out in the middle of it, wearing that same dress.

She had gone straight home and texted him. She hadn't even changed.

And he started to run toward her.

And she stood. Smiling.

"Penny," he said, when he reached her, "I came back for you."

It was true. It was why he was here. He was here for Penelope Case. He had been building a life for himself and Penelope Case, all this time. Because she had saved him all those long years ago, and all he wanted to do was live in heaven with her.

"I love you," he said.

"I love you too," she responded, throwing her arms

around his neck and kissing him. Deep and long. With all the passion built up inside her.

"Maybe we'll drive each other nuts," he said.

"No. Because we are still those people. The same people we've become. I like both versions of you. So much. I like everything about you. And on top of that, I've always had you in my heart. Always. I didn't have a dream. Not when you asked me. But now… Now I know. I don't just want a guy with a polo shirt. I don't want a life that looks a certain way. I want a life with you in it. I always have."

"Me too," he said. "Me too."

"We have the rest of our lives to find out all the things we've been doing for the last seven years. We have the rest of our lives for this."

The first time Jude James had caught a glimpse of salvation, she had been in pigtails. And she had been the love of his life.

She still was.

* * * * *

# Do you love romance books?

## JOIN

## on Facebook by scanning the code below:

A group dedicated to book recommendations, author exclusives, SWOONING and all things romance! A community made for romance readers by romance readers.

**Facebook.com/groups/readloverepeat**